This Time Tomorrow

Part One of The Searight Saga

R.P.G. Colley

Novels by R.P.G. Colley:

https://rupertcolley.com

This Time Tomorrow

Rupertcolley.com

Part One

Chapter 1: Departure – June 1915

He'd promised himself not to turn around. The horse-drawn taxi was ready to go; the smell of sweaty horse filling his nostrils. They all sat in silence; his father, sporting a black suit, chomped on his pipe, wearing an expression of resolute self-restraint, his mother and Mary one of foreboding. Only Jack, his brother, seemed to be relishing Guy's coming adventure. The taxi driver snapped the reins. The horse stepped forward. And he did turn around; he couldn't help himself. He saw his home receding into the distance. Just an ordinary detached house in a leafy London suburb, nothing special, but it was home, his home, and now that he was leaving it, he appreciated it more than ever.

The taxi seemed to take an age, the mid-morning sun blaring down on them, but half an hour later, they stood together on the heaving concourse at Victoria Station, surrounded by a dense throng of khaki, as men, laden with packs and rifles, jostled for space. So many men, so much noise. He tried to smile, tried to hide the unease that had settled in the pit of his stomach, refusing to budge. He had to remain upbeat; he knew what was expected of him.

Mary took his hand; Jack his rifle.

'You'd better not get too used to holding one of those,' said his mother to Jack. 'One son at war is enough.'

'One day, Mother, one day,' said Jack.

Why did his brother have to act so? Could he not sense what Guy was going through?

Guy looked at his mother, her eyes puffed up, clasping her handkerchief. 'Mother, please…'

'Oh, Guy, you're not going to tell me not to cry, are you?'

'I think he is, Mother,' said Jack.

'And am I the only one?'

'Edith, keep your voice down,' said Arthur, Guy's father.

'She's right, though: everywhere you look, mothers in tears,' said Jack.

'And girlfriends,' added Mary, squeezing his hand. 'Especially this one.' How pale she looked, thought Guy; she, at least, knew.

'Wait,' said Jack. 'Is this the time we leave you two alone?'

'Yes,' said Edith. 'There's a canteen here somewhere, rumoured to brew the strongest cup of tea in London. I could do with one.'

'And I think I can see it,' said Jack. 'Do you two want one? No? Follow me then, dear parents.'

Guy and Mary watched them snake their way through the crowds, Jack proudly bearing Guy's rifle. 'How does he do it?' she asked.

'What, the perpetual cheeriness? That's Jack for you.' There was much he could have added, but now was not the time, nor the place. He had to remain buoyant, for Mary's sake, as much as his own. 'And you,' he said, bringing her into his embrace. 'How will you remain cheery?'

She pushed up his cap and giggled. 'By remembering last night; that might help, don't you think?'

Guy guffawed. 'It most certainly will.' His hand, delicately around her waist, squeezed her buttock through the layers of her dress.

'Guy Searight!' She leaned up and kissed him. 'You take advantage of me.'

4

'Not nearly enough.'

'Oh, Guy, what am I going to do without you?'

'Wait for me. Will you wait for me?'

'You know I will.' They held each other, oblivious to the noise around them, one couple among many, shedding their usual inhibitions, kissing in public, unwilling, unable, to let one another go. He breathed in her scent, a hint of lavender, needing to take every bit of her, to lodge her very essence into his memory.

'Look at all these girls,' said Mary. 'Kissing their boys goodbye. You'd think we could form a club and give each other comfort. But we won't; we'll all go home alone to cry and count the days till you all come home again.'

'At least, you have your sister, and your job.'

'As if life in a bakery is so exciting.'

'And your mother to look after. I hope… I wish her well.'

'Ma? Oh, Guy, it's going to be so difficult looking after her when all I'll want to do is think of you.'

'Please, Mary, don't put your life on hold for me.' Did he mean it? He knew the thought of her would sustain him in whatever lay in store for him.

'Well, I'm certainly not going to do so for anyone else. Will you write to me?'

'Of course I will.'

She ran her finger down his lapel. 'You look so handsome in your uniform. I shall miss you; God, how I'll miss you.'

'It won't be long.'

'You don't know that. How can you say that?'

She was right, of course. It was the uncertainty of it all; not knowing what to expect. He'd heard the rumours; they all had, but few could believe it could be *that* bad out there. 'It can't go on forever.'

'It's gone on long enough already. You won't… when you're out there, I mean, those French girls…'

5

'They're meant to be very pretty.'

She thumped him playfully in the chest. 'Please, Guy, don't joke at a time like this.'

'I'm sorry. It's all I have.'

'Here they come.'

'With their tea. Never thought I'd see the day – my mother with a mug of tea in public. How standards are slipping.'

He could hear his mother berating his father; 'Black? I ask you, Arthur, what made you wear black, for goodness' sake, hardly the appropriate…. Ah, here we are. Guy, Mary, what a picture you make.'

'Love's young dream,' chirped Jack.

'Did you say platform eight, Guy?' asked his father. 'They're congregating.'

Guy glanced up at the station clock. 'I'd better go.'

'No,' gasped Mary. 'Not yet.'

'I can't be late.'

'Your sergeant will have your guts for garters,' said Jack, offering back Guy his rifle.

'Exactly.' He swooped up his pack and pulled down his cap. 'Well, this is it.' No turning back now, he thought. 'You might as well follow me to the barrier at least.'

Holding his rifle in one hand, and Mary's hand in the other, Guy led the way through the mass and noise of men and families, the scene of so many emotional farewells, but it was as if he could see none of them, hear not a sound but for the beating in his heart. His feet, heavy and awkward, led the way towards platform eight. They stopped at the barrier, guarded by a solitary soldier. No civilians beyond this point.

The train waiting there, many carriages long, let rip a puff of steam as men Guy recognised from training climbed aboard. He hugged his mother, kissing her on her cheek, now wet with her tears. 'Thank you.'

'Thank you?'

'For everything.'

'You have nothing...' Unable to continue, she reached for her handkerchief.

He turned to Jack. 'Look after them all, won't you,' he said, embracing him. 'Seriously, Jack, look after them. I'm relying on you now.'

'Of course I will. And you, brother, look after yourself. Come back soon; as soon as you can.'

His father shook his hand firmly, desperately trying to suppress the emotion in his Edwardian heart. 'We're all very proud of you, son.' Guy smelt the familiar pipe tobacco on his breath. He'd never particularly liked it but right now, at this strange moment, he'd have bottled it and taken it with him.

Finally, he took Mary in his arms again and hugged her hard. 'I love you,' he whispered in her ear.

'I love you too.'

He let go of her, far sooner and more brusquely than he'd intended, but he had to – for his sake, and hers, he had to.

The solitary soldier allowed Guy through onto the platform. Guy knew they were watching him from behind the barrier as he made his way towards the train, gradually disappearing into the sea of khaki. The platoon's sergeant was shouting, urging the stragglers to board. Around him, the sound of boots running along the platform, doors slamming shut, of men shouting and whistling. Finally, with all men and packs on board and the train doors shut, the conductor blew his whistle and waved his flag. The men fought for space along the platform side of the carriages, pulling down windows to lean out of, to catch a last glimpse of their loved ones as the train, emitting billows of steam, slowly pulled out of the station. Sandwiched between two others, Guy craned out the window. He saw them briefly – Mary skipping up and down, waving frantically, Jack and his parents

7

beside her. He waved back, like a child, oblivious to those around him, until he lost sight of them.

He took a seat, numb. Everywhere men, like himself, in uniform. As the train picked up speed, they settled down in their seats and sat in silence – no one was ready to talk yet. He had re-joined the company of men, an environment he'd experienced in training, and one which, for all their individual merits, he deeply disliked.

*

As the train sped through Kent and towards Dover, Guy closed his eyes and thought of his parents and the home that awaited their return from Victoria. He thought of Mary having to cope with an ailing mother and a sullen sister. But most of all his thoughts turned to Jack. He was alarmed by Jack's determination to join up. He may not yet have experienced life at the front, but Guy feared for his brother's temperament. They were different in personality. Guy was, in every way, the older brother – strong and forthright, a boy imbued with a determined sense of responsibility from the moment Jack was born. While Guy was thoughtful, conventional and studious, Jack had always been extrovert, rebellious and given to horseplay and jokes, but he was also small, and it made for a dangerous combination. Teased as a weakling at school, Jack kicked back at his tormentors with his sharp wit, but sometimes his tongue took him too far, and often Guy had had to come to his younger brother's rescue. How would Jack fare in the trenches? Guy shuddered at the thought.

He just hoped that the war, already almost a year old, would be over soon enough to spare his brother the ordeal of finding out.

Chapter 2: The Toast – December 1915

Jack had to hold onto the street railings as he retched. Bent double he spat out a mouthful of bile. 'God, never again,' he muttered, wiping his mouth with his sleeve. Groaning, he left the darkened street and wandered into a park. He was close to home but thought better of greeting his parents in such a state. Better, he thought, to try to sober up. As his eyes grew accustomed to the dark, he found a bench and plonked himself down. It'd been a cold day and now, almost eleven, it had turned freezing, the grass stiff with ice. He heard a group of men passing on the street, the other side of the railings and bushes behind him, laughing and talking gibberish. More revellers from the pub.

He'd gone to the pub with a couple of older friends to celebrate their joining the army. Apart from the occasional beer offered by his father, Jack was unaccustomed to drinking, certainly in this quantity. In the shadow of the pub's Christmas tree, he'd played the piano and sung some old music hall favourites and a couple of carols, to the amusement of all. He could play well but his singing, by his own admission, left much to be desired. He may have been the youngest there but Jack could never pass up the opportunity to entertain – especially when a piano was available.

One pint had turned into two; two into three and more. He knew he was drinking too much but it seemed churlish to deny his friends their celebration – they were both deeply excited by the prospect of leaving their mundane jobs behind, donning the uniform and finding adventure in a foreign place. And why not, thought Jack, he was excited for them. The minute he turned eighteen, he'd be down there at the recruiting station, signing his name on the dotted line. He'd heard of boys lying about their age in order to join up early but he couldn't do that – it'd break his mother's heart. Besides, she wouldn't let him.

It'd been six months now since Guy had gone over to France. There were days when he missed the old bastard and others when he never thought of him; but nonetheless he was envious, as envious as he was of his friends who would soon be joining him on the other side of the Channel.

'Mary,' he said aloud. No sooner had he said her name than he was on his feet, deciding to strike straightaway before he lost the nerve. Mary and her sister and mother lived not far from his parents, only a few streets away but in a location decidedly less salubrious than his own. It was their close proximity to each other that first brought Mary to his brother's attention. He'd always thought Mary was too much fun for the staid Guy. She deserved better, someone she could have a joke with. Guy, bless him, wouldn't recognise a joke if it slapped him in the face. And now, he'd buggered off, Mary was struggling to cope with her poorly mother and he, Jack, could extend the hand of friendship... or more.

He could see her front door. Could he do this? No, it wasn't right. Blast it; Guy's loss could be his gain. All's fair in love and war, as they say, and while Guy was at war, Mary needed love. Taking a deep breath of cold air, he marched up to the door, his shadow in front of him. He noticed a light on in the front room. Not allowing himself to consider the rights or wrongs, he stepped up and rapped on the door. A face appeared at the window, the

10

curtain pushed aside. It was Josephine, Mary's sister. Moments later she was at the door.

'Jack, what brings–' A darker version of her sister, tall, elegant, subtle green eyes; there seemed to be little family resemblance.

'I was passing, as they say. Is… is Mary in?' He realised he was speaking quickly, perhaps aggressively.

'Of course she's in; what would you expect at this time of night?' Her hair was darker and wavier, her skin positively pink in comparison to her younger sister's paleness.

'She's gone to bed?'

'No, but…' She spoke with a more pronounced Irish accent than her sister.

'Let the poor boy in, Jo,' said Mary from inside.

'Hello, Mary.' He realised he hadn't been inside their house before. The living room, although large, felt small with its drab brown wallpaper and cluttered with so much furniture.

'Jack, what a surprise.' She was standing in the living room next to a leather sofa, her back to the bay window as if she was expecting him. The fire in the grate was down to its last embers, a Christmas tree sparkled with lighted candles. On the wall a painting of Dublin, and on the mantelpiece, he noticed, a bust of Queen Victoria and a small silver cup with ornate handles with an inscription. He tried to read the inscription but, his head floating, found it too difficult to make out.

'What's the cup for?' he asked.

'Swimming.'

'Oh. Very nice. I've been to the pub.'

'I think I worked that out. Jo,' she said, turning to her sister, 'I reckon Jack could do with a coffee.'

'Yes, please. Make it strong.'

'Certainly, sir,' she said, affecting a curtsy. 'Coming right up.'

He waited until she'd gone to the kitchen before announcing to Mary his decision to join up as soon as he turned eighteen.

11

'That's good, Jack, but it comes as no surprise. I think I'd be disappointed if you didn't.'

'Would you, Mary?' He approached her. 'Be disappointed, I mean.'

'Of course. It's important…'

Jack lunged at her, his lips puckered. Mary sidestepped him, using the sofa as a shield. 'Jack, please, what do you think…?'

'Mary, don't think bad of me but I think I–'

'No, don't say it, whatever you're about to say, I beg you – don't.'

'No, you have to listen to me–'

'And I think you forget yourself.'

'Oh God.' The absurdity of his gaucheness suddenly hit him. 'You're right. I'm sorry, oh no. Forgive me.'

Regaining her composure, Mary forced a little laugh. 'It's OK. Just took me by surprise a little.'

'No, it's not OK. What an idiot, a bloody idiot. It's just that… I'm fond of you now but I shouldn't have…'

'It's fine, Jack; we'll pretend it didn't happen, yes?'

'Mary?' Josephine was at the door, carrying a tray of cups and saucers. 'Is everything OK?'

'Everything's fine.'

Jack stood at the window, sucking his knuckles, looking out through the gap in the curtain. Re-adjusting his focus, he could see them through the reflection, looking at him.

'Are you sure?' asked Josephine quietly, placing the tray on a low table at the centre of the room, pushing aside a newspaper.

Mary nodded and mouthed a yes.

Josephine coughed. 'I'll get the coffee.'

'What?' said Jack, turning around. 'Actually, I… I think I'd b-better get going.'

'So quickly? Are you sure now?'

'Yes, I ought to go. It's getting late.'

12

'If you wish,' said Mary. 'I do have an early shift tomorrow.'

'The bakery?'

'Yes, Jack, the bakery.'

'Yes, of course. Yes. I'll see myself out.'

'Are you sure you won't stay for a quick…'

He didn't hear the end of the sentence. Closing the front door behind him, a little too loudly, he thought, he found himself outside on the doorstep, the sharp winter night biting into him. He knew he'd made a fool of himself in there but he couldn't prevent the mischievous grin playing on his lips. She'd pushed him away, as she had every right to; as indeed, he'd expected her to. But he saw it, as clear as day, he saw it; the gleam in her eyes.

Chapter 3: The Order – June 1916

'Jack, have you sent that order through yet?'

'Order?'

'For goodness' sake, boy, what is the matter with you?'

Jack's father had returned from a meeting in Piccadilly, shaking the rain off his umbrella, and had found the shop empty of customers and his younger son gazing idly out of the window. 'Three rolls of cloth, two black, one light grey. All you have to do is write out the order form and post it. Surely even you can manage that.'

'Yes, sorry, Father, I got distracted.'

'Distracted? By what exactly?'

Jack was saved from further interrogation by a customer arriving in the shop, stamping his feet on the doormat as he came in.

'Ah, Mr Ince, how are you today, my good sir? OK, Jack, I'll see to Mr Ince, if you'd be so kind as to continue in the office.'

Thankful for the intervention, Jack acknowledged Mr Ince and made his exit.

Sitting in the back office, Jack set to work, filling out an order form and entering the details on the shop's ledger. After a few minutes, as he was writing out the envelope, he heard a new voice drifting through from the shop – the reason for his distracted concentration. The office door opened, and in came Mary. He rose to his feet. 'Hello, what a nice surprise.'

She laughed. 'Hello, Jack.'

'What brings you here?'

'You don't sound so pleased to see me.'

'Oh God, yes, I am. Thrilled even.'

'Steady, Jack.'

'I mean it.'

'Yes,' she said, lowering her voice, 'but that doesn't mean you should say it.'

'I know. Sorry.'

'It's OK. It's nice. But anyway, I thought you might like to know, your mother has invited me to dinner tomorrow evening. I saw her today.'

'Really? She never said.'

'Apparently, it's a year tomorrow since Guy went to France so, what did she say, it's not a celebration more an opportunity to mark the occasion.'

'A year already?' He picked up his pen, then immediately put it back down on the table again as the familiar stab of guilt pierced him, as it always did whenever he thought of his brother. It had surprised him how quickly he had adjusted to life without Guy; he missed him for sure but not to the extent he'd anticipated. And then there was Mary… He still cringed when he thought back to the occasion six months ago returning from the pub. Although neither had mentioned it again, the incident now hung between them. But if he'd feared it would sour their relationship, he was wrong – if anything he felt that Mary saw him now in a different light and there were often moments when she seemed to be positively encouraging him.

'What about your mother? Can you leave her for an evening?' he asked.

'The doctor came this morning. She doesn't have long, but we knew that; it could be any day now.'

'I'm so sorry.'

'Yes, well.'

Jack's father's voice came booming through from the shop. 'Jack, Jack – have you been to the postbox with that order yet?'

'Just going, Father.'

'How long does it take, man?'

'I've got to post this,' said Jack, waving the envelope at Mary.

'I'll come with you.'

Outside, the drizzle fell steadily. A horse and cart laden with fruit splashed them. 'Careful,' screeched Mary.

'Almost got me. Perhaps you shouldn't come tomorrow, what with your mother.'

'Jack,' she said, lowering her eyes, 'your concern is touching, I'm sure, but no, I'll be there. How could I not be? A year's a long time, poor Guy. Josephine can always ring the house if I need to get back for…'

'Whatever reason.'

'Yes, exactly.'

'Well, here we are – the postbox.'

'Yes, the postbox.'

'I'd better post this then.'

'Yes, you better had.'

He popped the letter in. 'Look forward to seeing you tomorrow then.'

'Look, Jack, I'll be there because of your brother. You know that.'

'Yes, of course, I know. I appreciate that.'

'Good.' She leaned over and planted a light kiss on his cheek. 'Until tomorrow then.'

He watched her leave, making her way along the crowded pavement, pulling her bonnet tighter against the rain. He resisted the urge to touch his cheek where she'd kissed him. It was only when she was out of view he realised he'd forgotten to put a stamp on the envelope.

*

'And so, I would like to propose a toast to Guy.' Arthur was standing at the head of the table, glass of white wine poised. 'To Guy.'

'To Guy,' returned the chorus of Edith, Jack and Mary, clinking their glasses.

They sat in silence for a few moments contemplating their wine. 'Have you heard from him lately, Mary?' asked Edith eventually.

'Not for a couple of weeks. The last letter I received had been so heavily censored it left nothing of interest.'

'Ah yes, those bold black lines,' said Arthur, attacking his shoulder of lamb.

'We had a letter a week ago, didn't we, Arthur? He seemed fine and said we weren't to worry and that he was in good spirits. He's been a good boy – writes to us a lot.'

'He never writes to me,' said Jack, chasing the peas around his plate.

'Oh, Jack, don't you know how to use a knife and fork? Anyway, don't be so churlish; when he writes to us he writes to all of us.'

'He won't have the time to be composing lengthy letters to each of us,' said Arthur. 'Anyway, boy, you'll be able to see for yourself soon. Then you can write the letters.'

'Arthur, please, don't remind me.'

'You're still planning to join up then, Jack?' asked Mary.

'Of course. You try keeping me away. Three months' time. Apparently, you only have to turn up and if the doctor looks into your ear and doesn't see daylight the other side, you're in.'

She smiled.

Arthur raised his glass. 'Good boy, give the Hun a bit of a bashing, eh?'

'Arthur, don't be so crude, you sound like a newspaper,' said Edith.

'So how does it work after you sign?' asked Mary. 'Do you have to go off for months of training, like Guy had to, or is it different now?'

'We'll find out when we go along, won't we, Jack?' said Edith.

'No, Mother, *we* will not find out when *we* go along; you're not coming with me. No other mums go along.'

'I am not any other mum, as you so eloquently put it.'

'Oh, woman, leave the boy alone; he's perfectly right, he doesn't need you there. He'll be eighteen years old, a proper man.'

'He'll still be–'

'Mother, don't say it; just don't.' He glanced at Mary who smiled into her dinner.

Arthur lifted the bottle of wine and peered in it. 'Could do with another, I think.' He rang the little bell on the table next to him. Within moments, Lizzie, their maid, appeared. 'Lizzie, another bottle, if you please.'

'In fact we're having a celebration soon, aren't we, Arthur? It's our thirtieth wedding anniversary, that's pearl.'

'Thirty years? Congratulations.'

'Thank you, Mary. We've hired the town hall.'

'And invited half of London.'

'Thank you, Arthur. We haven't sent the invitations out yet but you may rest assured, Mary, that your name is amongst them, and we would be delighted if you could join us. And Josephine of course.'

'That'd be lovely, thank you.'

'There's a piano there, isn't there?' said Jack. 'Would you like me to play?'

'No, thank you, Jack, kind of you to offer.'

18

From the hallway, the telephone rang. 'Who in the Dickens could that be at this time of night?' said Arthur.

'Oh dear,' said Mary, 'I hope it's not Jo.'

They fell silent and tried to make out Lizzie's muffled voice. 'Yes, madam, I'll tell her straightaway.' Knocking, she came in, holding the opened bottle of wine.

'Who was it, Lizzie?'

'Sir,' she said, placing the bottle on the table, 'it was the sister of Mary.'

'It's my mother, isn't it?'

'Your sister didn't say, miss, but she did say you are to return home straight away.'

'Oh gosh, that doesn't sound good. I'd better go.'

'I'll come with you,' said Jack.

'No, really, it's OK. If you would all excuse me.'

'Yes, naturally,' said Arthur. 'You rush along. Are you sure you don't want Jack to escort you back? It's getting late.'

'I'll be fine, but thank you for a lovely evening.'

'It's been lovely having you, dear. We just hope everything is OK at home.'

*

Two hours later, the table having been cleared, Jack tinkered quietly at the piano while his parents read – his father, his pipe clamped in his mouth, read *The Times*, his mother a book on gardening. 'Are you all right, Jack?' asked Edith, 'it all sounds rather melancholy, not your usual jaunty stuff.'

'Yes, I suppose it is.'

'Perhaps you should go to see her,' said his father, a puff of smoke appearing from behind his newspaper.

Jack stopped playing. 'Who?'

'Mary, of course – it's obvious you're thinking about her.'

'Jack,' said Edith, elongating his name, 'you're not falling for Mary, are you?'

'No, of course not. Why would you think that?'

'Because it wouldn't be right, you know.'

'Yes, I know that. I'm just concerned, that's all.'

'Like I said,' said Arthur, 'go see her, see whether everything's OK.'

'Arthur, I'm not sure that's such a good idea. I think we should allow them their privacy.'

'Yes, but then it seems like we're not concerned and after all, she could well be our daughter-in-law one day.'

'I hope not,' said Jack, perhaps too quickly. Edith raised an eyebrow. 'Maybe I should ring her,' he said.

'No,' said Arthur, 'what if the worst has happened? It'll be awkward on the telephone. Best pop round. Just say we are all worried and sent you around just to make sure everything is OK.'

'And ask if there is anything we can do,' added Edith.

'Right, I'll be off then,' said Jack with a quick arpeggio on the piano.

*

It was nearing half-past ten when Jack knocked on Mary's door. As soon as Josephine answered he knew by the redness of her eyes that the worse had happened. She didn't speak, just nodded and let him through. Inside their living room, unnaturally dark, a doctor was closing his briefcase. 'She was a good woman, your mother,' he was saying, 'never one to complain, strong-minded until the end.'

'Thank you, Doctor.' Mary acknowledged Jack with the briefest of smiles.

'Now are you sure you can wait for the ambulance until tomorrow morning? I can arrange for your mother to be taken away tonight if you prefer.'

'I don't think I could face the disruption now.'

'Tomorrow is fine,' added Josephine.

'Fair enough. I shall bid you goodnight and I leave you with my most sincere condolences. Good evening, young man.'

'I'll see you out,' said Josephine, leading the way, 'and thank you for everything you've done for us, Doctor, you've been so kind.'

Jack waited, leaning against the mantelpiece, as the doctor made his way out. He read the inscription on the silver cup: *Fourth Year Swimming Champion, Saint Dominic's Girls Secondary School, 1910.* 'I'm very sorry, Mary.'

'Knowing it's going to happen doesn't make it any easier.' She wiped her eyes with a handkerchief.

'It must be very difficult.'

Josephine reappeared at the door. 'I'm going to go upstairs. You OK, Mary?'

She nodded. 'You go.'

'Thanks for coming, Jack,' said Josephine as she took to the stairs.

'Yes, thank you, Jack.'

He ran his finger across the bust of Queen Victoria sitting on the mantelpiece. 'It's fine. I liked your mother. What do you say in Ireland? She was a good crack.'

'Yes, that's right. That she was,' she said in an exaggerated Irish accent. She sat down on the settee. 'She didn't have it easy. Come, sit next to me. Father ran off when we were young, I was fifteen. Ma told him, "It's me or the drink." He chose the drink. It was New Year's Day; we'd only been in London a month or two. So here she was, no family, no support, no one she knew, and not able to afford to go back home. Thirty years old and destitute. She got us through it though. Found work and grafted every given hour. Got us this place through sheer determination and hard labour.' Unconsciously, she had taken his hand. 'Not yet fifty years old.' She dabbed her eyes. 'It's no age to die, is it?'

'No.'

'It's not fair. A lifetime of struggle to die so young.'

'But she had you two.'

'Yes.' She laughed. 'She did indeed. She had us. Thank you, Jack, that's a lovely thing to say.' She squeezed his hand. 'She never saw us get married though. She never said but I think it bothered her.'

'That's not your fault. If it wasn't for the war, you'd probably be married to Guy by now.'

'I used to write to him all the time but in this whole year, I've only ever received one letter back. I know your father says it's difficult to write but I ask you, how long does it take to jot down a few lines to your girlfriend? He writes all the time to your parents, your mother said so. I can't help but feel hurt. It's like he's forgotten about me.'

'I'm sure that's not true. I thought you'd said he wrote to you recently.'

'It wasn't true. I couldn't face telling your parents that their son has neglected me.'

'He's a fool then, a bloody fool.'

'Well…'

'I wouldn't neglect you, Mary. Christ, if I was Guy I'd write to you every day.'

'Oh, Jack. I know…' She hesitated, 'I know how you feel about me and, well, I'm flattered. What I mean to say is…'

'I know – it wouldn't be right.'

'Exactly. It wouldn't be right.' And with the words hanging between them, still holding his hand, she leant towards him and kissed him delicately on the corner of his mouth. He touched his lips where she'd kissed him. She smiled, then slowly kissed him again, her lips fully on his. 'It wouldn't be right,' she repeated in a whisper.

'No, it wouldn't,' he echoed.

'This is so wrong.'

'Yes.'

'Where… where did you learn to kiss like that?'

Chapter 4: On Leave – September 1916

After fifteen months at war, Guy Searight was going home. And he was decidedly happy about it. The train from Dover sped through the countryside, hurrying the men back to London. Mostly, they sat in silent reverence, staring out of the windows at the passing landscape, the sun beating down. This is what they'd been fighting for – the lush green fields, the hedgerows, the villages and towns, the churches, the farms. Guy had never realised how beautiful England was. And with every passing station, the familiar names of the English towns tugged at his emotions. For this, all of this, they had endured the hardships and depravity of war; had lived daily with indiscriminate death, pain, boredom and fear. For this, they had sacrificed so much – their youth and the illusions that come with innocence. As much as he tried, Guy could not suppress his heart-stirring love and loyalty for the country that had asked him to do so much and, in the process, had taken so much. He was home.

Half of the men were returning because of wounds. Some of them, after a period of recuperation, would return to the war. The others, men like Guy, were simply coming back on leave. A Scotsman from Stirling had buttonholed Guy into a conversation he could have done without, preferring to daydream of dancing with Mary. The Scot was complaining that his nine days' leave started the moment he'd left base-camp. 'It bloody means by the time I've crossed the Channel,' he said loudly for all to hear, 'and caught a train to London and from there up to home, right in the north, mind you, I get two days at home then I have to bloody go all the way back again. But they don't think of that, do they?'

Once the Scotsman had fallen silent, Guy's thoughts returned to Mary. Sometimes over the months, he had tried not to think of her for he missed her so much that it pained him. It was surprisingly easy to forget – amid the mud, the cold and boredom, the mind fell into a numbness, devoid of thought, in which one could survive indefinitely. But when, just two days ago, the lieutenant had told Guy he was due his next bout of leave (he didn't like to remind the officer that it was not so much his 'next' bout of leave but his first), he'd thought of Mary and nothing but. Suddenly, he felt vulnerable. Every shell that fell he was convinced had his name on; every sniper had him, and only him, within their sights. If he could just survive the next forty-eight hours, he'd be safe. He'd made it this far, surely just another two days. And he had. Fifteen months without seeing her. He hadn't a photograph of her – never thought they'd be separated for so long – and so now, to his shame, he realised the memory of her face had faded. Fifteen months. Not long in a man's life but it seemed an eternity.

His brother would have turned eighteen just a couple of weeks ago. He wondered whether he went off and joined up, as he'd been so keen to do.

Having left the countryside behind, the train was approaching Charing Cross Station, cutting through the sprawling city, past the backs of houses, work yards, parks, and alongside streets, shops and people. So many people. Welcome back to London. Alas, there'd be no one there to meet him for he had had no time to let them know. Nor had he been allowed time to properly wash or shave. Not that it mattered on the train, amongst these men, united in their constant filth; it was a layer as natural as the top layer of their skin.

There was much excitement at Charing Cross, as hundreds of men, especially the wounded, were met by their loved ones; scenes of such raw emotion, thought Guy, screams, yelps, sobbing, as women, young and old, fell into the arms of their husbands and sons. But not for him; after all, no one was expecting him. Other women, their eyes full of desperation, roamed the platform shoving photographs in front of the soldiers, asking whether they'd seen their men, anxious to hear news of their missing boys. Escaping the pandemonium of the station, Guy caught a tube across south London to Charlton – home.

How strange it was to be back on the tube, to be back in society, people around him dressed in ordinary clothes. London – it felt like an alien city, a city in which he did not belong. But people smiled at him on the tube train. An old man in a bowler hat winked at him. For a couple of stops, two uniformed men, like him, sat opposite, privates from a Kent regiment. But their uniforms were clean, not covered in a layer of grime and emitting a stench, for Guy realised he smelt rank and although aware of it, he was immune to the assault on his sense of smell. One of the soldiers, carrying a bouquet of flowers, said hello. 'Just come back?' he asked.

'Yes. it's fairly obvious, I suppose.'

'Could say that. Well, welcome home, mate.'

'Thank you. Thank you very much.'

Stepping off the tube and emerging into daylight at Charlton, Guy's pulse quickened. It was a twenty-minute walk from the station to his parent's house, and his heart began to pound as he turned into Ladysmith Road, so named in honour of British success during the Boer War. How familiar the street was – the pavement lined with trees, the bend in the road, the houses of old school friends, the carefully maintained front gardens. How luscious everything seemed bathed in sunlight. His father had done well from the millinery trade and had always wanted to move to a larger house in a more fashionable part of London. But his mother had refused; this had been their family home, she knew people here, they had family close at hand, and she couldn't see the point in moving. And so they stayed put in their modest two-storey, redbrick semi-detached house in Charlton.

He didn't see the woman coming towards him, carrying a basket, her dress rustling as she sped along. 'Afternoon,' she said stiffly, as she passed him.

That voice! He spun round. 'Mother!' he called.

She stopped in her tracks. She turned slowly, as if she was unable to believe her ears. On seeing him standing there in the street, her hand went to her mouth, and tears sprang to her eyes. 'Guy? Is that really you?' she said dropping her basket.

He approached her and threw his arms round her.

'Guy, Guy, I can't believe it's you,' she said between tears and gulps. 'You didn't say… If only I'd known… Oh, how lovely.'

'Hello, Mother, you haven't changed a bit. How are you, how are you?'

'Oh, well, very well, all the better for seeing you. What a surprise. Guy, what are you doing here? Is everything OK? There's nothing wrong, is there?'

'No, everything's fine. I'm just on leave for a few days. I didn't have enough time to warn you, I'm sorry.'

'Oh, don't worry about that now. You're here; that's the main thing. How joyful. Come, let's go home,' she said, taking him by the hand.

'Weren't you on your way somewhere?'

'A few provisions; nothing that can't wait. Oh Guy, what a lovely surprise.'

'So has Jack joined up now that he's eighteen?'

She sighed. 'Yes, I'm afraid he has. Essex Regiment – like you.'

27

'I wouldn't worry; he's got months of training ahead of him. With any luck it'll be all over by the time he's finished.'

'I do hope so. Oh, Guy, I can't tell you how worried I've been about you. It's been so long. How long have you got? Please tell me you'll be here the day after tomorrow?'

'Yes, I've got three nights. Why?'

'Oh, perfect! Perfect. Thank heavens. We're having a party.'

'Really?'

And so his mother led him home explaining about the party. She sat him down in the living room while she made him a cup of tea and talked of the catering, the guests, the venue. Guy half listened, while enjoying the comfort of the settee, re-familiarising himself with a room once so familiar. The carriage clock still ticked noisily on the mantelpiece, flanked by the sepia family portraits, ornate vases of dried flowers and a small gas-lamp. He looked at the large mirror that hung above the mantelpiece, the paisley motif wallpaper, much despised by his father, and the various landscape paintings and commemorative plates that hung on the walls, pride of place given to the king, Lord Roberts and Baden-Powell – more references to the Boer War. His mind flashed briefly to the time when he stood here freshly dressed in his new uniform, haversack at hand, eagerly anticipating the adventures that lay ahead of him. Jack had stood by his side, envious and so keen to follow in his footsteps.

In the corner was the upright piano, its lid open. Guy ambled over to have a look at the sheet music. 'You're playing Chopin now, Mother? Don't say it's Jack.'

'Oh no.' She laughed. 'Far too difficult for me and not Jack's style, but Mary plays for us.'

'Does she?'

'Yes. Since you left, she comes to see us regularly and she entertains us with the piano. Usual sort of things – Chopin, Liszt, bits of Beethoven. She's really rather good.'

'And where are Father and Jack? At the shop?'

'Yes. Poor Guy, you must be exhausted. Why don't you go upstairs and have a bath perhaps?'

He laughed. 'Yes, I know I need one.'

'Well, I didn't like to say but now you mention it…'

*

A couple of hours later, Guy was still trying to get used to the idea of being clean, freshly shaven and wearing civilian clothes. He'd grown so used to the natural itchiness of the uniform it felt strange not having it. He wore a neatly pressed pair of dark trousers, a shirt and collar, and a blue pullover, and how lovely it felt. He sipped another cup of tea, idly flitting through *The Times* trying to find articles not about the war. His mother pottered about, doing her 'chores' and preparing the evening meal, talking constantly.

'Mother, what happened to my bedstead?'

'We removed it and donated it – a contribution for the war, they need the brass apparently.'

'Right. Great.'

He heard the key in the front door and the sound of familiar voices, and seconds later, standing before him, his father and brother.

'Guy, you're back!' screeched his father. He went to shake Guy's hand but then, uncharacteristically, decided to hug his son, slapping him on the back. 'Good to see you, boy.'

'Isn't it marvellous,' crowed Edith, her hands clasped as if in prayer.

'Guy, great to see you,' said Jack, following Arthur's example, and embracing his brother. 'Have you heard my news?'

'I have. Mother told me. Congratulations.'

'Thanks.'

'You looking forward to it?'

'You bet.'

'Yes, I feared you would.'

'What's that meant to mean?'

'Oh nothing.'

'You're back in time for the party of the year,' said Arthur.

'Yes, Mother's been telling me all about it.'

'So we won't need to hear it again from me. Well, where to start? So much to catch up on. You're drinking tea? Edith, couldn't you have offered the boy something a bit stronger? Have you been to see Mary yet? No? Bad news there, I'm afraid: her mother died. When was it, Edith? About two months ago, maybe three.'

'Well, she was very ill, wasn't she? Why don't you pop round quickly, just to say hello.'

'Yes, I might do that.'

'I think she might be out for the day,' said Jack quickly. 'So what's it like out there?'

Arthur intercepted. 'Jack, give your brother time to catch his breath. How long have you got, Guy?'

'Three days.'

'Excellent. Plenty of time.'

Maybe, thought Guy, but a small part of him almost felt as if it was too long. 'I'll go see Mary after dinner.'

'Good idea,' said Edith. 'She'll be delighted to see you.'

'Look,' said Jack, 'I've just got to pop out for a bit.'

'It's almost dinnertime, where would you want to be going at this time?' asked Edith.

'Shop. Cigarettes.'

'I've got a couple spare,' said Guy.

'No, it's fine, thanks. Won't be long.' And with that, he was gone.

Guy and his father watched him leave. 'He forgot his wallet, silly boy,' said Arthur, his eyes still on the living room door. 'You know, these last few weeks that boy's been acting ever so strangely. Have you noticed that, Edith?'

'I think he's worried about joining up. Despite the bravado.'

'Maybe, maybe.'

'Here,' said Guy, 'I'll take his wallet for him; I'll catch him up.'

*

Guy was surprised how much ground Jack had already covered. He could see him walking briskly at the far end of the street. He called his name, but with the passing traffic and people, Jack didn't hear. He walked after him, jogging a little to try and catch up. He saw him turn tight into Hatherley Road, a residential street without a shop in sight. Where in the heck was he going? He reached the turning just in time to see Jack take the second left along Hatherley Road into Barclay Street. Jack was going to Mary's; that much was now obvious. But why? And why the hurry? People passed him in the street, a couple said hello, but Guy didn't hear them, so intent was he on following Jack, wondering why he'd lied about going to see her. Why say he was going out for cigarettes? He was about to call out his brother's name again but stopped himself. He wanted to see the reason behind the sudden need to visit Mary.

He'd turned into Grove Road, a street lined with trees, in time to see Jack walk into Mary's house, after quickly glancing round to check he hadn't been followed. Guy darted behind a tree, its shadow falling long in the late afternoon sunshine. The door closed. Guy ambled up the street, worried now about what lay ahead of him.

He paused at Mary's gate and looked up at the house. Now, having come so far, he wanted nothing more than to turn tail and head home. Forcing himself on, he approached the front door, his whole being shaking with trepidation. Without advancing too close he tried to peer through the window, his heart thudding in his chest. Through the thick glass and net curtain he could see the outline of two people in an embrace. And so, conscious of the anger rising within him, he knocked on the door.

Josephine answered, her shock at seeing him immediately apparent. 'Guy? Oh hello, erm… Mary,' she shouted behind her, 'Mary.'

'I'll just come in, shall I?' said Guy, pushing past her.

Mary and Jack jumped away from each other, their faces turning red.

'Guy…?' Her voice sounded weak.

'What's going on?'

'Guy, calm down,' said Jack, 'I just wanted to tell Mary that you'd come back.'

'By kissing her?'

'It's not what it seems.'

'No? So tell me, how should it seem?'

'Mary's been upset, Guy,' said Jack quickly. 'You know her mother died recently.'

'Yes, I'm sorry to hear that. So you, Jack, you thought you'd offer your shoulder to cry on? Was that it?'

'You've not been here, Guy.'

'No, indeed I haven't. Bloody right I haven't.' He stepped towards him, his fist clenched. 'But that doesn't give–'

'Don't you dare,' shouted Josephine from behind him. 'Not in my house.'

'Stop, Guy,' cried Mary. 'Just stop, please.'

'Go on then, what happened?'

She went to take Jack's hand but seemed to think better of it. 'It just happened. Jack's right, Ma died and yes, I did look to him for support.' Guy noticed that Josephine had slipped away. 'And, like he says, you weren't here – I know that couldn't be helped especially as no man could have better reason but I was so sad, ask Jo, and Jack was so kind.'

'I bet he was.'

'No, Guy, you make it sound seedy.'

'Well, I'm sorry but it sounds fairly seedy from where I'm standing.'

'I know, but it wasn't like that; it wasn't Jack's fault, believe me.'

Guy paced to the mantelpiece. 'That's why you've been popping round to our house and entertaining my parents with your piano playing. So where does that leave me then?'

'I'm sorry, it wasn't meant to happen.'

'But it did.'

'And I'm sorry you had to find out in this way.' She approached him and ran her hand down his sleeve.

'Don't!' he yelled, yanking his arm away, then, violently, he swept the silver cup and the Queen Victoria bust off the mantelpiece onto the floor where they landed noisily without breaking. He stormed out of the room, out of the house, passing Josephine, and back into the street. He marched down the road, his mind spinning with the image of them embracing, tears pricking the back of his eyes. He didn't slow down until he reached Hatherley Road. He looked up to the sky and had to fight the urge to be sick. A gentle breeze rustled the leaves. He spat and wiped his eyes. An elderly woman crossed over to the other side of the street. He realised with a jolt that all he wanted to do was to get back into uniform and get back to France, and leave these bloody people behind, to forget them. All of them.

Chapter 5: The Party

'Well, Geoff, Belgium and France are now nothing more than estates taken over by the Kaiser. The man's an antichrist and any man who condones him is no friend of mine.' Guy's father, Arthur, was speaking in his usual booming voice, Guy on one side; Arthur's old friend, Geoff, on the other.

Geoff turned to Guy. 'You've done the right thing in joining up, this is the time for the young men of our country to stand up and be counted.'

The party was in full flow – thirty years of marriage was something to celebrate. Guy's parents worked the room, his mother's hands continually clasped at her bosom, wearing her newest gown, lilac and pleated, his father, as with all the men, in black tie but standing apart with his white waistcoat, holding forth, his voice audible at all times.

The town hall, hired for the occasion, was furnished with long tables adorned with white tablecloths laden with too much food. At the far end, upon the wall, was a coat of arms belonging to the borough, and beneath it a large portrait of George V. Draped across the walls were long sashes of red, white and blue, placed there by the borough the day war broke out.

Arthur was looking pleased with himself having just delivered a lengthy speech. He had thanked everyone in the room, which, in itself, had taken long enough. 'It's been thirty happy years,' he'd said, warming to the task, 'and so now I feel qualified to talk of marriage as an expert on the subject; after all, I've had enough practice. I truly believe a happy marriage is a matter of giving and taking... yes, the husband gives and the wife takes. No, really, I never knew what happiness was until I got married... and then it was too late.'

'Stop it, Arthur,' said Edith, sitting next to him.

'Edith and I have planned this occasion for a long time; after all, a man always knows when his wedding anniversary is,' he'd said to more male guffawing. 'But now that we're here; and Edith, don't misunderstand me, but it almost feels inappropriate, for, as we all know, we are at war. Is it right for such a celebration at a time when our young men are going off to fight?'

'Absolutely,' somebody shouted.

'Yes, absolutely, thank you, Geoff. If the Germans think we're all going to hide under the table, they have another think coming. And furthermore, my dear friends, they'll be quaking in their boots for they'll soon be facing another Searight – yes, my friends! As well as Guy, Jack has put his name on the dotted line and is now a proud member of His Majesty's forces.'

Everyone cheered and turned to look at Jack, who acknowledged the applause with a bow and a self-conscious wave of the hand.

More 'thank yous' followed, then, with Arthur's speech over, a quintet burst into life, playing easy tunes to dance to, and indeed people were dancing but Guy, conscious of his two left feet, as his brother called them, preferred to remain on the sidelines.

'Good speech, Arthur.'

'Thank you, Geoff.'

Geoff slapped Guy on the back, wished him luck, and went off to refill his glass.

'Everyone's very proud of you, son, both of you, this will be the making of you both.'

'Not sure if mother sees it that way.'

On saying her name, Edith approached, her arms outstretched towards him. 'Guy, Guy, my brave soldier boy.'

'Steady, Edith,' muttered Arthur.

'Don't steady me, I just worry for him.' She went to stroke his face but checked herself. 'My sons, both soldiers. It's not what I expected.'

'And they'll do a good job of it,' said Arthur.

'Of course, but it doesn't stop a mother fretting, does it, Guy?'

'I'll be fine, Mother.'

'Yes, of course. But what about Jack? Despite what he thinks, he's still a boy. Will he be all right out there, Guy? Will you look after him?'

'Of course I will.'

'You promise?'

'I promise.'

'And how are you both – you and Jack? If you don't mind me saying so, the two of you seem, I don't know, a little strained with each other.'

'We're fine, Mother, really.'

'If you say so,' she said, forcing a weak smile. 'And how are things with Mary? She's been so looking forward to you coming back.'

'She was?'

'Naturally. Where is she now? Why aren't you with her?'

'Leave the man alone, Edith, all these questions, it's like an interrogation.'

'Arthur, the Ways are here. Have you said hello to them yet?'

'The Rays?'

'No, Arthur, the Ways. Really, I think you do it on purpose sometimes. Come, we must say hello. We'll leave you to it, Guy. Plenty of pretty girls here tonight, don't you think?'

Guy lit a cigarette as Jack and Mary, together, zigzagged around the chairs towards him. 'Hello, Guy, you're not dancing?' asked Jack.

'I'm having to fight them off.'

'So I see.'

'Leave Guy alone,' said Mary. She was wearing a long blue dress, with a sash and a blue feather in her hat.

'Father's speech, eh?' said Jack. 'Typical father – *Edith, don't misunderstand me.* Ah, but we love him dearly.'

'Shut up, Jack.' Guy hated his brother for trying to act as if nothing had changed between them. 'So when are you two going to announce it then? When are you going to tell the world that you are a couple now? Mother's still under the impression that nothing's changed. It's not right.'

'Look,' said Jack.

'Yes, what? Or maybe you can't. Is that it? You can't face telling everyone your dirty secret? Too ashamed perhaps.'

'I'm sorry, Guy,' said Mary, 'really I am, but this is not helping. I didn't want to drive a wedge between you.'

'What did you think it would do?'

'Look, here's Josephine,' said Jack, waving at Mary's sister, glad for the distraction. 'Jo, Josephine, come and join us.'

'Hello, Guy.' She kissed him on the cheek.

'Jo, Jack's going to France,' said Mary.

'Honestly, Mary, I think I managed to work that out for myself.' She wore an embroidered top, finished off with a necklace, a green bow in her hair.

'Well, no, not straight away. They're packing me off to Salisbury Plain first.'

'To turn you into a modern-day killing machine,' said Guy.

'Guy,' said Mary, 'you don't have to be so vulgar.'

'Ha!' said Jack. 'Vulgar, she says, that's the kettle calling the pot black.'

'It's the other way round, you silly boy; anyway, it's simply not true. I'm not vulgar, am I, Jo?'

'No, of course not, you're the very essence of the refined lady about town.'

Despite himself, Guy laughed.

'So, do you have your uniform yet?' asked Josephine of Jack.

'Yes, I am now officially Private Searight of the Essex Battalion. Perhaps Private Searight junior might be more accurate,' he said saluting, looking at his brother. 'So soon it'll be off to France for me. Imagine, Mary, going to France.'

Mary shuddered. 'Couldn't think of anything worse – all those...'

'Yes?'

'Well, French people. Oh, I like this song,' said Mary, reeling around. 'Come, Jack, ask me for a dance.'

'I was going to have a smoke.'

'Jack...' She motioned with her head at Josephine and Guy.

Jack, taking the hint, sprung out of his chair. 'Mary, er, care for a dance?'

'Oh, I thought you'd never ask.'

Guy and Josephine watched them take their places on the dance floor, holding each other in their arms. Guy quietly groaned.

'They make a funny couple, don't they?' said Josephine before realising her tactlessness. 'Oh, God, I'm sorry.'

'Do they? I suppose they do.'

'They're as silly as each other.'

'I suppose.'

They watched them dance, jostling with others on the crowded dance floor.

'So, you didn't want to be an officer?' asked Josephine, sipping her wine.

'No.' She looked at him, and he realised his one-word answer wasn't enough. 'I don't know anything about being a soldier, I didn't want the responsibility.'

'There's plenty that do. No older than you.'

'Maybe but I don't want to make a career out of it.'

'No, I suppose with your father's business, you've already got a career, handed on a plate, so to speak. How old is your father now, if that's not too rude a question?'

'Old enough to retire.'

'Exactly.' They sat in silence. Guy watched his mother speaking to her sister-in-law, his Aunt Winifred, or Aunt Winnie as he knew her.

'I must go speak to Vera,' said Josephine.

'Vera?'

'Just a friend.'

He watched her make her way through the throng, moving at quite a speed, he thought. She was attractive, for sure, perhaps more so than her sister, but she was not the sort of woman whose company he would seek. But instead of finding her friend, he saw her leave the hall, exiting quickly via the main door.

He spent the next ten minutes buttonholed by Aunt Winnie, who extolled the virtues of her husband. Such a fine man and, like Guy, served his country faithfully. How easy it is, thought Guy, to revere the deceased. The man had been dead ten years. He had only a vague memory of Uncle Peter, his father's brother.

Guy needed a respite from the party – he wasn't used to these occasions, had lost the ability to enjoy such gatherings and joviality. He stepped outside. The night was warm, a slight breeze. The town square, usually bathed in the light of the streetlamps, was pitch black, the lights having been turned off at the beginning of the war. Stepping onto the grass, he stood next to a large tree and lit a cigarette. The time on the big clock at the top of the town hall showed ten past ten. He heard voices coming from around the corner of the building. Stepping closer, he realised they belonged to Jack and Josephine. Jettisoning his cigarette, he peered round the corner. Jack was there, down the side of the town hall, silhouetted in the shadows, talking in urgent tones to Josephine, who, pinned to the wall, looked like someone trying to get away. Guy stepped back round the corner and listened.

'Come on, Jo, you know you want to.'

'That I do not.'

'I've always liked you and I'd finish with her in a moment – you know that.'

'You're talking about my sister here, not some cheap woman off the street.'

'I know that but it's you I want.'

'And so what? What good would it do? Look, finish with her if that's your desire; you have to, you have to be honest with her but if you think I would entertain such an idea then you're wrong. Utterly, utterly wrong. Now if you'll excuse me…'

Quickly Guy darted away but realising he wouldn't make it to the main door in time, chose instead to hide behind the tree. He heard Josephine's steps along the path, walking briskly, heading back to the dance. For a moment she stopped but then carried on. Jack came up the path much more slowly. He stopped, close to the tree. Guy cursed the ridiculous situation he found himself in, hiding from his brother behind a tree. He could see his cigarette on the path still burning. Jack had seen it too and Guy watched as his brother picked up the cigarette, take a couple of puffs and then throw it away. It landed to the side of the tree where Guy watched it fizzle out in the wet grass. Finally, Jack ambled back to the party, his hands in his pockets. If he'd been stung by Josephine's rebuttal, he didn't show it.

A while later, having sneaked back in, Guy sat down and helped himself to another glass of white wine. He tried to think. His girlfriend had given him up for the most fickle man in London. He saw his parents dancing gingerly, hardly moving and taking little notice of each other, instead both acknowledging the waves and greetings from their fellow dancers. His father was in his element, being the host, the centre of attention. His poor mother, on the other hand, was putting on a brave face; Guy knew she was too worried about Jack's departure to enjoy herself. He knew that every day Jack was away would be a day of torment for her. Well, he didn't share her concern, not now. Jack's catalogue of immorality had taken him beyond the pale, and as far as Guy was concerned, he could damn well fend for himself out there. What happened to the scheming little bastard was his own lookout.

'Well, if it isn't my young cousin.' The voice belonged to Lawrence, Aunt Winnie's son. 'So, what's it like being in the army then?' he asked, shaking Guy's hand.

'Couldn't be jollier.'

'I bet.' Lawrence was a tall, dark-haired man, with a sharp pointed nose, a long beard and a pince-nez. A good ten years older than Guy, all Guy could remember of him as a child was his appearance at the occasional family get-together. And here they were doing it again. He had never, as far as Guy could recall, had a girlfriend. He was definitely the bachelor type, thought Guy.

'Could all be over by the time Jack gets out there,' said Lawrence.

'I doubt it. That's what they said last year. And what about you, Lawrence, you're not tempted?'

'The call-to-arms, eh? I think not, not really my sort of thing. But I admire those that do; I admire you, Guy. If the Huns think they can just walk through Belgium and set up shop in France, and not get a bloody nose for their efforts, they've got another think coming. Have you heard what they're doing out there?'

'I'm sorry?' The noise of the party was getting louder.

Lawrence raised his voice: 'I said, have you heard what the Germans are doing in Belgium? Raping nuns, for Holy sake, ravaging old women...' Two maidenly friends of Guy's mother looked over. Lawrence raised his glass at them. 'I've always considered the Hun to be barbarians. Now we know it, so I say hats off to you; go out there and show them what for. Say, have you got a spare cigarette? Good man.'

'Do you need a light?'

'Good man.' He drew on his cigarette.

'So what is it you do now, Lawrence?'

'Me? Still working for the government. Was transport, well, still is, but now, what with this blessed war, it's less your domestic transport and more to do with military, working with the high command, making sure we've got the right sort of transport at the right place and in sufficient number.'

'Important stuff.'

'I should say so. Listen, who was that tasty girl I saw you talking to just now?'

'That was Josephine.'

'Who?'

'Mary's sister.'

'Sister? Didn't know she had a sister. Don't look anything alike. So how's it going between you and Mary?'

'Well, let's say we're not together any more.'

'No? Oh, sorry to hear that. Listen, if you see the sister again, you couldn't introduce me, could you?'

Guy looked round for her. 'She went to find a friend.'

Lawrence put his arm round Guy's shoulder. 'Well, if you see her again, bring her over. Good to see you again, Guy.'

Guy could see Mary, wanting to approach him, unsure of herself. As Lawrence disappeared into the party, he beckoned her over. 'Come, join me, sit down.' He actually felt sorry for her.

'Thank you,' she said. 'It's a lovely party, isn't it? Thirty years, it's a long time. Your parents are so lovely.'

'Yes, lovely.' He had to tell her, to warn her about Jack.

'They were so supportive when my mother died.'

'Not the only one.'

She sighed. 'Guy, you know it was never meant to happen.'

'What wasn't?'

'You know what I'm talking about. It isn't your brother's fault. Don't take it out on him. It's just that everything got on top of me – my mother's illness and looking after her while working. I was happy to do it, of course, and Jo helped but she had her full-time job to go to every day, and it became such a strain on me. And then when she died…'

'Yes, I was sorry to hear about your mother.'

'Thank you. It's been a difficult time. I go swimming now to help me relax. It does my mind so much good.'

'Swimming champion.'

'Oh yes, fourth year, 1910. It wasn't *meant* to happen, you know, me and Jack. I didn't mean to cause you pain.'

'Oh but, Mary, you have. Listen, Mary–'

'You never wrote.'

'No.'

'You said you would.'

'I didn't know what to say.'

'I'm not using it as an excuse but I thought you didn't care, Guy.'

'So it's my fault?'

'No. No, but I honestly thought you'd forgotten about me.'

They sat in silence watching the couples on the dance floor. Guy spotted Jack, cigarette in hand, speaking to Lawrence.

'I think you're very brave, Guy.'

'You do?'

'Yes. What you're doing is such a noble thing. Oh, listen to me, I sound like a newspaper.'

'*The patriotic call to arms. Your country needs you.*'

'Yes, something like that. Not surprised everyone's joining up with that poster and that face glaring at you.'

'And his pointing finger.'

'Yes, it's enough to frighten anyone into joining up.'

'How's your work?'

'The bakery? Dull but it pays. I've decided to join up as well – as a nurse.'

'You have?'

'Yes. After all, I got a feel for it looking after Ma for so long. I want to join the Saint John Ambulance and take an examination, a first aid certificate. I'm hoping to become a VAD.'

'Voluntary Aid Detachment.'

'Yes.' She picked up a saltcellar and put it down again. 'I shall miss you.'

'You will?'

'Yes, of course. I know things didn't work out but I'm still very fond of you, Guy.'

He tried to catch her eye but she looked away. 'Thank you. Thank you, Mary, that means a lot to me.' Now, he thought, he had to tell her now. 'Mary, I think–'

'You be careful out there,' she said, watching the dancing guests. 'Come back in one piece.'

'I'll try.' The quintet started up a waltz. Guy could still hear his father's voice in the background, rising above everyone else's. He looked at her hands on the white tablecloth, fingers in the snow; how thin they were, how delicate.

'Oh, how maudlin we are all of a sudden. Of course we shall *all* miss you.'

'Yes, of course. I know that.'

'There's Jack, I'd better make sure he's not getting drunk.'

'Mary, wait a minute…'

But she was gone.

'It's a beastly business, all this.' It was a chap called Evans, Guy forgot his first name, but another of his father's acquaintances.

'What is, the party?'

Evans laughed. 'No, no, the war, I mean, not the party.'

'Yes, it's not a picnic, that's for sure.'

'Can't last for much longer, though, surely.'

'That's what they say.' He could see his brother and Mary, standing to one side of the bar. They were arguing. That much was clear from their gestures, the way they stood, the way their contorted mouths opened and shut.

'I was in uniform once,' said Evans, puffing out his chest. 'Never saw any action, mind you, but still proud. They're an arrogant lot, aren't they?'

Jack and Mary were standing very close, facing each other, trying not to make a scene and indeed those nearby, propping up the bar, seemed not to have noticed. But they were arguing all right.

'Hmm? Who?'

'The Germans, of course. Arrogant lot. With us and the French on one side and the Ruskies on the other…' Then, in mid-sentence, Mary spun on her heel, and walked briskly away, her dress billowing in her wake. 'OK, they've got the Austro-Hungarians on their side, but that's like playing football with a one-legged blind man in goal. No good to anyone. I do envy you, y'know, Jack. Being able to go out there, do something with your life.'

'What? No, I'm Guy.'

Jack leant against a wall, away from the bar, and lit a cigarette. He looked over and his eyes immediately set on Guy's. Guy tried to look away; he didn't want his brother to think he'd been watching them, but it was too late, Jack had seen him.

'Guy, yes, of course, Guy. How is that brother of yours?'

'You can ask him yourself – he's just here,' said Guy, motioning at Jack as he came towards him.

Evans could spot a furious man when he saw one and immediately leapt out of his chair. 'Well, lovely to talk with you again, Jack. Great man is your father, a great man.'

'That man called you Jack,' said Jack, scraping back a chair. 'Did you see that? Mary – flouncing.'

'Why, what did you say to her?'

'Nothing.'

'Didn't seem like nothing to me.'

'For Pete's sake, not you as well. I need a drink.'

Guy was exhausted. Half an hour later, he found himself alone; chairs all around him, empty plates littering the table, glasses half drunk, food stains spoiling the sheer whiteness of the tablecloth. He exchanged waves with various acquaintances and friends of his parents. Guy himself had had numerous brief conversations mainly with middle-aged men, friends of his father's. He did wonder whether Arthur had any real friends or were all these guests merely business pals. Had his business not been doing so well, Guy couldn't help but fear half of them wouldn't have made the effort. Making hats had been his father's life and after years of struggle, he was now enjoying the fruits of his many years of labour.

Suddenly, he had had enough; he couldn't face another conversation. It was gone eleven o'clock, far later than he was now accustomed to, and he needed to go to bed. Not that he'd yet slept in his bed – it was too soft and the two nights since his return, having tossed around, he'd given up and with a blanket slept on the floor. He wondered whether to tell his parents that he was leaving but he could see them, surrounded by friends. They'd understand.

The band had just finished another tune, and people were clapping as Guy made his way through the party, smiling and acknowledging people's hellos. He was almost at the exit, relieved

46

to be leaving, when he heard his name being called. It was Jack again. 'Where you going?' asked his brother.

'Home,' said Guy, pushing open the exit.

'Already?

'I've had enough.' Guy breathed in the night air. The stars shone brightly.

'I'll walk you back.'

'You don't need to.'

'Cold out,' said Jack.

'Is it? This isn't cold. Jack, you don't realise what you're letting yourself in for. All these people here talking about bashing the Hun and onward Christian soldiers – they've no idea what it's like over there. It's bloody awful and you're about to find out.'

'Steady on, Guy, it can't be that bad.'

'No. You're probably right, it's not that bad.'

'Well, is it?'

Guy lit a cigarette. The smoke danced in the night air.

'You'll be gone a long time. Like me. How will Mary cope? How do you know she won't do to you what she did to me?'

'She wouldn't.'

'How about cousin Lawrence, eh? There's still him, isn't there?'

'Sod off, Guy, she wouldn't do that.'

'Well, she has once already, as you and I well know.'

'Yeah, but maybe you were a mistake. You're old before your time, you know that? You're so much like Father, all stiff shirt and doing the right thing. You even sound like Father. Upholder of the family reputation. That may be your way but it's not mine. You may want to live your life with a straitjacket on but I want to live for *me*,' he said, jabbing his thumb into his chest.

'And what about you, then? Now that you've taken her from me are you going to remain the faithful boyfriend to Mary?'

'Yeah, of course.'

'Not tempted by Josephine then.'

47

'No.'

'You liar – I saw you, over there, earlier on.'

'What? Were you spying on me?'

'Don't be ridiculous, I just came out for a breath of fresh air, and I saw you pawing at her.'

Jack grappled for an answer, his eyes scanning the sky. 'You're right.' He sighed. 'I don't know what I want. All I know is I can't stay here any more, living up to *his* expectations, bloody Father. I need to get out. Take me with you, Guy.'

'Don't be so dramatic.'

Guy's words seemed to sting. 'Damn you to hell then,' he said, pushing his brother in the chest. 'You know, I'm right, you are old. That was it – Mary needed someone younger, someone with a bit of fun in them. You hadn't thought of that, had you, wallowing in your self-pity.'

Guy glared at him, clenching his fist. Nothing more he would like than to punch that pretty boy face, but no, he wouldn't stoop. He buttoned his coat, drew heavily on his cigarette and walked away.

'What's the matter, Guy, why are you running away?' Guy walked on. 'Scared of the truth, is that it?'

Ignore him, Guy said to himself, ignore him. But Jack wasn't finished yet. 'Running scared, are we, brave soldier boy?'

That was it. Guy spun round and marched back up to him.

'Whoa,' screamed Jack. 'What are you going to do? Bloody hit me?'

'Nothing I would like better.'

'Go on, then, I bloody dare you.'

Breathing through his nostrils like a bull, Guy threw away his cigarette. 'Listen, in a few weeks, you're going to be out in France shivering in a muddy hole in the ground experiencing the like of which you never thought possible in your worst nightmares. Remember as a kid that you didn't like thunderstorms?'

'I was a bloody kid.'

'Maybe, but I've seen men reduced to the state of kids. I just hope to God it doesn't bring it all back because God in all His anger,' he said shouting at the sky, 'cannot match what those big guns can do. And when *you* are running scared, as you call it, don't come running to me to protect you, 'cause there'll be nothing I can do. You'll be on your own. Oh, you hear all about soldiery camaraderie but when a man is scared shitless he is scared shitless by himself. So don't you ever talk about me being scared again. You got that?'

'All right, Guy, all right. What's the matter with you?'

'You'll find out soon enough.'

*

The following day, Guy found himself back at Charing Cross station, surrounded again by soldiers returning to the trenches, girlfriends and families in tears bidding their loved ones goodbye. Many of the families would never see their men again. The last time he embarked for France, fifteen months ago, Guy had never considered this option, why should he have done? It would never have occurred to him. But a man in combat learns quickly. How many within his battalion, his company, his regiment had already been killed, or wounded and shattered for life? Too many to remember, too many to count. He queued at the exchange kiosk and swapped a few pennies for French francs and thought back to the last time he left for France, from Victoria. Mary had come to see him off, his parents and his brother. Today, no one, he was alone. It's how he wanted it. He'd made it perfectly clear that he wanted no send-off, no emotional farewells on the concourse. His mother protested, his father demurred and Jack appeared shifty but relieved. Either way, Guy had made his goodbyes quickly, then, with his haversack slung over his shoulder, walked briskly to the tube station, the sun on his back. Most of the men now, around him, kissing their girlfriends, were new to the fray. How eager they seemed, how old he felt. How experience wearies a man; one both pities and envies the innocent. With his wallet full of francs, it was time to board. At the gate, he turned, wondered what they'd all be doing at home, then boarded the train.

Part Two

Chapter 6: Last Day of Innocence – 2 August 1917

Guy had ensconced himself in the warmth of the barn where, under the gloomy light and amidst the jovial banter, sixty or more soldiers were relishing every moment of respite, relieved to be temporarily away from the racket and mayhem of the trenches. Some of them sat round small trestle tables chatting and laughing, playing cards or dominoes, smoking and drinking copious amounts of tea. Some sat by themselves writing letters home, while others were content to lie back on the straw and contemplate. Guy had found a table of card-playing friends and joined in. He wasn't keen but at least, he thought, it would take his mind off things, for today he was expecting his brother.

Guy had been back at the front for almost a year since his return to France the previous summer. Letters from home had kept him informed of Jack's progress – his training on Salisbury Plain, then further training in France at the camp they called the Bullring at Étaples and his subsequent transfer to the rear lines and to this billet Guy was now in. He'd been told to expect him mid-afternoon, and it was now nearing five. It was early August, the war was exactly three years old, but the weather was far from warm and the steady drizzle outside added to Guy's downbeat mood.

Eventually, his friend, Robert Chadwick, came in from outside, bringing gusts of cold wind in with him. 'They're coming,' he said to the men. Guy's heartbeat quickened slightly but otherwise no one noticed or cared. Robert knew of Guy's apprehension at his brother's imminent arrival. 'You OK, chap?' he asked, patting Guy's shoulder.

'Yeah, guess so.'

'Don't you want to go out and meet him?'

'No, he'll find me soon enough.'

'Go on, Guy, go meet him. Bury the hatchet and all that.'

He remembered his promise to his mother that he'd look after Jack. 'Might as well,' he said, throwing away his cigarette end. 'I'm losing anyway. This rate I won't have any fags left.'

Guy followed Robert through the huge doors of the barn and into the rain. In the far distance, they could hear the faint rumble of shellfire.

Standing at the doors, he saw the rattling two-stroke making its way down the muddy track. Nearby, a French farmer and his inbred sons were bringing in a small herd of cattle, disturbing the hens en route. Guy muttered a *bonjour* but received a disdainful look in return. Barking instructions at his sons, the farmer prodded the cows into the direction of the archway at the far side of the courtyard. Ignoring them, Guy watched intently as the van drew into the yard and clattered its way over the wet cobblestones, coming to a juddering halt about twenty yards away. The back doors swung open and a small stocky sergeant with a ruddy complexion leapt out, landed in a puddle, and ordered his fellow passengers to jump down. A small group of ten soldiers appeared from the back of the van, each one lugging a large, cumbersome pack. Guy searched their faces, hoping his brother wasn't there, hoping that he'd be spared the ordeals awaiting him, but, more pertinently, not wanting to see him. But yes, there he was: the last one to appear from the back of the van. It'd been a year since Guy last saw him and the boy was now a fresh-faced soldier in a clean but slightly ill-fitting uniform. The sergeant ordered them to wait in line while he went off to find the platoon's commanding officer. Robert pointed him in the right direction before winking at Guy and returning to the barn.

As the sergeant disappeared towards the farmhouse, the young thin recruit approached Guy, his hand outstretched. 'Hello, Guy, you old bugger, how are you?'

'Fine, I suppose. You all right then?'

'Yes, fine. Mother and Father send their best.'

'How are they?'

'Fine. Well, fine as they can be with both of us out here. This pack here is half full with chocolate and cake and goodness knows what else. Typical Mother, of course.'

Guy smiled at the thought of his mother fretting. He remembered the last letter he received from her, full of concern over Jack. 'And how was training?'

'Bloody eleven months of it. And that last bit, the Bullring – bloody awful. Bunch of semi-retarded sadists. And that sergeant you saw who's come up with us, he was the worst of the lot. Wilkins is his name.'

'Nothing changes at the Bullring then.'

'Frankly, it's a relief to be out here.'

'I think that's the idea.'

The stocky Sergeant Wilkins returned with Lieutenant Lafferty, the platoon's commanding officer, who seemed unnaturally tall next to the sergeant. The sergeant called his new recruits to order, and then the lieutenant, smoothing his thin moustache, introduced himself. He informed his new men that they had only the evening to relax and get to know the other men before joining the platoon in its move back to the front at first light the following morning.

With that, the lieutenant bade the men good night and returned to the comfort of his quarters, leaving the sergeant to take over.

'Right,' said Sergeant Wilkins, 'you 'eard the lieutenant, no hanging around for you lot, straight into the fray, aren't we the lucky bastards? Any questions?'

Never one to resist having the final word, Jack put his hand up. 'Is there a pub nearby, Sarge?'

The sergeant's eye twitched with indignation; he clearly hated the cocky ones. 'Shut the hell up, you little shit. You think this is all a game, don't you? Well, one more peep out of you, Private, and I'll give you some fun 'n games. Got it?'

Guy could tell Jack was biting his tongue, curbing his urge to grin. Once the sergeant had dismissed the men, Guy took Jack into the barn. 'You're an idiot; you shouldn't talk to him like that.'

'Yeah, all right.'

Guy introduced him to some of his immediate friends and comrades. After much handshaking and sibling comparison, the men quizzed Jack about the news from home. He told them about the important stuff – the politics and the headlines, then amused a gathering crowd with humorous gossip, nuggets of scandal and the latest jokes from Blighty. He even entertained them with tales of his eccentric Aunt Winnie and her stuffed shirt of a son, Lawrence. Jack had always been a natural performer, always happy to play the piano, sing, make people laugh. Guy shook his head. Five minutes and his brother had already made more friends than he had in the whole year. Typical Jack.

With Jack's introductory performance completed to the enjoyment of the whole platoon, Guy sat him down and made him a cup of tea. 'You don't listen, do you? Don't make yourself too obvious too quickly. Otherwise, the NCOs will have your number. And once they know you, especially if they think you're too uppity, you'll be up for everything.'

'Listen, Guy, I might as well get this over and done with.'

'Go on – what?'

'Don't be angry but Mary and me – we've got engaged.'

Guy had been expecting it but nonetheless his heart tumbled at the thought of it. 'What do you want me to say – congratulations?'

'No, but… I'm sorry. For everything.'

'Yeah, well.'

'I proposed the day before I joined up. As soon as I get back, we're going to get married. I got her a ring as well.'

'All right, Jack, spare me the details.'

'Oh, sorry, I got a bit carried away there.'

'Telling me. I don't need to know, OK? I'm putting it behind me but I'm still sore about it, right? It's not every day one's girl dumps you for your brother.'

'Yeah, I know. So,' he said brightly, 'go on, tell me, what's it like out there? Met any Germans yet?'

'No.'

'You haven't?'

'I know, it seems strange but no, I haven't. I've been in the front trenches and I've heard them but I've not gone over the top yet, not seen a German face-to-face.'

'So is it really as bad as some are making out?'

What should he say? Should he tell him the truth and warn him of the horror, of how shocking the first death is, and equally how quickly one becomes immune to death in its many indiscriminate guises, or the gut-wrenching fear, the agony of hopelessness, the tedious sound of men dying, or the frightening intensity of the noise and the periods of unrelenting boredom punctuated by moments of sheer terror. 'You'll find out soon enough,' was all he could muster.

The two brothers were only four years apart in age but after two years at war, Guy, aged twenty-three, felt so much older. He envied Jack's naivety but pitied the inevitable disillusionment that was shortly to come, for this was surely Jack's last day of innocence. He would have to learn to fend for himself; whatever he'd promised his mother, he couldn't take responsibility for his brother's safety. Every man had to work out his own way of surviving and keeping one's sanity. Why did he have to join the same regiment and add to Guy's strain?

'Why did you join up; you didn't have to, you know?' he asked.

'Oh, but I did. You know I did.' He looked at the contents of his tin mug. '*You* joined up and I felt... well, envious, I s'pose. It seemed like such a glamorous thing to do. Of course, mother tried to persuade me against it. It was all right for you, she reckoned, you could look after yourself, but not me, not little Jack.' He paused. 'And you know father needed me to help with the business; hats don't make themselves, y'know. I was taking over where you left off. But dealing with all those bloody bills and invoices and accounts seemed so dull compared to what you were doing...'

'Yeah, well, maybe. Listen, you go and talk to one of your new friends. I need a kip.'

As he lay down at the back of the barn on a bed of straw, he wondered whether he'd imagined it or whether Jack had looked put out by his sudden departure. He hoped so. He thought about what Jack had said and tried to remember why exactly he had joined up. It was true, from the start of the war Guy felt drawn by the temptation of adventure in a foreign place. The patriotic call became louder, the tempting prospect of glory grew stronger, and the sense of national duty all the more acute. After just four weeks, Guy bowed to the inevitable, and in September 1914 volunteered. Nine months later he was on duty. His father had wanted Guy to try for a commission, which, with his education, he was amply qualified for, but despite what his father felt were his natural skills of leadership, Guy refused, not wanting the responsibility of leading men into battle. Meanwhile, if Guy's duty was to his country, then Jack's had been to the business, but it was not, it seemed, a role Jack coveted.

He saw in Jack his own recent but alien past and he shuddered to think that within a few hours, Jack too would have to suffer the same humiliations of fear that the new ones all experienced, and 'old boys' like himself, never forgot. How they all start off as keen as mustard and then shit their pants as they realised that this war was nothing like the adventurous wars their forefathers had told them about. But damn it, Jack was a man always out for whatever he could get in life, even if that meant trampling over his own brother. Guy realised this now; he'd spent all his growing up looking out for Jack, being the protective older brother, as instructed by his mother, while Jack did his own merry thing and hang the consequences – after all, he had his big brother to throw his weight around on his behalf. Well, not any more, little brother, not any more.

*

It was six o'clock on a mild and, thankfully, dry August morning. The sixty men of the 1st Platoon, D Company, 4th Battalion, Essex Regiment, lined up in eight lines on the cobbled stones of the courtyard. Lieutenant Lafferty stroked his moustache and gave the men their orders. They were returning to the front. Ahead of them lay a fifteen-mile route march from the billet up to the rear trench. 'There,' said the lieutenant, 'you'll be allowed to rest and have dinner before embarking on an evening march down the communication trench to the front – another three miles or so.' He ordered his men to put on their packs.

'Christ, it's heavy,' muttered Jack to his brother. 'I never knew we'd need so much. How much does this stuff weigh?'

'About seventy pounds,' said Robert, adjusting his shoulder straps.

'Blimey, that's half my body weight. They expect us to carry this for fifteen miles?'

The packs contained all manner of essentials: spare pair of boots, socks and underwear, groundsheet, blankets, quilted coat, shovel, gas mask, half a dozen hand grenades, four days' worth of food and water, soap, razor and of course, a rifle. 'I feel like a bloody packhorse,' said Jack.

'Jack,' said Guy, 'for Pete's sake, stop whining, will you?'

'Yeah, all right, I was just saying it's heavy, that's all.'

'Yes, and I think we get the point.'

Robert stepped in. 'Steady on, Guy old chap, it's his first time, remember?'

'As if I needed reminding.'

On Lieutenant Lafferty's orders, the men began the long hike. They marched in ranks of four, the brothers marching side by side. The platoon walked in silence, conserving their energies for the long day ahead. Only the sound of the marching boots, their panting breaths and the clinking of their bayonets broke the morning silence. With the warmth of the August dawn, the men soon began to sweat. And with the sweat came the lice.

'They don't seem to be bothering me,' said Jack.

'That's 'cause your uniform is still nice an' fresh,' said Robert. 'Don't you worry, old chap, they'll catch you up soon enough.'

'Shut it back there,' yelled Sergeant Wilkins from the front.

They traversed through the attractive French countryside; passing villages, cutting across fields, and through copses, but the men were soon too exhausted to notice or care about the scenery. Each hour, they were allowed ten minutes' rest.

As they marched the last few miles, the rumble of artillery fire became louder. Guy kept looking at Jack who began showing the first signs of trepidation, his eyes scanning the horizon at the large clouds of black smoke. Finally, after almost seven long hours, the platoon reached the reserve trench. It was early afternoon. The platoon was allocated two adjoining dugouts.

'These dugouts are sturdy things,' said Robert, 'about twenty feet deep, so need to worry here.'

Jack forced a smile. 'It stinks.'

'Does it?' asked Guy.

'Cosy, I guess,' said Jack, pulling off his pack. He removed his boots and rubbed his aching swollen feet, swearing under his breath. He lay on a bottom bunk and within moments was fast asleep.

Guy pulled himself onto the bunk above his brother and closed his eyes. He found himself tugging nervously on one of the metal buttons on his tunic. They were on the edge of Hell; in only another few hours they would find themselves in the midst of the cauldron. He remembered his own first time. Familiarity didn't take away the fear, but at least one knew what to expect. He wondered how Jack would cope.

*

Eight p.m.; it was getting dark, a damp chill hung in the air. After a dinner of almost indigestible stewed beef, the platoon was ready to move. Lieutenant Lafferty split his troops into four sections, each containing fifteen men. 'Remember,' he bellowed, 'thin out as you make your way down the communication trench. Keep your heads down, especially where there're gaps, or the Hun knock your blocks off. If anyone falls, you are to ignore them and carry on your way. No talking, no slacking, no smoking. Understood?' He paused. 'Leave your packs here. Transport will bring them up for you tomorrow. Your section commands will give you your loads.'

Jack and Guy reported to Sergeant Wilkins. The rugged little man assigned Jack a large crate of small arms ammunition to lug to the front. 'Bloody awkward, this,' said Jack, getting to grips with it. Guy was given a bag full of sandbags, which, although an effort,

61

seemed positively lightweight in comparison to his pack. With his men at the ready, Wilkins led them down the trench, which three miles later would bring them to the very epicentre of Hell itself.

The walk was torturous. The trench, deep and narrow, was too slippery underfoot to allow for any rhythm in their walking. Precariously, they trudged forward, each step an effort; the mud sucking their boots from them. The men within the section soon became separated from each other. Jack slipped and fell into a pool of mud, cursing as he landed on his backside. 'Christ, get up, Jack.' One couldn't tell how deep these pools were and his mind flashed back to the time he saw a man almost drown in a shallow crater of mud.

'You think I slipped on purpose?'

The barrage of noise intensified with every step. The ground shook as bombs and shells flew around, exploding at regular intervals nearby, showering them with fragments of flying earth and debris.

'Shit, what is all this?' Jack instinctively ducked every time.

'You get to know after a while.'

'Know what?'

'What the different sounds mean, and when to take cover.'

'Jesus, this smoke, it sticks to the back of the throat.'

Further up the line they heard a yell of 'make way'. Coming towards them were a couple of stretcher-bearers carrying a wounded man. They could hear the man groaning in pain. Guy and Jack pinned themselves against the trench wall to allow them to pass, but the width was tight. As they approached, the front bearer yelled, 'Lift.' The two men stopped to yank up their arms, lifting the stretcher above them, exposing the wounded man above the height of the trench, his uttered groans lost to the night skies. They squeezed past Guy and Jack, but the second man slipped as he struggled past. The stretcher tilted down at an angle and the brothers found themselves momentarily staring at the wounded man face to face, his features almost unrecognisable as human, a congealed mass of blood and grime.

As the stretcher-bearers scrambled away, Guy glanced at Jack. He saw the glazed look in his brother's eyes, the 'thousand-yard stare' they called it, when fear shocks the mind into numbness. He gave him some water. 'Come on, we've gotta carry on.' Still clutching onto the hefty weight of the ammo, Jack followed his brother, grappling with each painful step.

Five hours after leaving the reserve line, Guy and Jack staggered into the front trench, catching up with Sergeant Wilkins and the rest of the men from their section. The sergeant allowed his men fifteen minutes to catch their breaths. The men huddled around a brazier, lapping up its warmth, but Jack, too tired to stand, sat on the fire-step trembling with cold and exhaustion, slurping at his water.

After a while, the sergeant called the men to order. 'Right,' he bellowed, but then remembering he could be within earshot of a German patrol, lowered his voice. 'The battalion's holding about a thousand yards of trench here. Us and Second Platoon will hold this bit of front for three days while the third and fourth platoons stick around in support. We all swap around after three days. Don't expect anything less than three weeks up here. Any questions?' Jack muttered something under his breath. The sergeant stepped towards him, his eyes bulging with indignation. 'Speak up, Searight.'

'Nothing, Sarge.'

'No, come on, spit it out, man.'

'I was just wondering what that smell was.'

'That, young Searight,' said the sergeant gleefully, 'is the smell of death, of rotting corpses and rotting food. Chuck in a bit of shit and sweat, stir it all up, and *this* is what yer get!'

Jack looked around. 'Putrefying,' he said disdainfully.

The sergeant glared at him. He stepped up closer still, his stale breath filling Jack's nostrils. 'My, what a big word from such a small bugger. I think we need to get you a bit more acquainted with the sweet smell of roses. Perhaps, Private, you'd do us the *honour* of being our shit-wallah for the evening.'

Guy couldn't help himself – he laughed aloud.

'What's funny? What's so funny, Searight? If it's so bloody hilarious, you can bloody join him, right, Private Searight?'

Guy rolled his eyes.

'I said right, Private Searight?'

'Sarge.'

'Well, c'mon, git on with it!'

Armed with shovels, Guy and Jack made their way a few yards back down the communication trench while the sergeant issued orders to groups of working parties. Night time was the frontline soldier's busiest time. It was one a.m.; the noise of the big guns had died down; the welcoming party had come to an end, now the work of maintenance began.

Jack followed his brother. 'Guy, what are we meant to be doing?'

'All you have to do is find the latrine pits. If they're full, fill them in, but don't chuck the earth in from too high or else you'll get splattered with piss. Then you dig another pit nearby.'

'How deep?'

'Four foot.'

'And how do we find the old ones?'

'Follow your nose. Should be easier for you 'cause the stench in this place has dulled my sense of smell. It's easier during the day too, because you can spot them a mile off; you just look for the little black clouds of flies hovering above them. Here's one, full to the brim. Go on, start shovelling, I'll find another one.'

'Great, thanks, brother.' They started work.

After a while, Jack asked, 'Hey, Guy, can I ask… did you and Mary ever, you know…'

'What? You're asking me that? Sod off, Jack, mind your own bloody business.'

'Do you remember the party? When Mary and I had that little argument?'

'Go on.'

'It's because I asked her if… you know, she would. With me.'

'I guess from her reaction, she said no.'

'Well…'

'I don't want to know.'

'Of course.'

A flare shot up into the night sky lighting up the whole landscape.

'Keep still,' said Guy urgently. 'Don't move an inch.'

Jack watched as the light arched up and then fell back down with a hissing sound, gradually losing its light and extinguishing as it hit the ground. 'A Very light?' he asked.

'Yeah. You've gotta learn not to move when those are up, even if you're stuck standing up in the middle of no-man's-land. Move an inch and you'll be plucked off in an instant.'

Latrine duty was an hour's worth of work. The brothers laboured in silence, working steadily and rhythmically. Guy hated digging in the dark. The whole Western Front was a continual plot of shallow graves. Whether human or animal, if the corpse was recent, the fetor would warn you off, but otherwise you never knew what you were thrusting your shovel into. A few feet away, Jack had speeded up and was digging frantically, expending unnecessary energy.

'Slow down, you fool, you've got to learn to pace yourself.'

Jack stopped and caught his breath. He looked up at his brother.

Guy saw the tears streaming down Jack's shit-splattered face. 'It's OK, Jack, you're doing fine, it's OK.'

Chapter 7: Potatoes – 14 September 1917

The day was warm, the sun bright, the morning peaceful. An hour before their allocated stint of sentry duty, Guy and Jack were sitting on the fire-step, cleaning their rifles. Nearby, men tried to snatch a few moments' sleep. A corporal puffed on his pipe, his eyes blissfully closed.

'I got a letter from Mary today,' said Jack.

The sound of her name still made Guy wince. 'Oh. How is she?'

'She's fine. Sends her love.'

'I bet.'

'She's volunteered too, you know, a nurse, a VAD. She'll be based at one of those base hospitals on the coast. Calais perhaps, or maybe Le Havre.'

'Good for her. Aren't you meant to be peeling carrots or something?'

'Yeah, all right, I'm going. Still waiting on the potatoes. Reynolds should have been back by now. Look, here's Robert'

'Hello, chaps, lovely day,' said Robert, sitting next to Guy on the fire-step.

'Yep,' said Jack, 'but it's the dugout and a peeler for me. See you.'

'Hope this weather holds out till Saturday,' said Robert, watching Jack leave. In two days the platoon was due a rest behind the lines. 'Imagine – four days in the sun. Just think, we might even see sight of a bath.'

'Oh for such luxury.'

From inside the dugout, Guy could hear their chatter and laughter. Jack had been out for six weeks. So far he seemed to be coping but much of their time had been spent behind the lines.

A small group of men passed, carrying planks of wood, each bidding Guy and Robert a good morning.

'You seem to be doing very well over this girl malarkey.'

Guy sighed. 'It's this place, isn't it? Sort of puts everything into a different perspective.'

'I guess you're right but I reckon I'd have killed the little bastard by now. Watch out, here comes Father Christmas.'

A private called Reynolds was struggling up the trench, a large sack slung over his shoulder.

'Good God,' said Guy, 'how many potatoes has he got there?'

'They'd better not be rotten like the last lot. Hey, you lot,' Robert shouted to the men in the dugout, 'potato man's here.'

Jack and a friend by the name of Pickard popped out from the dugout. Jack's sleeves were rolled up, his hands wet. 'Reynolds,' shouted Jack, 'what took you so long?'

'Sod off, Searight, you try lugging this lot a mile and a half in this heat.'

'You got the easy bit, you don't have to peel them, do you?'

'Wow,' puffed Reynolds, sliding the sack off his back, letting it land with a thud. He pushed up his helmet and wiped the sweat off his brow. 'I'm knackered. Any tea going?' He looked up to the sky. In an instant his head was gone, blown to smithereens.

The eruption of noise froze their senses. 'Shit,' came the collective cry. Reynolds's body teetered, blood shooting from his neck like an overworked fountain, then buckled and collapsed in a heap. Men threw themselves against the trench wall. A second shell, a third and fourth, landed almost simultaneously all within close proximity. The earth shook. Then, a moment of stillness broken only by screams and cries, both close and afar. It lasted but a moment, and then the shells started falling afresh.

Guy and Robert pressed their faces against the mud, trying to disappear into the wall. Pickard had been hit, his tunic awash with blood, his arm clean away at the shoulder. He shrieked in agony and panic, his hand failing to stem the torrent of blood spurting from his stump. Clumps of earth and bits of metal fell onto Guy's helmet. A ball of mud flew into his mouth. He choked but managed to spit it out. The corporal was dead, his neck severed, his head hanging awkwardly but incredibly the pipe remained in his mouth, the tobacco still smouldering.

Shells burst overhead, shards of metal whooshed down like a swarm of gigantic wasps, cutting and piercing anyone unfortunate enough to be exposed. A pack of rats appeared out of nowhere, screeching en masse as they ran down the trench at great speed, some instinct taking them away from the noise.

Guy realised he was shivering uncontrollably, his legs shaking as if possessed by a banshee, while beneath him, the earth trembled. Robert's face, only inches from his, was blackened with dirt, his eyes squeezed shut. The noise, persisting and continual, assaulted Guy's ears not as a sound but as a physical presence that he could touch, a tangible being enclosing him like a devil's blanket. He tried to listen beyond the noise, trying to distinguish between one shell blast and another but all he heard was an unremitting roar. Beneath it, he could make out the cries and yells, sounds he never knew men were capable of. He hoped to God Jack was OK. His brother was wearing his helmet, not that it offered much by way of protection. Guy didn't know where he was – there was no way of seeing beyond a few inches such was the density of smoke.

The earthen wall of the trench shifted. Robert and Guy glanced up and then at each other. They knew what was coming. A man on the other side of Robert, a man called Bishop, was quick and dived out of the way as the wall collapsed. For a moment, engulfed in blackness, Guy relished the fact that the noise of the barrage was now muffled. But the earth was heavy and wet. The bile of panic rose in his throat. He knew he had to keep his mouth shut but still the mud found its way into his nostrils, beneath his eyelids. He couldn't move his arms, which were pinned to his sides. His ears pounded. The muffled sounds were no more as the soil in his ears compacted. His heart thudded. But there was movement, a shift of earth. He could move his left arm. Desperately he clawed at the earth. What calmness he experienced was now replaced by terror. Nothing so frightening as hope. His fingernails broke as he clawed at the earth. He pushed but didn't know whether he was pushing it in the right direction. His hand broke free and felt the air. He heard shouting. The soil moved again and he could move his entire arm. He tried to lift his head, swallowing small chunks of earth, his tongue coated with the stuff, cloying and suffocating. His arm was being pulled. His arm socket jarred but his head was freed from its grave. He took in huge gulps of air but, in the process, swallowed more mud. Unable to open his eyes, he rolled onto his front and vomited, his breath coming in violent bursts. Someone placed a bucket of water next to him. He still couldn't hear but he knew the bombardment had stopped. He plunged his head into the bucket. The water washed over him, cold and delicious.

*

Guy sat on a new mound of earth, shivering, shocked, still catching his breath. He surveyed the scene: a shell nearby had left a hole big enough to accommodate a haystack. All around, among the fresh heaps of earth and puddles of blood, were shreds of uniform, pieces of flesh, the odd helmet, most of them buckled, a bayonet, twisted, a shovel without a handle. Smoke lingered menacingly.

Robert came and sat next to him, slapping him on the knee. Neither could talk. They nodded. Robert's eyes were raw red, accentuated by his mud-caked face. Everywhere the sound of men in pain, men crying, men dying. Nearby lay bits of Private Bishop; where the rest of him was, no one would ever know. Ten feet away, Albert Jarrett sat upright, his hands cradling his intestines. His eyes seemed to be laughing. Guy inspected his fingers, throbbing and black, and grimaced at the lack of fingernails. He spat more dirt from his mouth. Someone screamed, the noise soon disintegrating into sobbing.

'Where's my brother?' panted Guy.

'Over there.' Guy followed the direction of Robert's pointing finger. Through the smoke, Guy could make out the vision of a man huddled in a ball, not far from Jarrett. Robert nodded, yes, that's your brother.

It took a couple of efforts for Guy to stand. His legs like jelly, he staggered over to Jack, across the ripped-up ground, stumbling over a body. A hand momentarily gripped his ankle. It was Jarrett, the goo of his stomach piled neatly on his lap. He muttered something. Guy wanted to ignore him. Jarrett beckoned him to lean over. The stench made Guy want to puke. 'What? What is it, Jarrett?'

'Shoot me. Please, I can't bear it.'

'Help will come.'

Jarrett shook his head; he couldn't speak any more. His eyes lolled around. Guy left him. As he approached his brother, he realised Jack was whimpering, his words unintelligible. He'd curled up on the ground, his knees tucked up beneath him, his arms covering his head, his whole body shivering. Next to him, lay a helmet. 'Oh, Jesus,' said Guy, 'what's happened to you?' He sunk to the ground next to him. 'Jack, it's me,' he whispered, trying to bend down low enough so that his brother could see him. 'Can you hear me? Jack? You can come out now, it's OK, it's stopped.'

Jack removed one hand from behind his head, then the other. He looked at Guy; he was crying. He tried to speak but, wheezing heavily, couldn't catch his breath.

Guy rubbed his shoulder. 'Don't worry, it's finished now, you're OK. God, look at you. This wasn't meant to happen, not to you, not to Jack.'

Jack attempted to sit up but his knees jarred. Slowly, still trembling, he stretched himself out. As he righted himself, Guy noticed a couple of stretcher-bearers arrive on the scene, their stretcher slack between them. They looked around, trying to decide where to start first. He pointed them in the direction of Jarrett.

Jack cursed as the life returned to his joints.

'You all right, Jack?'

Jack fought to speak between breaths. 'Guy…'

'Don't talk.' There was no blood on his tunic, or his trousers. He felt up and down Jack's legs, his arms, seeing if anything was broken. 'You're not hurt?'

Jack shook his head.

'Good. I think you're OK.'

The stretcher bearers had ignored Jarrett – he was too far gone to be salvageable. Guy watched them as they bore another to the First Aid post. With their heavy cargo, they struggled to maintain their balance over the bumpy ground.

'That was hell, wasn't it?' said Guy. 'I never knew sound could be so loud.' His brother wasn't listening. 'Jack, you OK? Jack – speak to me.'

'I'm sorry.'

'I said–'

'No.' He wiped his mouth. 'I mean, I'm sorry.' The words came slowly. 'So – so – sorry.'

'It's fine.'

'No. It's not. It's not fine. You're my brother. You mean more to me than anything in the world.'

'You don't have to say it.'

'No, I have to, I want to. It's just… you've always been there for me. Haven't you? And then I did that to you.'

'It's OK now.' Guy put his arm round his brother's shaking shoulders.

'You were out here, with all this shit, and me? What was I doing? Playing the dandy. What an idiot. She never meant that much to me. How could I have done that to you? Guy, I'm sorry.'

He stroked Jack's mud-streaked hair. 'It's OK.'

'You're my big brother. And I did that to you. I'm sorry, I'm…' The words faded into tears as he let his head droop into his brother's neck.

The smoke swirled, the only sound was of cries and pitiful groans. Jarrett's eyes were open but he was dead, finally out of his misery. Robert sat further down the trench, coughing as he tried to smoke a cigarette. A rat scurried past with its ugly naked tail. Guy couldn't move; his limbs heavy, his body sagging with exhaustion. He realised how thirsty he was, the taste of mud still at the back of his throat, the feeling of the stuff on his tongue. He tried to shout for Robert but he lacked the strength even to raise his voice and was too comatose to get to his feet. Jack had fallen asleep, his head on Guy's shoulder. Guy rested his head on Jack's and yawned. A deep, deep yawn.

Chapter 8: At the end of a Bayonet – October 1917

Guy was having a daytime sleep in a six-foot-long hole dug halfway down into the trench wall, a funk hole. He'd warned Jack against sleeping in these things, especially in the wet. 'I heard of a bloke suffocated by a collapsing funk hole,' he'd told his brother but it was only damp and after a week of intermittent sleep, Guy was happy to spread his groundsheet out and take the risk.

After four hours' sleep, Guy was stirred back into consciousness by an annoying tickling sensation against his chin. He opened his eyes to see the back of a huge brown rat resting on his chest, rising steadily up and down with his breathing, licking its front paws, its tail flicking against his chin. It took a few seconds for Guy to register and when he did, he hollered just at the moment a man was wandering past his resting place. Guy's scream made the man jump and the rat scampered off as Guy sat up hitting his head against the damp mud ceiling of the hole. The passing soldier instinctively lunged at the rat with the butt of his rifle and, amazingly, scored a direct hit, stunning and almost flattening the rodent. The rat was hurt and started squealing – a surprisingly loud, piercing scream. The soldier quickly twisted his rifle around and thrust the bayonet into the rat, the blade slithering through its back and out the other side through its stomach.

'Got 'im!' said the soldier gleefully. Guy recognised the thin, gaunt man as Charlie Fitzpatrick, same battalion, but different section. Fitzpatrick held his rifle up, the rat neatly skewered. 'Fancy a snack?' he said with a hint of a Northern Irish accent.

'Big bugger, isn't he?' said Guy, getting to his feet, slightly embarrassed by his alarmed outburst.

'Yeah, bloody horrid things. Anyway, I was looking for you. You're needed for a raid. You've got to report to the Savoy after dinner.'

Guy had heard that a number of trench raids were being planned. 'They're up to something big, aren't they?'

'Couldn't tell you, but I reckon they wanna catch a few Germans, y'know, get them talking.' He spotted Robert approaching. 'Ah, here's Chadwick. They want 'im too. See you along.' And with that, Fitzpatrick moved on, the rat still skewered on his bayonet, a thin trickle of blood oozing down the shining blade.

Guy stretched and yawned; he still ached with fatigue. He stamped up and down the trench, trying to warm his feet up. It was the sort of blustery October day when the sun popped in and out of view and couldn't decide whether it should be a warm day or not. He joined the others and waited for dinner to arrive, a time of relative quiet as each side respected the other's need to eat in peace. Guy saw Jack sitting down on the fire-step, busy running his fingernails up the seams of his tunic.

'How are the lice?' asked Guy.

'Trying to kill the buggers. They get bloody everywhere, don't they? Got them in my hair, my armpits, sodding everywhere.' Jack sighed. 'Fancy a fag?'

'Thanks.' He lit the cigarette. 'I'm going out on a raid later on.'

'Oh shit, are you?'

'I s'pose this is what it's all about, isn't it? Hand-to-hand combat, kill or be killed. It's what we're here for.'

'Your first time over, isn't it?' asked Jack.

'Yes.' Guy concentrated on his cigarette, hoping the effect of the smoke would help him relax and ease the nagging burden of anticipation. He glanced at Jack drawing on his cigarette, his fingernails stained with smudges of bloodied lice.

'Mine will come one day.'

'You've only been here two months – could be another year. Or more. Truth is, I'm not feeling too good about it. Listen, Jack…'

'Go on, I'm listening.'

'If anything happens to me, you know…'

'You'll be OK, they'll clear them out for you first.'

'I wish I shared your optimism.' Perhaps Jack was right, the preliminary bombardment should do the job, but whatever, he didn't want to think about it. His mind raced back to him and Jack as boys, charging round a churchyard. He smiled and shook his head at the memory. Jack the extrovert, the young daredevil, was always the one to come up with wayward schemes but, having started, often lacked the nerve to see them through, obliging the reluctant but faithful Guy to take over where his young brother had over-stretched himself.

Jack saw him smile. 'Penny for them,' he asked. He threw his cigarette away and watched it fizzle on the sodden duckboard.

'Do you remember the Albert Carr night?'

Jack smiled, the dimples showing on his cheeks. 'How could I forget?'

'I was, what, eleven, and you about seven? Twelve years ago.' He sighed. 'I can't say I was particularly proud of it, but–'

'Ah, the silly sod deserved it.'

They sat in silence, each casting their minds back to that mild autumn evening and the incident that seemed to define their growing up together. Guy remembered the church clock and the sound of it chiming nine o'clock…

*

It was already getting dark when the three boys stole into the churchyard. Shushing each other and suppressing their nervous giggles, the two eleven-year-old friends, Guy and Albert, led the way round to the back of the church, with Guy's seven-year-old brother, Jack, bringing up the rear. It was still warm, the nights had only just started drawing in and the full moon cast long shadows across their path. Guy could smell the dampness of the dew. He glanced up at the church clock, its Roman numerals showing a quarter to nine. Without warning, he ran ahead, full of bravado, rounded a corner and ducked behind a tilted headstone, hiding within its sloping shadow. Albert and Jack ran to catch up and although they couldn't see him, they could hear his ghostly voice hovering in the air near them: 'I'm coming to haunt yooou.' Drawing to a halt, Albert crouched down and crept forward while Jack followed, chortling to himself.

'Boo!'

Despite themselves, Albert jumped and Jack screamed. Then the three boys, standing in a circle, collapsed with laughter. 'Got you,' roared Guy, catching his breath between laughs and pointing at his friend.

'We knew it was you,' shrieked Jack. 'Didn't we, Albert?'

'Shush,' said Albert, raising his finger to his lips and glancing around with exaggerated nervousness. 'Someone's coming.' Immediately, the brothers stopped giggling and listened intently.

'I can't hear anything,' said Guy in a whisper.

'Is it a ghost, a real ghost?' asked Jack. Guy tried to read Jack's expression in the semi-light and wondered if his brother meant the question seriously.

'Run for it,' said Albert quickly, before speeding off along the grassy path between the jagged rows of headstones. The brothers

77

hastily followed him into the depths of the graveyard, their shadows sprinting in front of them, lapping at Albert's heels.

Finally, Albert stopped so abruptly that Guy ran straight into him. Untangling themselves, they realised they'd lost Jack. 'Come on, let's hide,' urged Albert. The two boys darted behind a sarcophagus and waited, kneeling on the damp grass, trying to control their panting breaths. A minute or two passed and there was still no sign of Jack. Crouching behind his friend, Guy scanned his eyes across the weathered stone of the sarcophagus. He could just make out the outline of what seemed like a pair of floating angels and beneath it, an inscription to a soldier, a casualty of the Crimean War, who'd died exactly fifty years previously. But where was Jack – what was taking him so long? Then, at last, they heard him, coming slowly up the path, quietly sobbing, then softly calling out for his brother, his voice edged with fright. Albert rose to his haunches, ready to pounce. Guy put his hand firmly on his friend's shoulder. Albert turned round and Guy whispered 'no' before rising to his feet.

'Jack? Jack, it's OK, I'm here.' His brother was only a few feet away, his eyes wide open, his body shivering. He could see the relief on Jack's face, his smile dimpling his cheeks.

'Where were you?' asked Jack.

'Are you all right?'

Jack nodded and wiped his nose with his sleeve. He was all right now, now that he was with his big brother again.

Albert stepped out from behind the sarcophagus, clearly annoyed that Guy had spoilt the fun. 'You weren't frightened, were you?'

Jack shook his head vehemently. 'No,' he said.

'Come on, we'd better go,' said Guy. He grabbed his little brother's sweaty hand and dragged him out through the main avenue, their shadows silhouetting against the leering headstones.

Albert followed, glancing behind anxiously as they went, ensuring that the bogeyman wasn't pursuing them.

A couple of minutes later, the three of them were standing silently in front of the church's main entrance. Eventually, Albert said, 'That was fun; we should come again when it's really dark.'

'No,' said Jack, under his breath.

'You were frightened.'

'So were you.'

Albert started laughing. 'No, I wasn't. You're the scaredy-cat. Scaredy-cat, scaredy-cat.'

'Stop it, Albert,' ordered Guy.

'Oh, don't start sticking up for scaredy-cat; what a little coward.'

'Leave me alone,' yelled Jack, his eyes filling with tears.

But his tears only encouraged Albert with further taunts. 'Oh, poor little Jack, the cowardly-custard!'

'Stop it!' Jack's pleading scream pierced the silent summer air.

'Cowardly-custard!'

'Stop!'

Jack's humiliation was too much for Guy.

He only meant to hit Albert the once, just to shut him up. Albert stepped back, more stunned than hurt, and looked at Guy, holding his lip, amazed that his friend had hit him. But then Guy punched him again. This time it hurt. Albert fell but immediately staggered back up. Jack caught his breath. Guy waited and then dealt Albert another blow, and then another and another. Blood started streaming from Albert's lip and nose, his arms flailing uselessly, trying to fend off Guy's persistent attack, the continual blows to his head. Guy should have stopped, but he couldn't, he simply couldn't. His brain turned fuzzy, unable to control his anger, the adrenaline feeding his strength. Albert was pinned down against the grass verge that banked onto the church wall, his body limp, his face ballooning with pain.

'Stop it, Guy! Stop!' sobbed Jack. 'Please stop!' The sound of the little boy's pleading voice immediately permeated Guy's brain and abated his anger. He stopped as suddenly as he started, his fist still clenched, his breath coming in short bursts. He noticed how Albert had rolled into a ball, his hands clamped behind his head, his elbows meeting in front of his face. Guy reeled back with exhaustion. Panting furiously, he bent forward, his hands on his knees, and spat. Albert lay on the grass and after a while, began to cry quietly. Jack, a look of horror frozen onto his face, stared at his brother. He knew Guy would suffer terrible consequences for this and Albert's face was too bloody to be patched up.

Albert sat up and put his face in his hands to try and ease the throbbing pain, the muffled sound of his sobs still audible. Guy rummaged in his pocket and offered Albert his slightly soiled handkerchief. 'I'm sorry,' was all he could say.

The minute hand of the church clock lurched to the top of the hour and the dreary chimes droned high above the three boys. It was nine o'clock. By now, it was properly dark.

Chapter 9: The Silence

Following the usual dinner of greasy beef and over-boiled potatoes washed down with tepid tea, Guy made his way back through the matrix of trenches until he arrived at the officers' dugout, optimistically named 'The Savoy'. There was already a small group waiting casually outside. Amongst them was Robert.

'Hello, Guy, you've been called on too, eh? All those hours spent practising raids weren't for nothing. Aren't we the lucky ones? Fancy a fag while we wait?'

During the following few minutes they were joined by others while the autumn sun made a concerted effort to break through the darkening clouds. Guy reckoned there must have been about thirty-five of them, all of whom he either knew or recognised from the different sections within the platoon. As the time passed, the men fell silent and waited anxiously, smoking and pacing up and down. Eventually two officers emerged from the Savoy dugout. One of them was Lieutenant Lafferty; the other Guy recognised as Major Smyth, a short plump officer with specks of grey punctuating his dark beard.

Lafferty spoke. 'OK, men, stand to attention.' He turned to the major and saluted.

'Good afternoon, men, at ease.' The major cleared his throat and spoke with a strident shrill. 'Now then, you men have been selected for a bit of Jerry-hunting. It's going to be a short, fast operation, and Lieutenant Lafferty here, will lead you. Your objective, apart from putting some good old-fashioned ginger into Jerry, will be to penetrate their lines, do a bit of damage, and, most importantly, to pull out a few Germans and bring them back here. The rest you can leave to us. OK? Now, I don't want any unnecessary heroics but I want to see Germans ready to talk. There'll be plenty of preliminary bombardment to cut their wire up for you, and you'll have ample covering fire to see you on your way, so you shouldn't have too many problems. Lieutenant Lafferty will brief you in greater detail. But remember, usual rules apply: work as a team, keep to your orders, and show the buggers what we're made of.' The major paused and looked approvingly at the men in front of him. 'Thank you, men, and good luck to you all.'

The men saluted as the major's shrill voice faded into the early evening air. Guy swallowed. It all sounded so simple. Before the lieutenant began, Sergeant Wilkins took a roll-call. On hearing his name and confirming his presence, Guy took a deep breath and kicked a stone. He'd been out in the trenches for over two years now, but he had yet to take part in any confrontational attack. He hadn't gone 'over the top', hadn't been on any raids, in fact, he had yet to see a German close to. The men had often practised trench raids on dummy trenches and straw enemy but this was the first time the section had had to do it for real.

'Shankland,' bellowed the sergeant, his pencil poised on his clipboard, his small darting eyes scanning the men in front of him.

'Sarge,' came the reply.

'Small.'

'Yes, Sarge.'

'Tasker.'

'Sarge.'

'Teale.'

Silence. Where was Private Teale?

'Teale?' repeated Sergeant Wilkins looking up from his clipboard. Still no reply. 'Has anybody seen Private Teale?'

A voice from the back shouted, 'He's out in no-man's-land, Sarge.'

'Well what the heck…' He shot a nervous glance at the lieutenant. 'Sorry, sir,' he said before turning his attention back to the men. 'What the *blazes* is 'e doin' out there? He 'ad orders to be 'ere.'

'He couldn't make it, Sarge.'

'Oh, could he not? And why is that?'

'He's dead, sir.' The men laughed.

'That's his excuse, is it?' More sniggering. 'OK, OK, quieten it, joke's over. Thatcher?'

'Sarge.'

'Thomas.'

The roll-call continued. Guy had known Archie Teale. Another victim, another son sacrificed. But what the heck, he got a good laugh. And just for a moment, Guy envied him. At least for Teale it was all over – none of this waiting, this foreboding sense of apprehension.

Lieutenant Lafferty briefed the men on the times and the exact details. The bombardment was due to start at 1745 hours; the raid would go fifteen minutes later, at exactly 1800 hours. He then assigned the men their specific duties. Guy was given one of the most important roles, and one of the most dangerous: he was to be a bayonet man. 'You know the drill,' said the lieutenant. 'Bombers first with the grenades; bayoneters next to kill any survivors. Then, following through, those of you detailed to capture a few unscathed Germans, although slightly wounded will do. You men will have an assortment of truncheons and clubs to subdue your prisoners.'

'What about knuckle-dusters, sir, can we have knuckle-dusters?'

'Yes. You can have knuckle-dusters. Old habits die hard, eh, Chadwick?'

'Well, I wouldn't say that, sir.'

'Lastly, the rear-guard to subdue any German reinforcements and stifle any attempt at a counterattack. Any questions? Good. Go prepare.'

Guy looked at his watch – it was 5.15. The men began by removing anything that could give the Germans clues as to who they were and what regiment they belonged to: buttons, cloth badges, and identification papers.

Charlie Fitzpatrick, the Irishman with the skewered rat, and Robert were both 'clubmen'. Robert secured a sturdy piece of lead to a long stick with a length of string. 'That should do the trick,' he said to himself.

Guy smiled as he fastened safety pins to his tunic in place of the buttons. 'You OK, chap?' he asked.

'Course he's OK,' interrupted Fitzpatrick. 'Nothin' like a bit of proper action, is there? What do they say? You're either bored stiff, frozen stiff or scared stiff. Makes a change being scared stiff, don't you think?'

Robert laughed. 'Well, right now, I think I'd gladly swap with bored stiff.'

'Soon be over,' said Guy.

'That's what I'm worried about.'

'Best time to get a Blighty, nice little wound to get you back home,' said Fitzpatrick.

'I've got a cold sore, will that do?' sniggered Robert.

'Only if it gets lanced by a German bayonet,' said Fitzpatrick.

Private Greene approached them carrying a tin bucket.

'Here comes Stan the Man,' said Fitzpatrick.

Stanley Greene looked like a man with fur balls in his mouth, constantly puffing his cheeks. 'OK, boys,' he said. 'Let's be having your badges an' buttons. Don't forget to black up.' Greene moved on with his bucket.

Guy scooped up a wad of damp mud and smeared it across his face. 'How do I look?'

'Oh lovely, old chap, quite divine,' said Robert. 'May I have this last dance with you, you look so beautiful tonight.' Guy flung a small ball of mud at him. 'Oi, steady on, old man. This was clean on four weeks ago!'

Guy picked up his Lee-Enfield and gave it a last-minute inspection, ensuring the bayonet was securely fixed.

'Remember,' said Fitzpatrick, 'it's not for killing rats.'

'What, no rat stew for dinner tonight then?'

'More like bacon an' lice.'

'Have you heard that Aussie joke?' asked Robert.

'Go on.'

'The officer says to the new Australian recruit, "Have you come here to die?" and the Aussie says, "No, sah, I came yesterdie".'

They heard Lieutenant Lafferty's voice. 'OK, men, let's be having you. Line up please.'

The men stood in two raggedy lines armed with an assortment of grenades, rifles and clubs; their faces blackened with mud or burnt cork. On the lieutenant's order, they filed up the couple of hundred yards to the front trench. As they made their way, the artillery bombardment began. Guy looked at his watch. It was 5.45. On reaching the front line, the lieutenant led them to a straight stretch of trench referred to as 'The Strand', which had been prepared with a number of wooden ladders for the men to climb out of the trench. The men shuffled around and lined up in two squashed lines, with the bombers and bayoneters in front. The lieutenant repeated his orders and walked up and down the line wishing his men good luck. The time passed quickly while the mass concentration of artillery fire pounded the strip of German trench opposite them.

'OK, gentlemen,' shouted Lafferty, clutching a whistle tied with a piece of string around his neck. 'Remember, move out on my order, don't dilly-dally, keep your heads down, if anyone falls, do not stop, proceed with your orders. On hearing the second whistle, retire. Fifteen minutes, twenty minutes max. OK then, get ready…' He looked at his watch. 'We go in one minute. One minute.'

One minute or an eternity, it made little difference now. Sixty seconds to prepare, but to prepare for what exactly? The men stood in total silence, waiting, heads bowed, perhaps lost deep in thought or offering a silent prayer, or perhaps their minds empty, numb. Guy gazed at his mud-caked boots, his rifle by his side, the gleaming bayonet. He took a deep breath, conscious that his whole body was trembling. He'd known fear before, but not like this, not this intense. It seemed to be invading every pore of his being; rooting him to the spot. He feared the fear would prevent him from moving but he'd rather die out there in no-man's-land than be left behind in the trench simpering like a coward. Pride was the most precious commodity for a soldier – to do and to act as one expected others to do and to act. To fail, to be brushed with the tar of cowardice was more fearful than death itself. He found himself praying. The very act of praying was something that had become alien to him. He thought of himself as a boy kneeling in church, his hands clasped, praying for a better batch of conkers, the presence of his parents either side of him. He prayed now that he may be granted the chance to see them one more time, the chance to feel their sobering presence either side of him. His father, who had invested his fighting spirit into his eldest son. If he died, his father would bathe in the glory of his son's bravery. If he lived, his father would embrace the man that his son had become, while his mother would mourn the loss of the boy that was. The boy who lost his youth and his innocence in the trenches.

The man in the trench stood, his eyes clenched shut, his hands clasped around the shaft of his Lee-Enfield. He prayed for courage, the courage to act like a man. He prayed for a Blighty. He prayed for a clean death. There were no halfway measures with death – like virginity, one either was or one wasn't.

Thirty seconds. His whole life had come to this, signposted to this place at this moment. This was the watershed, the moment that would forever divide his past and his future. If he survived, the rest of his life would be defined by what was about to take place – out there in a muddy field in a foreign country. His youth, if not his life, sacrificed to the greater cause. A cause worth more than his life and the life of all these men put together. Guy swallowed. Yes, this was fear all right. Fear of death perhaps; fear of pain most certainly; fear of letting your comrades down; fear of letting yourself down. The fear of being killed, the fear of killing. He gripped his rifle – his rod, his staff. The soothing words came to his head: "Yea, though I walk through the Valley of Death…"

'OK, gentlemen, at the ready…'

Guy picked up his rifle, his palms wet with sweat and mud. "I shall fear no evil…" He placed his left foot on the fire-step. One of the bombers stood at the foot of the ladder. The final hint of sun disappeared behind a sky of steely blue.

'Steady…' Lieutenant Lafferty raised an arm and put the whistle to his lips. Guy shivered.

This was it. "For thou art with me; thy rod and thy staff…"

How suddenly silent everything seemed to be. The big guns had ceased their work. The men were silent. A tin can rattled in the barbed wire.

'Steady…'

Was Guy imagining it, or was the lieutenant's hand shaking as he held it in the air, poised to bring it down.

The eerie silence was punctuated by the shrillness of Lieutenant Lafferty's whistle. 'Go, go, go!' he urged in a sort of subdued yell. The machine-gunners either side of them let rip with a fearsome tirade of fire in their attempt to give the raiding party some cover as they emerged from the trench. The bombers climbed the ladders and were out. Guy and the bayoneters followed, clambering over the parapet. A British artillery shell whizzed over their heads and hit the German line directly ahead of them. Surely there wouldn't be any Germans left at this rate.

*

Guy is out; he is on the edge of no-man's-land, the Valley of Death lies ahead of him, three hundred, maybe four hundred yards. The men crouch as they inch forward, their slow advance shielded by the clouds of drifting shell-smoke. With each step, they sludge through the mud, their boots sucking into the earth, soft and clawing. For a few minutes (or is it just moments? – adrenaline reduces time to a meaningless measure) they advance without a single shot being fired. But then a volley of machine-gun fire spews out from the German trench. The men instinctively hurl themselves to the ground. Was someone hit? If he was, he must be dead, for there's no sound. One of the bombers lets fly with a grenade. It explodes amongst the barbed wire, forcing the Germans to take cover. The men exploit the chance to race forward beneath the cover of the smoke. Another German volley, a couple of men are hit, one is killed, another falls screaming. Guy throws himself head first into a small convenient crater and plunges into the freezing water, only to discover a dead English soldier. It is not a fresh casualty; this chap has been here a while for the stomach is grotesquely bloated and will burst at any moment. What's left of his contorted face has turned into a shade of green; his eyes pecked clean away. Guy covers his nose against the vile fetor. The poor bugger must have crawled wounded into the shallow hole to wait for the rescue that never came. The English machine gunners step up their returning fire; it manages to subdue the Germans for a while. Guy moves forward, every yard an achievement, but every yard reducing the chances of survival as he approaches the German trench. The guns on both sides keep up a tremendous roar. A shell explodes close to Guy, casting up a shaft of black smoke and clumps of earth. Shrapnel falls in a shower of metal and mud, clinking and bouncing off his helmet. To his right, Guy sees a fellow private. He is trying to say something, passing a message on. He is barely four yards away, but his words are inaudible under the cacophony of noise. He leans forward to try and make himself heard. It is a mistake. As he opens his mouth, he is hit. A torrent of blood spouts from his head and he falls face down into the mud. Guy feels nothing, not even a momentary hint of sympathy. The German machine gunners are being pummelled into silence. The raiding party can advance forward again.

Guy suddenly realises his fear has disappeared. An overwhelming sense of joy, of freedom, washes over him. Every pulse within him surges with adrenaline. He would laugh if every ounce of energy were not being taken up with pure physical exertion. He is light-headed with it all. He wants to meet the enemy; he wants to kill.

The bombers are now within close range of the German line. They fan out into two distinct groups – to the left and right of the target area. They throw grenades into the trench at regular, short intervals. There appears to be no defensive reaction, maybe the gunners have done too good a job of clearing the trench. The bombers' job is almost done. It's up to the bayoneters to follow through and breach the German line. Guy has got as far as the barbed wire. He sees an English corpse caught on the wire nearby. Guy scrambles along on all fours, his uniform drenched in wet mud, until he finds a suitable gap in the wire. He spots one of the bombers. Guy signals to him and the bomber throws a grenade into the trench. Guy flattens himself against the soft earth and waits for the explosion. The ground shakes beneath him, there's a scream, and a cloud of blackened smoke billows out of the trench.

He wriggles through underneath the wire, freeing his trouser leg, caught on a protruding spike. He lies on top of the parapet and peers cautiously into the trench, his rifle at the ready. He sees a group of dead Germans lying huddled on the trench floor – four of them. But he thinks he sees movement, no more than a twitch. He moves quickly. It's too far down to jump, so he slides down the trench wall, but still lands awkwardly. As he regains his balance and manoeuvres his rifle, he sees a hand, a revolver. A German, five yards from him; barely clutching onto life, is staring at him and about to fire. There is a slight pause as they look at each other; a fleeting glance of acknowledgement passes between them. It's you or me. Guy is rooted to the spot, staring at the small black circle at the end of the revolver's barrel. The German fires, but Guy is still there. He has wet himself. Did he imagine it, or was there a tiny sound of a 'click'? He sees the look of utter panic on the German's face; his last lifeline has just failed him. It's you or me. The sensation of the warm urine slaps Guy's consciousness back into the present with an inexplicable anger. He flings himself forward, propelled by bloodlust, screaming with pure hatred, both hands gripping his rifle at waist height. He bears down on his terrified foe, who utters a single word: '*Mutter*' the moment before the point of the bayonet catches the German in the cheek. The blade slices effortlessly through, lodging itself in the back of the man's throat, spurting blood all over his face. Guy cannot extricate his bayonet; such is the force of the impact. He slams his left foot against the man's chest and pulls. The man grips the blade as if trying to help Guy remove the impaling metal. The bayonet gives and slips out, slicing the man's hands as it withdraws from his throat. The German, clinging to the last moments of life, fumbles in his tunic pocket. Guy fears he is reaching for another revolver. He attacks again. The second blow slices through the man's nose. The man's eyes are transfixed on the Heavens; he is dying. But Guy's anger remains undiminished and he lunges at him again. And a fourth time. The German is dead. Just for a moment, Guy hears a small boy's voice, pleading with him: 'Stop, Guy! Stop! Please stop!' Guy notices something in the German's hand. It is not a revolver. He reaches down and unclamps the gripped, bloodied fingers to reveal a photograph. It is a picture of a woman and two children, no more than about five or six, a girl and her little brother. Soon the image is obscured by the man's blood. Death is like virginity…

From behind him, Guy hears a frightful scream. He turns to see a German bearing down on him, bayonet fixed. Guy is rooted, too terrified to move, too shocked to defend himself. But amongst the noise, he hears a shot, a single shot that seems to come from above and behind him. Blood spouts from the German's head as he falls in a heap at Guy's feet. Guy thrusts his bayonet into the man's back and grimaces at the ugly squelching noise as the blade does its brutal work. Satisfied that the German is dead, he turns around, but his saviour has vanished.

Guy leans against the trench wall trying to catch his breath, clutching his rifle, his staff. The noise around him continues unabated and within it the screams and cries of men. Guy peers around the corner of the trench. No one there. He creeps along to the next corner and peeps around. Empty apart from a couple of fresh corpses – one German, one English. He moves on, carefully stepping over the bodies. He recognises the Englishman or rather Irishman – it's Charlie Fitzpatrick, the man who had skewered the rat just a couple of hours before, his tunic awash with blood, a hint of a smile on his parted lips. The next corner – still empty, but he's getting closer; he can hear the excitable noise of German voices. Cautiously, with his rifle at the ready, Guy glances around the corner and sees three German soldiers just a matter of yards away, shooting over the top. They are isolated; they must know that, but still they fight on. He hasn't been spotted. He steps back. He takes a deep breath, glances skyward, and then, with his rifle at the ready, steps fully into the new stretch of trench and fires. The first shot catches the nearest one in the head, killing him instantly. The other two don't have time to readjust when Guy fires again and hits the middle soldier in the stomach. The man plunges to the ground and writhes in agony. Just then, an unexploded grenade lands in the trench next to the dying German. The third man stares at it, his life flashes by. Guy silently steps back around the corner. Moments later, he hears the explosion. Still with his rifle at the ready, he takes a quick look. Amongst the smoke lay three motionless Germans.

Behind him, Guy hears the sound of someone scrambling into the trench. Guy quickly turns around ready to shoot. It's Robert. 'Didn't you hear the whistle?' shouts Robert. 'Come on, let's get out of here.' Robert pulls himself up the trench wall and lies flat on the parapet. He offers his hand to Guy and helps pull him out of the German trench. Guy looks around; the men are making their way back. He follows suit, casting his eyes each way, every sense straining to warn him of potential danger. Together they walk back, too exhausted to run. Around them, the British machine gunners continue to provide covering fire. He's half way back across the interminable stretch of no-man's-land, the British trench just one hundred and fifty or so yards ahead. Like an oasis looming in the distance, sanctuary and safety beckons. He's almost there; he's laughing, the next batch of conkers will be the best yet.

But then a searing pain explodes in the back of his leg. He falls onto his haunches; his mind shuts down, rendered useless with pain. His eyes glaze over. He wants to lift himself up, but his body is sapped of energy. Something tells him to lie flat. He allows himself to succumb and falls limply into a shallow indentation in the ground. The slight crater is full of rank, slimy water. Guy's face is briefly submerged in it; he takes in a mouthful of the vile liquid and spits it out. The pain pounds. He can't move. He remembers the corpse who waited for the rescue that never came. The fear that had been driven away by the adrenaline returns in abundance. He clutches his leg. Sticky, warm blood pours out between his fingers and mingles into the dark, filthy water. He sinks slowly into the mud, the water swirling around him. He knows he could drown in this. But like a drunkard, his head is swimming, he doesn't care any more. Suddenly the prospect of death seems almost inviting. It beckons him like a temptress, enticing him, luring him with promises of silence, of freedom from the pain and fear. And sure enough, as if answering his prayer, everything goes quiet, the pain is no more, the fear is snuffed out. There is nothing left but silence.

An eternal silence.

Chapter 10: The Strand

Sometimes being a spectator can be more stressful than taking part, like a parent watching a child competing in a football match. For the competitor, the physical exertion takes away the nerves, the stress and the fear. But the partisan onlooker is encumbered with anxiety for the duration of the ordeal. They mirror every action, kick every ball, jump every jump, urging the ball forward as if they could influence its direction by the intensity of their mental energy. Every miss-kick is a personal embarrassment, every goal a reflected triumph. And so it was for Jack, in the Strand trench, watching from the sidelines. He managed to get hold of a periscope and, through it, watched the progress of the raid. He tried to keep Guy in view. He saw him advance and he saw him throw himself onto the ground, but that was it. After that, it was too difficult to see anything, smoke and confusion clouded his view. The noise was intense. The individuals that went out had already merged into a homogeneous mass. Some had already fallen, but Jack had no way of knowing whether Guy was one of them. He did see some of the men disappear into the German trench but it was too far away to make any sense of what was happening. He gave up on the periscope and stamped up and down the trench. Someone spoke to him, but he was too self-absorbed to notice. He lit a cigarette and immediately threw it away, rendered furious by his inability to help, disabled by his lack of knowledge. The minutes ticked by.

Fifteen minutes they'd said, surely time was up. He lit another cigarette and had taken a few puffs when he heard someone say the whistle had blown. Full time. He wanted to look through the periscope again, but Stanley Greene had taken his place. The noise was as intense as ever. He could no longer tell what was coming from where.

The first couple of men from the raiding party returned, scrambling back into the safety of the Strand, their faces, beneath the coatings of mud and camouflage, a mixture of exhilaration, exhaustion and relief. Others soon followed; each of them helped down by their comrades. More arrived including Lieutenant Lafferty, but Guy wasn't amongst them. Jack's anxiety reached a state of panic as he searched the faces. Where was he? The next batch brought in a couple of captured Germans, pushed into the arms of British soldiers pointing their menacing rifles at them. How strange it was to be in such close contact with the enemy, their alien uniforms incongruous in the British trench. The trench was a mass of activity. The lieutenant ordered his returning men to report to The Savoy. Stanley Greene, still with the periscope, reported: 'Only a few more now.' Jack's heartbeat quickened. Three more slid into safety, but still no Guy, but one of them was Robert. Jack pushed his way towards him.

'Robert! Robert, have you seen Guy?'

Robert's voice was breathless. 'He got hit; he's out there. He's close, about a hundred yards, I couldn't stop.'

'Is he dead?'

'Don't think so.' Robert pushed Greene off the periscope. He scanned the terrain he'd just escaped from.

'There!' he said. He passed the periscope to Jack. 'Look. Can you see him?'

At first, Jack could not. But there, a slim view of a crumpled figure caught his eye. 'Yes, I think so.'

The lieutenant interrupted. 'Well done, Chadwick. Debrief at the Savoy please.'

Robert saluted. 'Sir.' As he turned to leave, he said to Jack, 'Look, old man, if he's alive, the stretcher-bearers will pick him up. I'll see you later.' Jack nodded and watched as Robert disappeared down the trench.

Sure enough, the stretcher-bearers had arrived, each with an armband bearing the letters SB. But there were only four of them. Jack watched as they climbed out of the trench armed with the two stretchers between them and paired off into no-man's-land to try and bring in some of the wounded. The guns fell silent; for once, the stretcher-bearers were allowed to work relatively undisturbed. And with the silence, Jack could hear the sound of the wounded men crying and pleading, trying to attract the attention of the stretcher-bearers. It was a pitiful sound, for the chances of rescue were slim; for what could two stretchers do, but carry in a fraction? Robert's assertion that Guy would be picked up had been optimistic; it was too much of a lottery. Jack held onto the periscope and watched the stretcher-bearers at work. He saw them move towards Guy, but stop to investigate another casualty. But they left him where he lay. He was either already dead or too much of a lost cause to be worth the effort. Then they moved away from Guy, further out to Jack's right. As far as Jack could see, Guy had made no attempt to wave an arm or try and attract their attention. He was dead, Jack knew it.

The fading light ended all further rescue attempts. The stretcher-bearers carried their wounded back along the lines to the first port of treatment, the Regimental Aid Post. With the night came the nocturnal routine of work. Tonight Jack had been detailed to trench maintenance, which meant filling sandbags and repairing damaged trench walls. He had an hour before work commenced. There were rumours that thunder had been forecast for the night. Jack shivered at the thought; how he hated thunderstorms. It was then he heard him. He wasn't sure at first and almost ignored it. But then he heard it again. He strained to catch, if not the words, then at least the sound of the voice. It was difficult to tell, for it wasn't an ordinary voice, but the pleading desperation of a wounded, frightened man. Even the slightest of wounds could prove fatal if the wretched soul was left unattended, exposed to the elements and without water for hours, if not days, on end. But yes, he still couldn't make out the words, but that was Guy. He was alive, perhaps only just, but he was still there, still hanging on! Jack's immediate relief was soon tempered by the thought Guy needed rescuing. He didn't know what to do. If he approached an officer or a NCO, he'd be told to leave him be, even if it meant death. They'd say no point risking two casualties for the sake of one. But this wasn't just a casualty – this was his brother. The older brother who'd always looked out for him, the brother strong enough to take the blame, the brother who beat up Albert Carr. He had to do something and he was prepared to die in the effort, for he knew that death was preferable to doing nothing. How could he face his parents if he knew that he'd listened to Guy die just yards away and had done nothing?

He had the advantage of the dark and he had almost an hour before Sergeant Wilkins would be harassing them into work. He saw a friend of his called Gregory and asked him to help pull Guy in. Gregory pulled nervously on a button; he was too concerned about breaking orders, operating without permission. Jack understood. He too would have been reluctant. He realised this would have to be a solo effort and he was almost relieved – he wanted to go alone. This was a Searight saga, why involve anyone else? *His* moment had come. This is what would redefine him for evermore in the eyes of those who knew him, especially his father. Jack, the little brother; Jack teased and bullied at school; little Jack who needed his older brother's protection. Whether he died in the attempt or not, all that was about to change.

*

It began raining. The stars were invisible. Jack managed to commandeer a flask in which he poured some water. Together with a bottle of rum and some biscuits, he stuffed it all into his tunic pocket. He removed his tin helmet, fearing the noise it would make if he dropped it and put on instead a woollen hat. He smudged burnt cork over his face and hands and lastly pulled on a pair of socks with the toes cut off, over his knees. Hoping he had everything he needed, Jack was ready to leave when he heard a voice call out his name.

'Oi, Searight, where d'you think you're going, man?' It was Sergeant Wilkins walking along beside Lieutenant Lafferty. How small but how wide the sergeant seemed in comparison to the tall, thin lieutenant. Both men wore greaseproof capes against the rain.

Jack decided he had no option but to tell the truth. 'I've gotta go, Sarge, my brother's dying out there.'

'What, and have two Searights killed instead of one. Leave him, if he's still alive, the stretcher-bearers will pick him up in the morning.'

'And is that what you'd do if it was *your* brother out there?'

'Why, you little… how dare you—'

'Oh, come now,' the lieutenant interrupted. 'I think young Searight has a point.' He looked at Jack. 'Do you know where your brother is, Private?'

'Yes, sir; he's about a hundred yards out.'

The lieutenant pondered Jack's answer. 'Well,' he said, 'you won't be able to pull him in by yourself, especially in this rain.' He hit upon an idea. 'Sergeant, you've been out on a number of night patrols, perhaps you'd be good enough to go out with Searight here, and give him the benefit of your experience.'

Wilkins glared disbelievingly at the lieutenant.

'Well, Sergeant, what are you waiting for?'

Wilkins tried to object. 'But he's probably dead already, sir.'

'No, he's not,' said Jack. 'I heard him – just a few minutes ago.'

'There you are, Sergeant, you shouldn't have too many problems; you'll be too far away for Jerry to bother you. Come on then, get on with it.'

Jack was delighted, he'd got one over on the sergeant, and it was worth it just to see the look on his little squat face. Five minutes later, the sergeant was ready and the password for re-entry into the trench agreed – cuckoo. The lieutenant nodded his approval and wished them both luck. Sergeant Wilkins placed a ladder against the trench wall and Jack climbed up, the sergeant behind him. The two men crawled beneath the wire entanglements and out into the dark expanse of terrain between the enemy lines and theirs. The cold night air was silent except for the soft patter of rain. In a reversal of roles, Jack led the way. They crept forward on their bellies over the sodden mud until they found a small crater to roll into. Jack could sense the sergeant's silent rage at being shown-up by Lieutenant Lafferty in front of him. But he didn't care, it wasn't his problem; all he wanted to do was to find his brother. It all seemed so dark out there. He blinked, trying to accustom his eyes to the darkness.

The sergeant nudged him. 'I'll bloody get you for this,' he whispered.

'What's up, Sarge, lost your nerve?'

'Don't you worry about my nerve, Searight,' he said, carelessly raising his voice. He checked himself, inched closer to Jack and spoke again in a whisper. 'But if you ever speak to me in front of an officer like that again, I swear I'll crush you, you understand, I'll bloody crush you.'

Something moved near them; there was a German lying just a few yards away. Jack steadied his rifle, his eyes, his ears acutely alert. He peered down the barrel. Perhaps it was just the breeze or perhaps the German was still alive. Then, with a sudden dash, two huge rats scuttled out from beneath the corpse and disappeared into the rainy darkness.

But where was Guy? His voice had fallen silent. Jack had an idea of where his brother was, but he knew how easy it was to lose oneself out here. He had heard the stories of men who'd become so confused, they'd walked straight into the German lines, thinking it was theirs. He tried to call out Guy's name, as loud as he dared, but little more than a whisper. No response. The sergeant hit him in the arm. 'Keep your bloody voice down, you fool.'

They inched ahead, moving slowly over the mud, crawling imperceptibly forward. The smell of death accompanied them; the very earth seemed infected with the putrid, rank stench of human decay. With their nerves taut and senses strained, every hint of sound took on a sinister edge, every object a menacing shape. In the darkness, inanimate objects seemed to come to life: a rusted revolver, a discarded helmet, a loose strand of barbed wire. Jack paused and whispered Guy's name again. Still no reply. He began to fear he'd gone too far forward or too far to the left. He crawled towards the right, keeping parallel to the trench. His hand felt something. He recoiled at the cold, soft touch. It was a blackened hand, the wrist still clad in khaki, a ring on the smallest finger. Wilkins saw it too. 'I'll 'ave that,' he said picking up the hand and pulling off the golden band. With the ring safely tucked away in his tunic pocket, he threw the hand away.

'That could've come in handy, Sarge.'

'Was that meant to be a joke, Searight?'

For a moment, Jack thought he heard a groan. He wasn't sure if he wanted to call back, for what if it wasn't Guy? He couldn't face the prospect of purposely leaving a man out here to die. He moved forward another few inches. Another groan, but too indistinguishable to be sure. He whispered hoarsely, 'Guy?' Silence. Should he call again? But then came the uncertain, frail reply.

'Jack? Jack, is that... you?'

Jack's heartbeat quickened. 'Hold on, man.' He crawled quickly forward, almost unable to contain the excitement of finding his brother. A few more yards and he was there. His brother's face, almost unrecognisable under the dried mud, smiled at him. Jack clasped his shoulder. 'Are you all right, Guy?'

'Yeah, it's just my leg, looks worse than it is.' Jack peered down, but it was too dark to see anything.

Wilkins caught up, grimacing with every movement. 'Can he move?'

Guy replied. 'Just, but it's bloody agony,' he whispered. 'I've lost a lot of blood. I put a dressing on, but it didn't stick 'cause I couldn't move my leg out of the water. I passed out for a while.'

They heard the dreaded, familiar hissing sound as a Very light went up, illuminating no-man's-land in a blaze of multicoloured light. 'Keep still,' whispered the sergeant as the three men lay motionless, feigning death. Beneath the whirling light, Jack saw a man lying nearby. At first, he assumed the soldier was dead, but he caught the agonised eyes blinking, staring at him through the drizzle. The man was still alive, but those tortured eyes knew he was beyond help; it was only a matter of time. The flare faded away and extinguished, and the dying man disappeared into the returning darkness.

'Here, let me pull you out a bit.' Jack moved himself around, put his hands under Guy's armpits, and pulled. He saw Guy flinch and bite his fist with the pain. Jack got to work quickly. He gave Guy the water, which his brother gulped down, and a couple of biscuits, followed by a tot of rum. While Guy consumed Jack's emergency rations, Wilkins undid the pouch on the inside of his tunic and produced a bandage, field dressing and a bottle of iodine. He swabbed the wound with Lysol, then applied a gauze dipped in iodine. He then quickly applied the dressing and bandage.

'Right,' said Wilkins. 'He can't crawl, he can't walk, we're going to have to carry him. With any luck the Bosch won't want to risk a full-blown scrap just to pluck us off.'

Guy tried to intervene. 'But—'

'Yeah, I know,' said Jack. 'But what choice do we have? It's only what, less than a hundred yards.' He nodded to Wilkins. 'Right, you ready? Let's go.' Jack knelt and helped steady his brother as Guy heaved himself up. Bracing himself between Jack and the sergeant, Guy stood up.

The walk back was long and hard. Despite the wet and the dark, Jack knew they were horribly vulnerable standing bolt upright in no-man's-land. Every step he feared would be his final stride, every breath his last. Guy's leg dragged; he felt so damn heavy. They were almost there, only a few yards to go. Jack called out, 'Cuckoo.' He could see men from his section waiting to bring them in. Their arms reached up, someone half climbed out and helped pull Guy in. Jack breathed heavily, thankful to have been relieved of Guy's full weight pressing down on him. His knees trembled as he slid down the trench wall. Sergeant Wilkins slithered in after him. They sat on the fire-step, breathing furiously, trying to catch their breaths, while Guy was carried off to the nearest Aid-Post. Jack laughed; he'd done it! He'd stepped into the jaws of the sleeping lion and had returned unscathed. Perhaps he'd done it more for himself than Guy and for a few moments, his exhaustion was forgotten in the exhilaration of what he had done.

'Well done, men.' It was Lieutenant Lafferty. 'Excellent work, well done!'

'Thank you, sir,' said Jack.

'Now why don't you both go off and get some sleep, you deserve it.'

Sergeant Wilkins stood up uneasily. 'Yes, thank you, sir,' but as he spoke, he turned to look at Jack, his eyes ablaze with rage.

'Anything to oblige the Searights.' With that, he turned back to the Lieutenant, saluted and disappeared down the trench.

As Jack and the lieutenant watched him zigzag away, the lieutenant said, 'Don't worry about Sergeant Wilkins, Private, it's just a bit of wounded pride, that's all. He'll get over it.'

'Yes, sir,' said Jack. But Jack wasn't convinced that the sergeant would get over it. He hadn't been in the army long, but he'd already seen enough to know there was nothing so dangerous as a soldier with a damaged ego.

Chapter 11: The Dream

As soon as Guy awoke, he was conscious of the faint, nagging pain around his left knee joint. He reached down awkwardly to explore and found that his trouser leg had been cut or ripped off halfway up his thigh. He could feel the huge dressing bandaged around his knee, but he couldn't reach further down. An awful thought occurred to him. He carefully lifted the stained moth-eaten blanket and pulled it back, praying his leg was still there. It was. The dressing had obviously been applied in a hurry, clumsily wrapped around numerous times, stained heavily by his blood. His shoes and tunic had been removed. He shivered and tucked himself under the warmth of the blanket.

He gazed around at his surroundings, and could tell he was in what they called an Advanced Dressing Station; this one was in a large, draughty barn. There were two rows of wounded men like himself lying on small, trestle beds. Doctors and staff of the Royal Army Medical Corps buzzed up and down the central aisle, each with the Red Cross armband on their upper arm. The ADS was close enough to the front to be within reach of the German shells. The windows had been blown out and the glass hastily replaced with hard, bleak sheets of corrugated iron. Part of the roof, to the far end, had disappeared. Guy noticed the floor was awash with potholes and littered with discarded bandages, dressings, bits of uniform stained red with blood, and general rubbish. The noise of the enemy shells made him feel uncomfortable, despite them being almost inaudible over the continuous noise within the barn – the sound of staff shouting requests and orders at each other, of soldiers yelling in pain, pleading for attention, muttering incomprehensibly, groaning in discomfort. He knew he was in the presence of death, lurking and intimidating. The unceasing flow of human traffic provided the only source of sorry entertainment: stretchers carrying their burden of wounded men in and – if they were lucky enough to survive that long – patched-up men out. A fair proportion came in half dead and left with the task of dying duly completed. Some hobbled in and out on crutches, others on foot but clasping blood-soaked bandages. It was, thought Guy, a real circus of atrocity.

Guy's attention was caught by the pitiful sounds emanating from the bed diagonally across the barn from him. At each corner of the bed stood four RAMC orderlies, holding three yellowing sheets between them to shield onlookers from seeing what ordeals the unfortunate occupant of that bed was suffering. Occasionally, Guy could see a RAMC officer's hat bob up from within the wall of sheets. After a while, the muffled screams fell silent. The officer's head re-appeared, the sheets came down and the five men walked away leaving behind a crumpled figure underneath the blanket. Just for a few moments, the men seemed subdued, but then another emergency beckoned and with it, their haste returned. Two minutes later, two stretcher-bearers appeared and, while comparing notes on sleep deprivation, removed the fresh corpse without a second glance. They left behind the rotting blanket and within moments a nurse came along and rearranged the blanket and sheets, removing all trace of the previous occupant. Within another three minutes, the bed had a new patient who clasped the still-warm blanket tightly around himself.

Guy had the uncomfortable sense he was being watched. He turned to look to his right. In the bed next to him lay stock-still a man whose age Guy couldn't tell. His eyes were fixed, unblinking and wide open, his mouth slightly ajar from which a trickle of blood oozed. Guy turned his gaze away and closed his eyes, unmoved by another death.

Guy's thoughts were interrupted by the sound of an officer's authoritative and low-pitched voice. 'And who do we have here then,' said the voice. The young, fair-headed RAMC lieutenant looked at the card attached to Guy's tunic lying at the foot of his bed. '8562 Private Searight, Fourth Battalion, Essex Regiment. Well, Private, looks like you've been in the wars.' The Lieutenant chuckled at his own little joke. Guy forced a smile. 'Let's see then,' said the lieutenant, clearing his throat and inspecting the bandage. 'Hmm, got a few maggots in there, I'm afraid; we'd better get you cleaned up. You've had your anti-tetanus – you probably didn't notice, you were a bit gaga at the time. Now it appears that a Bosch bullet caught you right in the back of the knee, went straight through and caught an artery. Afraid it's made a frightful mess. A frightful mess. But you were lucky; the mud stemmed the flow of blood and stopped you from bleeding to death. Now question is, can we save your leg.' He looked earnestly at Guy. 'Can't pretend it's going to be easy, I'm afraid. You see, we're too busy here doing the life 'n death ones, you know. So, what we'll do is get you moved up to a casualty clearing station ASAP and see what they can do for you there. In the meantime, Private, we'll get this dressing changed for you and wrap your leg up with a Thomas. OK?'

'Thank you, sir.'

'Goodbye for now then, cheerio.' With that, the lieutenant walked over to the opposite bed. Guy heard him say with a chuckle, 'Looks like you've been in the wars.'

Guy waited for someone to come and clean his wound, somewhat alarmed by the thought that maggots were gnawing into him as he waited. Presently, a glum-looking RAMC corporal came to change Guy's dressing carrying a dish with a red solution in it, which Guy reckoned was Lysol. The corporal did his work efficiently but brusquely, causing Guy to bite his fist in pain as the last twists of dirty, blood-soaked dressing were whipped from his knee, tearing away a layer of flesh. 'Keep still, son,' said the corporal, taking little notice of Guy's pain; he had become immune to it. 'This may hurt a bit,' he said. Taking a pair of forceps, the corporal dipped a swab into the Lysol and dabbed it clumsily onto the wound. Guy endured the pain of having his knee lifted and a new dressing applied. With that part of his job done, the sullen corporal told Guy to roll over to his side. Guy rolled over to his right in order not to put any strain on his left leg, leaving the corporal standing on the wrong side of the bed. The man tutted irritably as he lumbered over to the other side. He yanked Guy's trousers and pants down, exposing Guy's left buttock and then jabbed the needle in, with, thought Guy, undue relish. Guy flinched. Next, the orderly applied the Thomas splint – a padded ring placed around his thigh with two long, lateral bars that met under the heel. 'Right, job done,' said the corporal and disappeared without another word.

Guy was just dozing off when he heard his name being called. He raised his left arm and shouted back: 'Here!'

Two RAMC orderlies approached, one carrying a folded stretcher. 'You Searight?' he asked. Guy nodded. 'OK, you're being moved to a Casualty Clearing Station.'

'Is it far?' asked Guy.

'Yeah, we're taking you to bloody Vienna. Is that far enough for you?'

The second orderly stepped in. 'I must apologise for my colleague's unnecessary sarcasm,' he said just as sarcastically. 'It's about ten miles back.' He turned to his companion. 'Right, you're ready? One- two- three, *heave*.'

Guy was hoisted onto the stretcher and carried through the barn, past all the rows of wounded and dying men, until they hit the grey daylight and coldness of the outside. The artillery explosions rattled nearby. The orderlies shunted Guy into the back of a waiting ambulance – a small, black van with room for six casualties: three either side. They lifted Guy into the middle bunk on the left-hand side. Guy noticed all three places on the right were already occupied. The van doors behind him closed with a thump. Presumably, he thought, the other two bunks, above and below him, were also full. The engine spluttered into life and jolted slowly along a rough path until it came to a slightly smoother track. As the ambulance gathered speed, so the ride became bumpier and more uncomfortable. The mattress, wafer-thin, offered no comfort. Inside, with the doors shut, it was dark, with just two small, dirty windows at the back. The heat was stifling and the smell of diesel fumes and sweat oppressive. Guy broke out into a furious sweat, soon accompanied by the frenzied itching of the lice. He unbuttoned his shirt, desperate for air. The six men rode in silence, except for the sound of groaning at each pothole and, above Guy, the pitiful noise of a man quietly whining.

What felt like an age later, but was probably no more than an hour, Guy could hear the sound of gravel beneath the tyres of the ambulance. The van slowed and came to a halt and he heard voices outside. The back doors swung open and, much to his relief, a rush of cool air filled the van's interior. 'Christ, it stinks in 'ere!' said one of the two men who climbed aboard. They pulled out the man on the top right. Two more men came and took the second casualty who cursed with the pain of being so crudely pulled about. Then the third man went. Guy noticed his jaw had been blown away. How could men survive such horrific injuries? There was a delay before the first two men returned to take out the man above him.

'Stop a minute,' said the first.

'What's up?'

'He's 'ad it, poor bugger.'

Guy looked up at the wire mesh and the mattress above him. He noticed the large circle of fresh blood; slowly widening on the material like a stain of freshly spilt ink on a piece of blotting paper.

'We'll 'ave to come back for 'im later,' said the first. He peered into Guy's bunk. 'Are you still wiv us?'

'Just about,' replied Guy.

'Good, let's be 'aving you then.'

The first one took Guy by the shoulders; the second took his legs. The pain of being manhandled shot through Guy like a bolt. He screeched in anguish.

'Sorry, chum,' said the first as they laid Guy onto the stretcher. They carried him across the gravelled drive and into the building through the main door into a large, square hallway. The first stretcher-bearer said, 'You're going back to school, y'know.'

'Sorry?'

'This used to be a boarding school for boys till the army took it over. Lots of classrooms but not a teacher in sight. Just poor sods like 'im out there, and lucky sods like you here. You'll be nice and comfy in this place, and no bloody shells to worry 'bout.'

Guy listened. Here in the grand hallway, he could hear only the sound of lowered voices, of footsteps on stone floors. But no gunfire, no artillery shells, no bombs. This was the first moment of silence he'd had for months.

'We've got nurses here,' said one of the orderlies. 'You know, as in *women*. French and English. Nothing like the soft bosom of a cuddly nurse to get yer goin' again, is there?'

Guy smirked with relief. The man's speech was obviously a well-used one, but it had the desired effect. He had got away with a 'Blighty' after all, and he had warmth, silence and women to look forward to. Until that moment, he hadn't realised quite how much he'd missed, even craved, female company. He wiped away a tear, such was his relief and gratitude. All they had to do was to save his leg and his joy would be complete.

The orderlies stopped at the desk in the hallway and placed the stretcher carefully on the floor. A sergeant behind the desk told them to take Guy to a specific ward on the first floor.

'OK, hold on tight,' said the first, 'we're goin' up.'

Guy found himself smiling. 'That's fine. I say, boys, you wouldn't have a spare ciggie on you, would you?'

*

It was the middle of the night. The pain in his left knee had woken Guy up. Like a hammer pounding his knee from the inside, his whole leg throbbed with the pain as it rippled out from its epicentre. He writhed around on the bed, gripping his blanket, groaning uncontrollably. His throat was brittle, his insides burning. He needed water almost as much as he desperately needed a piss, but the pain pinned him down to the bed, not allowing him the freedom to move. The effort of trying to contain the pain took up all his mental and physical energy, he could think of nothing but the searing agony. It seemed as if the pain had become a being within itself, a parasite that lived off his wound, delighting in the dominance it held over its host, purposely tormenting him, relishing its absolute power. Within a few minutes, its intensity stripped him of his dignity and, no longer caring, Guy relaxed his bladder muscles and winced at the warm sensation cascading down his legs. He spotted a nurse. He put his hand up and called for her attention.

'Oh dear,' she said as she saw Guy, 'you are in a mess.'

'Please,' spluttered Guy, 'can you give me something, anything?'

'I'll see what the doctor says. Back in a minute.'

Guy clenched his eyes shut and began to count the seconds as if holding the nurse to the promised sixty seconds. A throb of pain caused him to jerk, arching his chest out, his head almost swallowed by the pillow. He wanted to hurt another part of his body, just to take the focus of pain away from his leg, to deny pain its total dominance over his wretched knee.

'Private Searight? Major Cartwright, how d'you do.' The doctor adjusted his glasses and looked at Guy's details on his card, rubbing the end of his greying, droopy moustache between his fingers. 'I see we're due to operate on you later today.'

Guy wanted to ask questions, but pain claimed his tongue and his ability to string a coherent sentence together.

The doctor continued: 'But for now we'll give you another dose of morphine to keep you going.' The nurse passed him a syringe. The doctor checked its contents. 'Turn over,' he said to Guy. Guy's buttock was exposed for another injection. Guy wished he felt embarrassed at being so exposed in front of the nurse, but the pain had stripped him of the luxury of dignity. 'Give it a couple minutes or so and it'll start to take effect. Now, we don't want you going into shock, so try and keep warm and nurse will bring you a hot cup of Bovril. I'll be seeing you later; I shall be performing the operation. Good day.'

And with that, the doctor marched off, his shoes echoing on the wooden classroom floor. The nurse remained and smiled. She was a large middle-aged woman with puffy cheeks and a sympathetic face. 'I'll come back when you're settled a bit and we'll see about cleaning you up, OK?'

The pain was still present but even the placebo effect of the injection began to take effect and question pain's authority over its unhappy host. Guy summoned his strength and biding his time, muttering: it won't be long, it won't be long. And it wasn't. Pain teetered, tried to cling on, and then collapsed, defeated by the conquering morphine. But whatever pain-free elation Guy experienced was soon crushed by the recollection of the doctor's parting words: "*I shall be performing the operation.*" What operation?

The comely nurse returned, carrying a bowl of hot soapy water and a flannel. 'Feeling better?' she asked.

Guy realised she was the first English woman he'd spoken to in over a year. 'Did the doctor really say I needed an operation?'

'Major Cartwright? I think so but there again my hearing's not what it used to be.' She flung Guy's blanket back and did not flinch at the stench of urine, sweat and blood.

Guy lay back and allowed the nurse to do her refreshing work, the warm invigorating flannel working its way over his chest and neck, and between his legs. For the first time, he noticed his surroundings and his fellow occupants. The ex-classroom was small, holding only ten beds, five on either side. Guy was struck by the silence, but it was too dark to see any faces. He was conscious that his painful groans had probably kept them all awake, but there were no complaints. Soldiers soon learnt to be stoical; no doubt they just pitied him and thanked God it wasn't their turn to suffer. He wondered why he needed an operation. The brief bed bath complete, Guy arched this way and that as the nurse replaced his bed linen from beneath him. She changed his pyjamas and finished off by plumping up his pillow.

'There,' she said, 'that should make you feel better.'

Guy bit his tongue, trying not to cry. 'Tell me,' he said, 'what's your name?'

She looked awkward, glancing left and right. 'I can't tell you that, not allowed to.'

'No?'

'It's in case you men get too, erm, let's say attached to us.' She laughed, 'Not that anyone in their right mind's going to get too attached to the likes of me.'

'Nurse, I wouldn't say that.'

'Oh, listen to you. Now, you get some rest; I don't want to hear another peep, you understand?'

Guy listened to the night time silence and smiled. This was what fighting soldiers dreamt of – silent sleep in a warm, comfortable bed. This was heaven.

*

Guy dreamt of Jack. Jack the boy had become Jack the man, a successful businessman. He is walking down a London street, arm in arm with a woman, smiling as he passes shop after shop selling 'Searight Hats – the finest hats in London'. People wave to him and strangers wearing his hats call him by his name. Everyone in London seems to know Jack Searight. He is on his way to a party being held in a large London townhouse, frequented by the fashionable set. His father is there too, holding court, basking in the reflected glory of Jack's success.

'But, Arthur, what's become of Guy?' asks an elegant lady wearing a feather boa, her arm linked with Albert Jarrett, still cupping his intestines.

'Now Guy is a fine young man,' his father replies. 'He's a war hero and we need our war heroes.'

Guy too is there at the party somewhere, hovering in the background, his presence unnoticed. He hears his father's words and brims with pride. But then his father adds: 'But a legless war hero doesn't put bread on the table, now does he? Whereas Jack here…' Everyone turns to look admiringly at Jack standing with his companion talking to a gathering of admirers. 'Jack here was a war hero too, but more importantly, look at him *now*.'

'No, no,' says Guy. But no one hears him.

His father continues: 'Poor Guy, what can he do? *He* won't be able to provide me with any grandchildren, will he, for no one will want him now?'

'No!' bellows Guy. 'I did it for you, Father; I did it for my country. You can't just dismiss me now, I gave my legs for you.' This time they hear him but they try to pretend he's not there; he's become an embarrassment. They want to forget the war, not be reminded of it by such an obvious demonstration of its impact. They ignore him and turn their backs.

'Jack, Jack, you still need me, don't you?'

Jack at least acknowledges him. He smiles at Guy. 'No, not any more, there's no Albert Carrs left now. Please, you must excuse me.' He returns his attention to his friends. Guy catches sight of his lady companion – it is Josephine. He wonders where Mary is.

Guy doesn't know what to do, it seems like a lifetime has passed him by and he's only just noticed. He sees a German face in front of him, the silvery blade slicing through his boyish looks. 'Mother, mother,' the boy pleads. He is the enemy; Guy is killing him, yet he understands Guy more than anyone else, including his own brother. Guy hands the German a handkerchief to wipe away the blood, but it is too late. There is no one else to turn to. Guy is a war hero; his father had said it, but a legless war hero. But no, it's not true, he still has his legs, he is still a man and he'll give his father as many grandchildren as he wants. But Guy glances down at himself – just to make sure. He is wearing a full-length khaki gown and suddenly he feels awkward. He hitches up the gown and stares in disbelief at the two wooden legs below. Attached to the left leg is a label. In large stark lettering, it reads, 'Property of the British Army'.

*

'Guy, you awake, Guy?' A familiar, friendly voice stirred Guy back into consciousness. He opened his eyes, but it took a few seconds to focus on the face looming above him. Guy blinked and the smiling face came into view. It was Jack, of course. What was he doing here?

'Jack, you still need me, don't you?'

'What are you talking about?'

Guy's throat was dry, his head ached.

114

'Guy, are you OK?'

'Yeah, I'm sorry, I feel, I don't know, a bit odd, it's so damn hot in here. What time is it?'

Jack looked at his wrist but there was no watch. 'Don't know, I've lost my watch somewhere. Must be about four. You sound hung-over, what have they been giving you, eh? Spicing up your tea with a bit of rum?'

Guy tried to move but was too numb. He seemed to have no control over his body. 'I feel as if I've been asleep for days. God, I feel thirsty – and hungry.'

There was a glass of water on his bedside table. Jack handed it to Guy, who drank it eagerly, dribbles of water dripping down his chin, cooling his sweat-drenched chest.

'What's this doing here?' asked Jack, picking up a bullet from his bedside table.

'I've no idea.'

'You've not seen it before?' he said, passing it to his brother.

'No.'

Jack laughed. 'You know what it is, don't you? It's the bullet that got you. They must've removed it for you and left it here as a little souvenir.'

'How thoughtful.'

'But it is, that's exactly what it is. You have to keep it, Guy, keep it forever.'

Guy rolled it around in his fingers. From a bed nearby, a soldier started singing: *Pack up your troubles in your old kit bag...* His voice sounded strained as if singing through gritted teeth. *And smile, smile, smile.* A nurse was changing his dressing. Guy realised the poor chap was singing in an attempt to distract his mind from the pain. *Smile, boys, that's the style...*

'So how are you feeling?' asked Jack.

'Bloody leg hurts still, but I s'pose there's worse than me.'

'Telling me.' He leant towards his brother. 'Have you seen some of 'em in here, it's bloody grim stuff, and I just think of Father who still thinks of all this as a bit of fun, you know, maketh the man and all that stuff.'

'I know, Jack, I know, but there's no point getting all hot about it.'

'I feel like dragging him here, show him what war's like now.'

Guy didn't want to talk about his father. 'Listen, I don't know how to say this, but–'

'Then don't say it, there's no need.'

'You should have left me, y'know, you could've got yourself killed.'

'You would've done the same.'

'Perhaps. How did you get the sergeant out there?'

Jack laughed. 'Ha, he had no choice, Lieutenant Lafferty ordered him out with me. He was furious, reckoned I'd showed him up in front of the lieutenant. He's still sore about it.'

Guy shook his head. 'Be careful of that bugger, he's all talk, reckons he's been through it all, but it's just bullshit, he gets as scared as the rest of us. Seriously, Jack, be careful, I saw the look in his eyes, he was more petrified out there than you were, and he knows it; he knows we've seen it.'

Jack produced a packet of Gold Flakes, offered one to Guy, and took one himself. The brothers sat in silence, smoking. After a while, Jack spoke: 'It's getting to me, you know, Guy.'

'It does.'

'I can stand the sight of death and the work, the cold and the rest of it; it's the bloody noise, it drives you mad. Afterwards, I'm shaking so much; I'm like a gibbering idiot. It's like having a low ceiling above you, so low you can't stand up properly. I sometimes think I could reach up and touch it. The heavy guns, the field guns, the machine guns, the rifles, and then you got our side throwing the same stuff back, it's… well, I don't know why I'm telling you, you know what it's like. You saw how I was that time.'

'I know. Everyone has something, like a pet hate, something that gets to them.' He threw his cigarette to the floor.

'Knowing what to expect doesn't make it any easier 'cos each time it just gets worse. I've only been here nine weeks and I'm a wreck. I didn't know it was going to be like this, not this bad. When that noise starts up, I can't help it, Guy, I just start trembling, I can't control it. Look at me now, just the thought of it and I go all shaky. It's horrible, I start slavering and I can hardly talk. It's like when I was a kid, y'know, with the thunderstorms and that.' He smoked the rest of his cigarette quickly, hoping to be calmed by the rush of nicotine. 'I'm having nightmares too. There's all this noise and I'm surrounded by bodies lying on the ground, pointing at me and grinning. You warned me, didn't you? You tried to tell me what to expect.'

'Let's not worry about that now, eh? Have you tried seeing the MO about it?'

'No. Bloody doctors, wouldn't make any difference, would it?'

'Perhaps not, but it's worth a try, surely.'

'Perhaps.'

'Listen, I need to go to the loo,' said Guy. 'God knows how long I've been flat out, but my back is stiff as hell.' He tried to move, but a sharp convulsion of pain in his leg pinned him back to the bed.

'There's a bedpan here.'

'No, I need a toilet.'

'Oh,' said Jack. 'Here, let me help you.' Jack took Guy underneath the armpits and helped pull his brother upright.

It reminded Guy of being rescued from no-man's-land. He caught his breath.

'You ready?' said Jack.

117

'It's bloody difficult.' Guy swung his right leg from beneath the bedding and onto the floor. With Jack steadying him by the shoulders, Guy cupped both his hands around his left thigh and clenched his eyes as he endured the pain of manoeuvring his leg out of the bed. With all his weight on his right leg, Guy pulled himself up to his full height, while holding onto Jack. He saw the look of panic in Jack's eyes for a split second before losing balance. As he fell to his left, Guy tried to clasp Jack's arms, but he was too unbalanced and he collapsed onto the floor shrieking in pain as he hit the wooden deck. The initial shock of pain receded. 'Bugger, that hurt,' he said looking up and reaching his arm out for Jack to help him back up. But Jack's face wore an expression of horror; his eyes focussed on Guy's leg. Guy followed his brother's gaze. It took a moment for it to register. But then with horrifying clarity, he saw what Jack was staring at. He quickly turned away, his head spinning, his fingernails gripping the wooden floor as he vomited on an empty stomach.

The lower left leg was gone. It had been amputated slightly above the knee, the stump wrapped in a blood-stained bandage.

Chapter 12: The Doctor – 1 November 1917

Jack had had enough. He feared he was going mad and had asked Lieutenant Lafferty's permission to see the battalion's Medical Officer, a Captain Butler. Jack was waiting in a silent queue outside the MO's tent in the reserve trench, shivering from exhaustion and cold. He looked around at his fellow patients. These were not wounded men or at least not seriously wounded. There were a few bandages and dressings evident, but most, like himself, seemed to carry no outside sign of their malaise. Jack wondered what sort of reception he could expect from the MO. All the men in front of him seemed to be in and out within two minutes. Perhaps the MO had a secret potion he could prescribe and perhaps God would answer his prayers and pluck Sergeant Wilkins off the planet. Since his rescue of Guy, the sergeant had seen to it that Jack went out on every working party, on numerous night-patrols and more than his fair share of sentry duty. The worst was sentry duty in a sap, a forward trench that jutted out from the main trench on the frontline. There you were, in the pitch black, stuck halfway out into no-man's-land, totally by yourself, your ears out on stalks, listening for the slightest movement or a snatch of enemy conversation. It played havoc on one's imagination – the bits of debris and litter blowing around, a rat scurrying about, the wind gusting in the barbed wire. Jack had never realised that silence could be so noisy, so frightening. The experience reminded him of the Albert Carr night, but at least then, he had his brother around.

He was at the front of the queue now, another few minutes. He stamped his feet and wrapped his arms around himself. He hadn't slept well for days and when he did sleep, he had tremendous nightmares. Always the same one. He was advancing alone across no-man's-land under a wall of noise that seemed so intense he feared walking into it. But he kept going, trudging on, wondering why he was out here all alone. Eventually, he would come across a crater filled with corpses. Then, under the illumination of a Very light, he would see the dead all looking up at him, their arms outstretched, beckoning him, their expressions fixed with mischievous grins. That horrible supercilious grinning, the unceasing noise which would wake him up with a start, shivering and drenched in sweat.

The more he thought about it the more he envied Guy. OK, he may have lost a leg but he was out of it now; he was safe. What Jack would do for such a wound – anything to get a Blighty ticket back home.

'Next!' The voice bellowed out from within the Nissan hut. Jack stepped in, closed the metal door behind him and stood to attention. The MO was sitting behind a table, scribbling down some notes. 'Number, rank and name,' he asked in a sharp staccato voice, without looking up from his papers.

'8112, Private Jack Searight, sir.'

Captain Butler jotted down the name. 'At ease, Private. So, what's t'matter with you then?' Jack noticed the curly tufts of hair swirling out from beneath the captain's cap.

Jack coughed. 'Erm, I feel in a bad way, sir. I had weeks of patrols and sentry duty and…'

'So what's so unusual about that?' Captain Butler was an older man, short and plump with small eyes and saggy jowls and a bushy moustache.

'I think my nerve's gone. I just need a rest, that's all, a few days out of it and I'll be as right as rain again.'

'Hmm, they all say that.'

Jack looked at him. Did the MO really think he was making it up? 'No, really, sir, I have these awful nightmares and some days my vision becomes blurred and I have these terrible headaches, and other days I lose all sense of taste and smell.'

The Captain laughed. 'Count your blessings, I'd say. The rot they serve up here! Well, let's have a look at you then.' The Captain examined Jack. He shone a light into his eyes and ears, placed a stethoscope to his chest, asked Jack to poke his tongue out and felt his pulse. 'Hmm, have you sustained any injuries?'

'No, sir.'

'Any illnesses recently?'

Jack shook his head.

'Any instances of ill-discipline you need to tell me about?'

'No, sir,' said Jack incredulously.

'How are your feet, got any trench foot?'

'No, had them checked over recently.'

The Captain tutted, removed his cap and scratched his head. Jack was surprised to see that above the circle of curling hair, the Captain was bald. 'Can't see anything wrong with you.'

'No, sir, it's not my–'

'How are your bowel movements?'

Jack was taken aback by the question. 'Well, I haven't been, erm... for days.'

'Well, that's it then. What you need is a good dose of laxatives, that'll see you right.' The Captain reached to a pile of wrapped tablets ready to hand on his table. 'Here we are, take two of these and if it doesn't work, take another two tomorrow morning. Works wonders this stuff, you'll see.' Jack stood still; staring at the little packets the MO had given him. The captain returned to his seat behind his table and scribbled down a few notes. 'Oh, and take a couple of these as well.' He handed Jack two white pills.

'Aspirin?'

'Well, you said you get headaches.'

'Yes but…'

'Anything else, Private?'

'Erm…'

'Well, if that's all,' he said standing up again, 'I've got many more to see to. Good morning.' Captain Butler led Jack to the door. 'Now, pull yourself together, man, and you'll be OK.' And with that, Jack found himself back outside, clutching his tablets. He glanced back to see another private enter the Nissan hut. He hadn't known what to expect, but he expected more than this. Much more.

Chapter 13: Nurses

Two days had passed since Guy's left leg had been amputated from just above the knee. The day after the operation, he received a blood transfusion to prevent post-operative shock. As he was getting ready, Major Cartwright, the surgeon, told Guy in a matter-of-fact tone, 'Had the leg been sterilised and drained a bit earlier, we could've saved it but it'd become infected with gas gangrene.'

'Gas gangrene?'

''Fraid so, Private, a gas-forming bacilli, which, once it infects a wound, can only be treated by amputation. What can do you, eh?' Guy took this as a vague apology but he knew this wasn't the place where surgeons had the luxury to worry about what might have been. They concerned themselves only with the here and now, and if a surgeon believed an amputation was needed, off it came, no time to seek a second opinion. Guy's leg would have been chucked into a bucket, along with numerous other limbs, and some poor nurse detailed to take it away and throw the grim contents into the furnace. In the meantime, Guy had had a bath – his first proper bath in over two months. The water had to be almost cold so as to not cause further pain to the stump. The water turned black as soon as he lay down in the metal tub, sparing Guy the trial of staring at his shorn leg. Once finished, he found it impossible to drag himself out and, much to his embarrassment, had to call for assistance.

Within those two days, Guy had almost come to terms with the loss of his leg. How long would it have taken under normal circumstances? But these were far from normal circumstances. Here, mangled men with wounds severe and life-threatening surrounded him. What was a leg to a jaw or charred skin or the poisonous effects of inhaled gas? Guy's leg ached – a dull, incessant pain which served as a constant reminder of its absence. Guy lay on his bed for two full days, barely acknowledging his fellow patients. He needed to be left alone, allowed time to absorb his new self, his new being. At least his war was over, but it was a high price to pay, one hell of a Blighty. How long would it take to be strong enough to go back to England? he wondered. And once home, what would he do then? He had no concern for his financial future – he could simply slot in with the family millinery business. With Jack at his side, they could take over and allow their father to enjoy his long-sought-after retirement. He sniggered at the thought of his father being unable to resist offering his advice and being incapable of relaxing for fear his sons were cocking it up. No, Guy's concern was more for his personal future. He was considered a good-looking chap and he had had the pleasure of a few short-term acquaintances, but never a serious girlfriend, with, perhaps, the exception of Mary. But who would be interested in him now – an incomplete ex-soldier? What woman would want to share his bed, to have his children, to provide his father with a grandchild, the grandchild he was so looking forward to? He remembered his dream; his scathing father complaining about his legless war hero of a son. In removing his leg, the surgeon had cut off his future; the women he could have had, the bride that would never be.

At least now, in this hospital, Guy felt safe, cocooned from the outside world, his wound like a membership card to a unique club of contorted and mutilated men. Here, he was one of many, they were all one of the same, victims of the same cause. They understood him and Guy understood them. They'd all seen, felt, smelt and experienced the same emotions of fear, boredom, hatred, deprivation, apathy, love, comradeship, pity and self-pity. A generation of young men, just like himself, united by the experience of war. Surely, *their* sons and grandsons would never have to experience or suffer as they had experienced and suffered?

But would the outside world understand? Here, among the cripples, the wholesome and healthy staff were the odd ones out. But out there, back in England? Would *they* understand; would they try to? Out there, isolated from each other, he and his fellow victims would stand out like lepers. Guy shuddered at the thought.

After the third day, Guy began to take more of an interest in his surroundings and his fellow inmates. In the bed next to him was a man in his thirties who had lost his right arm, a Devonian with a pockmarked face, a corporal named Lampton, who spent his time learning to write with his left hand.

According to Lampton, they were in Ruby Ward. With just ten beds, it was one of the smallest wards and contained only the lightest casualties – the not-so-badly wounded, or amputees or potential amputees. There was little sign it had ever been a classroom. The walls, which had been painted yellow, looked dirty and uneven. The wooden floorboards were dusty and unswept, the windows filthy and cracked, two large but dim lights swung from the high ceiling. Two paintings broke the monotony of the peeling yellow paint – one, an alpine scene, the other, a portrait of King George. Guy was tempted to salute each time he looked at the earnest monarch and his piercing eyes. By each bed stood a small table for their meagre belongings. Guy's table was empty, so Lampton gave him his copy of Dickens's novel *A Tale of Two Cities*.

The corporal introduced Guy to each of his fellow occupants. Opposite him a chap called Stephen Browne – Browne with an 'e'

– and either side of him, two men whose names Guy couldn't remember but whom he christened Smith and Jones. Jones, poor chap, was a basket case – he'd lost all four limbs, various tubes were attached to him, leading to a huge demijohn beneath his bed. Guy, to his shame, shuddered with revulsion. Smith, for his part, had lost his right arm and his right leg. Further down, a Welshman with part of his jaw missing and bits of food smeared across his shattered mouth. None of them were in a fit state to talk or acknowledge Guy's hello. And this, thought Guy, was a ward for the lighter casualties?

Browne seemed ridiculously young, his fresh complexion belied by his dark eyes. Although quiet, Browne was able to offer his own explanation, 'Got caught by a piece of shrapnel,' he told Guy. 'Gouged out my thigh. But I was lucky; they saved it in time.'

Each had his own sorry tale, similar to Guy's. And now together, in Ruby Ward, they found solace in each other's company, swapping stories, jokes, cigarettes, optimism and encouragement.

Later that afternoon, the autumn sun shone and the nurses encouraged the men to go outside and exercise, and enjoy the fresh air. One of the nurses brought Guy a pair of crutches. He struggled to use them and found the effort exhausting. He asked for a wheelchair but the chairs were in short supply and reserved for officers or those like Smith and Jones in greater need. It put into perspective the nature of his suffering. So, he persevered with the crutches. It was difficult at first, fearful as he was of falling over at any moment. Lampton accompanied him as he stumbled precariously around, the corporal promising Guy to help him if he looked like he was about to fall over. Guy wondered what Lampton could do with his one arm, but he was grateful for the offer. Once outside, Guy was surprised to see the lawn covered in long wooden huts and even a series of marquee-style tents.

Lampton anticipated his question. 'They've been put there,' he said, 'ahead of the next big push.'

'Expecting a lot of casualties then?'

'Yes. How fast we learn, eh? At least we're out of it. They'll move us out soon; we're taking up too much valuable bed space.'

'Home?'

'Yep, home – a beautiful word, don't you think? Not so sure about Browne though,' he added, lowering his voice.

'What do you mean?'

'Well, poor chap, he reckons he's got himself a Blighty but I'm not so sure.'

'You reckon he'll get sent back?'

'Yeah. It all depends on the Blighty nurse.'

'The what?'

'The doctors – they're so rushed off their feet they ask the nurses what they think. So on Ruby, the Blighty nurse, I don't know which one it is, but she seems to have the authority of who gets sent home and who doesn't.'

'Good God, that's some responsibility.'

In the far distance, the men could still hear the rumblings of war. For some, the sound was too much and even at this safe distance, they preferred to stay indoors, closeted from the audible reminder of what had brought them here.

The nurses were mostly well-to-do English ladies, attached to the Voluntary Aid Detachments, but there were a few French nurses in attendance. Guy found the contact with women such a humanising effect. For two years, he had lived with men in an unreal, unnatural environment where the thought of women seemed such a trivial distraction and where death made a more natural if unwelcome bedfellow. As such, he had forgotten how much he missed the company of women. For the first few days, whenever a nurse spoke or touched him, Guy felt thankful, almost tearful, for their attention. It wasn't the women's sexual being that so moved him; it was the sense of comfort, of maternal security and well-being that was so blissful. Once, in those early days, when a nurse rested her palm against his forehead, Guy felt his muscles relax, the inert tension ease and his mind drifted away. He wondered whether she was the Blighty nurse that Lampton had mentioned. But there were, of course, a few nurses who were considered particularly attractive and the subject of much lurid discussion. The men regarded the nurses with either maudlin sentimentalism or lewd crudeness. Guy was relieved that at least in front of the nurses, the men always behaved impeccably. They all preferred the English nurses, women who could talk to them of England and the things that reminded them of home. The French nurses were fine, but even if they spoke good English, and some did, the men felt alienated by their accents, the lack of common ground. And Guy couldn't help but agree. After such a long absence from home and away from women, talking to an English nurse was like touching home. Whether she represented your girlfriend, your mother, your sister, you felt the bond, the hand stretching across the Channel resting on your forehead, soothing one's whole being.

Chapter 14: The Ridge – 3 November 1917

Sergeant Wilkins was leading the working party across the open terrain trying to keep to the mud-tracked road, followed by his small group of twenty men including Jack, Gregory and Robert. They walked in silence, mindful of the holes and craters that pockmarked the road and the shallow ditch that ran alongside it. It was eight at night and dark, only a few stars visible, but at least the big guns on both sides had fallen silent, and even the rain had eased off; however, the legacy of an earlier downpour made progress difficult. Jack was exhausted. He'd only had a matter of a few hours' sleep during the whole week. The sergeant knew of his 'little visit to the quack' a couple of days earlier and had promised Jack to keep him busier than ever. 'That'll teach you to go running to an officer,' the sergeant had said sadistically. The lieutenant warned them the Hun knew that the two-mile road was a key supply route to the brigade depot and that they kept a careful eye on it in the hope of disrupting the British chain of supply. But the alleged 'couple of miles' seemed unending.

'How much further, Sarge?' asked Jack.

'What's it to you, Private?' the sergeant snapped back.

Eventually, they came to the depot from where the men were loaded up with an assortment of supplies: wiring, spades, axes, duckboards, sandbags, buckets, and other assorted things. Laden with their hoards, the men knew that the return journey would prove to be far more arduous. It was virtually pitch black as they staggered slowly back, and every few yards they had to stop and wait because someone had slipped in the mud and spilled their burden.

The road took a slight incline upwards. Jack groaned with the effort, his throat parched dry, his temples pounding. The pace was excruciatingly slow, one laboured foot in front of the other, each step an effort through the sucking mud and the puddles of slimy water. Gregory had fallen behind. 'Not in line,' he shouted. The advanced group stopped for Gregory and the other stragglers to catch up. Jack listened. Beyond the rasping of his own breathing, all he could hear was the uneasy silence. He didn't like it; the silence couldn't last. They were so exposed out here on top of the ridge and very much alone. The darkness that engulfed them offered little comfort. He wished the stragglers would catch up; they had to get back, it'd only be a matter of time before the Germans realised what they were up to. He realised that the closer they got to their lines, the more vulnerable they'd be to an attack. There was another way, a longer but safer route through a copse. He stood right behind Sergeant Wilkins, wondering whether the sergeant had thought of this too, and dare he ask. He decided he had little option.

'Sarge, will we be going straight down the road near Fritz or should we circumnavigate the trees?'

'Circumnavigate, eh? Is this a question or a suggestion, Private?'

'I just thought it might be—'

'I don't give a damn what you think, you little upstart.' Warming to his task, Sergeant Wilkins leant towards Jack until their noses almost touched, his foul breath filling Jack's nostrils. 'Listen, you useless piece of shit, don't think your big words impress me, cos they don't, see. Now get your arse in line, right?'

'Sir.'

'Don't "sir" me, Searight, I'm sergeant to you; I work for a living, gottit?'

'Yes, sergeant.'

The stragglers caught up, panting, bent double under the weight of their loads. They huddled together, each realising, like Jack, how precarious their position was, and how far they still had to go. Then, as if to compound their fears, a Very light shot up in the sky, illuminating the stark landscape. The men stood stock still, their hearts thumping with the dread of what would follow.

'Shit,' uttered Robert, looking around anxiously.

'That's blown it,' whispered Gregory.

Jack agreed. 'We're going to be sitting ducks up here.'

'Stop your whining,' barked the sergeant, but Jack could hear the uncertainty in his voice. 'C'mon, let's get the hell out of 'ere.'

Jack spoke; once again, he didn't want to, but he had to: 'Shouldn't we lie low for a while, Sarge?' Sergeant Wilkins spun round to face him. Jack flinched; for a moment he thought the sergeant was going to hit him.

'Your nerve snapping, Private?'

'No, but it'd be suicidal to go forwards now.'

Through gritted teeth, the sergeant hissed, 'You don't listen, do you, Searight? I don't give...' He stopped. He heard it. They all did. The eerie sound of the *whoosh* steaming across the night sky. They all threw themselves onto the ground. It exploded a little way further up the track in front of them, some thirty or forty yards away. Moments later, a second shell landed at the same distance, throwing up huge wads of earth.

The sergeant waited for a short while and then rose to his feet. 'Let's go,' he said just loudly enough to be heard. Jack stood up unsteadily, repositioning the awkward load on his back while gripping his rifle, which he knew had been rendered useless in the circumstances. He edged forward, every nerve frayed, compounded by the debilitating exhaustion that reduced his legs to jelly. The party began to elongate and sub-divide into smaller groups again. The sergeant seemed intent on leading the men straight towards where the shells had exploded. Another flare lit up the sky, quickly followed by another shell, which burst behind them shaking the ground. As they dived down, a couple of the party were hit, obliterating one man into bloodied shreds, while the other clasped his pummelled head, his piteous screams ringing out into the night. Jack lay prostrate on the wet track, his cumbersome load jettisoned next to him, his head so low his lips touched the muddy gravel. The Huns had them now, he thought; another couple like that and they'd all be done for. The wounded man started crying hysterically. Jack noticed some of the men had taken shelter in the roadside ditch. He crawled towards it and grovelled into the thin channel of mud as another shell exploded nearby, the noise deafening him. He crawled up to Robert. They could hear the sergeant's rasping voice ordering his men to proceed but no one heeded his demands. Jack realised he was shaking uncontrollably, that noise was having its usual effect again. Another was coming; Jack buried his head into the mud as the shell exploded. More screams. He began to whimper pathetically; his mind collapsing in on itself.

'The Huns seem to be making a lot of effort on our behalf,' said Robert.

The screeching *whoosh* sounds became continuous. One landed precariously close, showering the crouching men in clumps of earth. 'Just make it stop, in Heaven's name, make it stop,' muttered Jack to himself. He had to get away, but the noise trapped him in the ditch. He waited.

Robert sat up. 'It seems to have stopped, come on, let's make a run for it.' They clambered nervously out of the ditch and crept forward, holding their rifles. Everywhere there were men lying flat on the ground, most of them dead, some blown apart, others screeching as men do in the painful and lonely realm that lies between dying and death. Jack saw Sergeant Wilkins, groaning, clutching his leg. Jack reached down to him, grappling for his emergency dressing pack. But then another shell bore down. He should have thrown himself down flat, but as if hypnotised, Jack remained still, kneeling beside the sergeant. The air thumped him hard on the back of the head with the force of being hit by a damp sandbag, followed by a terrifying noise as the shell exploded on impact. Immediately, came the sound of hundreds upon hundreds of lashes swishing through the air as great pieces of jagged shell flew in every direction. Something caught him in the shoulder, the force pushing him over onto the sergeant. But he barely noticed; the pain was unable to permeate through his blank mind. His vision blurring, bewildered and dazed, Jack staggered up and breathlessly zigzagged across the road, tripping over himself, pulling himself back up, oblivious to his surroundings. He stumbled through the maze of men, wounded, dying or dead. Unable to control the whimpering, nonsensical noise emanating from his mouth, Jack lurched forward, before finally collapsing in a heap.

Chapter 15: Stranger in the Midst

Private Christopher Webb was having a late-night stroll. It was almost ten; lights out would be in a few minutes. His platoon was halfway through a six-day rest and stationed in a couple of billets a few miles south of the village of Saint Omer. He and his fellow privates had spent an exhausting day clearing the local road of mud following a forty-eight-hour downpour. But after four p.m. each day, the men had the evenings to themselves. Dinner had been a couple of hours ago. Back home, Webb had always been partial to an after-dinner walk. The big guns had fallen silent and the evening was wonderfully still and quiet. The two adjoining billets backed onto a small forest and Webb breathed in the smell of the fir trees. In three days' time, the platoon was due to go on another tour. The prospect didn't worry Webb unduly because, assuming he survived it, he was due his first bout of leave since arriving in France ten months previously. Webb was thirty-five years old, a veteran of the Boer War, married with three children. How he longed to see his family again. The youngest would have almost doubled in age since he last saw him. He appreciated that he would be a stranger to the little chap, but he still couldn't wait to hold him.

Webb had just lit a cigarette when he became aware of a figure coming up the track towards him. At first, he assumed it was one of the men returning to the billet after a more adventurous late-night walk than his own. But there was something in the way the man slouched that made Webb realise that this was a stranger. For a fleeting moment, he thought it was a German, but then he saw the khaki of the British uniform. The man seemed to be heading straight towards Webb but his head hung low and Webb reckoned the man hadn't yet realised he was standing there. The stranger was muttering to himself. With barely ten yards between them, Webb called out. Immediately, the man stopped and looked up at Webb, clearly surprised to have bumped into anyone. The two men stood in silence gazing at one another, each suspicious of the other, each wondering what to do or say next.

Webb could see that the stranger looked filthy, exhausted and cold, and was panting heavily. He also appeared frightened, his eyes began darting this way and that, as if looking for an escape route. He was young, perhaps not yet twenty. He was short, his slouched posture emphasising his lack of height, and he had dark, almost black, unkempt hair. His eyes, however, looked anything but young; they looked bloodshot, thought Webb, lined and weary. He had no helmet or hat and, Webb noticed, no rifle. In his arms, he cradled his greatcoat which was wet and splattered with mud. His face and hands were almost black with grime; his trouser leg ripped in the right leg. His puttees looked ragged and his boots misshapen by layers of dried mud. The man looked as if he'd just come back from the front, thought Webb.

The stranger spoke. 'I've gotta get back.'

'Back?'

'Yeah.' He paused for a few moments, trying to catch his breath. 'Have you got any water?' he panted.

'I think you'd better come in, mate,' said Webb nodding his head towards the billet.

'No, gotta…' He bent forward and put his hands on his knees, his breathing still laboured. He muttered something, but Webb didn't catch it. Then, suddenly, the man fell to his knees, looked up momentarily at Webb, and collapsed in a heap.

Throwing away his cigarette, Webb sprung forward and felt for the man's pulse. It was still strong, very strong. He concluded that the man had simply collapsed from exhaustion. He noticed a wound in the shoulder; a large damp patch of blood stained the back of his tunic. Webb ran back into the billet and headed for the communal room, which was a hive of men chatting, laughing, and drinking and smoking. A crackly record played in the background. Webb recognised the tune as 'Come Under My Umbrella'. Near the door sat three men playing cards. Webb beckoned them and urged them to come outside and give him a hand to 'carry in some bloke who'd appeared from nowhere and just collapsed'. In no time, the three soldiers were up on their feet, following Webb outside to where the stranger lay. They each took a limb and heaved him indoors, laying him on the floor of the hallway to catch their breaths and to decide where to put him. Webb remembered there was a spare bed in the downstairs dormitory, near the kitchen. They lugged him through, thankful not to have to carry him upstairs, and laid him on the bed.

'He's just a boy,' said one. Webb sent one of the men to fetch the captain while he stayed with the stranger. A few minutes later, the gaunt-looking Captain Ellis appeared. Webb told him his story of how the stranger had emerged from nowhere. Ellis listened intently and then sent someone off to find the first aider. With the help of the others, Captain Ellis propped the man up on the bed and removed his boots and rotting socks. His tunic gave no clue as to what regiment he belonged to – the buttons having been replaced by pins. He searched his pockets for the man's papers, but all he found was a half-full pack of cigarettes, a box of matches and a photograph of a young girl. Pretty thing, he thought, young, probably late teens, nice eyes. While no one was looking, he slipped the photo into his pocket.

136

The first aider appeared and made Webb repeat his story while he checked the man over, checking his feet for trench foot and carefully inspecting the wound in the shoulder. 'He's all right,' he declared while rubbing the circulation back into his feet. 'Looks like he got caught by a piece of shrapnel, painful, but he'll live. Better get him to a CCS tomorrow and meanwhile, I'll disinfect it.'

Webb addressed the captain: 'Do you reckon he's a deserter, sir?'

Captain Ellis rubbed his chin and watched as the first aider did his work. 'Yes, first thing I thought of, Webb, but no, thinking about it, I don't think so. Firstly, he wouldn't have come here, would he, and he would have been more on his guard. And secondly, or is that thirdly, you say he said he wanted to get back somewhere.'

'Yes, sir.'

'So, presumably, he got sent out on some errand, got lost, wandered around a bit and ended up here, hence his need to get back. I'll question him first thing tomorrow, find out where he's meant to be and get him sent up to the CCS.'

'Yes, sir,' said Webb. 'Do you think someone oughta go with him, in case he gets lost again?'

'What, and have one of you fools get lost as well?'

'Well, sir, we could vouch for him, in case they think he deserted.'

'Hmm, I'd thought of that, Webb.'

'Yes, sir.'

'He looks young, doesn't he? I found no identity papers, which seems strange.'

'What about a photo? His sweetheart perhaps.'

'No, no photo.'

'But he's no deserter, is he, sir?' said Webb.

'No, not this chap.'

The first aider had done his work quickly, cleaning the boy up and applying a dressing to the wound. 'That should do him,' he said.

The captain looked around at the little congregation of men. 'Well, nothing more we can do for him now, might as well leave him to it.'

'Sir, do you think we oughta put a guard on him, you know – just in case.'

'Yes, I thought of that too, but no, probably no need to – look at him, he's out for the count. He won't be going anywhere.'

'Yes, sir.'

The men turned to leave. Private Webb took a final look at the mysterious wanderer. Somehow, he knew this boy had a story to tell, but they would have to wait until morning to find out what it was.

Chapter 16: Provisions – 4 November 1917

Jack woke up. The dull pain in his shoulder ached but the thought occurred to him that, for the first time in weeks, he had slept soundly and in a proper bed, without the routine scourge of a nightmare. He had no idea where he was or what time it was. It was dark, although a dim light shone through a slightly ajar door next to his bed. Around him, he could hear the comfortable snoring of men and smell sweat and dirty feet. He guessed he was in a dormitory, probably in a billet behind the lines. Slowly, it all came back to him. He remembered the bombardment on the ridge the previous night, the terrifying feeling of exposure, squirming in the shallow ditch at the side of the road. Jack trembled at the thought. He vaguely remembered the blast that sent him flying and knocked him for six, and then waking with the pulsating pain in his shoulder. He'd staggered for what seemed like hours in a sort of daze. No one stopped him or asked him where he was going. He remembered at some point asking for the nearest aid post, and trying to follow the confusing directions and getting hopelessly lost. And then of course, bumping into the soldier outside the battered-looking house. Jack had said something to him but he couldn't remember what.

He began to panic. What should he do next? Should he stay put and rejoin his section the following day? But what if someone had seen him walking away and reported him? He was so hot, suffocating under the blanket, breaking out in a sweat. He thought of Sergeant Wilkins, if that bastard didn't have him up for desertion, then he'd have him for every raid and patrol going. His hands started shaking, the sound of the shells pounded in his head. Visions of men torn apart, of blood flowing in torrents swamped his mind. And in the midst of it, came Wilkins's face, contorted with venom: 'I'm going to break you.' He couldn't face it, he wanted to go home, he wanted to see Guy, to see Mary and her sister. Jack sat bolt upright, his heart pounding with panic; his breath coming in short bursts. He wasn't going back.

He crept out of bed, wincing with the pain in his shoulder, and followed the dim light, half expecting there to be a soldier standing at the doorway. To his surprise, there wasn't. He went into the hallway and peered up and down. The corridor stretched out to the left, but to his right, just a few feet away, was a glass-fronted door. The hallway light shone through the glass and, stepping up to it, Jack saw that this was the door to the kitchen. He realised how hungry and thirsty he was. Quietly, he turned the doorknob and thanked his luck that it wasn't locked. He sneaked in and noticed the large stove, the generous sink and the backdoor with the pantomime-sized key still in the lock. Carefully, he opened a few cupboards; there was just enough light from the hallway to make out the shape of tins, bottles and containers. He found some bread and hurriedly broke off a chunk and ate it. He found a beaker and drank a cup of water. How pure this water tasted, he thought. He'd become accustomed to the taste of water tinged with the repugnant hint of fuel having been carried to the front in petrol cans. Jack then returned to the dormitory. The man sleeping in the bed next to him stirred. Had he opened his eyes, Jack would still have been OK. He could have simply told the truth – he was hungry and had gone off in search of food. The sleeping soldier stirred again, and in doing so, he'd repositioned himself in an odd position, his head resting to one side, missing the pillow entirely. It was then that Jack had the idea. He crept over to the man's bed and carefully removed the warm pillow. As he stepped back, Jack kicked something soft at the end of the bed. Jack knelt down to feel it, perhaps it was a spare blanket he could use in his deception, but no, it was an empty canvas haversack; equally, if not more, useful.

Jack returned quietly to the kitchen and stuffed the bag full of bread and various tins, including a half-full tin of Golden Syrup. He opened a few drawers, hoping to find a tin opener. In one of the drawers, he found a heap of entangled kitchen utensils, but Jack was too worried about the noise to rummage through them. Instead, he opted for a sturdy-looking butcher's knife, and, for good measure, a spoon. Next to the sink, he saw a half-full bottle of red wine, its cork pushed part of the way back in. Pulling out the cork, Jack took a few sips of wine and drained the rest away into the sink. He refilled the bottle with water, gently running the tap, and finally pushed the cork back into the bottle.

By now, Jack was almost ready and itching to make his exit. Leaving the haversack on the kitchen floor, he crept back into the dormitory, pushing the door slightly further ajar to allow more light in. He found his trousers and greatcoat draped over the end of his bed and his tunic hanging on the bedpost. He slipped on his trousers and then his tunic, noticing the large bloodstained rip in the right shoulder. He couldn't, however, find his boots, despite groping around in the darkness under the bed, but in the shadows, he saw the outline of a pair of boots next to his neighbour's bed. He moved over, picked them up, and noticed that a sturdy pair of socks had been stuffed inside. He put on his greatcoat, which was still wet and heavy. He thought about finding another one, but that seemed too low; he felt bad enough taking a valued pair of boots, without adding further to the crime. Then, carrying the boots, Jack returned again to the kitchen and picked up the haversack, swinging it over his shoulder. He gently turned the chunky key in the backdoor anti-clockwise and carefully pushed open the heavy wooden door, cursing the creaking noise of the hinges. Not wanting to open the door more than necessary, he squeezed through, holding his breath, and stepped out into the night, gently closing the door behind him.

Once outside, Jack noticed that dawn would soon be upon him, the stars were fading. It was already just about light enough to make out the outline of the shrubs and bushes in the garden, the wall at the end of it, and the tops of the trees beyond. He sat down and put the socks and boots on. They were a good size too big for him, but still preferable to his own knackered pair. Bracing his shoulder, he climbed over the six-foot-high wall, something he couldn't have done before six months of training, and jumped over onto the other side, letting out a little groan of pain as his right leg landed heavily on the damp earth. Ahead of him lay the forest. He started walking, the dim dawn light disappearing as he entered the canopy of trees. His wounded shoulder ached, but the adrenaline of escape dulled the pain, his heart beating with a mixture of exhilaration and trepidation. For the first hour, he made slow progress, tripping over roots or fallen branches, stumbling into small holes and indentations in the soft ground. He stumbled onwards. But then daylight permeated through the trees and Jack kept going, his sense of urgency pushing him on.

Finally, after two hours of solid walking, Jack stopped. Exactly where he was, and where he was heading, he had no idea, as long as he was a safe enough distance away from the billet. He circled his shoulder; the pain had dulled but its presence was still there.

The soldiers would be up by now, he thought, and they would know he had done a runner. Jack reckoned that even if they did send a search party out, they'd have too much other work to do to worry about him for long. He decided to camp down and get some sleep. He opened the haversack and fumbled around inside and wondered why everything felt sticky. The stickiness seemed to have spread everywhere – onto the bread, the bottle of water and the tins. Jack smelt his fingers – it was the Golden Syrup. He removed the syrup tin, flung it to the ground, and sucked his fingers clean. From the haversack pocket, he took the butcher's knife and stabbed it into the top of a baked bean tin. After a few minutes of jabbing, the tin finally buckled and Jack poured small amounts of beans onto the syrup-soaked bread. It made for an unusual mixture, but not altogether unpleasant. He found a small hollow in the ground lined with damp moss and laid his greatcoat on top of it. He gathered a few branches, snapping them into smaller pieces, and collected large handfuls of leaves and placed them on top of the coat. He then slid himself carefully under the coat, trying not to disturb his crude attempt at camouflage, and settled down. It took a while to get used to the dampness of the moss, but there were times, Jack thought, when he would have given anything for a bed as comfortable as this. Soon fatigue overcame the damp discomfort and Jack fell into a deep sleep.

Chapter 17: Alarm

The reveille sounded at six a.m. Private Reginald Scales woke up feeling cold and his right shoulder stiff from having slept in an awkward position. He stretched his arm up trying to relieve his aching muscles and turned his head to the right, facing towards the stranger's bed. The evening before, the news of the lost boy, as he became known, had spread throughout the adjoining billets. The men speculated about where he'd come from and how he ended up here. Despite Captain Ellis and Webb's denial, the consensus was that the boy was indeed a deserter. Some of them had urged the captain to phone the Military Police, but Ellis stuck to his guns, preferring to wait until the morning so he could at least hear the boy's side of the story. Scales's bed was next to the boy's. Lights out was at ten, but Scales had had difficulty getting to sleep owing to the deep snoring emanating from the sleeping boy. Eventually, the toll of a day's shovelling sent Scales to sleep.

Scales yawned. The boy was still asleep, huddled underneath his blanket, oblivious to the sound of the reveille. As Scales stepped out of bed, he realised his blanket was missing. He looked under his bed, but no, it wasn't there and he wondered where his boots were. The other men in the dormitory were up and about chattering to each other.

'Our "lost boy" still asleep then, is he?' asked one.

'Looks like it,' replied Scales. Then turning to the sleeping figure, he said, 'Oi, c'mon, Sleeping Beauty, time to get up.' But there was no response. Scales leant forward and shook the boy. From the softness of the touch, he knew immediately that the bed was empty. He threw the blanket back and there, on the bed, was his pillow and his blanket. 'The little sod,' he murmured.

The other men joined Scales, all staring speechlessly at the empty bed. At that point, Captain Ellis appeared, his footsteps echoing on the wooden floor. 'Is he up yet?' he asked as he entered the dormitory to be confronted by the sight of six gormless soldiers. He followed their eyes and, for a few moments, was also struck dumb. Scales glanced at the captain and could see the look of panic coming to his eyes. Ellis cleared his throat. 'Maybe he's just popped out for a jimmy-riddle.'

''Fraid not, sir,' said Scales. 'He's tricked us, that's why all this stuff's on the bed.'

'Oh my word.' The captain was clearly shaken. He looked at Scales and the others. 'Well, don't just stand there, go look for him,' he bellowed.

'In our pyjamas, sir?'

'Now!'

The men hopped barefoot into action, telling passers-by what had happened, while Captain Ellis returned to his makeshift office. Soon the word spread, and the whole billet and surrounding area was a hive of activity as semi-dressed soldiers searched frantically around the house and gardens. After fifteen minutes or more, Private Webb, fully dressed, reported back to the captain. 'He's definitely gone, sir.' The captain bowed his head and cursed quietly to himself. 'I'm sorry, sir,' added Webb. He knew the captain would have to face some awkward questions over this. Ellis may have been a fairly ineffectual officer, but he was generally a decent bloke and Webb liked him.

Scales reappeared. 'He's taken a load of food from the kitchen, sir, and, what's more, the blighter's gone and nicked me boots and haversack.'

Ellis stomped up and down his office. 'Damn, damn, damn. Damn him, I knew he was a deserter.'

'Yes, sir,' said Webb.

'There's only one thing for it,' said the captain, 'I'm going to have to inform the authorities. They're not going to like this.' He stormed out of the room muttering to himself. 'They're going to have my guts for garters for this. Damn him.'

Chapter 18: The Forest

Jack woke up. It took him a few seconds to register where he was and how he came to be lying under a blanket of his greatcoat and leaves. The realisation hit him and induced a sense of panic. He was now no more than a fugitive and he had no option but to carry on. He'd been missing too long to go back now, burdened as he was with a catalogue of theft, absconding and deception. He was amazed he'd evaded capture for so long, walking straight out of the lion's den early that morning. Above him, the tall beech and fir trees loomed, their branches swaying gently in the breeze, the cool sun shining through the gaps leaving a mottled effect on the ground. He breathed in the smells of the forest – the pine, the moss, the damp leaves. How fresh everything smelt. It was only a few miles behind the lines, but here in the autumn forest, Jack was reassured somehow that nature cared nothing for man's petty squabbles. He had no idea what time it was, but he guessed it was around midday.

His shoulder ached. He reached back and felt it. Someone had applied a bandage; he wondered when that had happened.

Eventually, having stirred and brushed off the bits of forest from his clothes, Jack decided to move on. He guessed that if a search party had been sent out to find him, he would have heard it by now. He knew the town of Saint Omer lay somewhere to the north of the forest, but where exactly he didn't know. The forest itself wasn't too big, but big enough to get lost in. This had both its advantages and disadvantages. He also knew that if he walked long enough, he would eventually reach the edge of the forest, and then he would be able to follow its perimeter until he came to Saint Omer. He'd been there before and the place teemed with Allied soldiers of different nationalities, so despite his unkempt appearance, he hoped to be able to blend in with the crowd and make his way unnoticed. He had no money, so he would have to steal or scavenge to survive, and that was risky, for any soldier caught stealing would immediately be questioned. Then came the even trickier business of boarding a train heading back to the ports. He hoped, somehow, that Saint Omer would provide him with a solution. He reckoned he had enough provisions to keep him going for about two days. He had plenty of tins, but his supply of water worried him. He shook his greatcoat free of leaves and moss and heaved it on. They weren't the most practical of things, these coats, they kept you warm but they absorbed water, dampness and mud. He'd be able to walk quicker without it, but equally he knew it would be foolish to ditch it. With the haversack swung over his good shoulder, Jack began walking. It was going to be a hard slog, but after five continuous weeks on the frontline, he didn't care; anything was preferable to going through that again.

As he walked, Jack's mind went back to the night before his embarkation, his last night in England. He liked Mary and the more time passed, the more he thought of her with affection. Then, when he was able to join up, he decided he had to be a man to do a man's job, so he asked her to marry him. Fortunately, events moved quicker than he anticipated and there was no time to marry, at least not in the grand manner that Mary desired. Even more fortunately, she was able and willing to accommodate him as her fiancé. And so, they made love; only the once, but it was enough, he could go to war a man. But what would he do come the end of the war? Did he love her enough to want to marry her? Despite the letters he'd written to her expressing his undying love, the doubts lingered. He rummaged in his pockets for his photograph of Mary but having searched each pocket a number of times, he had to conclude the photo wasn't there. Pity. He so wanted to see her face, to be reminded of her lovely eyes.

At first, Jack thought he'd imagined it. He stopped and listened, but there was nothing but the sounds of the forest, the breeze shuffling through the leaves, the assorted shrills of birds, the drone of insects. But then he heard it again. He ducked down and strained his ears. He heard the sound of voices. Jack cursed and glanced around for somewhere to hide. He couldn't tell how far away they were or how many, but the voices were definitely English. Were they men on exercise or were they coming for him, hunting him down like the fugitive he was? He began to shiver. There was nowhere obvious to conceal himself, so he had no choice but to pin himself against the trunk of a hefty tree. He wanted to run, to flee, but with great determination, he stayed put, fearing that even his breathing would betray his position. The voices seemed to be coming from everywhere, closing in on him. He could see someone, not forty yards from him. His heart lurched, the sweat pouring down his back. But then the voices seemed to be fading. He dared to peer round the trunk and sure enough he saw them moving on through the woods, about eight of them. Jack slunk to the ground and breathed a heavy sigh of relief.

*

The old man barked at Jack in French, his lips moving incomprehensibly under the thick bush of his grey moustache, finishing off with a raucous laugh. Jack smiled, relieved that the man seemed friendly enough.

'Saint Omer?" he asked, shrugging his shoulders in an exaggerated fashion. *'Ou est Saint Omer, s'il vous plait?'* he asked, each word painfully articulated.

'Saint Omer?' The old man launched into a long dialogue, seemingly unaware that the young English soldier had no idea what he was saying. But he pointed to his right, jabbing the air with an outstretched finger.

'Over there?' said Jack, pointing in the same direction.

'Oui, oui, Saint Omer.'

Jack bowed. *'Merci, monsieur.'* He thanked him again and started to walk.

The old man shouted after him, laughing out loud at his own joke.

*

Jack had no idea how long he'd been walking but he reckoned many an hour. The night was drawing in but now, finally, he could see the village ahead of him, perhaps another mile, a church spire dominating the horizon. He trudged on, his shoulder aching still, both thankful to be closing in on his destination but fearful of what lay in store there. He was cold and hungry – he had some provisions left but had rationed them until he found somewhere to sleep. He hoped the village would offer new sources of food.

He'd walked through the last field, where he decided to rest, leaning against a stone wall, and wait until dark. He closed his eyes and fell asleep.

By the time Jack woke up, it was properly dark, the half-moon mostly obscured by clouds. He couldn't tell what time it was but he felt better for having eaten and rested. The ache in his shoulder seemed to be fading. With his eyes accustomed to the dark, he decided that now was the perfect time for re-joining his fellow man. He climbed over the wall and, landing on the other side, was pleased to feel the solid tarmac beneath his feet. Taking a deep breath, he walked up the steep road towards the silhouetted village in front of him.

Not a soul was about as Jack made his way down the various narrow streets, not a single light in the houses either side. Conscious of the noise of his boots, he began to worry that the village might be under a curfew. Walking slowly, he made his way to the central square. Again, total darkness, not a street light, not a sound. Somewhere a dog barked. There, in front of him, was the church, its presence dominating the square. The time, according to its giant clock, was half-three. Scanning the square, he saw a café, its tarpaulin fluttering in the breeze, its windows covered by wooden shutters. Closer to, Jack saw its name – Café Vincent – and outside its front door, a dustbin. A cat scurried off on his approach. Jack was hungry but he wondered whether he was *that* hungry. Perhaps not yet, but he soon would be. Holding his breath, he lifted the lid. Immediately he was hit by the smell of beef. But it was too dark to see inside. He couldn't face plunging his hand into a goo of mixed-up leftovers. He'd rather beg or steal than subject himself to this. Quietly, he replaced the lid and turned back towards the church. A road sign caught his eye, *Gare*, so at least now he knew which direction to take to find the railway station.

Jack climbed the steps leading up to the church and approached the huge wooden doors. He turned the brass ring and, to his relief, found the doors unlocked. Despite their size, the doors opened quietly and Jack slipped inside.

Having slept so much that afternoon, he wasn't tired. He lay on a pew at the back of the church. The church clock rang each hour with such volume as to awaken the dead. The last chime signalled six o'clock. Jack needed a pee. Outside, despite the sun, the air felt cold. Going back inside, he found a room at the back of the church to the left of the altar which was obviously the priest's office. Peering inside various cupboards, he duly found a breadbin and, to his relief, inside, was half a loaf of white bread. It was stale, but Jack ate huge chunks, his jaw aching as he chomped. A quick further search, and he found two bottles of communion wine, one opened with about a quarter remaining. He took a couple of swigs. The liquid made Jack shudder and he laughed.

Having feasted on his communion breakfast, it was time, he decided, to catch a train.

Half past six and already the town buzzed with activity but in such a way that made Jack shiver with apprehension – everywhere he looked were men in uniform – both army and Royal Flying Corps. He remembered that the RFC had a large base on the outskirts of the town. Gaggles of relaxed men, their uniforms clean, their boots polished, their faces fresh. Among them, he knew he stood out – the soldier who looked dishevelled, his boots caked in mud, unshaven, his breath rank and tinged with alcohol.

He made his way towards the train station, his eyes fixed on the pavement, hoping not to attract attention. For a while, he walked alongside a horse pulling a cart laden with potatoes and turnips. Behind him, he heard the quick step of boots on cobblestones. He made to go into a bakery, opening the door. He thought of Mary and her work in the bakery. In the reflection of the door glass, he saw a group of men jogging past in formation. He sighed with relief, hovering at the door. '*Bonjour, monsieur,*' a man's voice called from inside. He was serving a middle-aged woman, wearing a wide-brimmed hat of straw. At her feet, her shopping basket. The aroma of freshly-baked bread wafted through and for a moment Jack felt weakened by the gorgeous smell. He smiled weakly at the man in his pristine-white apron. He went in, nodded a *bonjour* at both, then set himself to consider the variety of breads on sale. He reached inside his haversack and touched the kitchen knife. He didn't mean to do it and he knew he would hate himself for it. The shopkeeper and his customer resumed their conversation and feeling himself ignored, Jack made his move. Nimbly, he stretched down, grabbed the purse from the handbag and ran out of the door. The woman in the straw hat, on realising what had happened, screamed at him to stop. He ran, faster than he thought would be possible, his boots echoing on the cobbled streets. Some of the jogging men turned at the sound of the woman yelling from the door of the bakery, wondering what she was trying to say. They looked around but Jack had already raced ahead of them, turned a corner and headed for the station.

The train station was a mass of soldiers on the move; the intermittent shout of a Frenchman cut through the excitable voices of Englishmen. Jack was out of breath. He looked round, reassuring himself that he wasn't being followed. The purse tucked away in his inside pocket made an uncomfortable bulge on his conscience. A train stood on the platform, emitting occasional belches of black smoke. According to the clapperboard, it was due to depart in ten minutes; its destination was Calais, just forty kilometres away. Calais – even the sound of the word in his mind made his mouth water. He saw a sign for the men's toilet, and popping in, he fished the purse from inside his tunic and looking within found a note or two and a bit of change: twelve, perhaps fifteen francs altogether. Enough, he thought, for a while yet. He pushed the money into his pocket and found a bin for the purse, pushing it down to the bottom, obscuring it with various bits of litter. He needed to get on that train. Less than eight minutes to departure.

Getting a ticket from the ticket office proved easy, even with his pidgin French: '*Billet, s'il vous plais.* Calais,' was all that was necessary. Two francs later, he was ready to go. But a commotion outside on the platform made him stop short. Peering through the ticket office window, his heart surged on seeing the woman from the bakery, and, alongside her, a policeman, his black uniform shining in the sun, men in khaki passing by either side of them. Jack pulled back from the window. Around him, the office was almost empty, only an elderly French couple in the corner examining a pamphlet. He was trapped. Outside, waiting, the train. The clock inside the office showed five minutes. 'Oh, Lord,' he said aloud. The elderly couple looked at him; the woman raised a plucked eyebrow. In the corner, a wooden chair. Should he sit on it; try to appear normal?

He turned instead to face a poster on the wall. A painting of a puffing train emerging from a tunnel. His mouth turned dry. He could hear the woman outside, talking loudly, whether to the policeman or to all within earshot, he couldn't tell but it was enough to interest the elderly man. '*Ce qui est?*' he heard him say. The train outside blew its whistle, a conductor shouted, '*Quatre minutes.*' Four minutes. He felt the eyes of the couple on his back. The puffing smoke in the picture seemed to swirl. The Frenchman spoke again. Jack examined his ticket, trying to think what he could do next to appear normal, an ordinary soldier, albeit a scruffy one, about to board a train. A glance out of the window told him the woman and her policeman had moved further down the platform. The Frenchman repeated himself but louder. It was obvious the words were directed at him and they were not friendly in tone. Three minutes. He turned to look at the man. His wife was behind him pretending to be leafing through the leaflets. The chair. The door. A solution came to him, a ridiculous solution. The man was now standing directly in front of him, his aftershave faintly apparent. The man spoke again but this time, leaning back towards the ticket man behind his grille, all the time his eyes remained fixed on Jack.

Outside, the conductor was shouting, the train whistling, train doors slamming; inside, the ticket man shouting, the old man threatening, his wife pleading. Jack could see the seconds tick by on the clock behind the man's head. It had to be now. '*Au revoir, monsieur*', said Jack. Quickly, he picked up the chair, but the old man read his intention. Surprisingly nimble, he grabbed it. The two men tussled for the chair. *'Qu'est ce qui ne va pas? C'est vous qu'ils recherchent?'* asked the Frenchman, his tone threatening, mocking. *'Claude,'* he called to the ticket man. *'Appelez le policier.'*

Jack recognized the word *policier* and with it, let go of the chair and plunged his hand into his haversack, pulling out the kitchen knife. The man put down the chair, not taking his eyes off Jack. *'OK, c'est bon, c'est bon,'* he said, putting his hands in the air.

'Get back,' said Jack, gesticulating with his knife towards the man's wife. 'And you,' he shouted at the ticket man. The man muttered something but did as was told, appearing from a door next to his booth. 'Over there, I'm sorry about this, this wasn't meant to happen.'

The clock showed one minute to go. The three of them huddled in the corner next to the leaflet stand. The train emitted another whistle and a puff of black smoke drifted over the platform. Taking the chair, Jack strode outside, returning the knife to his haversack. He slammed the chair against the doorknob. The train had started to move. He could see her straw hat at the far end of the platform. The old man was rattling the doorknob from inside the ticket office, pushing at it.

Jogging up alongside the train and seizing a door handle, Jack began to feel exhilarated. He heard her yell, *'Il est là,'* just as he opened the door and jumped up onto the train. He lowered the window and leant out. He saw the chair being kicked away, and the old man tumbling out, screeching, *'Oi que pensez-vous que vous faites.'* The policeman was sprinting down the platform, waving his helmet, yelling, *'Arrêtez, arrêtez.'* But it was too late; the train had already gathered too much momentum; the driver would never hear the policeman with his flailing arms. Jack could see them all, rapidly receding into the distance: the policeman bending down to catch his breath, and, further behind, the old man and the woman waving her straw hat. Jack leant against the door and slid down.

His shoulder hurt. He hated himself for having subjected them to that – the woman, the elderly couple, the ticket man; what had led him to such desperation? But for now, at least, he was safe.

Chapter 19: The Piano – 5 November 1917

With the ticket in his hand, Jack made his way down the train corridor, pushing past soldiers, trying to find an empty compartment, but each one seemed to be full of men, shouting in good heart, laughing. Making his way, he saw at the end of the corridor, a lieutenant. The soldiers wouldn't question him, but an officer? It was too risky. Instead, he turned back. Eventually, on the fourth carriage, towards the back of the train, he found a compartment with just a woman and a child inside. This will have to do, he thought.

Sliding the door open, he muttered a *bonjour* to the woman and sat down heavily, relieved to catch his breath. The woman responded with an accented 'hello'. She was about thirty, thought Jack, wearing a brown jacket with large buttons, a daffodil brooch in the lapel, a matching hat and bright red lipstick. On her lap a newspaper. Next to her, wearing shorts, her son, probably about eight, reading a book with a cowboy on its cover. Jack, in his awkwardness, wished he had something to read. Instead, he leaned against the window and watched the countryside rush past. He thought of what lay ahead of him – how would he get on a boat to England; the train to London. It was all too daunting. At least now he had the money. He thought of the woman with her straw hat and pitied the anguish he had caused her. He knew the policeman would telephone ahead; that they'd be waiting for him at Calais and possibly every station in between. He could try and merge in with the soldiers but it wasn't without its risks, especially in the state he was in. The little boy laughed at something in his book. His mother spoke fondly to him, then smiled at Jack.

'He's always reading,' she said.

'You speak English?'

'Yes.'

'I read a lot at his age. Always adventure stories. Africa, India…'

'Are you going back home to England?'

'Yes. England.' How simple it seemed.

'You have a ticket,' she asked.

'Of course.' What made her ask that?

They sat in silence for a few minutes and Jack tried to concentrate on the outside. She broke the silence by speaking to her son.

'Why do you not sit with your friends?' she asked, turning to Jack.

'Oh, I've seen enough of them to last a lifetime.'

The compartment door slid open with a flourish. '*Billets, s'il vous plait.*' The ticket inspector's call made Jack jump. The inspector, wearing a cloak, took both the woman's and Jack's tickets, punched them and handed them back.

Jack couldn't help but let out a sigh of relief as the man slid the door behind him. He could hear his voice asking for tickets in the next compartment.

The woman picked up her newspaper, opened it randomly and started to read. On the front page, a picture of Henri Pétain, the French commander-in-chief, with his square little hat. 'You can't get off at Calais,' she said from behind the paper.

'I'm sorry?' asked Jack, sitting up.

'They'll be waiting for you.'

'I don't understand, who will be…' He slumped back in his chair; what was the use? 'How did you know?'

She put down the newspaper. 'I saw them from the window at the station. The woman, the policeman. They were looking for someone. They were looking for you.'

The two looked at each other, their eyes locked. The spell was broken only by the boy pointing at something out of the window. She humoured him, and said to Jack, 'He saw a bird, I don't know the name of it in English. Big, colourful. You come off the train with me at the station before, Les Attaques.'

'Peacock?'

'No, not peacock.'

'They could be waiting for me there.'

'They will be expecting you in Calais, not Les Attaques. More brown than a peacock. Has a green head.'

'But why? Why should you want to do this?'

'We walk together, with Pascal here. Husband and wife. Yes?'

'Pheasant.'

'Yes, it was a pheasant, *un faisan*,' she said, picking up the newspaper.

*

Thirty minutes passed without another word between them. Occasionally, the boy would chuckle at the pages of his book. After a while, she closed her eyes, and drifted off. He looked at her more carefully. She wore her hair in a hairnet, pulled back beneath her hat. The hat and jacket were made of a heavy cloth, almost masculine, but countered by the flower. Perhaps she was older than he originally thought; there were lines at the corner of her mouth, crow's feet around her eyes. She looked tired; she looked as if she would be perpetually tired.

159

The train stopped a few times but the woman did not stir. Only as the train slowed for perhaps the fifth time, did she open her eyes. 'We are here,' she said, repeating the phrase in French for the boy. Jack breathed deeply, trying to calm his nerves. He knew what lay ahead could be awkward. She took her handbag and thanked Jack as he slid the compartment door open for her. The boy glared at him as he passed. He spoke to his mother as they alighted onto the platform of a tiny-looking station called Les Attaques, questioning her. She tried to soothe him.

'Come,' she said to Jack, 'walk next to me. Stay close. *Pascal, venir ici.*' There were very few people about, the station seemed small. Ahead of him, he could see the ticket barrier and an elderly ticket inspector in uniform, a pair of glasses, but not, that he could see, a policeman. He caught the eye of a soldier still on the train. The man winked at him. He wished he could take her hand, to appear more like a married couple. He stopped in his tracks, seized by a moment of panic – could he trust her, was she taking him into her confidence only to betray him at the barrier? As if reading his thoughts, she smiled at him and motioned him forward with the slightest nod of the head. He had no choice.

She walked quickly now, taking Pascal by his hand. Jack knew why, she wanted to crowd into the family ahead of them. He heard the inspector asking for the tickets. If need be, thought Jack, the old man could easily be pushed to one side. '*Billets, billets, s'il vous plaît.*' And of course, he still had the knife.

'*Vous avez votre billet?*' she asked him. 'Your ticket?'

Jack nodded, unable to speak, the ticket in his hand. Without a word, the ticket was taken from him. '*Merci, monsieur,*' said the man, taking the ticket, a glint of light reflecting in the rounded glasses. '*Mais c'est pour Calais.*'

He didn't understand but he didn't like the tone. The woman spoke, '*Il faut changer de plan.*'

'*Ah bon.*'

And then they were on the other side, the train station in front of them, largely deserted, barring their fellow passengers. 'My word,' said Jack, the relief pouring out of him. 'We did it, we… we did it.' He beamed at her; she smiled back but between them came the irritated voice, '*Arrêtez*.' Young Pascal, thought Jack, was one jealous little boy.

'Are you hungry?' she asked as they strolled towards her home, through the empty streets flanked by tall, grey-bricked houses. The clouds were dark, the atmosphere strangely oppressive. He noticed a sign with the words *Les chiens doivent être tenus en laisse*, with a picture of a dog with its lead.

'Yes, very.'

'So, what is your name?'

'Jack.'

'Jacques – that's the name of my husband.' She told the boy of the coincidence and the boy reacted to this new nugget of information with a tirade of angry-sounding words. He seemed surprised as if only his father had the right to use that name eliciting a verbal riposte from his mother. He walked on, a boy cloaked in sullenness.

'And what's your name?' asked Jack.

'And here we are. This is where we live.' The house, although two-storied, was small and sat on a bend in the road. The front door opened straight into the living-room, and Jack's eyes had to accustom to the dark until the woman flung open the windows and pushed open the shutters. A large table dominated the room, a faded carpet, a coat rack, small oil paintings on the wall, a photo of a man in uniform and, in the corner, an upright piano. She told her son to take Jack's coat and things to his room. Why not the coat rack? thought Jack. She offered him the armchair and promising something to eat disappeared into the kitchen. Pascal, having done his errand, sat at the table and pulled his book out from his satchel. He half-heartedly flipped through the pages but Jack knew he was being watched by the boy.

'Is it good – your book?'

The boy made no response but merely stared at him, troubled, resentful. '*C'est bon?*' said Jack, trying again. Still no response. The boy was dark, almost black-haired, large, prominent eyebrows on one so young. Jack gazed at the pictures on the wall, hoping the boy would stop staring at him. The boy snapped shut his book and left, flouncing out and back up the stairs. Jack sympathised – it must be difficult having your mother invite a total stranger into one's house.

Stretching his legs, he ambled round the room. On the coat rack, a man's coat – the only sign, thought Jack, of the man of the house, except, of course, the photo. A good-looking man, staring into the distance, a prim moustache, his hair combed back. The work of a studio. And then there was the piano. The lid was peeling and on opening it, the keys had faded yellow. Jack sat down on the stool and ran his fingers down the keys. It'd been a long time since he played, such a long time… He should have asked, he knew that, but the sight of the keys had had a strange pull on him. With his left hand, he held down a chord, most gently, barely audible. To his surprise, these notes were in tune. Then closing his eyes, and throwing his head back, he lunged into a melody. His heart soared for a moment, the first time in such a long, long time. His fingers skirted across the keys, the melody not attractive, harsh to the ear, jagged and twisting but the joy, the joy it brought him, the freedom. *Arrêter Arrêter Arrêter* . The word, repeated ever angrier, came to him. He saw her from the corner of his eye, to his right, her hands on her cheeks. He stopped mid-tune, his hands levitating above the keyboard, the last chord hanging between them. '*Que faites-vous?*' she asked. 'What are you doing?'

To his left, the boy had come running back downstairs and stopped on the bottom step, as wide-eyed as his mother, muttering something.

She answered back, her voice laced with concern. The chord had gone yet it still sounded in their ears. More calmly now, she said to Jack, 'No, you must not play.' Stepping forward, she gently closed the lid. She looked at him intently. 'No one plays this piano.'

'OK. I understand,' he said, understanding nothing.

*

Jack sat on the sofa, feeling awkward, but clean. He'd taken up her offer and had had a bath. But she hadn't offered any clean clothes, those belonging to her husband. And so, although clean, he sat in his dirty uniform. She was in the kitchen, preparing a meal. He offered to help in some way, peeling potatoes, but all offers were politely if firmly put down. Eventually, she called through from the kitchen and asked him to tell Pascal lunch was ready. Jack went upstairs. There was a French flag pinned to one of the doors. Knocking gently, he opened the boy's bedroom door. Pascal was standing next to his bed and wearing Jack's tunic. The look of shame swept across his face as he stood there with the arms hanging down, the hem reaching his knee. Jack laughed and immediately regretted it. The boy looked so pathetic, his eyes filled with hurt.

'I'm sorry,' said Jack. 'I didn't mean to laugh at you.'

In a flurry of indignity, the boy pulled off the tunic and flung it to the floor. The two of them looked at it, the boy's breaths coming in short bursts. Gently, Jack picked up the jacket as the boy stepped back. 'Don't worry,' he said. 'It's OK.'

'*Je ne veux pas de toi ici*', the boy yelled.

'Hey, no need to shout at me, young man.'

'*Il faut s'en aller.*'

163

'What are you saying? Stop shouting. Your mother will—'

'Will what?' She was standing behind him. 'What's going on here? *Qu'est-ce qui se passé?*' she said, addressing her son.

Pascal didn't answer, instead he turned his back and folded his arms.

'He's upset, that's all. He'll get used to you after a while.'

After a while, thought Jack, how long did she expect him to stay? 'I'm sorry if I upset him.'

'Come, let's have something to eat.'

For Jack, it was a luxury to be able to eat at a table with a knife and fork. Dinner consisted of a small cut of mutton with boiled potatoes and a glass of wine, which went straight to his head.

Afterwards, Pascal went to his room, and the woman and Jack reclined on the sofa in silence. His shoulder ached again, and he reached back and rubbed it. Eventually, he said, 'I'm sorry about earlier – the piano.' He hoped it would open up a conversation about her husband, her Jacques.

'No, I am sorry; I should not have reacted the way I did.'

'No one plays it now?'

'No. No one plays it now. It is never played.'

'Right.'

'Your shoulder – it hurts?'

'Yes, a little.'

'Here, let me look at it.'

'Really? Well, OK.' Jack squirmed at having to take his shirt off in front of the woman and felt vulnerable sitting, perched on the edge of the sofa, while she examined his wound.

She peeled off the dressing. Jack winced. 'Why do you make a fuss? Keep still. It's just a scratch. Wait a moment.' She disappeared into the kitchen and returned seconds later with a bottle, cotton wool and a bandage. 'Keep still,' she repeated, dabbing the wound with disinfectant.

'You haven't told me your name,' said Jack.

'We should take you to a doctor – to make sure. Tomorrow I take you.'

'OK, thank you.'

'But now, I think it is time to go to bed. There is no spare bed but you can sleep here – on the sofa.'

'Thank you, thank you for everything.'

*

The sound of a door slamming stirred him from his sleep but it was the shouting of the boy's name that brought him to. He sat up on the sofa and pushed the blanket to one side. The clock on the wall showed eight.

'Pascal, Pascal!' she screamed from outside.

'What's the matter?' he asked as she came back in, wrapped in a dressing gown, her face flushed.

'It's Pascal,' she screeched, 'I can't find him. He's gone.'

'Gone? Are you sure?'

'It's not a big house,' she snapped, 'of course I am sure.'

'Perhaps he's…'

'Yes? *Pour l'amour de Dieu*, I should never have allowed this. How stupid of me.'

Jack had slept in his trousers. Pulling on his shirt, he said, 'I'll go find him.'

'You won't know where to go.'

'It's not a big village, is it? He can't have gone far, maybe he's gone to buy bread or… or something.'

'Yes, perhaps. Go then, hurry. I'll stay here in case he comes back.'

'OK. Look, I'm sorry to have…'

'Please, just go.'

*

It was cold out, a slight drizzle, the clouds dark. She lived about a quarter of a mile from the main village, such as it was. There was a café and a *boulangerie*, both already open. He looked in both, asking, '*Un petit garçon?*' In the bakery, he was understood, despite his accent, but received only apologetic shakes of the head. He was in too much of a rush to take notice of the smell of freshly baked bread. In the café, they stared at him vacantly from behind the cigarette smoke. A burly-looking man, unshaven, an oversized cap on his head, approached Jack, barking at him. Jack shrugged he didn't understand. The coffee smelt divine but Jack needed to leave. But the man felt Jack's lapel and shouted at his friends behind him. They laughed. Jack pushed the man's hand away. The man's eyes narrowed, Jack clenched his fists at his sides but recoiled from the size of the man. The man sensed his fear, this little Englishman in his uniform. With a laugh laced with contempt, he rejoined his friends, picking up a cigarette he'd left burning in the ashtray.

Back outside, Jack looked up and down the main street with its small houses, unkempt and squalid. That brief encounter had unnerved him. The church, try the church. The church, small and squat, a much poorer cousin of the grand church in Saint Omer, sat at the end of the village. Too dark inside to see beyond irregular shapes, he called out the boy's name, his voice muffled in the darkness. He walked up the aisle, looking left and right, thinking he must be here, he must be here. He was not. This was not a church where one came to feel the kindness of God, but to bear His anger. Here, in this small church, in this dreary village, he felt His displeasure. Man had failed Him; Jack Searight had failed Him. He had to find the boy, to repay the woman's kindness, to leave her feeling gladness in her heart. He realised he still didn't know her name. He called out Pascal's name again. *I should never have allowed this.* Her words came back to him. It was obvious he had to leave. But first the boy. He exited the church, his legs straight, his heart staggering. Outside the drizzle had given way to rain. No one was about. Where now?

It was perhaps an hour, maybe more, when Jack finally had to give in to defeat. He'd circled round the village, looked in fields, traipsed through mud, trespassed onto farms, avoiding dogs, checking barns. Sodden, he trudged back towards the house, hoping to God that the boy had returned. He wanted to find Pascal, for sure, but it was the mother's gratitude he sought, that and a huge breakfast, and he had failed her. He saw the house ahead of him, on the bend of the road. At first, he thought himself mistaken but no, he heard it all right – the piano; someone was playing the piano. Perhaps it was coming from elsewhere but there was no elsewhere – it was coming from within the house.

He slowed down, the rain dripping off his face; why the piano, who was playing it? She was so flustered the previous evening, as if the instrument was the unique preserve of someone no longer there, her husband. He stopped, poised just yards away from the house, squat and ugly with tiny windows. He saw the reflection of the dark clouds in a puddle, the raindrops causing the smallest ripples. The tune was a hearty one, she played well, if indeed it was her. The boy must have come back, why else would she be playing? But it didn't seem right; something was wrong. Why so loud; she seemed to be hammering on the keys. The realisation caught him in the throat – she was warning him. He had to leave, he had to run. Everything he had was in the house – haversack, clothes, money. But he knew now with certainty – she was telling him, don't come in.

He turned to leave, a rumble of thunder, then the boy's scream. The piano stopped. He looked back, he was there at the window, Pascal, his face white against the dirt of the pane. The door swung open and out charged two policemen. Jack ran. The policemen called, *arrêtez, arrêtez,* the boy was screaming, '*Vite,*

vite.'; his mother called his name, '*Non, Pascal, non, non.*' He could hear their footsteps on the wet tarmac. Glancing behind, they were closing in on him, two hazy figures in black. He pushed himself on, running, his breath pounding in his chest, his boots stamping through the puddles, the rain a mask before him, the lane, the dotted houses all a blur. *Arrêtez!* He had to keep going but the tunic, so heavy, laden with rain. But where to? In the distance, he could hear Pascal screaming, urging the policemen on. He was running, still running through the village, approaching the church; the policemen's yells followed him, their boots thumping behind him. A fleeting look back, they were still there, minus their caps, dropped in the chase. The blow to his body upended him. He lay on the road, his chest heaving. The clouds so dark seemed to be moving rapidly across the sky. Excited voices circled round him when a face came into view, peering at him from above, the man who had stepped out in front of him, the man from the café with his huge cap. He was laughing, enjoying the moment, the capture of the fleeing beast. Then, the man leant down, growled something in French, and spat at him.

Chapter 20: Basket Cases

Guy sat in a sturdy chair at the dormitory window trying to concentrate on *A Tale of Two Cities*. The ward was almost deserted. His fellow inmates had been given permission to visit the nearby town that afternoon and there were whispers that a visit to the local brothel was on the cards. Corporal Lampton invited Guy along and although tempted, he resisted. After months on active service, the luxury of experiencing the pleasures of a woman was more than simply sex; it was a part of the process of rehabilitation. The thought of satisfying or being satisfied by a woman signalled, albeit temporarily, a return to normality. But not for Guy; the thought of anonymous sex held no appeal. Later that afternoon, the men returned in buoyant mood, their mission satisfied, their ten francs apiece well spent in the company of a Frenchwoman doing her bit for the Allied war effort. But Guy knew that amongst these outwardly satisfied men, some would be harbouring the disappointment of failure when expectation exceeded reality; when trepidation overcame the moment and the opportunity to taste freedom became too oppressive.

Guy received a rare visit from Major Cartwright, the surgeon who had amputated his leg. A nurse removed the bandages, causing Guy to wince with the pain. The major adjusted his glasses, inspected the stump carefully, and declared himself content with its progress. He asked Guy a few questions relating to his mental well-being, the degree of physical discomfort and his bowel movements. Satisfied with what he heard, the major congratulated himself on a good job done and then informed Guy that he would soon be perfectly fit enough to make the trip up to a base hospital near the coast.

He thought of Jack; he knew he could no longer be of any use to his younger brother, but the thought of leaving him behind made Guy uneasy.

On the seventh day, two nurses came to attend to Smith and Jones. Guy watched them, as they stripped the two men beneath their blankets, and set to them with flannels and a detached sense of determination. A quick drying with a towel, then Smith and Jones, who both took in the proceedings with a glazed look of disinterest, were cleanly dressed. The whole process had taken only a few moments and was completed with brutal efficiency. As they finished, Browne called for one of the nurses, 'Sister, can I have a bath today?'

'No, Stephen, not today; too much on.'

A few minutes later, two orderlies appeared and lifted Smith onto a stretcher, swept his few belongings into a bag, and carried him off. Five minutes later, they returned and took away Jones. What an odd sight Jones made, all four limbs blast away. A basket case. 'You can guess where they're going,' said Lampton.

'Poor buggers, what sort of future can they expect back home?'

'We'll be joining them soon, won't we, Corporal,' said Browne.

'Any day now,' said Lampton.

Their beds must have still been warm when two new occupants took their place, Major Cartwright and a couple of nurses following the stretcher-bearers as they placed the new casualties onto the beds either side of Browne. Both men were asleep. The major checked them over, seemingly satisfied with the amputations, while the nurses checked on the other men. Guy wondered whether one of them was the Blighty nurse Lampton had mentioned. Browne certainly thought so – Guy heard him say, 'You're not going to send me back up the line, are you, sister? I'm not well enough, you know that, don't you?'

'Of course, Stephen. You'll be pleased to know we're sending you in the other direction, back to a base hospital on the coast. And from there – home to England.'

'Oh! Oh, God, thank you, sister, thank you.'

After the staff had left, Browne, his face radiating relief, called across to Guy and Lampton, 'Did you hear that? They're not sending me back; I'm going home.'

'Congratulations,' said Lampton.

'Oh God. It's all right for you two, they can hardly send you back up the line, can they, hopping into battle? But me, I was worried sick; hell, I was worried.'

'We'd guessed that.'

'But not any more, eh? I'm going home; I'm bloody going home.'

*

Guy caught sight of Robert entering the ward and looking around. He too was now using crutches. He said hello to a nurse cleaning the floors with a mop. Guy waved his arm and shouted out his name. Robert saw him and approached with a gentle smile, but, Guy couldn't help but notice, with an anxious look in his eye.

'Robert, how nice to see you,' said Guy.

'Hello, Guy, old chap. How are you?'

'Fine, but more to the point, how are you?'

'Yeah, got hit by flying shrapnel. Not too serious, unfortunately. Not enough to get me home anyway. I was sorry to hear about your leg, but heck man, look on the bright side, at least you're out of it now. Couple more weeks in here and you'll be off home.' Robert perched himself awkwardly on the edge of Guy's bed. 'So, erm, what's the book?'

He was clearly ill at ease, thought Guy, as if only visiting under sufferance or duty.

Guy broke the awkward silence. 'Just a novel'

'Oh, fine.' He reached into his pocket, pulled out a handkerchief, and blew his nose.

'Are you all right, Robert?'

'Yes, fine. Fancy a fag?' Guy shook his head. Robert produced a packet from his tunic and lit himself one. Guy noticed that Robert's hands were shaking slightly. Robert sneezed.

'Bless you.'

'Thank you, I've got a bit of a cold coming on.'

'So I see.'

Robert looked earnestly at him. 'Listen, Guy, I've got some bad news for you.'

'I guessed.'

'I'm not sure how to tell you this…'

Guy's stomach lurched. 'It's Jack, isn't it? He's been killed.'

Robert sighed. 'If only it was that easy.'

Guy sat up. 'What do you mean?' He must have been wounded, thought Guy, in bad shape, critical perhaps.

Robert took a deep breath. 'I'm sorry to have to tell you this, Guy, but Jack's been arrested.'

'Arrested?' A shiver ran down his spine; he hadn't expected that.

Robert nodded. 'For…' He hesitated as if the word was stuck in his throat. 'For desertion.'

Guy's heart dropped. 'Oh, Christ no,' he muttered.

'He was found missing a few days ago and was caught yesterday morning, they'd tracked him down in some village not far from Calais. They're holding him under arrest.'

172

Desertion. The word conjured up so many terrible connotations; men dreaded the accusation of desertion more than death. Robert was right: it would have been easier to be told that Jack was dead. Death was at least clear cut; you were either dead or were not, but desertion was so subjective, so acutely sensitive.

'Is there going to be a trial?'

'Yes.' Robert drew on his cigarette. 'I'm afraid it's happening tomorrow. They've given him Captain Ainsworth to act as his defence. Prisoner's friend, they call it.'

Guy tried to smile. 'Well, he's got some chance then.'

'I'm sure Ainsworth will do his best.'

'Yes. I can't ask for any more than that.'

Chapter 21: The Trial – 8 November 1917

'Left, right, left, right, left... halt! Left turn, stand to attention. 8112, Private Jack Searight, sir.'

The major thanked the court sergeant and turning to Jack, asked, 'Can you confirm that you are 8112, Private Jack Searight?'

'Yes, sir.' Jack glanced around the Nissan hut. In front of him sat the major, the President of the Court, a greying, square-jawed man, his tunic ablaze with medal ribbons. Either side of him, another two convening officers. They sat behind a row of upturned boxes covered with an old blanket on which flickered a number of candles.

Jack's stomach lurched at the formality of it all. These three men were charged with establishing the facts of his case and, on the face of it, the facts seemed fairly damning. To one side of the three officers sat another two men with pen and paper poised. To Jack's right, Captain Ainsworth, the man charged with his defence; to his left, Captain MacDonald, the prosecuting officer, and behind him a small number of others, standing guard or witnessing the proceedings.

The major continued. 'This is a Field General Court Martial, the hearing is now open. I am, for the record, Major Hopkins. To my left Lieutenant-Colonel Hughes-Wilson, to my right Lieutenant-Colonel Corns.' The major picked up a sheet of paper on the table in front of him and, putting on his glasses, read,

'Number 8112, Private Jack Searight, Fourth Battalion, Essex Regiment, as a soldier of the British Army, you are hereby charged with attempting, while on active duty, to desert His Majesty's services, and that you discharged yourself from duty without permission from your Commanding Officer on November third, 1917, to your arrest at approximately nine hundred hours on November sixth. And that in the intervening time, you held up a French civilian at knifepoint and forced another French citizen to provide you with shelter.' The major adjusted his glasses and looked directly at Jack. 'How do you plead – guilty or not guilty?'

'Not guilty, sir.'

The major scribbled the words down on his sheet of paper. 'OK, Private Searight, stand at ease.' Jack stepped back a few paces. The major signalled to Captain Ainsworth. 'Thank you, Captain, you may proceed.'

'Thank you, sir.' The captain rose to his feet and glanced at his notes. He had been volunteered to act as Jack's counsel; it wasn't a job he relished. He had received the Summary of Evidence the day before and only managed to interview the prisoner the one time. The bare corrugated iron sheets of the Nissan hut shook under the pressure of a gale blowing outside and, despite the presence of a large brazier in the corner of the hut, the captain shivered under his greatcoat. He cleared his throat. 'My client, the accused, did indeed absent himself and was later arrested as the court describes but he is not guilty in the sense that at the time he was not in full possession of his faculties. His absence from duty was not a premeditated act of defiance, nor a deliberate dereliction of duty for while maintaining a balanced state of mind, the accused would no more have considered deserting than he would have painted a cow. However, at the point of his departure, his mind had been pulverised to the point of mental damage.' He paused while the court scribbled notes. 'I would like to call my first witness, Private Christopher Webb.'

The call for Private Webb echoed outside. Emerging into the courtroom from the adjoining Nissan hut, Webb was marched in by the court sergeant. 'Left, right, left, right... halt!' The private saluted the bench and stood to attention a few feet away from the convening officers. A court orderly handed him a bible. Webb took it in his right hand and repeated the oath dictated to him by the orderly. 'I do solemnly swear by almighty God that the evidence I shall give before this court shall be the truth, the whole truth and nothing but the truth.'

The captain strode purposefully towards him, his arms clasped behind his back. 'Private Webb, am I correct in believing you apprehended the accused at your billet near the Saint Omer woods on the third of November?'

'Yes, sir.'

'Could you tell the court exactly what happened?'

Private Webb related to the captain and the court his tale of how Jack approached him in the grounds of the billet; of how Jack staggered about and talked of 'getting back', but where to, he hadn't been able to ascertain. He talked of how Jack had collapsed from pure exhaustion; and how they carried him into the billet where the platoon's first-aider checked him over, and then how they left him to sleep. This part of Webb's account played neatly into Captain Ainsworth's hands. The fact Jack had walked straight into the grounds of the billet was not the action of a deserter. This had to be his main line of defence. If only he had said where he wanted to get back to. The captain skimmed over the second part of the story; the part concerning Jack's disappearance the following morning and his subsequent capture.

Ainsworth's old friend, Captain MacDonald, a tall angular man in his mid-forties, sporting a thin, carefully trimmed moustache, led the prosecution. The prosecuting captain focussed his attention on the second part of Private Webb's story. If Jack's initial mental state had suited Captain Ainsworth's defence, then the deliberate stealing of food and Private Scales's socks, boots and haversack, and his disappearance into the woods and escape to Les Attaques suited MacDonald's. Jack's behaviour at that point indicated the predetermined actions of a man in full control of his faculties.

The second witness called was Captain Ellis, the Commanding Officer in the billet that fateful evening. The captain was unable to add anything of substance to Private Webb's testimony, but the court took the opportunity to castigate the captain's role in the sorry affair. Why, for example, had he not placed a sentry at the accused's bed, why had it been so easy for the accused to raid the kitchen and make good his escape? Captain Ellis squirmed under the pressure and wished Jack the comeuppance he was surely due.

Next came the Medical Officer, whom Jack went to see shortly before his absence during a fit of desperation. Captain Butler took his oath in a sharp and staccato voice as if he was a man in a hurry. The captain addressed the doctor. 'Captain Butler, can you tell the court whether you recall seeing the prisoner on the morning of the first of November, this year?'

The doctor shot a quick look at Jack. 'Yes, I remember him.'

'What was his complaint?'

'Usual thing, said his nerves were playing him up.'

'And did you believe him?'

'No,' snapped the doctor.

'No?'

'Of course not, I see men like him several times a day, every day, all complaining of their nerves.'

'But was he not suffering or said he was suffering from the usual symptoms of what we call shellshock, I mean, for example, nightmares, shaking, a continual state of agitation?'

'Yes, but nothing unusual in that. And I wouldn't call it shellshock, no such thing in my opinion, just another way of saying cold feet.'

'So, in seeing so many men in a similar condition, you feel able to dismiss all of them as one of the same. Does it not occur to you that perhaps some of the men might be a little more deserving of closer inspection?'

The captain seemed agitated by the accusing nature of Ainsworth's question. 'No, I tell you, I haven't got time to pander to these imaginary illnesses of the mind. I knew exactly what he was angling for.'

'Which was…?'

'Well, to be sent back home as an invalid, of course.'

'And did he actually say that?'

'No, but–'

'So how could you be sure, were you able to read his mind?'

The MO glared at Ainsworth, how dare he question him in such a manner. 'No, of course not, but he did request leave.'

'And did you grant him leave on medical grounds?'

The MO laughed.

'Obviously not. Did you prescribe anything for him?'

'Yes, I prescribed him a laxative and aspirin.'

'A laxative and aspirin? Did you really think that a man showing the classic symptoms of shellshock could be dealt with by prescribing him the humble aspirin?'

'Shellshock, my eye. There was nothing wrong with him and I told him so, told him to pull himself together. This war needs soldiers, not shirkers.'

'You say that there was nothing wrong with him. So, tell me, Captain, in your opinion, is a man wandering around in a daze for a whole day the sign of a man in a normal state of mind?'

'That was after I saw him but in my mind any man can have the wind knocked out of him for a while. He knew *exactly* what he was doing, no question in my mind.'

Captain MacDonald cross-examined the doctor. He began by asking Captain Butler to confirm that a man with enough forethought to steal provisions was not a man under any particular mental strain. The doctor readily agreed. MacDonald then asked, 'After he reported to you on November the first, what, Doctor, was your final assessment of the prisoner?'

'That he was fit for duty as any other man and that he merely had to be kept under firm discipline and discouraged from malingering. The man got cold feet, that's all there was to it.'

'Thank you, Captain Butler, no more questions.'

Jack stood impassively watching the proceedings unfold in front of him. Were they really all talking about him; was it really happening? It all seemed so preposterous. He felt like an outsider looking into somebody else's world, somebody else's misfortune. The fact that his life was at stake seemed so incredulous as to be unreal.

Captain Ainsworth then called Lieutenant Lafferty as a character witness for the defence. Yes, the lieutenant believed that Jack had been a fine soldier, as evidenced by his brave rescue of his brother. He described how, under the cover of darkness, Jack and Sergeant Wilkins had crawled out into no-man's-land to rescue Guy and pull him in. The captain thanked the lieutenant for bringing to the court's attention the prisoner's previous display of tenacity and courage. He continued, 'From what you know of the accused, Lieutenant, would you say he was acting under considerable mental strain directly before his disappearance?'

'Yes, I would say so; he had lost his former verve and chirpiness.'

'Thank you, no more questions.'

MacDonald continued on the same theme. 'Surely, Lieutenant, there must've been others under your command who showed equal degrees of strain?'

'Well, yes, I suppose so.'

'Can you offer the court any real evidence of the prisoner's condition?'

'Yes, as I say, he lost that verve, became withdrawn and er–'

'But surely, all the men go through periods of depression. If you had noticed anything untoward about this particular case, you would have done something about it, would you not?'

'Well…'

'And did you? Did you do something about it?'

The lieutenant blushed. 'No. Perhaps I thought he'd get over it.'

'Perhaps, with respect, Lieutenant, what you're trying to say is that this man was no more in a mental state than any other soldier…'

'No, I–'

'Thank you, Lieutenant. No more questions.'

Ainsworth was worried. His case for the defence was complete. He wasn't sure how well things were going but he knew that Searight's guilt was already established in the minds of Major Hopkins and his colleagues. The prosecution had the head start, and it was up to him, as Jack's Defence, to rid them of their preconceived prejudices, to persuade them beyond any doubt of the man's extenuating circumstances. Lord knows he himself had to be persuaded. It was like an army gut reaction – a man runs, he is a deserter and a coward and he has to be punished. He fell for it as much as any other man. But after ten minutes with Jack, Ainsworth knew that this boy's mind had been pulverised by war.

He simply could not cope and fell foul of military law as a result. But did he deserve to be shot for it; was it really his fault? This was not a hardened soldier after all, but a civilian in uniform, who, in the spirit of the times, had volunteered.

The next witness, Ainsworth feared, was only going to make matters worse. The prosecution called for Sergeant Henry Wilkins. Wilkins entered the hut with his arm in a sling, a souvenir from the attack on the ridge. Major Hopkins asked after his health, then handed over to MacDonald. MacDonald began by asking Wilkins about Jack's attributes as a soldier. But, according to Wilkins, there had been nothing in Jack's conduct that could redeem him. The sergeant described in detail that fatal night on the ridge; how the shells came over, how after being wounded, he'd been unable to contain his men who retreated in disarray. And Private Searight? Yes, he had disappeared with the others, and no, he hadn't been in the least bit surprised to learn later that the accused had absconded.

Captain Ainsworth's witness. He eyed the squat little man with the ruddy complexion. 'I would like, if I may, to draw the court's attention to the evening of twentieth October this year. Sergeant, correct me if I am wrong, but the prisoner was concerned about his brother who, at the time, was stranded, wounded in no-man's-land?'

'Yes, sir.'

'And that you tried to convince him that any attempts at rescuing his brother were doomed to failure?'

Private Searight's words came back to the sergeant. 'What'd you do if it was your brother out there?' the private had said. The sergeant remembered it all so well but he had never really considered the answer. His brother had been killed at Ypres, and yes, he probably would have done the same.

'Sergeant Wilkins?'

Despite the cold, the sergeant was aware of the perspiration on his brow. He looked at the captain. 'Well, I wouldn't say that exactly. I mean, if we had to rescue every wounded or stranded man, we'd risk even greater casualties. And I told him – told him that the stretcher-bearers would bring him in.'

'And yet you did rescue him?'

'Yes.'

'So what made you change your mind?'

He remembered the lieutenant's smarmy smile and his condescending words: *'Sergeant, you've been out on a number of night patrols, perhaps you'd be good enough to go out with Searight here, and give him the benefit of your experience.'* Benefit of experience, yes – he had plenty of that but to be bamboozled into it by a private…

Ainsworth pressed home the point. 'It wasn't because you were actually ordered to by Lieutenant Lafferty?'

'No, sir, I suppose I reckoned he wasn't so far out as I'd originally thought. But, looking back on it, the lieutenant did give us his encouragement.'

'Would it not be fair to say, Sergeant, that the accused showed a great deal of valour in attempting such a risky venture?'

Yes, he had, thought Sergeant Wilkins, but could he admit such a thing? 'Well…'

Major Hopkins interrupted, 'Captain Ainsworth, is this really relevant?'

'I am merely trying to show, sir, that, through his past actions, the accused has proved himself endowed with great courage. With the court's permission, I would like to read a report attesting to the accused's gallantry and quickness of mind–'

'That is as maybe,' said the major impatiently, 'but the accused is not being tried for his former feats of courage but for his recent act of desertion. If you please, Captain Ainsworth, we're not in a civilian court now and we don't have time for such niceties here, so please stick to the case in hand.'

Ainsworth nodded. It was time to try another tack. 'Would you say, Sergeant Wilkins, that you held a grudge against the accused, a grudge compounded by this incident with his brother?'

Yes, thought the sergeant. Yes, he had wanted to crush the little upstart; he wanted to see him scared shitless, even to have copped it, but not in this way, not in front of a firing squad. 'No, sir,' he said. 'I may've been a bit harsh on him on occasions, but no harsher than I am with the others. We are talking about soldiers here.'

'Of course, but you didn't think you owed him one for having shown you up in front of the lieutenant?'

However accurate it was, the sergeant still bristled at the accusation. 'No, absolutely not.'

'Hmm, OK, Sergeant Wilkins, thank you, no more questions.' The captain sat down and sighed.

Sergeant Wilkins stood motionless for a few moments. He glanced at Jack. Yes, he'd crushed him all right, but he hadn't wanted it to come *this* far. He knew he could have said *something* to save him, and as he stood there, he knew he still had the chance. He had only to say that the boy had displayed remarkable courage that evening and shown a determined strength. OK, eventually the boy may have flipped but as he searched into his soul, he knew why. Because of his own wounded pride, he'd exposed the boy to far more than his fair share of danger; that he had sent the boy out on numerous patrols or working parties night after night after night. He never gave the boy a moment's rest. And did not the boy try to come to his aid when he was hit that night on the ridge? He just needed the courage to say it and the strength of mind to admit his own weakness. But for a man who lived off his strength, how could he expose his own deficiency in front of the court? As the sergeant stood there fighting his conscience, he knew he still had the chance to save the boy's skin.

Major Hopkins looked up from his papers and realised that the sergeant had not stepped down. 'Anything else, Sergeant?'

Sergeant Wilkins looked at the major. His own cowardice was more damning than the accused's. He opened his mouth... and then closed it again. He looked down and plucked an imaginary bit of dirt from his tunic. He shook his head. 'No, sir,' he said quietly.

'Thank you then, Sergeant, you may stand down.'

Sergeant Wilkins nodded and, as he turned to leave, he caught Jack's eye and for the briefest moment, he thought he saw a flicker of a smile. The sergeant walked quickly out of the Nissan hut. Someone said something to him but he ignored them and carried on walking as fast as he could away from the scene of his crushing cowardice. Finally, he stopped. He took out a handkerchief from his pocket and wiped his brow before bending over and vomiting.

Finally, Jack took the stand. He stepped forward and stood to attention, his hands clasped behind his back, his stomach churning. His legs buckled under the pressure of the accusing eyes surrounding him. MacDonald launched straight into his attack. 'Up to the point of your... absconding, how long had you been in active service, Private Searight?'

Jack quickly calculated the time in his head. 'About two months, sir.'

'Two months, is that all? A bit quick to have come under such strain. Why did you desert, Private Searight?'

'I don't reckon I did desert, sir. I was caught by a shell blast and I sort of got disorientated, I had no idea what I was doing.'

'So what went through your mind as you walked away from the ridge?'

'I don't remember, don't remember a thing about it.'

'But you knew enough to get up in the middle of the night, tuck away enough provisions to keep you going for two or three days and quietly slip out of the billet under the cover of darkness.'

Jack bowed his head. 'Yes, sir,' he said in a sotto voice. 'But I was in a panic. I'd been missing for so long, I just thought if I went back there and then, no one would believe my story.'

'Oh come now, surely it was less of a risk than running for it? Did you ever intend to return to your platoon?'

No, thought Jack, he had no intention whatsoever. 'Yes, sir.'

'Isn't that somewhat contradictory? You say you wanted to return but you headed straight for the woods, then made your way right up to the last village before Calais; why was that?'

'As I said, sir, I was in a panic, I wasn't thinking straight, hadn't been for a couple of weeks.' He thought of all the night patrols the sergeant had sent him on, crawling across no-man's-land on all fours; of the hours spent on sentry duty in the solitude of a forward sap, the threatening silence of the night, his sweaty palms gripping his Lee-Enfield, the aching tiredness, the overwhelming need to sleep.

MacDonald continued. 'Private Searight, you must've known what you were doing was wrong?'

'I… I didn't really think it through.'

'You didn't think it through? You disappear into the night from the billet with a sack full of provisions and someone else's boots, you steal money to get on a train, you force a defenceless Frenchwoman to give you shelter and you end up just one stop away from Calais. Yet you say you *didn't think it through*. And where did you hope this little escapade would eventually take you?'

To Saint Omer, to a warm barn, to England, to his parents, to Mary's bed, anywhere. 'No idea. Like I said, sir, I didn't think it through.'

'And when you talked about "getting back", where were you hoping to get back to?'

'I can't really remember, but I suppose I would've meant my platoon.'

'Your platoon? Or England perhaps?'

Yes, England, he thought, that far-flung place, that near-mythical haven viewed through dewy-eyed longing. 'No, sir, not England.'

'But you say you can't remember?'

'I can't, but…'

'No more questions. Your witness, Captain Ainsworth.'

The captain smiled weakly at Jack; he knew the odds were mounting against them. 'Private Searight, describe to us, if you would, your condition after the shell blast.'

'I don't remember a thing about it, sir. I just remember waking up in this billet feeling very confused.'

'But you didn't have a plan, did you, no identifiable reason for absconding as you did?'

'That's right, sir.'

'And how were you feeling before the shell blast, before that night on the ridge?'

'I felt terrible, kept having these nightmares and I couldn't stop shaking, I just couldn't think straight. It was the noise, you see, it just got to me, that continuous noise. That's why I went to see the MO. I've never been good with loud noise. I know it sounds pathetic, but I can't help it.'

'Going back to when you volunteered. Did you want to join up?'

'At the time, yes. You see, my older brother had joined up a year or so before me and I felt… well, envious, I suppose. I also wanted to do my bit for the country.'

'Yes, I see, that's good. Now, I understand you don't remember what happened after the attack on the ridge on the night of the third of November, but tell us, in your own words, exactly what happened before and during the attack?'

'Well, we were bringing back supplies from the depot. The enemy must've caught sight of us as we were crossing the ridge. We were terribly exposed and suddenly all hell broke loose. Men were falling all over the place. I got blown over by a shell blast and a piece of shrapnel hit me in the shoulder. The wound wasn't too bad, but I suppose the blast left me dazed because I can't remember a thing after that. All I remember is waking up in the dark with no idea of where I was and, like I said to Captain MacDonald, I suppose I panicked. I managed to get into the woods where, after a while, I fell asleep. When I came to, I thought I'd better get back, but I had no idea from which direction I'd come. So I wandered around for a while, not knowing where I was going. I suppose I should've given myself up there and then, but y'know I panicked again, because I knew that having disappeared in the middle of the night, they'd think I was a fugitive. So I'm afraid, I made a run for it.'

'Had you tried to desert before?'

'No, sir.'

'Had you thought about it?

'No, sir; never entered my head.'

'Thank you, Private Searight. No more questions.' He sat down and Jack stepped back and, on the court sergeant's barked order, stood at ease.

Major Hopkins finished writing his notes. After a few moments, he asked, 'Any more witnesses?' The two captains, Ainsworth and MacDonald, shook their heads. 'In that case,' continued the Major, 'Captain Ainsworth, you may address the court now on the prisoner's behalf. Be brief, please.'

'Thank you, sir.' Ainsworth returned to his feet, conscious that he hadn't yet managed to dispossess the court of their prejudices. Things were still against him and that every word in his summing-up had to count.

This was his last chance, he thought, glancing at his notes. Outside, the wind was still blowing a gale. He looked at the three officers who, with their pens poised, fixed their attention on him. 'This man is *not* a deserter in the true sense of the word,' he began. 'If he was, he would have planned it before, waited for his opportunity and acted on it. He would have prepared from the outset, with provisions, clothing, food, and money. That may have come later but not at the point he absconded. No, this man's absence began when a massive blast from a shell blew the spirit out of an already dispirited man. Away from the scene of slaughter, he walked in absolute bewilderment. And surely, ask yourselves this, would a true deserter walk straight into a soldier's billet? It would be akin to walking into the lion's den. And then, would he start talking about the need to get back if "getting back" was meant to mean England? No, he had no plan to return to England, for he was too exhausted and dazed, to use Private Webb's words, to have any such plan. No, all he wanted to do was to get back to his platoon and his comrades. And then the prisoner's account of finding himself in a strange place is, I'm sure you'll agree, entirely plausible. This is a man, who, barely more than a boy, joined to fight for his King and Country, a volunteer – not a trained professional soldier. Yet, he showed tremendous courage in rescuing his wounded brother. This man is not a deserter and I beseech you, gentlemen, to find him not guilty. Thank you.'

The three officers remained expressionless. One of them scribbled a few notes on his paper. The captain sat down, drained, and pretended to write some notes of his own. All he managed was a doodle of a crucifix.

Major Hopkins said, 'Thank you, Captain Ainsworth. Captain MacDonald, if you please…'

The captain rose to his feet. 'Thank you, sir. This, I'm sure we all agree, is a distressing and unpleasant duty. I don't want to see a man sent unnecessarily to his death. But a duty it is and a duty we have to observe, for this man is clearly guilty of failing to do *his* duty. While his comrades stand at their posts and do *their* duty day in and day out, this man took it upon himself to dispense with his obligations, his duty. That he deserted is clear. That it was on his mind is also clear, for Doctor Butler gave us the example of the prisoner's earlier attempt to duck out of his duty. Granted, he may have lacked the foresight to have a determined plan, but do deserters ever have much of a plan? I believe not. They act on impulse and then aim to get as far away from the fighting as possible and worry about the rest later. In this case, it took him almost all the way to the coast. Along the way, he stained the British Army's good reputation out here – a soldier in uniform threatening civilians with a knife and forcing a poor woman to give him shelter. What sort of actions are these for a man wearing the King's uniform? I also believe the prisoner has blemished the good record of his comrades, his platoon, his battalion and the whole regiment. And say, gentlemen, you decide to act with leniency? What sort of example does that give the men? That it's OK to fail in one's duty and not expect any more than a slap on the wrists. Is that the message we want to convey? I don't think so. For the sake of example, you must find the prisoner guilty and impose the maximum sentence as seen fit by military law. Thank you.'

'Thank you, Captain MacDonald.' Major Hopkins nodded at his colleagues. He cleared his throat. 'The hearing is now closed. The prisoner will be escorted back to the guardroom. We will reconvene in twenty minutes. Sergeant, if you please.' The court sergeant called Jack to attention and quick marched him out of the Nissan hut. The major turned to his colleagues. 'We'll proceed immediately to deliberate.' The two captains and the

189

various personnel within the hut stood while the three men of the court retired.

Captain Ainsworth slumped in his chair and rubbed his eyes. Captain MacDonald gathered his papers. He looked at Ainsworth and smiled. 'Well, at least that's over.'

Ainsworth sighed. 'Never again.'

'Horrible business, eh?'

'Ghastly.'

'I think I need a drink. Care to join me?'

The captain nodded. 'Absolutely,' he said.

*

Outside, it was raining. The court sergeant, revolver in hand, and two privates escorted Jack back to the guardroom. 'Hurry up,' said the sergeant, pushing Jack. 'You're going down for this, you know that, don't you?'

Jack tried to ignore him as he made his way through the trench avenues, the wooden slats oozing mud. Soldiers passed him either side.

'They're going to take you out and they're going to shoot you.'

'Leave him be, Sarge,' said one of the privates.

But the sergeant, with his bulging eyes, was only warming up to his task. 'Oh, such heart, Miller, you want to spare his feelings, our blushing bride, here.'

Miller could only shrug his shoulders.

'Go on, move along. We might as well shoot you now, you're as good as dead already,' said the sergeant, waving his revolver in Jack's face. 'Shooting's too good for you. If I had my way I'd hang you, let you swing.'

'They might let him off, Sarge, extenuating circumstances and all that.'

'Yeah, and my mother's the Kaiser. No, they know what's what; they know a coward when they see one.'

They'd reached a small wooden hut, the guardroom. The sergeant pushed Jack inside. 'Get in there, you bastard, and not a peep out of you until we're ready, right?'

The hut was tiny, inside nothing but a chair. The rain leaked through the hastily assembled roof, wind whistled through the slats in the wood and through them Jack could see the comings and goings outside. He could hear their voices, shouts and orders, a snatch of conversation. He sat down and put his head into his hands. He felt hungry but his stomach was too tight to eat, not that he was likely to be offered anything. He couldn't think, snatches of memory circled round his head, crashing into each other. This was not his life, he told himself, it was happening to someone else. They would let him off; they would take pity on him, everyone, surely, was allowed a second chance, he was a mere nineteen-year-old who wanted to do what was right, to do his best. What would he have done differently? He would have been a man. Too long he'd hidden behind his quick wit and sharp tongue believing somehow they made him into a man, but they did not; they were merely a disguise; it fooled no one. Strip away the disguise and what was left? A boy. And here he was, in a windy hut, the rain dripping onto him, a boy in khaki wanting his mother. He put his hand out and caught the drips of water, watching the tiny pool form in his palm, listening to the quiet splatter of raindrops on his skin. He couldn't understand why they would want him dead. He was Jack, no more, no less. He'd harmed no one, he hadn't hurt them, he was just a boy. A boy from London that somehow had taken the wrong path but he didn't deserve this. He clenched his fist and the water disappeared.

*

As Jack re-entered the Nissan hut, everyone was already in place. Major Hopkins and his two lieutenant colonels either side of him, sitting behind the upturned boxes with the blanket thrown over; the scribes nearby; Captain MacDonald to his left, Major Ainsworth to his right – exactly as it was before. Ainsworth nodded at him.

'Stand to attention,' barked the court sergeant. '8112, Private Jack Searight, sir.'

'Thank you, Sergeant,' said Major Hopkins.

He picked up his papers and adjusted his glasses. 'The Field General Court Martial presiding over the case of Private Searight is now reconvened and ready to declare its verdict.' He picked up a fountain pen and tapped it on his pad of papers. Jack tried to focus on the major but his face blurred, his glasses dancing on his face. 'Firstly, I would like to thank Captain Ainsworth and Captain MacDonald and their respective witnesses for their contributions. My colleagues and I have listened to both sides of the case and taken into account your recommendations. We have taken everything into consideration and having discussed the case we have reached a conclusion.'

The major's face had merged in with his fellow officers behind the boxes; Jack's head began swaying, his eyelids getting heavier.

'The court martial hereby finds Private Searight guilty.'

Jack thought he could hear laughing, somewhere far away, a familiar laugh. Was it his father? Was it Guy, Sergeant Wilkins? No, it was his own, his own laughter. Then as abruptly as it'd started, it stopped and everything went black.

Chapter 22: Days of Old

Brigadier-General Julian Sykes had had a busy day of meetings and paperwork. There seemed no end to it: dispatches to read or write, memoranda, letters, orders, reports and so on. Even now, at eight o'clock in the evening, he still had a small pile of paperwork to get through. He was tired and was tempted to leave it all, but he knew it would only increase the workload for the following day. He sat at his desk in his office, which used to be a drawing room in this rather fine house that the army had commandeered as the regimental headquarters. He poured himself a small whisky from his flask, diluted it with a splash of water, and sat back down at the desk with a sigh. He opened the first memo; it was an update on the latest planned offensive, which was due to kick off within a week or two. It was all still very hush-hush, but from what little he knew, it was going to be another joint affair with the French with the British thrust based around the area of Cambrai. He was also privy to the fact that the Allies were planning to use tanks in mass for the first time. He wondered whether they might employ gas again, not that they were allowed to refer to it as gas, but by its euphemistic name, the 'accessory'. The Germans had been the first to use gas, at the battle of Ypres in April '15, and what a hullabaloo we made of it, accusing the Hun of using devilish, ungentlemanly means; but just five months later, we were resorting to the same despicable tactics.

Almost an hour later, Brigadier-General Sykes was coming to the end of his evening's work; he had just the one envelope to deal with. His heart sank as he noticed the wording on the thin blue envelope; it read *Papers from the Field General Court Martial of 8112 Pte.J.Searight, 8/11/17.*

He opened the envelope, hoping it wasn't going to be another death penalty case. He skimmed his eyes over the paper and, to his disappointment, found it was exactly that. He had a case like this just six months ago, and he'd hoped not to have to deal with another so soon; it reflected badly on the regiment. There were the various reports pertaining to the case: conduct sheet, medical reports and a summary of the offence. According to the conduct sheet, the man had barely been in the army five minutes, but somehow that didn't surprise the brigadier. It was all very well applauding the huge numbers of civilians joining-up but frankly the calibre of these volunteers left much to be desired. It seemed like the accused had already tried to play the shattered nerves routine, said he'd got the wind-up. Well, the brigadier had little sympathy for such fun and games. If all the other men could stand it, why should he be allowed special dispensation; what if they all tried it on? There'd be no one left to fight. A deserter in the ranks has a dangerous influence on the others, leads to all sorts of panic. The officer in charge of the court-martial, Major Hopkins, had written, *'The Court has found Pte Searight guilty of desertion but we would recommend clemency.'* Typical, thought Sykes, condemn the man then plea for clemency – always the easiest way – satisfy your superiors and ease your conscience. What did the Medical Officer say? *'I hereby certify that I examined No.8112 Pte. J. Searight, 1st Essex on 1ª Nov 1917 and that in my opinion, his general physical and mental condition was satisfactory, Captain Butler.'* And what about his Commanding Officer, Lieutenant Lafferty – what does he recommend? *'Despite a sharp tongue, this man has shown bravery in the field in rescuing his wounded brother from the scene of battle. On account of his youth and lack of experience, I would recommend mercy.'* But nowhere did it say how old Searight was. But this was interesting: 'sharp tongue', and then this 'bravery in the field', but somehow, the fact it involved rescuing his brother rather diminished the validity of the action.

Brigadier-General Sykes laid the papers on the table and got up to stretch his legs. This was difficult: on the face of it, he was quite happy to recommend punishment but this plea for mercy from the CO threw a spanner in the works. He poured himself another whisky – just a small one, no water this time. His thoughts wandered back to the Sudan in '98 and the proudest moment in his military career: the battle of Omdurman. What a morning that was – some 25,000 British and Egyptian troops led by Kitchener himself, facing an army of Dervishes, twice their number. There were no shirkers in those days, and the sight of those savages bearing down on one was a sight to behold. Not that the plucky fellows stood much chance, armed with just their spears and the odd rifle. Poor buggers: thousands of them slaughtered and in return, we suffered a mere handful of casualties. Our Maxim guns just mowed them down in waves, all over in a matter of hours.

With the warmth of the whisky still flowing inside his veins, the Brigadier sat back down at his desk. He was certainly tempted by the CO's plea, but the other case, six months ago, nagged at him. It was an identical case: man got the wind up and deserted, found guilty by court-martial but recommended to mercy. That time, the Brigadier had gone along with it. He sent the papers up to the Divisional Commander who, on paper at least, had agreed with his view. The sentence was commuted and the chap was let off the hook. But then a few days later, the Divisional Commander came down to see the brigadier and questioned his judgement. He'd gone along with it, because he hadn't wanted to show him up, but his own view was that the man should have been shot. Well, the brigadier wasn't prepared to risk that embarrassment again. He picked up his pen and quickly wrote:

'I consider this is a case where, for the sake of example, the sentence be carried out.'

Seventeen words. How simple it was to condemn a man. But no, he wasn't condemning him, he was merely expressing an opinion, offering his recommendation. And hell, he meant it: if other men saw chaps running off and getting away with it, what would they think? No, this was more than simply a sop to his Divisional Commander; sometimes we have to face up to these things head-on, if only for the sake of example. He signed the papers and quickly folded and stuffed them back into the thin, blue envelope and wrote his Divisional Commander's name on it and then placed it in his 'out' tray. From the Divisional Commander, it would work its way up the chain of command to the Corps and Army commanders for their recommendation, and finally, to the Commander-in-Chief himself for the ultimate decision. How long would it hold his attention? wondered Sykes. A matter of seconds probably and it was very unlikely he would change anything. He would simply glance at it and write something like *'Sentence confirmed'.* Then, from the rarefied heights of power, the blue envelope would boomerang back down the system to hit the condemned man squarely between the eyes. The whole process would take but a couple of days. Well, frankly, he deserved what was coming to him.

The brigadier yawned, it'd been a long day and he was beat. He looked at his watch and decided to avoid the mess and have an early night. Ah yes, Omdurman 1898, now that was what you call a proper war.

Chapter 23: The Ghost – 10 November 1917

Guy was in the common room sitting in his bath chair and idly gazing out over the pastures and the woodland beyond at the back of the hospital. It was a dull day and there was little to hold Guy's attention. Behind him, men were finishing their lunches, cutlery against crockery, the flow of conversation, the occasional hearty laugh. God, he felt lonely. Since Robert's visit two days previously, his every waking moment was dominated by the thought of Jack. He'd hardly eaten or slept, drained with anxiety. The day before, the day of the court-martial, had been such an ordeal.

Guy didn't hear Robert's approach and jumped when his friend appeared at his side. He was now managing with just the one crutch. 'Robert?' He saw the grave look on his friend's face. 'Oh Lord, you know, don't you?'

Robert nodded. 'I'm sorry, Guy...'

Guy groaned and put his head in his hands; this was too much to bear. The whole world seemed to go quiet, the intrusive lunchtime commotion obliterated by the sound of his own panicked breathing while somewhere, in the background, Robert carried on talking, something about a rejected recommendation to mercy. Guy thought he'd succumb to tears, he wanted to, but none came. The agony of waiting with its forlorn sense of inevitability had been a strain. But at least when he tried hard enough, Guy could isolate a degree of hope, the last vestige of a desperate man. Like a drowning man in the dark clinging onto a rope, there was always a possibility, however slim. But now with Robert's confirmation, the rope had slipped from his grasp, the last lifeline disappearing into the blackness. He remembered lying out there in that ditch, waiting for death to come and take him. The sound of his brother calling his name. The Very light lighting up the world, the sight of Jack, the dimple in his cheeks still visible under the smearing of mud. He clenched his eyes and wished Robert would shut up.

'I know it stinks, I'm sorry,' concluded Robert.

He owed his life to Jack. He owed his life to Sergeant Wilkins. But what could he give his brother in return now? He wished he'd been left to die out there and been spared this ordeal of inadequacy. British military justice had built a wall between them, and nothing Guy could do could breach it. He was powerless. He wanted to be sick. He tried to control his breathing. Through his breathlessness, he asked, 'Do you know how he is?'

'Apparently, he's bearing up, considering. One of the guards reckons he's showing more courage than anyone can appreciate. I mean, if that was me, I would've totally cracked up by now, I don't know how he does it.'

Guy had a thought, a slant of light above the wall. 'Can't we appeal?' he asked expectantly.

Robert shook his head. 'I'm afraid not. They may allow the commonest criminal the right to appeal, but a man who has voluntarily given his services to his King and Country is denied such a right. That's military law for you.' The wall just got higher.

'I wish I could go to him,' Guy muttered more to himself than to Robert.

'You can. I took the liberty of applying on your behalf. Normally they wouldn't allow him visitors but as a sibling your request, so to speak, was considered exceptional. It's all arranged. He's being kept at the second battalion's HQ, which is at Arques, southeast of here. I even managed to cadge a lift for you with an ambulance that's detailed to pass that way later this afternoon. Are you up to it, old man?'

No, he wasn't up to it. Would anyone be? The thought of seeing his brother seemed terrifying; he'd rather walk naked across no-man's-land. Robert, in his presumptuousness, had meant well, so how could he refuse, what earthly excuse could he come up with? What would he say, what does one say, what words of condolence could he offer? A bitter taste lingered at the back of his throat. He looked down, avoiding Robert's eyes, and shook his head. 'I can't,' he said quietly.

He didn't see Robert's puzzled expression. His friend took his hand. 'You must. You must or you'll regret it for the rest of your life. The ambulance will be waiting for you in the courtyard at three.' He patted Guy's hand. 'Go to him, Guy, say your goodbye.'

Guy nodded and watched Robert take his leave, hoping his friend would turn around in order to catch a look of encouragement in his eyes but Robert, with his head down, walked out of the common room.

Guy looked round at his fellow comrades. His loss of calf seemed bearable amongst these wounded freaks. He found himself staring at a man sitting alone sipping a mug of coffee. The whole right side of his face was blackened and mottled by burns, his eye obscured by the folds of charred skin, the hairline unnaturally receded in an instant by the flame. His left hand gripped the coffee mug but the right hand lay limply on the table, his fingers glued together by the web of translucent skin. But at this moment, Guy almost envied him, and would have gladly swapped places. The man, conscious of Guy's prying eyes, looked up. The two men held each other's gaze for a few moments. He noticed him placing his good hand over the other. Guy wondered whether he was hiding the brutal evidence of his misfortune or trying to accustom himself to the tender texture of his charred skin.

*

The ambulance dropped Guy off outside the Nissan huts that made up the headquarters of the Second Battalion just outside the small town of Arques, the next town on from Saint Omer. He saw a hut with the sign 'Office' over the door. He knocked and entered. Once inside, he approached the young corporal sitting behind a table scattered with papers and saluted. Mumbling, Guy introduced himself and the purpose of his visit.

'Sorry,' said the corporal, narrowing his eyes, 'didn't catch that.'

Guy sighed; he didn't want to have to repeat himself. He realised the words shamed him. The corporal told him to take a seat and sent a message to a Sergeant Dunn who would come to see to him. As he waited, Guy tried to concentrate on what he could say. Words like courage and faith kept coming to his mind. He wished he had an ability to pray as he'd prayed in the trench before the raid, as he'd prayed as a boy in church standing between his parents. Guy had barely taken in his surroundings when the sergeant appeared. Guy stood up, saluted, and introduced himself again. Sergeant Dunn eyed him suspiciously, and beckoned Guy to follow him. The sergeant strode ahead, making no concessions for a man on crutches. Struggling to keep up, Guy was led past the row of Nissan huts, across a muddy patch of grass that could almost have been called a lawn, and finally to an isolated hut erected behind a large, looming oak tree. Guy recognised it as a red oak; they had one in the local park at home. Sergeant Dunn approached a corporal standing guard outside the hut. The corporal saluted.

'This is the prisoner's brother,' said Sergeant Dunn. Then, turning to Guy, said, 'You've got five minutes, right?' Guy nodded. The sergeant marched off without another word. The corporal repeated the sergeant's instruction and knocked gently on the corrugated iron door of the hut. From within, Guy heard the door being unlocked and a face appeared at the gap. His heartbeat quickened.

'A visitor,' said the corporal. The soldier within nodded and opened the door just wide enough for Guy to push through. The poorly ventilated hut smelt of burning coal from the roaring brazier in the darkened corner. Guy blinked. In the half-light of the dimly illuminated room was Jack sitting at a table smoking, poised with pen and paper. Another private, reading a newspaper, sat with him. The table was laden with bottles, overflowing ashtrays, books, paper, cards, and a half-eaten dinner. At Guy's entrance, Jack looked up.

'Guy, is that really you?' Jack staggered to his feet.

'Hello, Jack,' said Guy quietly, hardly able to hold onto his crutches for trembling.

Jack made his way towards his brother, his mouth set in a half-smile, his forehead furrowed. Stopping two feet away from Guy, he whispered, 'I knew you'd come.' Then he stepped forward and flung his arms around Guy with such force, Guy staggered back. Recovering his balance, Guy put his arm around his brother and was surprised by how thin he felt. Jack was shivering, yet his body burned. He muttered, 'Oh, my little brother, my poor brother, what's happened to you.' Eventually, Guy loosened his grip.

Jack stepped back, his eyes red. He rubbed his eyes with the palm of his hand. 'I couldn't help it. Lord knows I couldn't help it.'

Guy swallowed. 'I know, I know.'

For a moment, Jack's legs gave way and he lost balance. Guy reached out his hand and, dropping a crutch, almost lost his own

201

balance. Jack took Guy's arm and, supporting each other, they tottered back to the table and sat down. The private, who had been reading the newspaper, smiled apologetically and stood up and joined his colleague at the brazier at the far end of the hut.

The two brothers sat in silence, each unable to speak for fear of where their words might take them. The few words Guy had prepared failed him, refused to be spoken, too inadequate for the occasion. Eventually, Jack pushed a bottle of rum towards Guy. Guy shook his head. 'Don't blame you,' said Jack. 'They keep plying me with the stuff, but the more I drink, the less effect it seems to have.' He looked at Guy. 'It's been confirmed, you know, they rejected the court martial's recommendation. I've had it.'

If only he had the means to contradict him, to offer him a ray of light, the faintest possibility.

Jack took a cigarette from the packet of Gold Flakes and twirled it in his fingers. 'You've always looked out for me, Guy, but not even you can help me this time. By this time tomorrow…' His voice trailed away as he snapped the cigarette in two.

Guy stared at Jack, unable to take in the frightening reality of Jack's words. *'By this time tomorrow'*. Here he was, his own flesh and blood sitting before him and by this time tomorrow, he'd be no more. Never again would he hear Jack's voice, see that dimpled smile, be able to touch him. It was as if he was already sitting next to a ghost. He clenched his fist at the senseless absurdity of it, his own inability to alter the course of events. If it hadn't been for his leg, he would have considered doing something rash and stupid, just for the sake of doing something, anything, and blow the consequences, he no longer cared.

Jack picked up the metal mug, swilled the contents around and stared at the rippled pattern of dark liquid. 'Forgive me,' he whispered.

'Forgive, what's there to forgive?'

'I'm going to my grave as a deserter, as a coward who couldn't stick it—'

The word coward pierced Guy's heart. 'Stop it, Jack, just stop it. You're not a coward and you know it. You got the wind up, but hell, who hasn't from time to time?'

Jack looked up, his face flushed with anger. 'What am I then?' he bellowed, causing his two guards to glance over. 'What am I if I'm not a coward, a bloody coward?' He took a swig of rum and then slammed the mug down on the table. 'I thought I could take it, just like you did. But oh no, I couldn't. A bit of bombardment, a bit of noise and I shat it, bloody shat myself.' Gripping his fist around the mug, he took another mouthful of rum and choked on the burning liquor. His eyes met Guy's. He leant forward and whispered in rushed tones, 'I don't want to die, Guy. I'm sodding nineteen years old, I'm not meant to die, not like this. If only they'd let me go back to the front and let me die the proper way, the honourable way. That's why I ask you to forgive me, cos of the shame this will bring to you, to Mary, to Mummy and Daddy. Tell them I'm sorry, I'm really sorry I've let them down. Poor Father, he'll be mortified. I don't expect them to understand, but tell them, tell them what it was like and just ask them to find it in their hearts to forgive me.'

Guy moved his chair closer to Jack's and put his arm around his brother's shoulder. Jack shuddered at the bodily contact. For so long, he'd been alone, shunned, accused. The warmth of his brother's contact reminded him that among the hatred and accusation, there was still love.

'You know, Jack, I wouldn't be here if it hadn't been for you.'

'Damn right, your name was on the rat's menu that night. The sergeant saved you too, you know. Saved you, condemned me. He spoke against me at my court-martial. He seemed rather pathetic standing there under oath.' He remembered Wilkins's expression as he marched out of the Nissan hut, trying to hold up his shoulders. But he saw it in the sergeant's eyes. He knew all right.

'I hope he rots.' Jack smiled; he'd heard that the sergeant had gone to the MO, his nerves shattered. He wondered whether the laxatives had done the trick.

'And Mary, look after her for me. She'll be OK after a while; she'll find herself someone else. Someone to replace me. Tell her to keep the engagement ring forever. At least…'

'Go on.'

'At least we managed, y'know…'

Guy tried to smile.

'Just the once, the night before I embarked.' Jack smirked at the memory. 'You know it was her sister I was after really.'

'Why did you propose then?'

'Don't rightly know. Suppose I needed someone at home, waiting for me. Someone I could write to, someone I could call my sweetheart. I keep thinking of them both. The one I almost married and the one I wanted to marry. Don't tell her, will you, Guy? Don't tell Mary – or Josephine, I'm going to my grave with enough shame as it is.'

Guy nodded. 'She'll never know.'

'I know I've said it before but I'm still sorry about, you know, taking Mary off you like that.'

'It's passed now.'

'I wouldn't do that now.'

'We all learn.'

'Do you remember the day you embarked? What high hopes we had, thirsting for adventure, and now look at us. What fools we were, eh? You know, ever since you reminded me of the Albert Carr night, I can't stop thinking about it. You gave him a heck of a hiding for laughing at me.'

'And Father gave me a heck of a hiding for my trouble.'

'Yes, I remember, you couldn't sit down for a week. Albert never laughed at me again though, did he?'

'No, he rather avoided us after that; can't say I blame him.'

'You see, I was a coward even then.'

'Hell, you were only seven, we were all frightened, Albert included. He was just trying to deflect his own fear onto you.'

'I wonder where he is now.'

'Probably caught up in this bloody war himself.'

Jack smiled. 'D'you remember that time we went to Southend?'

'What, when you fell off the donkey?'

'I didn't fall off; I just got on and slipped off the other side. Wasn't my fault the saddle hadn't been tightened.'

'And Mother was worried in case you got trampled under the hooves.'

Jack laughed. 'As if it could be bothered to move.'

'Yeah, I don't think it was quite up to running the Derby.'

And so, huddled together, their heads touching, the brothers shared their memories of childhood, of boyhood adventures, of mishaps and games, of their shared innocence when life still held unending possibilities. Lost in the memory of happier times, Guy and Jack shared their last moments together.

'Promise me, Guy, promise me you'll live life to the full and live it for me.'

Guy pulled Jack tighter. 'Yes,' he whispered, 'I promise.'

'You'll have to hop though, you silly bugger; why did you have to lose a leg?'

'I had one too many, I guess.'

'Thank you, Guy.'

'Thank you?'

'You know, for looking out for me over the years, for… for, sod it, for being a good brother to me.'

Guy clenched Jack's shoulder and wiped his eyes with his other hand; he didn't want to cry, not now, not in front of him. 'Christ, Jack, I shall miss you.'

The corporal from outside opened the door to the Nissan hut. 'OK, boys, I'm sorry, but it's time.'

'Oh no,' said Jack. 'This is it.'

The two brothers rose to their feet. Jack took one of Guy's crutches and, with their arms wrapped around each other; they edged slowly towards the waiting corporal. As they reached the door, they stopped, turned to face one another and hugged for all their worth, terrified of letting go. Guy breathed in Jack's aroma. He would happily have drowned in it. The unwashed odour, the stale sweat, the hint of rum, the stench of fear. But beneath it all, was the unmistakable smell of Jack, his brother, a Searight, his own aroma. By this time tomorrow, he thought.

'Remember,' whispered Jack into Guy's ear. 'Live your life for me and don't you dare ever forget me.'

Guy clenched his eyes shut, trying to hold back the tears, and uttered, 'I'll live for both of us, I promise.'

'And don't let Mummy or Father, or Mary forget me.'

'How can we forget you when we all love you, you silly sod?'

'I think perhaps I loved Mary after all.'

'Don't worry, I'll look after her, I'll see she's OK.'

The corporal cleared his throat. The brothers reluctantly loosened their grip on each other. Then, suddenly, Guy grabbed Jack by the sides of his head and kissed him on his forehead.

Jack tried to smile his dimpled smile. 'Don't forget this,' he said, handing Guy back his second crutch. Guy took it, and stepped past the corporal and through the open door. Summoning up all his strength, he turned around to see his brother one final time. Jack stood, his legs buckling, his fists grasped at his sides, his face contorted with fear and pain. 'I'll s-see you again...'

'Yes,' said Guy, trying desperately to check the choking clamminess in his throat.

'But not too soon, you hear, not too soon…'

With an apologetic look, the corporal closed the door. From within, Guy heard the key turn. He walked away, towards the red oak on the muddy patch of grass masquerading as a lawn. In the distance, he saw a group of men bayoneting clumps of straw within string bags hanging from a wooden frame, the shouts of the sergeant bouncing off the Nissan huts. He could barely walk and his hands trembled so much, he had difficulty keeping his crutches steady. Guy looked up to the heavens, screwing his eyes shut. He bit his lip with such severity he thought he'd cut it. He approached the tree and noticed the snarled roots disappearing into the soft earth. He dropped his crutches and fell to the ground, exhausted by the speed of his heartbeat. Then, turning around to ensure he was alone, he finally succumbed. He meant only to cry; instead, crumpled on the grass in the shadow of the tree, he let out a scream that contorted his body with its intensity. A scream of despair that disappeared into the French air.

Chapter 24: Scoop, October 1988

'OK, it should be working now.' The reporter switched off her tape recorder and placed the little microphone on the occasional table. She smiled apologetically at the old man in front of her sitting in the dilapidated armchair. It was obvious this was where he sat all day long, watching television and doing little else. He was a tall slim man, wearing an old suit with collar and tie; his regimental tie, he'd told her. He'd obviously dressed up for the occasion, she thought. He was looking apprehensive and kept puffing his cheeks. She was conscious that she had bamboozled him into granting this interview. Might as well get going, she thought, he might relax once he'd got talking. She'd come to the old man's house to record an account of his time fighting during the First World War as part of her newspaper's seventieth-anniversary feature. 'Are you ready?'

'As much as I'll ever be,' he said in a deep, throaty voice.

She decided she'd let him talk and only ask questions if he looked like he was running out of steam. She removed her cardigan; it was stiflingly hot in his house. Poor old thing, his living room was bare, to say the least. The threadbare carpet had almost lost all its colour, there were no books, no photographs, just a television and a cat tray that needed a good clear-out but no sign of the cat. And it was so damn hot. She sipped the weak tea he'd made her. 'Well, let's make a start then. I'll just say something into the mike to introduce you and then I'll pass it to you, is that OK?' He nodded. She knelt down next to the microphone and hit the record button.

'Twentieth of October, 1988. A soldier's account of the First World War, recorded to commemorate the Armistice Day seventieth anniversary issue for the *Essex Guardian*.' Turning to the man, she smiled. 'Mr Greene, if you're ready.'

He sat up, stared at the microphone, and cleared his throat. 'My name is Stanley Greene.' He looked at the reporter. She nodded. He continued: 'Stanley Greene. They used to call me Stan the Man – not very original, I grant you. I served as a private in the Great War for over three long years on the Western Front. Being a local lad, I joined the Essex Regiment, Second Battalion. I was twenty at the time, I'm ninety-three now. I was one of the first to join up, back in fourteen. Keen as mustard I was. Is that OK?'

'Yes, excellent.'

'During my time on the Western Front, I saw and experienced many horrid things, the sort of things you never really forget and not the sort of things one ought to talk about, especially to a... a woman. Anyway, I will tell you one story, which wasn't so gruesome but which still gives me nightmares, more than anything else.' He paused, as if uncertain whether he could bring himself to tell his story.

The reporter was intrigued. 'Carry on, you're doing fine,' she said.

'Well, I remember it was a Saturday in November seventeen, a cold wet, miserable day it was. It was just before the battle of Cambrai. There weren't many of us left after that little affair, I can tell you. We were stationed in some billet a few miles behind the lines, I can't remember where. Some time in the afternoon, we were told to gather in the square behind the camp. I remember noticing a small table there, but no chairs. We stood waiting to attention in the drizzle for a few minutes, probably expecting our orders. Anyway, after a while, we saw the major approach. Samson was his name, followed by the sergeant-major and three privates walking in line. The middle private had no hat and no rifle; it looked odd. We soon realised this was the man they'd been keeping in detention but we had no idea what for or who he was. Good-looking chap, very young, no more than a boy really.

'So they made him stand in front of the table and the sergeant-major called us to attention. Major Samson comes forward and he has this piece of paper and he reads it out to us. It was a promulgation–'

The reporter interrupted. 'A what?'

'Promulgation, you know, like a statement. The young boy was called Searight. I've never forgotten that name; couldn't if I tried. Jack Searight, Essex Regiment, one of us, but different battalion. Apparently, he'd been tried by a court-martial for desertion and found guilty. Sir Douglas Haig himself, the commander-in-chief, had confirmed the sentence and he was to be shot at dawn, the very next day. The major said, "God have mercy on him". I remember him saying that because I thought much the same. Then the sergeant-major ordered him to be taken back to his detention.

'I can't tell you the effect it had on us. We were all stunned, couldn't believe it. We were dismissed and were making our way back to the huts in a state of disbelief. We'd heard of executions before, but we were volunteers, we couldn't believe they'd shoot a volunteer. We thought maybe they were just doing it to frighten us, you know, keep us on our toes. Anyway, then I heard my name being called out by the sergeant-major, so I had to walk back to that table. After a while, there were about a dozen of us, wondering why we'd been called back. I suppose, looking back, it was obvious, but at the time, I had no idea. Major Samson told us that the captain was in charge of arrangements. Captain Handley – a nice fellow, I liked him; got blown to smithereens about six months later. Anyway, Captain Handley waited till we were out of earshot from the others and then divided us into two groups. He said to my group, eight of us we were, that we'd been selected because we was all handy with a rifle. I still didn't understand, and then he said, "For the sake of everyone, especially that poor sod, don't miss". Well, then the penny dropped, I can tell you. My knees went like jelly. The other group was to be the burial party. They had to go off and dig the grave there and then. I'd have gladly swapped places, believe me.

'So then, this Captain Handley and the sergeant-major marched us over to some deserted farmhouse about half a mile away. Usually, it was used as another billet, but not that day. He pointed to an outhouse where the prisoner was spending his last night and another where we was sleeping. He took us to this large cobbled farmyard, and next to the wall was this chair. Little, delicate thing it was – like a lady's chair. Then the captain told us what would happen. He said we'd be given loaded rifles but one would contain a blank. The prisoner would be tied down to the chair and would have a white handkerchief tied to his tunic over the heart. We were to stand about ten yards away. He said he'd issue his orders silently with a red handkerchief which he had on him. And he went through the motions. When he raised his arm, like this, we were to take aim. And when he brought it down, like this, well, that was our signal to fire at the white handkerchief. To give him his due, the captain looked as uneasy about the business as we did. I remember him saying it was an unpleasant duty as we'll ever be ordered to do, but we were all under orders and there was nothing any of us could do.'

Mr Greene paused.

'Can I get you a cup of tea?' asked the reporter.

'No, it's all right, love. Talking about it doesn't affect me, not any more, but when it appears in my dreams, then it's horrible.'

'Does it happen often?'

'No, thank the Lord. Used to, but I suppose I've had seventy years to get used to it.' He coughed. 'Anyway, after that, we were shown our quarters for the night. What a night that was, seemed to last forever. Dinner was brought to us, but I don't think any of us had the stomach for food. They also brought various things to keep us occupied and an urn so we could make our own tea; well, we certainly drank gallons of the stuff. There were many nights during the war when I felt worried about the coming day, but none compared to this. We couldn't talk. We just sat there, not reading the newspapers they'd given us, or playing cards or dominoes, nothing. I remember staring out of the window and looking at the small building where I knew they were keeping him. And after a while, I saw the padre go in. Later on, one of the red caps came to see us—'

'Red caps?'

'Military Police. He came to wish us good luck. "Luck" didn't seem the right word really, but he meant well. We asked him what the prisoner was doing. Apparently, he was trying to write a letter, but kept screwing it up and starting again. He was also trying to drown a bottle of rum and trying to ignore the padre, but neither with much success! Poor bastard – oh, 'scuse my French. I remember thinking, how does one come to terms with one's last night on earth. You know, the prospect of going over the top was pretty terrifying, I know – I did it a couple of times. But at least you could pray to be spared or, even better, to get a Blighty.'

'And what's a "Blighty"?' the reporter asked.

'Oh, it's a type of wound we all hoped for – the sort that was bad enough to send you home, but not too bad to be long-term.'

She smiled at the desperate logic.

'The sergeant-major woke us next morning before dawn. Doubt if any of us had slept well. Morning of November eleventh it was, a Sunday. The war had exactly one year to go. After a quick cup of water each, he took us outside. It was all grey and misty and I couldn't stop shivering, but whether that was from the cold or my nerves, I couldn't tell you. And there, waiting in front of us, was that chair, all wet from the dew. And then Captain Handley appeared. Soon after, the door to the outhouse opened and my heart went mad. First out, came the padre reading from his bible. Then came the prisoner with his hands tied behind his back and surrounded by three red caps. At first, the prisoner seemed composed, but then, about twenty yards from us, he saw us standing there in line, our rifles at our sides, and that did it for him. His legs went to jelly and he had to be helped up by the red caps and dragged to the chair. He started screaming, pleading for mercy. Oh, I've heard those screams every night for years, that terrified high-pitched sound. Horrible, horrible.'

He paused again as the memory returned, the screams punctuated by short, panicky gasps. The reporter could see this was becoming difficult for the old man but having come so far, he had to finish. 'Would you like to stop for a bit?'

'Yes, I think I'll just nip to the loo. If you'll excuse me.' He pulled himself up from the armchair and tottered uneasily towards the living room door.

The reporter stopped the tape and congratulated herself on finding such an extraordinary tale. She'd done four interviews already and had heard all about the mud, the lice, the bodies, and she'd expected this to be a variation on the same theme, but no, this was different. This was going to make fantastic copy. What a shame it had to be wasted on the people of Essex, such a limited readership. Maybe she could try and sell it to one of the nationals and make a name for herself.

Mr Greene returned from the toilet and sat down with a heavy sigh. 'That's better,' he said. 'Where was I?'

'Erm, the prisoner screaming.'

'Ah yes. Well, the red caps had quite a struggle to get him to the chair and tie his arms and legs down, I can tell you. They had no choice but to be rough on him. For such a weedy-looking boy, he seemed to have superhuman strength so it took them ages to tie him to the chair, prolonging our agony. One had to hold his head still while another put the blindfold on. Then the sergeant-major went over and stuck the white handkerchief over his heart. It was a triangle shape. Finally, everything was ready, but he kept struggling and shaking furiously. He started calling out for his mother. Pathetic it was, truly pathetic. And I mean that in the old-fashioned sense of the word. Then, Captain Handley took out his red handkerchief and raised it in the air. We lifted our rifles and took aim, focusing on that piece of triangular cloth, each of us praying that ours contained the blank. I really couldn't see myself hitting him anyway; I was shaking so much. I saw the red handkerchief fall and I erm…' He paused. 'I, well, you know, I pulled the trigger.' He paused as the sound of the eight rifles echoed through his mind.

'You'd think that'd be it, wouldn't you, but no. He slumped forwards in his chair but he was still moving. He sort of fell forward taking the chair with him and staggered towards us groaning. He must've come about five, six yards before collapsing in a heap, shaking from the convulsions. I can't tell you how appalling that was, I felt so sorry for him, but there was nothing we could do.

'The medical officer went up to him and felt for a pulse and I remember praying "please let him be dead". But no, the MO shook his head. Captain Handley had to go up and deliver the coup de grace. He looked white as a sheet. He drew his revolver and pressed the nozzle against the prisoner's temple and his hand was shaking like anything. God, it was like seeing a horse put down, the poor man. He pulled the trigger and finally that was it.'

'My word, how awful,' she said.

'It took us a while to take it in, we just stood there. Then this chap next to me bent over and was sick. I'm afraid my legs went. I fell to my knees and dropped my rifle. I remember looking to the sky and begged for His forgiveness.'

'But like your captain said, there was nothing you could do.'

'The padre started reading from his bible again and the MO confirmed the prisoner was dead. The captain took the dead man's boots off.'

'Why did he do that?'

'Well, you don't want to waste a good pair of boots, now, do you? Apparently he'd stolen them anyway. And then the burial party put him on the stretcher, covered him in an old blanket and took him off.'

'Good God. So was he guilty; had he deserted?'

'Well, I suppose so, otherwise they wouldn't have found him guilty, would they? But it scared us, I must say. Probably all of us had to fight the urge to run off and hide at some time. I know there were times I felt so frightened, the thought entered my head. But something holds you back, I don't know what. But I knew that there, but for the grace of God, that boy could've been me or any one of us. It feels funny telling a woman how frightened I was, it was something I hardly admitted to myself for years, but now I think, so what? What have I got to hide any more?'

'Well, I can't imagine anyone I know having to go through what your generation did.'

'Ah well, if you have to, you have to. You have a sense of duty and not doing it seems worse than doing it. I was wounded soon after that, nothing serious, but it got me out of the line. I'd done

215

more than my bit – I'd been there a whole three and a half years. But after that day, I felt different from then on. I was fighting only for myself and me mates, just wanting to survive. Somehow, I'd lost faith in the King and Country bit.'

Mr Greene stopped and his eyes seemed to drift back to November 1917. The reporter knew the old man had nothing else to add. She switched off the tape recorder and placed it carefully back into her handbag. 'Well, Mr Greene, I can't thank you enough, it's been an education.'

'Hmmm?'

'Is there anything I can get you?'

'No, no.'

She stood up and gathered her coat. 'Will you be attending a Remembrance service?'

'No. I don't go out if I can help it. I'll do what I do every year – I'll have a glass of sherry and toast my mates, that's enough for me.'

As she made to leave, she asked, 'What was the prisoner's name again?'

He puffed his cheeks again. 'Searight, Jack Searight. Strange to think he too would be in his nineties now; what a waste, eh?'

'Yes, indeed.' She smiled. She thanked the old man again and left.

*

An hour later, she was back in her office, almost skipping with glee at having found such a damning testimony of British military justice during the First World War. She was sure she'd be able to sell the article on to a national, and from there, doors would open and the road to journalistic fame beckoned. She was sick of covering diamond anniversaries, cats stuck in trees and local muggings, there was more to life than this provincial treadmill. This sort of thing only happened once in a blue moon, and she was going to milk it for all its worth. Originally, her heart sank when she'd been assigned the First World War project, but surely this was an aspect of the war that, seventy years on, was not widely known to the public. It would make a great top line to pitch. Of course, she'd told Mr Greene that it was only for the local rag; she could ask his permission later before going further with it. Surely, he'd be pleased at helping uncover this murkier side in the history of the British Army. Anyway, he was ninety-three, so he wouldn't be around for much longer; what would he care?

She sat down and placed the tape recorder on her desk in front of her, plugged it in and pressed rewind. While the tape rewound she found a pair of earphones in her drawer. This truly was going to make a riveting read; she couldn't wait to get going. As she grappled around looking for a pen, the tape recorder started making odd gurgling noises. She peered at it and wondered if something was wrong. She quickly pressed the stop and eject buttons and pulled the cassette out. To her horror, there was a stream of tangled tape spewing out of the cassette and into the mechanics of the machine. She tugged at it, but the more she pulled, the more the tape poured from the cassette, twisting in an unending coil of brown, stretched plastic. Flushed with panic, she pressed play in the hope that the machine would allow her to extricate the tape. But, within moments, the spools sucked in more tape into the dark abyss of the recorder. She hit the stop button and looked at the mesh of snarled tape. She tugged at it but it made no difference. In frustration, she pulled at it again with greater determination. The tape snapped. She swore and smacked her palm against her forehead. She tried to think. Surely, she could remember what the old chap had said. Immediately, she started writing, but somehow it wasn't working, she simply couldn't recreate the scene he had so vividly described in his understated manner. She'd lost that urgency and her words seemed so lifeless in comparison. She still had the essence, but the telling detail had gone and, more worrying, the spirit had gone too.

Chapter 25: Farewell – 14 November 1917

'I've got good news for you, Private Searight.' Major Cartwright's voice took Guy by surprise. He was lying on his bed trying to finish the Dickens novel, annoyed with himself that he had gleaned such little pleasure from it.

'Sir?' Guy wasn't at all convinced that what the major deemed good news would entirely coincide with his own interpretation.

Major Cartwright grinned with the expectation of one who was looking forward to receiving gratitude on imparting good news. 'We're transferring you to a base hospital just outside Le Havre. Short notice, I'm afraid, but there're rumours of a big push soon, so we'll probably need every bed we can get. You leave this afternoon.'

As feared, Guy was right and he didn't know what to say. He'd half expected it, but not so soon nor with such little notice. The major seemed nonplussed by Guy's lack of enthusiasm; this was the sort of news that was usually greeted with huge relief and heartfelt thanks. The least he expected was some acknowledgement of pleasure, but no, Private Searight remained silent as if the news wasn't entirely welcome. 'Well, aren't you pleased to be going home, Searight?'

'Yes, I suppose I am. I'm sorry; it took a while to sink in, thank you, sir.'

That was better, thought the major. 'Good lad. Report to the courtyard for two o'clock. Transport will be waiting. You'll be taken to the station and from there a train to Le Havre and a base hospital. Once there, they'll decide how long you should stay but I don't imagine it'll be long before you're shipped back to London, probably somewhere like the Prince of Wales Hospital. Once in London, you'll have time to recuperate and get your strength up. And while you're there, they'll fix you up with a new leg. That'll make things easier for you.' The major could see that Guy wasn't really listening. He leant down and said in a softer, reassuring voice, 'You'll be all right when you get back to England, son. You've had nothing but good reports while you've been out here. I heard how you played a pivotal role in that raid; they got some useful intelligence out of it, and if you're lucky, you'll get yourself a recommendation for a medal. Wear it with pride, son; you've been a brave lad and you should be proud of yourself. I've seen too many shirkers around here, but you're not one of them. Go home and hold your head high, you've done more than your bit and the country owes its gratitude to boys like you.'

Guy listened to the major's earnest speech, which he knew was well meant. 'Thank you, sir,' he said, trying to look suitably humbled. Major Cartwright placed his hand on Guy's shoulder and then left to continue his tour of the wards. Guy watched him approach Browne. 'I've got good news for you, Private Browne.'

Guy closed his book and leaned back on his pillow. The major had said he'd seen 'too many shirkers'. Is that what Jack had been: a shirker? A deserter? Guy promised himself he would never use the word. A boy scared witless; a boy who was never meant to be a soldier; a boy with his life ahead of him, who, unable to cope, was made to pay for it with his life? And what about himself? According to the major, Guy was up for a medal, a hero. What had made *him* a hero? The answer was simple: fear. Fear for his life, fear of fear. What a thin line separated hero and shirker. Both of them had been driven by fear; it was pure luck that Guy had managed to channel his fear in the right direction. But the result was one got a medal, and the other got the firing squad.

Browne was up on his feet, unable to contain his relief that he was heading north. He hugged Lampton who'd also been given the good news. Browne went off to have a shave.

And now, Guy had to go home without his brother to face his parents. How he'd looked forward to going home, but now the prospect chilled him and the vast empty expanse of his future frightened him. The thought of slotting back into his old life seemed incomprehensible. War had changed him as it changed every man and two years older, he was no longer a young man. He knew, back in England, he'd resent those too old to fight and spend the rest of his life envying those too young or not yet born. And he hated the thought that his leg would mark him forever more as a victim, an object of pity, that people would see the leg first, not the man who lost it. He didn't want to go home, but equally, he had no desire to stay. The realisation of what he really wanted to do made him shudder – he wanted to return to the front where he still had friends. Guy wanted to join them again, to hear the sound of the shells, to feel the cloying mud, to smell the stench of battle and decay, to live hourly in the company of death. The prospect of the trenches filled him with less dread than the prospect of returning home and having to face the questioning eyes of his parents, of trying to explain the inexplicable. He would rather live through the nightmare all over again, rather than try and describe it in words palatable for those who could never comprehend. At least the events of the past had taken him unawares, like falling suddenly down a well – it was horrible but it happens quickly, leaving you no time to fear it. But the contemplation of the slow, exhausting climb out seemed all the more frightening.

Guy also realised he would have to face Mary. He remembered with unease Jack's inept attempt to woo Josephine at his parents' party.

Nevertheless, Guy was pleased by the prospect of leaving the CCS. He'd noticed how the men were already subtly distancing themselves from him. These men, who were so accustomed to commiserating each other over the loss of friends and comrades, were not sure of what etiquette of sympathy applied to Guy's situation. Jack's crime was taboo and, by association, Guy's company was, if possible, to be avoided. He was a freak amongst freaks. His mother would, of course, grieve for Jack, but only in terms of *her* loss. Guy needed someone who could help him grieve for *his* loss. He felt a sudden desire to seek out the men who had been guarding Jack when he went to visit his brother. They'd understand. They had, after all, witnessed for themselves the courage of a condemned man, a man who knew all too well what fate awaited him and bore it with such fortitude and dignity. A courage that far outstripped Guy's own instinctive bravery on the battlefield.

Time was getting on. Guy decided to get ready. He got up and, taking his crutches, went off to the communal bathrooms where, bumping into Browne, he had a wash and a shave. He had been growing a moustache, but decided to shave it off. He wanted to return to England the way he left it, albeit minus a leg. When he returned from the bathrooms, he found Robert waiting for him. His friend looked glum and so Guy took him to the common room.

'This time tomorrow, I'll be back at the front,' he said. 'Just in time for the new offensive.' He leant forward and whispered, 'You know, there're rumours they're planning on using masses of tanks.'

'As long as we don't resort to gas.'

'The accessory, you mean. It's all bloody awful, if you ask me,' said Robert leaning back in his chair.

Guy gazed around the room. He noticed the burnt man sitting at the same place he was the afternoon Guy had gone to see Jack for the last time. The man nodded, a faint hint of a smile, the sudden glare of white teeth, accentuated by the blackness of his face. Guy nodded back and turned to face Robert. 'They're sending me to base hospital,' he said tonelessly.

'You don't sound too pleased about it.'

'I'm not sure how I'm going to cope.' He didn't dare tell Robert he'd gladly swap places.

'Do you remember the raid, Guy? The Hun who charged at you with the bayonet?'

Guy noticed the twinkle in his friend's eye. 'Was it you… who killed him?'

Robert winked.

Guy smiled. Of course he remembered it; he remembered it every night he closed his eyes. The frightful scream; the German bearing down on him, bayonet fixed. Guy rooted to the spot. The shot, the single shot that came from somewhere above and behind him. The German falling in a heap at his feet. He remembered thrusting his bayonet into the man's back and the ugly squelching noise as the blade did its brutal work. He remembered turning around but his saviour had vanished.

Robert accompanied Guy back to his ward and sat on the bed while he gathered his few belongings. Browne and Lampton had already packed and gone to wait for the transport half an hour early. Robert talked about the things he'd do when, and if ever, he got home. The home in the country, the horse he would buy, the young country girls he would date. Guy envied him his dream. Then Guy joined him perched on the edge of the bed and the two of them reminisced about people they knew and missing friends. After a while, Robert declared he had to go. They bid each other farewell with a hug. 'I hope to see you soon then, Guy. I'll invite you out to my country estate and we'll drink until dawn.' Guy watched his friend leave, his hitherto unknown saviour.

Guy had less than half an hour before he was due to leave. It didn't take him long to pack his meagre possessions into a haversack given to him by the hospital: his soap, razor, and the book. He gathered his crutches and made to leave. As he passed each bed, he wished his fellow wounded friends farewell and received, in turn, their wishes and utterances of good luck. At the door, he turned around to take a final look at the ward that had been home for the previous week. He tried to imagine it as a classroom – the rows of desks, the young French boys listening attentively, the sun shining through the windows. He imagined the teacher rattling out the milestones of French history – the Revolution, Waterloo, the Crimea, the Franco-Prussian war, and now this. The Germans on French soil again, a thirty-man British raid on a small strip of German trench; nine killed, eleven wounded, a thirty-three per cent survival rate. His own insignificant contribution in a forgotten incident in a gigantic war.

The envious eyes of his now ex-wardmates were on him. He smiled, almost apologetically, glanced up at the portrait of King George, saluted and left.

With his haversack slung over his shoulder, Guy made his way down the long echoey corridor with the huge windows overlooking the tents and marquees set out neatly on the lawn. The pain in his leg grew more acute. His crutches felt awkward to move. Staff ran in all directions in the hurried pursuits of urgent duties; a stretcher passed - its occupant's face totally hidden beneath blood-soaked bandages, groaning as the stretcher-bearers hurried down the corridor. He saw a young Frenchwoman dabbing her eyes with a handkerchief; a doctor leaning against the wall, looking skywards, drunk with fatigue; a soldier in a wheelchair embarrassed by the damp circle between his legs. Wounded soldiers idled this way and that; a priest overtook Guy and almost bumped into a kitchen orderly carrying a bucket of vegetable peelings. No one noticed or acknowledged Guy as he made his way to the desk in the grand hallway. By the time he reached it, he was quite out of breath, the pain in his leg causing him to grip the desk until his fingertips turned white.

'You alright there?' said the man behind the desk.

'Yeah. Just a minute,' stuttered Guy as he waited for the pain to wash over him.

'Do you want to sit down?'

Slowly the pain receded, leaving Guy panting in relief. 'I'm... I'm OK now. Thanks.'

The man signed Guy's name off his register and handed him his medical papers.

Outside, it was cold and blustery. Guy shivered. It was fast approaching two o'clock. He saw his transport – a horse-drawn carriage with room for six passengers, Browne and Lampton had taken their places, Browne talking excitedly. The driver stood next to the horse, stroking its neck. Guy hobbled across the gravelled courtyard towards the carriage.

'Private Searight.'

Guy recognised the voice. On turning he was surprised to see coming quickly towards him Sergeant Wilkins, his arm in a sling.

'Private Searight,' he repeated, slightly out of breath, 'I see I've caught you in the nick of time.'

'Sarge.'

'They told me inside you was just leaving.' Having found Guy he looked like a man who wished he hadn't.

'Yes, I'm being sent home via a hospital on the coast.'

'That's, erm, that's good,' he said, nodding his head furiously. 'Yes, that's good.'

'How's your arm?'

'This? Oh, it's nothing. I'll be back up the line soon.'

The two men stood facing, unable to look at each other. Wilkins spoke. 'Look, the reason... I mean, what I wanted to say...'

'Sarge?'

Wilkins looked at the carriage, with the driver climbing aboard, reins in hand. 'I just wanted to say... to offer...' Then, finally, he looked Guy straight in the eye, 'To offer my condolences on the death of your brother,' he said quickly.

Guy opened his mouth to speak and found himself unable to form any words.

'Your brother, he was a good lad.' His hand shot out and it took a moment for Guy to realise that the sergeant was offering his hand.

He focussed on the fingers, stubbly and rounded, a gold band on one.

'A good lad,' repeated the sergeant.

'Yes, thank you, Sarge,' said Guy, taking the proffered hand limply and having his hand shaken.

The driver coughed.

'I'd...'

'Yes, you'd better go.'

Guy climbed aboard, let his bag drop to the floor of the carriage and acknowledged his fellow passengers. As the horses lurched forward, Guy looked back and watched the sergeant walking back towards the hospital. The carriage juddered through the large, black iron gates and around the corner. The sergeant was no longer in view. Guy's attention and that of his colleagues was taken by the passing of an ambulance travelling at speed towards the hospital. Its driver wore a look of grim determination as he took the latest batch of wounded to the hospital that used to be, before the war, a boarding school for boys.

Chapter 26: A Cabinet of Curiosities – 14 November 1917

The hospital train, eight carriages long, had emblazoned on it a series of red crosses but, Guy noticed, it carried the scars of having been hit – broken windows patched up by tape, woodwork splintered. One of the carriages, he learnt, had been requisitioned as an operating theatre. The platform was a mass of activity; men laid out on stretchers, many, like Guy, on crutches, others propping each other up, men asleep standing upright, men with bandages over their eyes and around their heads, so many gaunt, expressionless faces, a continual hum of groans. There must have been over three hundred men and nurses milling about, crowded onto the narrow platform, paying no heed to the fine drizzle of rain. Most were still in their filthy uniforms, having been brought directly to the station from the battlefield, sidestepping the casualty clearing stations; others, the more fortunate like Guy, had been given fresh uniforms. Nurses and orderlies buzzed round, making sure their charges were OK.

Now, with the evening drawing in, they waited to board. 'Doubt we'll get first class,' said Lampton.

'No, we're not wounded enough.' He pointed towards the rear of the train. 'We'll be in with the horses.' On the side of the rear carriages were notices painted large with the words *Hommes 40, chevaux 8.*

'What does that mean?' asked Lampton. 'Men and horses?'

'Yes. Question is does it mean forty men *or* eight horses, or forty men *and* eight horses.'

'We'll find out soon enough. It'll probably stink'

'Yes, poor horses.'

'Get on board, get on board,' came the shout from a sister who had the air of one in charge. The nurses and orderlies helped the men on board, the stretcher cases were lifted and manhandled in among the grunts and yelps of pain.

'Come on,' said Guy to Lampton, 'we don't need help, let's get on.'

The carriage door had been slid open, and along with a host of men, Guy and Lampton hauled themselves up the steps and in. The place did indeed stink and the carriage consisted of wooden benches, each piled with blankets. Guy sat at the end of one bench and pushed his haversack beneath him and rested a blanket on his knees. 'Very nice,' he said. 'Could be a lot worse.'

It took almost an hour for every man to be hoisted on board and made comfortable. With the doors closed, the fifty or so men in the horse carriage were left without light save for whatever daylight pierced the cracks in the wooden sides. Most of them were amputees, but every one of them had at least the one leg. Those without were made more comfortable in the better carriages nearer the front. Eventually, the train pulled out.

The train seemed to move at an excruciatingly slow pace, stopping frequently. Within a couple of hours, it was dark and the men lit a number of hurricane lamps. It was cold and without heating, the men huddled in their blankets. At the centre of attention was an Indian soldier, a man with a long wispy beard, wearing a turban, missing his left arm. His name, when asked, was Kiran Singh.

'Can-he-sing? Strange name,' said Browne.

Kiran giggled. 'No, listen,' he said, articulating the syllables, 'Ki-ran Singh; it means ray of sunshine.'

'Ray of sunshine? In this place?'

'So where's the sun, then, Ray?'

'Where I come from, there is much sun.'

'And where's that?'

'A small village in India.'

'My God,' said one. 'You've come a long way to fight for king and country.'

'Yes, a long way. But I am happy.'

'Hah? Happy? Then you must be a ray of sunshine,' said Browne.

'And what is your name?'

'Stephen Browne. Browne with an 'e'.'

'And what is the matter with you, then?'

'Leg wound.'

With a whoosh, the huge side door slid open and there appeared a nurse, a large bag on her back.

'How did you get in? The carriages aren't joined,' asked one of the men.

The woman laughed. 'There's a footboard, isn't there?' she said in a sing-song Welsh accent.

'Nonetheless.'

'Don't you go worrying about me, soldier, this train is so slow I could walk to Le Havre faster than this old thing.'

'How fast is it going anyway?' asked Browne.

'No more than twelve miles per hour. It's regulation.' She swung the bag onto the floor. 'Well, boys, I come with goodies – cake and smokes. Proper dinner will come later. Wait, wait, your turn will come.'

'Where's the toilet, nurse?'

'Surely you mean the lavatory, Private. Halfway down. You'll have to wait until the next stop.'

As the men dozed off on their hard benches, wrapped in blankets, Guy thought of Mary. He wondered whether he might find her in Le Havre. The town, by all accounts, had a couple of large base hospitals brimming with VADs and it was to one of these hospitals that they were scheduled to go.

*

The following morning, having slept as well as they could on their wooden benches, the men grumbled as the train made yet another stop, this time held up at a junction. But their irritation soon vanished when the side doors opened, letting in a blast of cold but welcome fresh air and a shaft of wintery sunlight, and, queuing up outside, a number of French women, mostly old and all dressed head to toe in black, bearing baskets covered with tea towels. '*Mesdames*,' cried Lampton, '*Qu'avons-nous ici?* What have we here?'

'*Bonjour, Messieurs, bonjour. Comment allez-vous?*' they said as they reached into the baskets and started handing out hunks of bread, bits of fruit and cigarettes. '*Des petits cadeaux pour nos Anglais courageux.*'

The men fell over themselves in their thanks. Guy took an apple and thanked the grizzled old women profusely. The old women were particularly taken by Ray, as Kiran Singh had now been christened, intrigued by his turban. Ray, aware of his novelty value status, bowed several times and smiled. Shouts came from the front of the train that they were ready to depart. The men crowded near the open door and waved at the gaggle of old women as the train slowly pulled away. They returned to their benches with their little snacks and ate in silence. The gifts may have been modest but the men, as one, were touched at their generosity, the simple show of support.

*

Finally, after two exhausting days, the train pulled into the station at Le Havre. Transports of varying sorts were waiting to take them to their new home, a hospital. Most were placed in ambulances but Lampton, Browne, Ray and Guy took their seats in one of the many horse and carts, theirs driven by a Frenchman smoking a ridiculously large pipe. As it made its way through the narrow streets flanked by high buildings, French children ran alongside, enjoying the sun, shouting and saluting. The men saluted back. The town was a heaving mass of soldiers, outnumbering by far the locals; ambulances whizzed by, columns of men heading in every direction.

After a ten-minute bumpy ride along the cobbled stones of *centre ville*, the driver took a smoother road where, after a further twenty minutes, he turned and drove through an ornate gate and onto a gravel drive of a grand-looking building. Lampton whistled. The *Hotel Saint Jacques*, as the sign informed them, was a huge, palatial hotel, a stone staircase leading up to the reception, three floors, huge windows, those on the first floor with balconies, on its roof the tricolour of the French flag. The driver, his pipe puffing blue smoke, weaved his horse through a number of similar vehicles, announcing '*Voici*,' as he pulled his horse to a stop.

A sister with small spectacles greeted them, 'Welcome to Hotel Saint Jacques,' she said, shielding her eyes from the sun. 'If you would like to follow me…' The four men did as instructed, and with their bags and holdalls, followed the sister. Browne touched Guy's arm and gestured with a nod of his head to a shed at the side of the courtyard. Its doors were open and just inside Guy could make out a pile of wooden crosses. The two men raised their eyebrows at each other.

The sister led the men into reception with its two-tone marbled floor. The whole area was covered with men laid out on stretchers with nurses moving between them, stepping over them, trying to answer their calls. Many were having their uniforms taken off, usually by a nurse wielding a large pair of scissors to slice through the heavy fabric. Behind the reception desk, two further nurses.

'Your names, please,' said one, trying to raise her voice above the din.

With the formalities done, an orderly led them to the lift. As they waited, Guy caught sight of the men on stretchers with their gaunt expressions and bloodied bandages.

Once inside the lift, the orderly spoke. 'You OK, chaps?' he asked of no one in particular. 'You'll be glad to know that you're on the top floor, away from all the chaos.'

'Is it always like this?' asked Guy.

'Oh yes, it never lets up, I can tell you. But you lot are considered fit, I mean what's a leg or an arm between friends? Don't get too comfortable here, though, you'll all be off tomorrow, back home. There's a thought for you all, eh?'

'Tomorrow?' said Browne. 'Music to my ears.'

'Yep, thought you'd be pleased to hear that. Your beds are too valuable. No one stays on the top floor more than one night.'

Coming out of the caged lift, the orderly led them to their room. 'Wow, this is something,' muttered Lampton as they made their way down the carpeted corridor with its chandelier lights.

'Here we are, gentlemen,' said the orderly, opening the door. 'Make yourselves comfortable. Dinner is at eight downstairs in the restaurant. Don't expect anything fancy, mind you, it may have once been a hotel, but it's the usual army fare, I'm afraid.'

'That's fine by us,' said Guy.

'Cheerio then,' said the orderly.

The room was small; Guy guessed before the war this was the sort of bedroom used by staff or perhaps servants of the wealthy guests. But as small as it may have been, it boasted a huge window, with heavy draped curtains.

Lampton placed a piece of metal on his bedside table.

'What's that?' asked Guy. 'Shrapnel?'

'Sure is, and not any old piece of shrapnel but the very bit that shattered my leg.'

Guy fumbled in his holdall, finally finding his bullet. Holding it up triumphantly, he said, 'Swap!'

'Hey, we could make a collection.'

'Yes, our very own cabinet of curiosities.'

Ray pulled open the curtains. 'Look,' he said, 'what a beautiful view.'

Guy and Lampton joined him at the window and looked – they were at the back of the hotel and ahead of them a long stretch of lawn, overgrown perhaps, but still a wonder to see the fresh, unspoilt grass, and a small copse of trees to the right. In front of the trees was a small cemetery, a series of wooden crosses haphazardly placed. Beyond the lawn, the sea – nothing but the sea and, to the left, the wave of cliffs.

'Listen,' said Ray.

The men listened and it took Guy a few moments to realise what he was listening out for. It was the sound of the sea, the waves, the seagulls, the silence. His leg gave way, momentarily, as he realised he'd never heard such peace.

Lampton, wide-eyed, said softly, 'Isn't it the most beautiful thing you've ever heard?'

Guy, unable to speak, nodded. The sea: how alluring it seemed, glistening beneath the blue sky, reflecting the sun. He looked at his new-found friends and noticed that Ray had tears in his eyes.

*

Guy was dreaming of the German, of the bayonet, the screams. 'I'm sorry,' he heard himself say, 'I'm sorry, forgive me, please.'

'Guy, Guy.' The German boy's hands, slender and surprisingly clean, are on the bayonet, helping Guy extricate it from his cheek. 'Guy, it's me.' 'Yes, I know.' The blood oozes out between his fingers, startling in its brightness. 'Help me. Mother.' 'I'm trying, Lord knows I didn't mean to do this.' He slams his foot against the boy's chest, but having the one leg now, loses his balance. As he lies on the mud, his rifle still skewered in the boy's face, tottering, he sees a spurt of red jut out of the boy's mouth, his eyes rolling over. Guy tries to look away only to find the mirror image on his other side. He looks to the heavens and the German is still there, his mouth a bubbling pool of blood. 'Guy, Guy, wake up, it's me…'

'No,' he muttered half-asleep. 'Leave me be, go away.'

'Guy, please…'

He opened his eyes. Leaning over him he could see the outline of a woman wearing the blue uniform of a VAD, a bonnet on her head. 'Who is it?' he said, his breaths coming in short bursts. 'Leave me be. Who are you?'

'It's me, it's Mary.'

'Mary?'

'Shh..'

'No,' he whispered, 'it can't be.' He tried to prop himself up. 'Here, let me help.'

As his eyes adjusted to the dark, he could see her now.

'I can't believe it's you,' she said, her hand clasped to her mouth.

'Nor I,' he said, trying to calm his breathing.

'Oh, Guy…'

'It's okay, come now, it's okay.'

'I… I don't know what to say.'

He stroked her arm. 'You don't have to say anything.'

She put her arms round him and the two embraced. Guy smelt her warm, youthful skin; his nose tingled at the incongruous mixture of lavender and iodine. He found himself breathing in her smell, intoxicated by the pleasure of this sudden and unexpected presence.

'I'm sorry,' she said. 'It's been so hard. I've seen so much, and I've not cried, I've not had time to cry.'

'I know.'

'You just move on. From one emergency to the next. They say the good nurses are the ones who don't feel. And I've tried, Guy, I've tried to be a good nurse, not to become so emotionally attached that I'm no good to man or beast. But when I saw your name on the register, I just crumpled. It's been so difficult; I never thought it'd be like this.'

'The war?'

She nodded, her hand clenched against her lips.

'I guess none of us did,' he said.

She fumbled in her gown for a handkerchief. 'Look at me,' she said, forcing a little laugh. 'Three months, I'm your stoical, no-nonsense nurse, a good nurse, now two minutes with you and I'm a wreck.'

'It's okay.'

'Mustn't wake the others.'

'I don't think anything could wake these chaps.'

'Do you know them?'

'Not really, but they're good men, all of them.'

'I'm so sorry to hear about your misfortune.'

'Yes, well.'

'How are you?'

'Glad to be alive.'

'Yes, of course,' she said.

'I can't believe it's you.'

'I know. Your name on that register, it gave me such a turn, I had to come see you straight away. I'm sorry for waking you. I think you were in the middle of a bad dream. I ought to go, I'll be missed, Matron will have my garters. I'm sorry. I wake you up then I'm gone.'

'Don't worry, I understand. Will I see you again?'

'Oh yes, a lot in fact. I'm going back with you.'

'To England?'

'Yes, it's one of my jobs, to transport patients back home, to nurse them along the way. But I never get to step on home soil. As soon as we dock, the ship turns round, comes back here and a couple of days later I do it all over again. I'll still be busy, it never stops, but we should snatch a few moments to catch up. Oh, and tomorrow morning, early. Inspection.'

'Inspection?'

'It's another one of my jobs – to check over amputees to see if they're fit to make the journey home.'

'And when do you get a chance to sleep?'

'Every other Thursday. I really ought to go. Tell me, have you seen Jack?'

'Not recently.'

'I do miss him; barely an hour goes by when I don't think of him. At least once a day someone comes in all bandaged up and I think, oh no, it's my Jack. He hasn't written for a while now. Oh dear, I said that about you once, didn't I?'

'Yes, but it doesn't matter now.'

'Yes. Well, look, we might have a chance to catch up on the ship.'

'I look forward to that.'

'Me too.' She leaned down and kissed him on the cheek. 'So lovely to see you, Guy. Seeing you again, well, it's like touching home. Sleep tight.'

'Goodnight, Mary.'

'And Guy…'

'Yes?'

'Try to dream of something nicer.'

236

'I'll try.'

Guy lay in his bed, unable to get back to sleep, his mind whirling. Mary, he'd seen Mary. It didn't seem possible. But at some point, he knew, he was going to have to tell her about Jack. It wasn't a prospect he savoured.

*

The following morning, Ray pulled open the curtains and let in the sunshine. The men smiled, happy to have had the most comfortable night's sleep for months. Guy remembered being unable to sleep in his own bed when on leave but somehow, in a hotel masquerading as a hospital, it was different. Gazing outside, Ray and Guy watched silently as a small party of men dug a couple of fresh graves in the cemetery.

Having washed and changed, Guy and his roommates went down for breakfast. It was like being in a proper hotel, remarked Lampton. Guy looked round the refectory, heaving with activity, hoping to see Mary. He wondered what time she'd come to do her inspection; she'd said early. A nurse armed with a clipboard approached their table and told them to be packed and ready and back in the foyer by ten – they had two hours, during which time they could expect a visit from a Major Heathcote. Breakfast, although basic, was welcome; the tea strong enough to strip varnish.

Back in their room, packing took all of a few moments. From outside, through the open window, came the sound of a man's voice, clear in the morning air: 'Lord most holy, O God most mighty…'

Guy looked out to the scene – a funeral, a small gathering of nurses and wounded soldiers, the coffin wrapped with the Union flag, the padre reading from the bible.

It was then that there was a rap on their door but before anyone had a chance to respond, it swung open and in came a major and in his wake, Mary, her uniform clean, her hair tied back in a bun. 'Good morning, gentlemen,' said the major, a short man, barrel-chested and sporting a monocle.

The men stood to attention.

'At ease. How are you all, this lovely morning? My name is Major Heathcote, and this,' he said introducing Mary, 'is Nurse O'Dowd.'

Mary bowed to the men. 'Good morning. Hello, Guy, nice to see you again.'

'You know each other?' asked the major.

'Yes.' She smiled at Guy. 'We go back a long way and I am engaged to Guy's brother.'

'Hearty congrats,' said the major.

Guy tried to smile back but the image of Jack flashed through his mind as the words drifted through from outside... 'Most merciful saviour, thou most worthy judge eternal...' Turning, he saw a nurse drop a bouquet of flowers into the grave.

'Right,' said the major, 'let's see how you are. Let's start with you, Private. I guess you'll be Private Singh.'

'Yes, sir, that is all correct, sir.'

And so Major Heathcote made his round with Mary at his side, taking just a few moments with each of them – a quick look at their stumps and, for Guy and Browne, an evaluation on how they walked up and down the dormitory. He made a few ticks on the scrap of paper attached to his clipboard.

The major took a deep breath to address the men as outside a bugle played the first notes of the Last Post. 'OK, thank you, gentleman. I can certify that with the exception of one you are all fit and healthy enough to take your place on board the ship today. On landing in Dover, you will be transferred by ambulance train to London and the Prince of Wales Hospital in Marylebone. The exception is you, Private Browne. The wound in your thigh is still liable to infection but is not, in my considered opinion, of sufficient severity to have you sent back to England.'

'No, that can't be.'

'I will instead be recommending that you spend the rest of your convalescence here in this hospital where we can monitor your progress until such time that we deem you fit enough to be returned to active service.' The last note on the bugle faded away.

'No, please, you can't do that.'

'I will remind you, Private, to address me as sir, and that yes, I can do that. My priority here is to the forces of His Majesty and not to the whims of the individual whatever their circumstances. Good day to you all. Nurse O'Dowd, would you stay and distribute the men their boarding chits?' And with a click of his heels, the major spun round, clipboard tucked under his arm and left.

The funeral party, Guy noticed, was slowly making their way back to the hospital. A soldier was carefully folding the Union flag, ready to use another time – soon. Browne, shaking his head in disbelief, sat down on his bed. 'I can't go back,' he said quietly, sounding like a man on the verge of tears. 'Guy, Ray, don't let them take me back. I won't stand a chance.'

'But the major's right,' chipped in Ray, 'look at you, there's nothing wrong with you.'

'What? How dare you–'

'I come all the way from India; I want to go back and fight. I didn't come halfway round the world to sit in a hospital.'

'Why, you Indian bastard–' Browne said, springing to his feet

'See,' said Ray. 'See how nimble you are?'

'Sit down, Private Browne.' The voice belonged to Mary.

Browne looked from Ray to Mary and back, his fists clenched, his breathing heavy. Then, seized by an idea, he jabbed his finger towards Mary. 'It was you, wasn't it, sister, it was you. You told the major I was fit enough.'

'I did no such thing.'

Running his fingers through his hair, Browne started pacing up and down. 'I don't believe you,' he yelled, 'I saw you whispering to him, you're the Blighty nurse.'

'Major Heathcote is perfectly qualified to come to his own diagnosis without–'

'You're all in this together–'

'That's enough now, Stephen.' Guy tried to take Browne by the arm, to steer him back to the bed. Browne yanked his arm free, his eyes ablaze.

'Help me, Guy.'

Guy turned to Mary. 'There's nothing we can do?'

'Perhaps.'

Browne rushed up to her. 'Yes, go on, tell me.'

'We're expecting a lot of fresh casualties very soon, which is why we'll be transferring men through double quick – two ships a day. We'll be needing every bed we can get. Private Browne would be occupying a bed that could be of better use to another.'

'Can you speak to the major?' asked Guy.

'I'll try. I'll go see him now.'

'Thank you, nurse, thank you,' said Browne reaching for her hand to kiss it. 'You are an angel.'

'And me?' quipped Ray, 'am I still an Indian bastard?'

Outside, the mourners had all gone; the gravediggers had returned and were shovelling the mound of earth back into the hole, on top of the coffin.

The men waited while Mary went to catch up with the major. The men sat on their beds, Browne and Ray together on one. 'I'm sorry, mate,' said Browne, wringing his hands, 'I shouldn't have said that.'

'It is OK, Stephen. These are difficult times. Now we wait.'

'Yes, now we wait.'

The men watched the gravediggers at work. Another wooden cross to add to the rows already planted, a few adorned with a bunch of flowers. The padre reappeared, walking quickly towards the cemetery, his black cassock flowing in the breeze. The men with shovels stopped to acknowledge him, removing their caps. He nodded back and appeared to be looking for something. The men began searching too, their eyes scanning the grass. Soon, one of the men held something up, a piece of metal. The padre clapped his hands in relief and smiles all round brought the little exchange to an end. The padre, with a grin on his face, briskly made his way back as the men resumed their work.

'What was that?' asked Lampton.

'I think it was a ring.'

'Obviously meant something to him.'

The door swung open. Browne shot up as Mary marched back in. Wordlessly, she held out her clipboard to Browne, who snatched it from her. His eyes, wide and terrified, skimmed the words. He screamed, then flung his arms round Mary. The men cheered as one, loud enough for the gravediggers to look their way. Releasing Mary from his hug, he turned to his friends, tears in his eyes, and shook their hands one by one. 'Oh my Lord, the gods are shining on me today, my friends.'

'What does it say?' asked Guy.

'Here, look.'

Among the list of names was Browne's and the major's note, which had said, *Patient is fit enough to be returned to active duties following another fortnight's convalescence* had been scored out with two thick lines of black ink.

'So you're coming back with us, Stephen; well done, man,' said Guy returning the clipboard to Browne. 'How did you do it, Mary?'

'Well, you know, powers of persuasion and all that.'

'I can't thank you enough, sister. Will you marry me?'

Mary laughed. 'Just think, this time tomorrow, you'll all be waking up in a cosy bed in England.'

'Far away from all this mess,' added Lampton.

'I can't believe it, I've got my Blighty ticket,' said Browne, re-reading the sheet of paper as if ensuring he hadn't got it wrong. 'I thought I'd had it.'

'Come,' said Mary, 'you boys have a ship to board, we should go.'

Chapter 27: The Ship – 17 November 1917

The ship was due to set sail at midday. The whole process of embarkation had been tiring, the usual mayhem of bandaged men, stretchers, and the walking wounded, with the nurses and orderlies trying to maintain a sense of calm, organising and cajoling. Guy saw little of Mary who occasionally, in her blue uniform, passed in a blur. There seemed precious few nurses and orderlies to cope with such an array of men. Guy had stuck with his motley crew, as they nicknamed themselves – Lampton, Ray and the chastised Browne. The ship, the SS *Derby*, with its two funnels, was some three hundred feet long, at least so Lampton reckoned.

The men, perhaps four hundred or more, trooped on board; Guy and his friends, as the least wounded, were among the last. There was, Guy thought, a palpable sense of excitement at the prospect of going home. Lampton kept winking at him, and Ray, who had never been to England, sung aloud in a foreign tongue and talked of how thrilled he was at the thought of seeing the mother country. Browne, who had the greatest reason to be happy, was instead subdued, perhaps realising how close he'd come to a return to the front.

The dock was full of ships and boats of varying sizes. An English troopship had just docked, bringing from England the newest batch of young men to face the fray. Guy could see their joyful faces. 'Silly bastards,' said Lampton.

'I was like that when I arrived all the way from India,' said Ray.

'Me too,' said Browne.

'You come from India also?' asked Ray.

'No, what I meant… doesn't matter.'

Ray winked at Guy.

A small crowd of locals had gathered on the quay yelling, '*Vive l'Angleterre, vive la France!*' Some of the men waved back, shouting, 'God Save the King, Long Live France!'

Finally, with everyone on board and settled, the ship blasted its foghorn and pulled out of the harbour. Guy and Ray had been assigned a cabin together, with Browne and Lampton next door. The men looked out of their portholes and watched Le Havre, cloaked in a wintry sunlight, fade into the distance. A destroyer, acting as escort, sailed to the side of the ship.

Guy and Ray settled on their bunks and found life jackets under their pillows and a nice surprise – hot water bottles, still warm. 'This is the life,' said Ray, lying on his bunk. Soon he'd dozed off while Guy turned his attention to his Dickens. After a while, he decided to take a stroll in the hope of bumping into Mary. He knew that with only half a dozen nurses on board, she would be busy but the thought of some sea air appealed.

Climbing the ship stairs with his crutches proved awkward and once completed he had to stop to catch his breath. The decks were mostly deserted. The sun was shining, the sea calm. The presence of the sleek destroyer glinting in the sun running alongside half a mile off was reassuring. Two nurses rushed past him along the deck carrying fresh supplies of bandages. He found a bench and sitting down, thought back to his first voyage across to France. It didn't seem possible he was the same man. At the time it seemed the most natural thing to do, to join the cause, and he remembered the sense of excitement and anticipation.

Now, on his return, he had been determined to remain angry and embittered; it was a state he rather enjoyed in a perverse sort of way. It gave him a sense of direction, of power even. The power to view his life and his circumstances with a detachment born of a new-found cynicism. He couldn't shake off the ridiculous desire to return to active service, as Ray had expressed, but he'd come to hate the army. The army had killed Jack, not the war – he could have coped with his brother's death at the hands of the Germans, but he couldn't forgive the army for what they had done to him.

'Guy, hello.'

'Mary.' As much as he'd half expected to see her, it still took him by surprise.

She was carrying a jug with a long spout and a length of tubing. 'How are you feeling?' she asked.

'OK, I guess.'

'Do you mind if I join you?'

'Do you have time?'

'No,' she said, sitting next to him. 'I've been cleaning these things out.'

'What are they for?'

'For feeding some chap with lockjaw.'

'Poor sod.'

'So, looking forward to returning home?'

'Yes, but it'll be strange.'

'Yes, it might take you time to readjust. Have you any plans?'

'Not really. I guess Father will be expecting me to return to the fold and help him out with the business.'

'Do you want to?'

'No, but what else can I do? And you?'

245

'Me? When all this is over? I'll become a nurse; a qualified nurse. God knows I've had the experience now.'

'Yes, I suppose you have.'

'I can't afford to do this as a volunteer forever. Guy, tell me, when was the last time you saw Jack? How was he?'

He took a deep breath. 'Mary, I've got something I need to tell you. This might not be the best time but I don't know when I'll see you again.'

'Oh no, I don't like the sound of this.' She hastily placed her things on the bench next to her.

'Yes, it's not going to be easy for you.'

'He's dead, isn't he?' she asked, her voice quivering.

'I'm afraid so.'

Her hand went to her mouth as she let out a squeal of pain. 'Oh no. Please, Guy, tell me it isn't so.'

'If only I could.' He offered his hand; she took it, clenching it tightly.

'Jack, oh, Jack. When?'

'A week ago, eleventh November.'

'Oh, Jack, my poor Jack.' She grappled for a handkerchief from her pocket. 'How? How did it happen?'

'Do you need to know? Isn't it enough just to know he's not with us any more?'

She thought for a moment, circling an engagement ring on her finger which he hadn't noticed before. 'Yes,' she said, 'I need to know.'

'This is not easy, Mary.' He took a breath.

'Please, tell me…'

'He was shot for desertion.'

Her eyes seemed to glaze over as she adsorbed his words. She sprung to her feet. 'No, not Jack, you've got that wrong, that can't be true.'

Guy stood up and reached out for her. 'He didn't deserve it, it was unjust—'

'Unjust! You're lying...' She pummelled him in the chest. 'He wasn't shot; were you there? Did you see it, you're lying; tell me the truth, tell me.'

With one hand he tried to catch her arms, his other hand holding onto his crutch. 'Mary, stop.' He fell back onto the bench.

Drained by her outburst, Mary looked as if she was about to faint.

'Sit down, Mary.'

'Desertion. It can't be true. Guy, please, tell me the truth.'

'I'm sorry.'

'So what you're saying is true. Jack, my Jack, was shot for desertion?'

'Yes.'

'Oh my dear Lord. What am I going to do? I can't carry on now, knowing...'

The tears came. She fell onto Guy's lap, resting her head, while he stroked her hair. A seagull flapped by, squawking; the ship's funnels belched their smoke. 'You have to carry on,' he said. 'Look at what you're carrying – someone needs that; some poor blighter is depending on you. Think of them all here, on this ship, many of them their lives ruined – they need people like you. Go now, go to the man who needs this.'

She sat up. 'And you, Guy, is your life ruined?'

'My life has changed. The leg, that's nothing; Jack – it's something we'll all have to learn to live with. The war, it's part of us now, we can't alter that but we can learn to live with it. My life's changed, but no, it's not ruined, far from that.'

'Guy, always the optimist.'

'Sometimes it's the only way to get through all this. You'd better go.'

'Yes. I suppose I had. You're right, someone is waiting for this.'

'Next time you're in England, will you come visit?'

'Of course.' She kissed him on the cheek. 'It's not as if we live far apart. Guy, you know, I'm still sorry about what happened, you know, between you and me.'

'I understand now. It took Jack's death to make me understand but I do.'

'You're a good man, Guy Searight.'

'I know. Off you go.'

'Yes. Goodbye, Guy.'

He watched her with her jug and tubing as she walked away from him, slightly unsteady with the swell of the sea. As she reached the door, she turned and waved. He waved back.

Guy made his way back to his cabin, and found Ray still fast asleep. He lay on his bunk and thought of Mary and realised, with a slap of guilt, that he had transferred a bit of his grief to her and that somehow the weight that had been pressing down on his shoulders since his last visit to Jack had ever so slightly been lifted.

An hour later, Guy peered out of the porthole. 'Ray, wake up, wake up.'

'What? What is it?'

'Look…'

'Oh my word, are those the white cliffs everyone keeps talking about?'

'They sure are.'

'I can see why – they're beautiful. So, this is England?'

Guy's heart surged with pride as he said, 'Yes, Kiran Singh, this, my friend, is England.'

No sooner had the words left his mouth, an explosion ripped through the ship; a tremendous crash, the cabin ceiling buckled.

The men lost their footing as the ship tilted violently. 'What was that?' shouted Ray.

'We've been hit.' Immediately, the floor of their cabin began filling with water. 'Shit, I can't move.'

'You OK?'

'No, I'm stuck.' Guy's good leg was clamped within a mesh of metal wrapped around his ankle. A momentary desire to laugh at the absurdity of his plight was soon replaced by fear rising as quickly as the water.

'Good God,' said Ray, 'the bunk seems to have trapped your leg. Is anything broken?'

'I don't know; I can't feel anything. Just get me out of here,' he said, trying to quell the intensifying panic within him. 'See if you can prise the metal apart.'

With his one hand, Ray pulled and tugged at the pieces of metal. 'It's difficult... I can't see, the water's too dark.'

'Oh shit, this is not looking good,' said Guy, the panic rising in his throat.

'God, I'm trying.'

'Ray – the life jackets. My crutches too.'

'Yes, life jackets, crutches.' Ray snatched both jackets and helped Guy wriggle into one, securing the ties at the front.

Outside, down the corridor, men were rushing amid shouts and screams; many on crutches but sliding on the slippery incline of the ship's tilt. 'Hey, someone help me,' shouted Guy, his voice lost within the mayhem.

'My fingers – they're frozen from the water,' cried Ray. 'I'll try pulling you up.'

'That won't work.'

Ignoring him, Ray stood on the twisted bunk behind Guy, wrapping his arms beneath Guy's armpits, while Guy jabbed at the coil of metal with his crutch. 'Brace yourself,' said Ray, trying to heave him up. The metal dug deeper into Guy's leg, he screeched with pain as the two men fell over, causing Guy's leg to lean at an awkward angle. The pain was acute and Guy swore until he was able to right himself. The water had risen to the height of their waists.

'I'll try again.'

'No, get someone to help.'

But as soon as Ray stepped into the corridor he was knocked over in the rush of panicked men and fell awkwardly. Guy could see him. 'I need someone's help,' yelled Ray, getting to his feet. 'You, sir, can you help me?'

The water was now swirling round Guy at stomach height. Its weight was pressing into him. 'Ray, you go, mate.'

'What? And leave you here?'

'Yes, absolutely. It's an order, you hear.'

'You can't order me about, you're a private as good as I am and you know it.'

'Please, Ray, leave me. Before it's too late.'

'No, I stay here with you.'

'Ray, Kiran, we've only just met; you don't have to do this.'

'I can't–'

'Just go, you stupid Indian bastard.'

It did the trick, Ray put on a show of hurt and waddled through the water, his arms held high.

Guy used his crutch to pummel the metal but to no avail, the water was now up to his chest, squeezing the air out of him. He knew now that the end was close; he had a couple of minutes. A thousand thoughts crashed through his mind – his mother, his father, Mary, even his cousin Lawrence and Jack, especially Jack. He tried to pray but found that the words refused to come. At least he'd managed to tell Mary about Jack – far better it came from him than anyone else. *I'll see you again,* the words came back to him, filling his mind, *but not too soon, you hear?* The water lapped at his throat. Well, this was fairly soon, not even a week. He tried to think of Jack, of Mary, to keep the panic at bay the last few moments but instead the German boy came into view, clutching the bayonet, urging Guy to join him.

He was now having to stretch his neck in order to keep his mouth above water. The German boy's face, which had always been a blur, now came sharply into focus – a long face, solid chin, deep eyes, his uniform impeccably clean. The boy was mouthing the Lord's Prayer in English, encouraging Guy to follow suit – *Our Father, who Art in Heaven…* But Guy's mouth was clamped shut as the water rose still further, inching up towards his nostrils. The strain of stretching his whole body was beginning to tell, the pointless but inescapable need to delay the inevitable a few moments longer. *Hallowed be thy name, thy kingdom come, thy will be done…* A huge cranking noise filled Guy's ears and the ship tilted violently, throwing Guy into a swirl of water, spinning round, before throwing him against a cabin wall. It took him a few moments to realise the jolt of the ship had freed him. But now immersed in water and holding his breath, he grappled and swam his way into the corridor and from there could see a faint light coming from the top of the steps. In his mind he told himself to keep calm, the German boy was still there, reassuring him. Using the corridor walls as a guide, he swam hard towards the light.

Still under water, he reached the steps, pushing away a body, face down, swaying slightly. Guy reached out for the rail and pulled himself up, his chest aching from pain. He feared he wasn't moving, as if his efforts were in vain but the light seemed to rush toward him and in an ecstasy of deliverance he broke through the water and released his breath into the clear air. His chest pounded as he bent double at the top of the stairway, still clutching onto the rail, retching, wanting to be sick. His ankle was bleeding, the blood swirling into the water, but he felt no pain. Guy took in the scene in front of him: men yelling, many of them amputees, clinging onto the deck or gripping the ship's rail as the

251

vessel listed portside, trying not to slip overboard. The bow of the ship had gone under up to its fore funnel but the incline to the stern was gentle enough to climb – at least for now.

There was hope in the air – the portside lifeboats had been lowered and, better still, sailing alongside, twenty, maybe thirty yards hence, the destroyer had drawn level, its crew urging the stricken men to jump and swim across. The more able were helping the basket cases, carrying them, helping to lower them down to the awaiting lifeboats. Amongst them, a couple of nurses, working feverishly, making sure the men had their life jackets on. Guy wanted to help but as soon as he got to his feet, without his crutches he slipped and fell.

'Guy, you're all right?' It was Lampton.

'Yes. You?'

'Let me help – you have to jump.'

'No, not yet, there's still time.'

'Not long – look.' The ship was still going down, water seeping up the deck.

It was then he saw her. 'Mary!'

She screeched back and waved at him, an odd gesture, he thought, as if she was waving at him from across the moors.

He struggled towards her, akin to climbing up a hill covered in sheet ice, as she bundled a double amputee towards helping hands. 'Mary,' he screamed, 'where's your life jacket?' Her face was white, her hair blowing in the wind.

'There's only enough for the passengers.'

'Here, take mine,' he yelled as he reached her. Behind her a couple of bodies, their limbs flayed out awkwardly.

'No, Guy, I can swim. Please go, jump if you have to.' Her hands were covered in the blood of the men she was helping. He tried to help her with another invalid but managed only to lose his balance and fall, landing on his poor leg. The pain shot through him and took his breath away. On opening his eyes, he noticed one of the dead men. It was Browne, Stephen Browne with an 'e', his eyes wide open, his lips blue. 'Oh no, Stephen, not you,' he muttered. He pulled himself up, his arms flailing to keep balance. Mary was helping a blinded lieutenant, sodden bandages falling off the congealed mess that was once his eyes.

'Guy, please save yourself. Think of your parents. They've already lost one son. This way, Lieutenant, you can do it, careful.'

'What about you?'

'You've done your job; this is mine. I'm staying. This way, that's it.'

Another pair of hands took the blind lieutenant. 'I've got this one now, sister.'

'Mary, please, you'll go under.'

'I've lost Jack; I don't care what happens to me now.'

For a few moments, the two of them stood face to face, momentarily aloof from what was happening all around them, shut off from the noise, the shouts and screams. A flock of seagulls circled noisily above them. This was the moment to admit to Mary, as well as himself, what he always knew in his heart to be true – that he loved her and when he thought about it he realised he always had. 'Please, Mary…'

'No, Guy, no.'

He felt himself being dragged away, an arm under his armpit. 'I may be an Indian bastard, but I'm a faithful Indian bastard.'

'Ray?' He threw his arm around his friend's shoulder.

'This time, I'm not letting you go, you understand?'

'Yes, OK, whatever you say.' He realised, with a shock, that he was crying. When he turned around, Mary had gone.

*

Dozens of men had been taken on board the destroyer, Guy and Ray among them. Given a tot of brandy and a cup of hot tea, they were soaking wet but covered with blankets provided by the crew. They watched with morbid fascination as the SS *Derby* looked set to vanish beneath the waterline, its engines still working, the propellers spinning uselessly as the stern hovered in the air. The second funnel had almost disappeared from view. There were still plenty of men in the sea, bobbing like corks, even those lacking limbs, trying to reach the two lifeboats treading water halfway between the ship and the destroyer. 'They'll be OK,' said Ray, 'they've all got lifejackets.'

'But there're still some on the ship, including nurses and they haven't got jackets.'

'Is your friend there?'

'Mary – I don't know. I don't know and it's killing me.'

'They still have time.'

'But not much. Once she goes, they'll be sucked into the vortex. Oh God, Mary, where are you?'

The white cliffs seemed so ridiculously near; how could this have happened so close to home? Had they been torpedoed or had the ship struck a mine?

He shouldn't have told her about Jack; it had drained her of life, of wanting to live. His presence had counted for nothing; she'd only wanted Jack. The crew were helping more men out of the water. Despite their outer appearance of calm, he could see how grateful they were to find themselves on the solid deck of the destroyer. He'd felt the same, shivering, in shock, but thankful to be in the arms of safety and the warmth of a blanket. The tea and brandy had helped. But where was Mary? How could she put him through such torment?

'I've got to go back.'

'What?' asked Ray. 'Where to?'

'I've got to save her; to get her off the ship.'

No sooner had he thrown off his blanket than he was tackled to the deck. 'Oh no you don't, my mad English friend.'

The two men grappled on the floor. 'Ray, I can do it; it's not far.'

'You almost drowned once; I'm not letting you drown yourself now.'

'Get off me, you Indian bastard.'

'Ha, that won't work this time.'

'What the hell's going on here?' bellowed a passing crewman.

'Help me,' shouted Ray. 'My friend here wants to take a swim.'

'Is he bloody mad?'

'Just help me.' But Guy's strength had already deserted him.

A sinister noise of creaking metal stopped them in their tracks in their tangle of limbs and stumps. The three men watched in horror as the *Derby* breathed its last, the huge metal corpse plunging into the sea, the propellers still spinning as the water claimed the ship for itself. Clinging on, the last few men and nurses screamed as the ship sucked them down to their deaths. In its wake, the water bubbled as if boiling. Then came the stillness. On board the destroyer and the lifeboats every man stood in silence and saluted, gazing at the empty space on the water where, moments before, the ship had been. Guy turned away, clenching his eyes shut, his mouth open, contorted, as if letting rip a scream.

Part Three

Chapter 28: The Homecoming – mid-November 1917

As the destroyer sailed into Dover harbour, Guy saw a small crowd of people, English people, gathered on the quayside watching their arrival, cheering and waving flags at the returning soldiers. The men waved back but few felt like cheering. This was England. A cold and damp November morning in England, but still and forever England. Most of the men hadn't stepped on home soil for months, even years.

Some were naked beneath their blankets, their pyjamas ripped off by the strength of the sea. Ray and Guy allowed themselves to be shuttled off and onto the train that would take them to London.

Guy's every waking moment was taken up with Mary. The uncertainty was tormenting him; had she survived, had she been one of the nurses that stayed to the end, that had given their lives to be with the last men? He shuddered at the thought of her being sucked into that vortex. He should have done more. Why hadn't he saved her? He couldn't dislodge the image from his mind – Mary on the deck, without a life jacket, calmly ushering the blind lieutenant as if leading him on an excursion. She knew she was approaching death but seemed almost to be welcoming it. And that hurt – the thought that he'd made no difference.

Once in London, Guy and his travelling companions were transferred by ambulance to different hospitals, depending on the severity of their injuries. He'd expected things to look different from what he remembered and was amazed at how little had changed in the city. Everything seemed so normal, so annoyingly normal. What right had London to remain unaltered while he had changed so immeasurably, both outside and in? But after a while, he noticed something that was different – there were so few young men around and he couldn't help but view the ones he did see with a certain degree of suspicion.

Guy and Ray were transferred to the Prince of Wales Hospital in Marylebone, formerly the Old Central Hotel. Somewhere, hidden within his anguish, Guy was tremendously pleased to be back in London; he hadn't realised how much he missed the sights and sounds of the capital. The trams, the motor vehicles, the horse-drawn traffic, the shouting of the street traders, the automated music of the barrel-organs, the nauseating smell of the coal-fired smog. Ray merely seemed bemused by it all. 'A far cry from your village in India, I guess,' said Guy.

'Oh yes. It's all so marvellous. Guy, are you OK, my friend?'

'Yes.'

'Yes?'

'No.'

Guy and Ray were shown to separate wards. He stood at the doorway and cast his eyes around. Everything seemed so large and spacious and so quiet compared to what he'd been used to. On a small table near the door, a vase full of pansies. A nurse showed him to his bed, next to which stood a small bedside cabinet and a chair. A dressing gown draped over the end of the bed. He thanked her.

'Are you alright there, mate,' said a man from the neighbouring bed, his arm in a sling and one eye heavily bandaged. 'Nice here, ain't it? Lovely comfy beds here, everything nice and clean, even the food's nice.'

'Wonderful.'

'Yep, sure is the best hotel I've ever stayed in.'

The man was right; everything seemed so sanitised after the chaos of the CCS in France. Guy lay on his bed, exhausted, and realised with a thump of dismay that everything ahead of him was blank. He didn't know how to fill the next five minutes, let alone five months.

'So where you come from?'

'What?' It was the man next to him. 'Oh, erm, local.' He could think only of Mary, doll-like, her arms folded neatly on her chest, being tossed around the whirlpool, smiling, as she disappeared, spinning, into the dark.

'Yeah, me too. London born, London bred. It's good to get back, hey? Nightmare out there. You know, there was this lad I met out in France, yeah, and he was saying...' Even beyond his freshly dug grave, Jack had the ability to render him impotent with jealousy. He would have saved her had he been fit, had God not rendered him a cripple; he could have saved her still.

'So I said, right, not bloody likely, the sergeant would have our guts for garters for that...' It was the calmness in her eyes that haunted him. How could she have been so calm; how could Jack have given her such strength? He felt suffocated, and looked around for a window, but realised it was the memory of the sea crushing his chest that pressed on him; the water, rising, tickling his nostrils, like a feather on the breath of God.

'I warned him, you know, I told him it was stupid. But he wouldn't listen. Once he got the idea in his head...'

He listened to the sound of his breathing and remembered the gagging sensation of the wet mud choking him, buried under the earth as the shells landed nearby with unerring frequency. He remembered his breathing then too, his lungs like bellows, gasping for air.

'You should've seen the look on his face. Picture, it was. That'd got him, the silly sod. So how long was you out there for? Hey?'

But Guy had fallen asleep.

*

Guy dreamt of Mary sitting at his bedside, wearing a long, dark blue dress with puffed upper arms, buttoned tightly to the top. Her right arm was covered with a cast and on her lap a pile of seaweed. She smiled at him and said, 'We're safe now, everything's OK. We can't come to any more harm.'

'But you've gone,' he said in a voice that seemed detached and far away. 'You didn't have to go; I could've saved you.'

'Guy, it's me, wake up.'

'No, no, I can't. They're waiting for me. I have to get back; I've got to save them.'

*

When, finally, he awoke, he found not Mary but Ray sitting at his bed. 'Ray. Hello. What time is it?'

'I don't know but I fancy it is soon time for dinner. Fancy. It's my new word for today.'

'What?'

'How are you, my friend?'

'I don't know. Fine. Terrible. My leg aches.'

'Which one?'

'The other one. D'you know, I can't tell. God, I feel odd. Anyway,' he said with a yawn, 'how are you?'

'Very well. I've learned to roll a cigarette with one hand. Fancy that?'

'Yes, fancy. I didn't know you smoked.'

'I don't. The doctors said they'd send me home if I had a home to go to here, so they're transferring me to Oxford. Fancy that – Oxford? It's so famous in India. I can go home and tell everyone I've been to Oxford and all the girls will want to sleep with me. Just fancy.'

'Yes, indeed, fancy. So they're letting you out already?'

'It's just an arm, isn't it? A flesh wound, they told me.'

'Then what?' asked Guy.

'Home, I suppose. India.'

'Yes, I do know where you come from. You must be looking forward to that.'

'I think so.'

'Anyone waiting for you back home?'

'Yes, oh yes, indeed.'

'Yes?'

'Yes, the debt collector.'

'Ha, you fool.'

'It will seem like a different place, I think.'

'Yes, I know the feeling. Thanks, Ray. You know... for everything.'

'Is that it? I save your life and that's the best I get?'

'Yeah, but don't forget you deserted me also.'

'Hah, so that evens things out? You English, you think us Indians strange. Yet there's no stranger race than the Englishman. I have learnt to find the true meaning of what an Englishman says by listening to what he doesn't say. Now, my friend, I'm going downstairs to watch a film. Charlie Chaplin. He's so funny. Do you want to come?'

'No, I'll stay here.'

'Okey-dokey.' He laughed at the expression. 'Oh, before I go, I have news for you. Important news. Your friend, the nurse, Mary.'

'Yes?'

'I just saw her.'

'Good God, where?'

'Here. In this very chair. Oh yes, she has a little room all to herself, just down the corridor from me. She broke her arm, but she is well. Yes. She sends her love and says she will come back soon. Isn't that good news? Fancy that. Guy, my friend, speak to me, what's the matter with you; has the cat got your tongue…?'

Finding a pair of slippers under the bed, Guy donned his dressing gown and followed Ray down a long corridor and along another. 'This way, this way,' said his friend, as if leading him on a mysterious expedition. He stopped outside a door with a small plaque bearing the number eleven.

'Here we are,' he whispered. 'You knock. I go. Good luck, my friend.'

'Thank you, Ray.'

'Goodbye, my friend.'

'Come in.' Guy's heart thumped at the sound of her voice.

She was standing next to her bed dressed exactly as he'd seen her in his dream. She was holding a shawl, dark green.

On seeing each other, they rushed to embrace. 'Guy, oh, Guy, heavens, it's so nice to see you.'

'I thought I'd lost you.'

'No, I'm still here. Remember, fourth-year swimming champion of 1910?'

'I really thought… It doesn't matter now. You're here and that's all that matters.'

'Yes, that's all that matters. Come, sit next to me on the bed. How are you?'

'I'm fine now, just fine.'

'We live to fight another day, eh?'

'Well, you perhaps, not me. So, you're out of uniform.'

'Yes, it feels strange wearing normal clothes. And out of hospital. I've already been discharged. I'm leaving this afternoon. I'm moving back in with Josephine.'

'Of course. How is the arm? Ray told me you'd broken it.'

'Who on earth is Ray?'

'Kiran.'

'Oh, Kiran, why do you call him Ray?' She laughed. 'Anyway, it's fine but I broke both bones in the forearm. Funny thing, I have no recollection of doing it. Isn't that strange? I was lucky, you know. I jumped in with this poor chap who couldn't swim; he was petrified, even with the life jacket. One of the boats picked us up and took us all the way back to shore. It wasn't far, of course. They say it was a mine that did it.'

'Yes, so I heard. How long do you have to wear the cast?'

'About six weeks, then, if I was returning to some little job in an office or a shop somewhere, I'd be OK to go back to work. But not France, the work there is too strenuous. They won't let me go back for months. By then the war will be over.'

'Not such a bad thing.'

'No, of course not. But…' She sighed. 'It gave me a purpose in life. And I need a purpose even more now than ever. What am I going to do? Sit around all day and think of my life as it should've been – marrying Jack, being a wife. Perhaps a mother one day. I miss him so much, Guy.'

'You and me both. Listen, Mary, I'm thinking of visiting my parents tomorrow afternoon. Come with me.'

'Oh, Guy, I'm not sure.'

'You have to face them sometime. We can go together, get it over and done with.'

'I suppose I will be just round the corner from them again.'

'So will you come?'

'I don't know. OK, yes, I'd love to.'

Making his way back to his ward, Guy stopped at the communal telephone booth and telephoned his mother.

'Oh, Guy, Guy, oh Lord, is it you?'

Guy grinned. 'Yes, Mother, it's me.'

'Guy, my boy… how lovely… Arthur, Arthur, it's Guy…' She trailed off, her voice caught between sobs. 'Are you OK, Guy? Tell me you're OK. Yes, Arthur, Guy, it's Guy on the telephone.'

'I'm fine, Mother, really I am. Can I come visit? Tomorrow afternoon?'

'Oh, yes, yes, please, please do…' She said more but her words were lost to grateful tears.

And so it was arranged – three o'clock the following afternoon. Mary would join them a little later.

*

And so, after lunch the following day, dressed in a new uniform and a coat loaned from the hospital and with his left trouser leg pinned up, Guy caught a tube from Marylebone to Charing Cross and from there a train to the suburb of Charlton where his parents still lived. He noticed that people on the streets and on the tube, complete strangers, would say hello to him, tip their hats, ask him if he needed any help, offer their seats. Although only a short walk from the station at Charlton to Ladysmith Road, his journey so far had tired him out and he caught a horse-drawn taxi the rest of the way. Guy's heartbeat quickened as the taxi turned into Ladysmith Road, and he wondered whether there'd soon be a Loos Road or Ypres Avenue. He remembered how anxious he felt returning here over a year ago on leave. But this now was worse, far worse. It began to unnerve him, he wasn't ready for this; he desperately wanted to turn around and run back to the safety and anonymity of the hospital. It had been fifteen months since he last saw his parents, fifteen months and a whole lifetime. 'This is it,' he told the driver.

Guy stood outside the gate. Like London, he expected the house to look different somehow, but then, why should it? He had changed irrevocably but it didn't necessarily mean the whole world had changed with him. Guy opened the gate and walked steadily up the front path, each step of his crutches echoing on the diamond-patterned tiles. He rang the bell and straightened his tie.

Lizzie, the family maid, opened the door. 'Mr Searight!' she exclaimed as if he hadn't been expected.

'How d'you do, Lizzie?'

'Oh, fine thank you, sir. Come in, come in, I'll tell Mr and Mrs Searight you're here. They'll be delighted.'

Guy waited in the hallway, re-familiarising himself with his family home: the parquet floor tiles, the sturdy banister, the dark floral-patterned wallpaper and the stained glass, squared-shaped lampshade on the hall table. Presently, Guy could hear the excited shrieks of delight as his mother came to greet him. She stopped in the hallway to look at her son, tears streaming down her face. She took in his uniform, his cap, his face and, of course, the crutches and the missing leg.

'Hello, Mother,' he said simply, removing his cap.

'Oh, Guy.' His mother wept as she flung her arms around him. From behind her, Guy saw the figure of his father emerging into the hallway. Guy prised his mother off and offered his hand to him. His father took his hand and shook it vigorously.

'It's good to have you back, son,' said Arthur, clearly suppressing his own emotion at seeing his son again after such a long, worrying time. 'I see you bear the scars of war.'

Guy laughed. 'If only it was a scar.' The two men looked fondly at each other, still gripping hands. Guy smelt the pipe tobacco on his father's breath and noticed that he was wearing his 'Sunday Best'. The two men seemed unsure of what to do or say next, but then Arthur, hesitating for a moment, clasped Guy's shoulder, leant forward and kissed his son on the cheek. Although taken aback and rather embarrassed by his father's uncharacteristic show of paternal affection and slightly alarmed by the brief sensation of feeling his father's beard against his cheek, Guy nonetheless felt touched. Subconsciously, he rubbed his cheek where the bristles had made contact.

Guy's mother, still flapping with excitement, ushered him into the drawing room. Lizzie came to take his coat and cap, and Edith asked her to bring them a round of tea and sandwiches. The drawing room hadn't altered a bit since Guy last saw it. His parents sat down together on the large dark sofa and watched Guy as he wandered around the room. He remembered being in the trench, waiting to go over, praying that he might be granted the chance to see his parents one more time. And now, he was here. His mother and father sat watching him, knowing not to speak and to allow him a few moments to absorb being back home. Guy looked at himself in the large mirror that hung above the mantelpiece and smiled at the thought that his mother still persisted in keeping the paisley motif wallpaper that his father always loathed. The landscape watercolours and the commemorative plates still hung on the walls, the piano still stood in the corner but now with its lid closed. On the tapestry-covered table stood an aspidistra. 'Is this new?' he asked.

'Yes, I bought it the morning I heard of Jack's death. I don't know why, I don't even like it very much. But now I can't seem to be able to get rid of it. Jack's death has been difficult for us, Guy, I'm sure you can imagine. There's no one we can talk to. Everyone has their own grief, no one has the strength to listen to someone else's.'

'We don't even know if Mary's been told the bad news,' said Arthur.

'She knows,' replied Guy. 'I've met her. I saw her in a hospital in France and now she's back in London. I told her.'

'Poor girl, it must've been hard on her.'

'Yes. In fact, we're expecting her any minute. You don't mind, do you?'

268

'No, no, of course not,' said Edith, 'but why? What is she doing here? Is she OK?'

'Edith, so many questions, give Guy a moment to explain.'

And Guy did. He skimmed over the details of the sinking of the ship, merely saying that they had got into difficulties and had to be escorted back, and that in the process Mary had broken her arm.

'Oh, the poor love,' said Edith. 'It'll be delightful to see her again. Guy, we must say we were sorry to hear about what happened between you and Mary.' She glanced at her husband.

'Quite,' said Arthur. 'We didn't approve of Jack stepping into your shoes like that—'

'But with death we forgive all,' said Guy.

'Well, I wouldn't put it quite like that but maybe you're right. Fact is, we weren't too approving of Mary either, skipping from one brother to the other. Edith wouldn't have her in the house.'

'Good for you, Mother.'

She laughed. 'Yes, I thought so at the time but then one day, soon after Jack had left for France, we heard from Josephine that she'd gone off to be a volunteer nurse. She never came to say goodbye.'

'You know they got engaged?'

'No!'

'You didn't know? The day before he embarked for France, he asked and she said yes.'

'Oh dear, he never said. It's our fault, I suppose, ostracising her like that, but could he not have told me, his mother? And you, Guy, how did you feel about that?'

It was a question he'd asked himself a hundred times. Resentful, hurt, jealous. But now all those emotions seemed so petty and self-pitying. 'I got used to it,' was all he could say.

'We know of so many families who have lost loved ones,' said Edith, 'but grief remains such a lonely experience. Your Aunt

Winnie tells me to pray, but I can't. Anyway, it's easy for her, she just has Lawrence safely hiding in the background pretending to be all high and mighty.'

'Wet rag of a man,' added Arthur.

'It's easy for her to criticise me for losing my faith when I consider my poor boys: Jack killed and you crippled.' She pulled out a handkerchief and blew her nose.

Arthur stood up and started pacing the room. 'So, Guy, how's it going out there? Sounds to me that we're not actually getting anywhere. Are we making any headway?'

'Don't think so. We've used chlorine gas, phosgene gas, mustard gas, you name it, often with disastrous results when it blows back in the faces of our advancing troops and does no end of mischief. Vile stuff, I never thought we'd resort to such barbaric tactics.'

Edith sat listening with her hand over her mouth.

Lizzie appeared with a tray of tea, cucumber sandwiches and scones. Edith thanked her.

After she'd made her exit, Arthur asked, 'People keep talking about the conditions out there. Is it really as bad as that?'

How could he explain, wondered Guy, how could they even start to understand? Perhaps he owed it to them not to even try. His mother interjected with a question.

'Tell me, Guy,' she said, pouring the tea, 'you don't fight on Sundays, surely? And what if it's raining; they don't make you go out in all weathers, do they?'

Fortunately, his father huffily intervened. 'Oh, for goodness' sake, woman, this is war, you don't think they make allowances for a bit of rain, do you?'

'Yes, of course, I'm sorry,' she said, sweeping back her hair. 'Even Lizzie's been affected. She's upset about Jack and her own brother. Jack was so excited about joining your regiment. Tell me, how was Jack the last time you saw him?'

270

Guy sighed at the memory. 'It wasn't long before he was killed. He seemed… well, I met many a brave man in France, but Jack had found a courage that surpassed anything I saw. It was a special kind of bravery, an unrecognised one. I was told he met his death quickly and painlessly, and…' He paused, wondering how to finish his sentence.

'And…?' his mother urged.

'Apparently, he uttered your name with his last breath, Mother.' He immediately wondered why he'd said that. Perhaps he had, but he would never know. And now, having said it, he could never unsay it.

She gasped and clasped her handkerchief to her mouth.

Arthur spoke, his words unusually soft. 'What do you mean when you say Jack possessed a special kind of courage?'

Guy swallowed, perhaps he shouldn't have said so much. But before he could speak, the doorbell rang.

'Might that be Mary?' asked Edith.

Guy and Arthur stood up as Lizzie showed Mary into the drawing room, wearing a long, dark green dress with puffed upper arms, buttoned tightly to the top. After a muted exchange of hellos, everyone stood, hampered by awkwardness. Edith broke the atmosphere. 'Come, give me a hug, Mary.'

Mary fell into her arms and the two women embraced silently. 'Let's have a cup of tea.' Everyone sat down, sighs of relief everywhere. 'Oh dear, no cup. Let me ring for Lizzie.'

Mary greeted Guy with a kiss. Arthur enquired whether Guy or Mary would be staying for dinner, to which both thanked him but refused. Mary sat down next to Guy's mother on the sofa, perched on the edge of the cushion, her knees locked together. Guy had the impression that she wasn't intending to stay for long. He noticed she was wearing her engagement ring. She appeared anxious and pale and, after a passing comment on the weather, remained silent.

'So, Guy,' said Edith, as she passed him a plate of neatly cut sandwiches, 'I don't suppose you've had a chance to think of your future plans.' Guy shook his head. 'You know,' she continued, 'you can always come back here once you're fit enough to leave hospital.' He thanked her.

Arthur, leaning against the mantelpiece, stuffed a whole sandwich into his mouth. 'Well…' he waited until he'd swallowed enough to talk. 'There's no need to worry about work.' He emptied his mouth and continued. 'You'll be wanting to come back to the shop and take over from where you and Jack left off. I'm getting too old for it anyway; it needs a younger man. It's all yours, Guy, give yourself a couple of years and when you're ready, I'll bow out.'

Guy sipped his tea. He knew it made sense and that he should be thankful, but he wasn't sure if it was what he wanted any more. His father continued, extolling the potential of the business. Granted, the war had caused a downturn in their fortunes, but plans were afoot for expansion into ladies' headwear. Guy smiled. Before the war, he tried to persuade his father that they needed to expand beyond the gentleman's market, but his father, not knowing anything about women's tastes in hats, had rejected his suggestions out of hand. But now that war had diminished the male demand, Guy's father talked enthusiastically of shawls, bonnets and cowls, implying that the idea was his.

'Is that your engagement ring, Mary?'

'Yes.'

'Isn't it pretty.'

Lizzie re-appeared with a cup and saucer, and a small pot of tea for Mary. 'Another sandwich?' asked Edith.

'I wonder where Jack got the money to pay for it. The ring, I mean.'

'Arthur, please,' said Edith. 'Don't ask such things. You paid him a salary didn't you?'

272

'Mother,' said Guy, changing the subject, 'did you receive a letter – about Jack, I mean.' His mother sighed and nodded. 'May I see it?'

She went to the bureau, opened a drawer and produced an envelope which she passed to Guy. He looked at his parents' typed name and address. One could tell immediately that this was an envelope that contained bad tidings. He wondered what sort of words the army had used to inform his parents that their son had been executed. His hands shook slightly as he opened the flap and unfolded the small slip of paper. The words were few, the tone cold and formal. It read:

"Dear Mr and Mrs Searight,

I am directed to inform you that your son, 8112 Pte. Jack Searight of the 4ᵗʰ Battalion, Essex Regiment, died on active service on the morning of 11ᵗʰ November 1917.

I am Sir / Madam,

Your obedient Servant

Capt. R.H. Handley, Essex Regiment."

They didn't know. They didn't know that their son had been executed. 'It's brief,' remarked Guy.

'Brief?' said Arthur. 'Downright discourteous, if you ask me.'

Should he tell them? They had to know.

'Yes,' agreed Edith. 'It doesn't tell us anything. I remember about six months ago, Mrs Evans lost her son and she received a lovely letter saying how keenly his friends and officers missed him, what a popular boy he was and how they mourned his death. And even Lizzie, she's lost her own brother, out in Palestine, said her mother had received a charming letter from his officer. But *this*… it's so… so impersonal. It's as if this Captain Handley had no idea who Jack was, or, if he did, perhaps he simply didn't like him.' She looked imploringly at Guy. 'How could anyone not like Jack, he was such a kind person. I can't bear to look at the letter; it's so short, so brutal. I don't understand and I daren't show it to anyone.'

'Guy, I think you should tell your parents.' The quiet voice had said the words slowly, carefully. Guy, his mother and father all turned to stare at Mary, still sitting rigidly on the edge of the sofa, her knees squeezed tightly together, her eyes focused on her hands resting neatly on her lap.

'Not necessarily.'

Arthur broke the astonished silence. 'What did you say? Do you know, Guy, do you know how Jack was killed?'

'Isn't it enough to know he was killed, that he won't be coming back?'

'No, frankly.'

His mother leant forward. 'Guy,' she said softly, 'if you know, you have to tell us. As his mother, I need to know.'

All three of them were looking at him, full of nervous anticipation. He realised that he hadn't yet told Mary what happened – that she only knew of his execution.

'Apparently, one day Jack was reported missing. Everyone thought he'd been killed or lay wounded somewhere. But he hadn't. He wasn't dead or wounded.'

'Go on, Guy,' urged his mother.

'They found him two or three days later, hiding in some French woman's house near the coast.'

'What was he doing there?' asked Edith.

'What are you trying to say?' asked Arthur.

Mary said it for him: 'He'd deserted.'

Guy's parents stared at Mary in total disbelief, unsure what to say, unable to say it. The word hung between them, unexplained, unqualified, simply left to fester in their minds.

'Deserted?' said Arthur quietly, still grappling with the significance of the word. He shook his head. 'No, surely not, not

Jack, not my son.' His voice was faltering. 'They'd have shot him if he had.'

Mary looked down and whispered: 'They did.'

Edith gasped and reached for her handkerchief. Arthur gripped the mantelpiece as if in need of support. Guy wanted to say something, to qualify Mary's stark statement, to defend his brother. But the words wouldn't come.

'Guy, this can't be true?'

'Yes, I'm afraid it is.'

'But... I don't understand,' said Edith, 'who was this French woman?'

'No one knows. We don't know her name and we don't know why he stayed with her or who she is, or whether they knew each other beforehand.' He noticed Mary grimace as he spoke of this unknown woman.

Arthur rang the bell for Lizzie and paced up and down as he waited for her. Lizzie entered breezily and immediately sensed the strained atmosphere. Arthur asked her to bring him a whisky. Lizzie glanced at Edith as if seeking permission to provide drink at such an unusually early time. 'Yes, you heard me correctly,' snapped Arthur. Lizzie jumped, muttered an apology, and left to fetch Arthur Searight his drink.

Edith, still clutching her handkerchief, turned to Guy. 'This is awful. Poor, poor Jack.' Her words, softly spoken, could not contain the anguish welling up inside her. 'You didn't just tell us because of Mary, did you, Guy? You were going to tell us at some point?'

'Of course he wasn't,' bellowed Arthur, now clearly agitated. 'Because he's ashamed, that's why. Ashamed of having a deserter as a brother.'

Guy stood up but, forgetting his crutch, quickly had to sit down again. 'No, that's simply not true,' he shouted back.

Edith spoke. 'Guy, tell us, what happened after they found him – do you know?'

'Yes, Mother.' Lizzie re-appeared briefly with Arthur's drink. Guy waited until she had left the room and then continued, knowing he owed it to Jack's memory and dignity to recount his tale fairly. 'It was too much for Jack and if truth be known, it was too much for me too. But Jack was caught on a ridge, which was under a sustained attack. Many of his mates were killed. Unfortunately, his sergeant, though wounded, survived.'

'Unfortunately?' echoed his mother.

'Yes. Well, you know what Jack was like – cheery and confident and I suppose to the sergeant, Jack came across as a bit arrogant and of course he didn't like that. But what really got the sergeant was that he thought Jack to be weak, but he wasn't. Jack saved me from certain death once and the sergeant, Wilkins was his name, had been forced to help him, and I suppose it was too much for his brutish pride. So when they found Jack, the sergeant was a witness against him and took his revenge in the cruellest way. They found him guilty and, yes, they…' he hesitated before saying it, 'they shot him. Firing squad,' he added quietly. Edith winced at Guy's use of words and clenched her eyes shut. Guy continued. 'I saw him the afternoon before he was shot; they let me visit him. That's what I meant, Father, when I said he had a special kind of courage, having to endure all that. He told me to tell you – all of you – he was sorry. And he said he was sorry for the shame his… his death would bring to you. Funnily enough, I saw the sergeant as I was about to leave the CCS. He offered me his condolences and said that Jack had been a good lad.'

'A good lad, eh?' Arthur remained standing next to the mantelpiece and began filling his pipe with tobacco. Edith absorbed her son's tale silently for a few moments. Then suddenly, she could no longer contain herself. She let out a guttural cry that seemed to emanate from the pit of her stomach, the desperate sound of maternal anguish, a mother's grief for her son. Mary slid an arm around Edith's shaking shoulders but offered no words of comfort, the woman was beyond consolation.

Guy took his crutches, stood up and crossed the carpet to speak to his father, whose pungent tobacco smoke choked the room. 'Father, please, there's no need to feel ashamed—'

'Oh, but I do, Guy, I do. I know I shouldn't but I can't help it.' He gulped his whisky. 'You say he got you out of an awkward spot, well, how can a man who's capable of such a feat then disgrace himself? I did my stint as you know and I never saw—'

'But, Father, with respect, that was over thirty years ago. Things have changed since Egypt; things have changed even since South Africa. I fought beside men who'd seen service in the Boer War and they said it was a picnic in comparison. We live within spitting distance of the enemy day and night for weeks, months at a time and those heavy guns are huge now, they can blow a man to smithereens.'

'Stop it, Guy.'

'And I've seen men mowed down in their hundreds by unrelenting machine-gun fire. And gas. Imagine, Father, using poisonous gas to kill men. And flamethrowers. Do you know what a flame thrower is, Father?'

'No, but the fact remains, he still deserted.' He grimaced as he said the word. 'He let his fellow men down, those prepared to fight. No one else ran off, did they, *you* didn't desert?'

'No, but there were times when I almost did; we all did. I saw men shit their pants out there, sorry, Mother; it was terrifying. And it's still going on – now, as we speak. This leg – it's a small price to pay, believe me. And Jack, he was just a boy; remember, Father, he was only nineteen, a nineteen-year-old volunteer, he was never a soldier, you know that, not like you'd been.'

'That's all very well, but you try telling *them* that,' he pointed towards the large bay window, 'the white feather brigade; your sentiment won't carry much clout out there.' All at once, he marched towards the window, pulled down the Venetian blind, and clumsily closed the heavy, red curtains.

Mary and Edith looked up, confused by the sudden darkness. The only remaining light was a small gas lamp shining dimly on the side table. 'Arthur, what on *earth* are you doing?'

'What do you think I'm doing? I'm closing the curtains.'

'But why? It's not even dark yet?'

'I forbid them to be opened again, is that understood?'

'No, Arthur, it is not.'

Arthur fought with his words. 'I loved Jack and always will. But he has brought shame to this family and we have to face up to that.'

Guy tried to contain his repulsion at his father's pathetic gesture. 'And is this not drawing attention to yourself?'

Arthur pointed towards the window again and the world beyond, his hand shaking. 'They'll know soon enough. Jack has put us in an impossible situation. We cannot show our faces in front of those parents out there who have lost their sons in an honourable manner. I have only the one son now.' He looked at Guy; his eyes still flushed with anger. 'I only ever had the one son.'

Mary let out a shriek of pained distress, her hand over her mouth. His harsh words had pierced her to her heart. Edith tried to take her hand but she waved it away, staggered to her feet, and reeled towards the drawing-room door. She turned to Arthur and blurted, 'You… you devil. I… I won't forget him, *I* won't disown him.' She hurried out of the room, bursting into tears as she left. Moments later the front door was shut with a slam that reverberated throughout the house.

The three of them remained silent, avoiding each other's gaze, each unsure as to what to say next. Arthur took a self-conscious slurp of his drink. Eventually, Guy spoke. 'I have to go too,' he said quietly.

'Oh, Guy, please stay,' pleaded Edith.

'I'm sorry, Mother, I can't. Please, don't disturb Lizzie, I'll see myself out.' Holding his crutches, he leaned down and kissed his mother. 'You have nothing, *nothing* to be ashamed of; you do know that, don't you?' She nodded. As he made to go, he turned to his father, who was puffing self-consciously on his pipe. 'You are so wrong, Father. One day you'll realise it.' Studiously, his father stared at Baden-Powell's image on the commemorative plate to the left of the large mirror. Irked by the man's stubborn silence, Guy added, 'Until you see the error of your ways, Father, consider yourself without *any* sons from now on.'

Edith gasped. 'No, Guy…'

But Guy had closed the drawing-room door gently behind him. Taking his hat and coat from the mirrored hat stand, Guy stepped outside and, without looking back, closed the front door to the house that had been his family home. His and Jack's.

*

Once outside, Guy buttoned his coat against the chilled late afternoon air. He realised he wouldn't be able to hail a taxi in the middle of Ladysmith Road, so he resolved to make his own way back to the station. Ahead of him, he could see the figure of Mary, walking very slowly with her head bowed. At first, Guy decided to hang back, as he had no desire to continue the ordeal. But he found himself walking faster and by the time she had reached the top of the road, he had caught her up.

She turned around at the sound of his crutches. 'I'm sorry,' she said as Guy stopped in front of her. 'I shouldn't have made you tell them.'

'I would have told them in my own time, you know.'

'Yes, I'm sorry.'

'It wasn't right just to spring it on them like that. It needed building up to.'

'I suppose I'm still in a state of shock, I never thought…' Her voice trailed off.

'Now look at them – Mother's distraught and Father… well, you saw his reaction.'

'Don't be angry with me, Guy.'

'What did you expect?' He started walking and Mary had to jog to catch up.

'For a man on crutches, you do walk fast.'

'You get used to it.' A middle-aged couple said hello as they passed but Guy ignored them. After a while he slowed down as he realised he was walking towards Mary's house. 'You called my father a devil. That was good – he deserved it. I doubt anyone's ever called him that before. Although I could think of a few more choice words, I must say.'

'Yes, but I shouldn't have forced you into it, I should've let you do it in your own time, like you said. Do you forgive me?'

'No.' But he knew he didn't mean it.

They walked slowly in silence. After a while, Mary said, 'I know it didn't work out between us, Guy, and I shall always feel bad about that–'

'I've got over it by now.'

'But I did love your brother very dearly.'

'That's fine. He could be an annoying tyke at times, always showing off, but that was Jack for you. We were very different, he and I. But yes, I loved him too.'

Mary smiled. 'Just think, had we married, I'd be a nineteen-year-old widow now.'

'Unfortunately, you wouldn't have been the only one.'

'Yes, I suppose you're right.'

They continued in silence until they reached Mary's gate where they stopped and faced each other. 'Do you want to come in?' she asked.

'No, I ought to get back. It's a long way and I feel tired. I still get tired very easily.'

'I suppose it's goodbye then.'

He offered his hand but, ignoring it, she leant up and kissed him on the cheek. 'I'm sure it's OK to kiss my brother-in-law.'

'Thank you very much.'

'You know I can't go back to your house again. Not now.'

'You could come and visit me if you like.'

She smiled. 'Yes, that'd be lovely.'

Chapter 29: The Advice

For the first few days following his visit to his parents, Guy remained in a state of shock. His father's outburst had upset him and no matter how he tried to reason it, Guy found the man's reaction beyond comprehension. Arthur had always been a proud man, keen to do the right thing. But surely, thought Guy, love ran deeper than public acceptance. Could his father really shun his youngest son for something that had been out of Jack's control? Jack had asked Guy to beg his parents' forgiveness and Guy had failed to break through Arthur's public persona, his outer skin. It was a shock to realise how cold his father's heart was. He put it down to the jolt, the sudden realisation that his son had died a dishonourable death. He hoped time would do its work, strip away the hard outer layers of the man and reveal the father within.

After just a couple of days in his new surroundings, Guy relaxed in a way he never had chance to in France. The pace was so much less frantic, the staff attended to their duties at walking pace, bidding the men good day, dressed in clean and neatly pressed scarlet and grey uniforms. Guy thought of the nurses at the front and their perpetually stained uniforms, the surgeons hacking off limbs day and night and the doctors working non-stop while the next influx of casualties awaited their attention.

In the fortnight since seeing his parents, Guy received several visitors at the Prince of Wales Hospital. His first visitor, much to his surprise, was his father's sister, his Aunt Winnie. If she knew about Jack's so-called disgrace, she certainly didn't mention it. She asked a couple of kindly meant but bewildering questions about life in the trenches, to which Guy smiled and answered as vaguely as he could. After a few half-hearted questions about Guy's health, she furnished him with all the latest gossip in Charlton. She spoke of people Guy had either forgotten about or didn't care for, or people he'd never heard of. And all the while she knitted. She told him she was knitting him a jumper. At one point, she made Guy stand up so she could get a rough measure of his size. She left, half an hour later, promising to return once the jumper had been completed.

The following day, Aunt Winnie's son, Guy's cousin Lawrence, also paid him a visit, still sporting his pince-nez. It was soon apparent that Lawrence was only there under sufferance, obviously forced into it by Aunt Winnie. Lawrence hadn't fought in the war; he still had his important job in transport and logistics, which had excused him from active service. Aunt Winnie had said he was doing his bit behind the scenes, but when pressed, knew not the details. Lawrence wasn't forthcoming either – still something to do with military transport but refused to be drawn in further. He stayed for as little time as possible without appearing rude and then made his excuses and left. Frankly, Guy was relieved, for he couldn't help but resent Lawrence's preoccupation with trivial matters. This was a man whose self-esteem was still intact, who still had the luxury of vanity. Vanity, Guy had soon learnt, was always the first luxury to be jettisoned amongst the depravity of the trenches and he was coming to resent those who still entertained it.

A couple of days after Lawrence's visit, a Regimental Brigadier arrived and updated Guy on the regiment's progress in the trenches. He confirmed that Guy was to be awarded the Distinguished Conduct Medal for his display of tenacity and courage in the field.

Guy's next visitor, again to his surprise, was his mother. She still looked upset and distinctly unwell.

'Oh, Guy, how are you? Are they looking after you?' She'd brought him a tin of biscuits. She took off her shawl and placed it on her lap. 'I wrote to the War Office, you know, to see if I could see the papers from Jack's court-martial.'

'Really – did they write back?'

'Yes, they wrote back, at least, but no, it's an absurd situation – they can only disclose the papers to the prisoner and since he's, you know… there's nothing they can do.' She sighed. 'Please, tell me, Guy, what was he like the last time, the last time you saw him?'

'Oh, Mother, how can I tell you, how can I describe such a thing?'

'Please, Guy, try,' she said, wrapping her shawl around her hand.

'He was frightened, of course, what man wouldn't be? But he was strong, so, so strong.' He told her the best he could of the hut, of the cigarettes, of the guards ashamed of being assigned such a duty, of his deep courage, of his love for his mother, the love for his father. She listened, her eyes filling with tears, taking in every last word, every image, searing it onto her memory. On finishing, Guy fell back against the pillow, exhausted.

They sat in silence for a while. Eventually, she whispered, 'Thank you, Guy. Thank you for telling me.' She stroked his cheek with her finger. 'You were always a good boy to your mother, both of you, such good…'

'How's father?'

She pulled a face, one of embarrassment and resentment. 'He's upset, of course.'

'Has he opened the curtains?'

She looked away, her eye caught by the appearance of a nurse pushing a trolley of medicines.

'Mother?'

'No, Guy, he hasn't.'

*

His mother's visit left Guy depressed, but the next day, he received the visitor he had been looking forward to the most.

'I'm sorry I didn't come sooner,' said Mary, after the initial exchange of pleasantries, 'but if truth be known, I wasn't going to come at all.' She appeared paler than usual. Her arm was in a cast but she had discarded the sling. 'I thought that if I was to start again, I had to make a break from your family altogether. But I can't. I can't stop thinking of Jack. I know I'll never see him again, but when I look at you, I can see him in your eyes. You're quite similar to each other in many ways. Perhaps not in the way you are, but in the way you look. I'm sorry, it makes it sound as if I've come for the wrong reasons.' Whatever the reason, Guy didn't mind and tried to reassure her of the fact.

Their conversation was dominated by Jack. She talked of the future that would have been – the wedding she'd planned, where they would have lived and even potential names for the children that would never be. Guy, in turn, spoke of the past – of growing up with Jack, the fights they had, the scrapes they got into, family day-outs and the family business. He told her of the Albert Carr night. As much as his mother's visit had wearied him, Mary's visit lifted him. But at the back of his mind lay the uncomfortable truth that Jack's love for Mary was not as complete as she believed it to be. He consoled himself with the thought that she would never have to know the extent of her illusion.

Over the next month or so Mary visited frequently – two, three times a week. Her visits became the highlight of Guy's hospital routine. Each time, she would stay a bit longer. On one occasion, a nurse almost had to forcibly evict her from the hospital. She envied the nurses' workload and the genteel way they could conduct their administrations. As time went on, they spoke less of Jack, although he was never far from their thoughts or their lips, and spoke more of themselves. Here, thought Guy, were two people whose lives had been turned on their heads by the war and the death of one young man. Two people who were fast becoming dependent on each other. They spoke more about the important small things in life and not just their haunted pasts and their uncertain futures.

*

On one occasion, Mary brought her sister Josephine. 'It feels like years since I saw you last,' she said, kissing him on the cheek. Jo was as attractive as Guy remembered her, lovely green, wispy eyes.

'I've brought you some biscuits,' said Mary. 'Oh, I see you already have some.'

'My mother's been. She brings me biscuits and, bit by bit, my whole wardrobe. She thinks I should look smart for when I go out.'

'And she's quite right.'

'Yes, of course.'

'So, how are you, Guy?'

'Feeling much stronger. It's doing me good being able to do nothing but rest.'

'Do they feed you well in here?' asked Josephine.

Guy patted his stomach and winked at her. She chuckled.

'How are your parents?' asked Mary. 'I do miss them, you know. I feel I've been cast out by them twice now.'

'My mother came to see me just last week. She'd come more often but it's a distance for her. She's... well, you know, it's a difficult time.'

'Yes. Yes, of course.'

'I've been to see your Aunt Winnie.'

'You have?'

Josephine lowered her head. 'More than just once, Mary.'

'Yes, well.'

Turning to Guy, Josephine said, 'Her visits seem to be quite a success with a certain–'

'Yes, thank you, Josephine,' said Mary.

'Go on,' said Guy.

'There's nothing to say, ignore her.'

'That's not the impression I got when I saw him.'

'You mean Lawrence?' asked Guy.

'We do indeed,' said Josephine, nodding her head. 'Taken quite a shine to my little sister, he has.'

After they left, Guy couldn't help but feel slightly aggrieved that Mary should swap her affections so quickly from one side of the family to another.

While he was alone, Guy's thoughts often turned to his time at the front. A time and place, which although all too recent, Guy preferred not to dwell on. Sometimes it seemed so unreal, as if it belonged to someone else's past. Not that he could escape it, it was ingrained within him and he knew no matter what happened to him now, no part of his life would ever occupy such a definitive watershed. And he was, to a degree, still living it. Here he was, in an army hospital, surrounded by soldiers who could only talk of the war. Guy didn't mind, in fact he rather enjoyed the banter, the familiar stories, the similar experiences. But, to the others, it was still as real to them as being physically out there. He would lie awake at night and listen to their pathetic dream-induced mutterings. Guy, at least, was able to make the distinction; for when he was out there, he still had a brother; by the time he came back, he did not and he envied the others who could talk of brothers and friends killed in action. He knew in being able to make a clear distinction between the past and now, he could move on.

*

During his stay at the Prince of Wales, Guy was fitted with an artificial leg. An overly cheerful man with poor skin fitted the heavy wooden contraption, fastening it onto his thigh with various belts and buckles. After a few trips to the limbless hospital in Roehampton, the fitters constructed the leg, cutting the wood so that it could fit his stump exactly. 'You'll take a month or so to get used to it,' said the cheerful man, slapping the wooden limb, 'and you might get a few blisters along the way, so you might have to resort to the crutches, but that's to be expected. And then there are the phantom pains, not dissimilar to a dull toothache, you know the type. Could lay you low for a day or two but as you get more used to walking with the leg, the pains will soon go. Any questions? No? Good.'

At first, Guy was convinced everyone could hear the clanking noise it made as he trundled down the street, but after a while he realised that no one could hear it. And anyway, London was a mass of walking wounded. You'd only have to walk a few minutes before seeing a man in a wheelchair or a man made ageless by a face of burnt skin. But worse than the sense of self-consciousness were, as warned, the blisters that the false leg caused to the stump.

A week after the initial fitting, the hospital gave Guy notice that he was fit enough to be discharged. The thought of being cast out on his own filled him with a mixture of excitement and apprehension. He could either go back and stay with his parents or the hospital administration would help him find private lodgings. He knew it would be easier to go for the first option, but while his father refused to acknowledge Jack, he felt he had no choice but to opt for the latter.

*

A couple of days later, Mary visited again. 'I've brought someone to see you,' she said.

'So I see. How do you do, Lawrence? Take a seat.'

'Good morning, Guy, good to see you again.' He'd trimmed his beard and a pair of glasses had replaced the pince-nez. He looked slightly younger for it, but was it Mary's influence, Guy wondered. He hoped not.

'Lawrence and I have a little disagreement, don't we, Lawrence? You see, Guy, I think I need a new job, just while I get fit enough to return to France.'

'Of course you don't,' said Lawrence. 'I've told her, if she's ever short of anything, I'm always here. Jack, God rest his soul, would never have wanted you to work.'

'Well, I don't know.'

'Listen, this war will be over soon and then the men will be back in their droves wanting their jobs back. What could you do anyway?'

'You know I used to work in a bakery once.'

'Oh for goodness sake, Mary, I can't have you working in a bakery, what sort of work is that? And this talk of returning to France…'

Guy listened to the to and fro of their argument and to his annoyance knew he was intimidated by his cousin's dull but authoritative presence. 'I've been given a job,' he announced.

'You have?' asked Mary.

'Yes, with the army – a desk job in Woolwich. And I've been given a date for discharge from this place.'

'Oh, Guy, that's wonderful news. When?'

'A week's time.'

'Will you go back to your parents?' asked Lawrence.

'No, the hospital has found me some lodgings in Lewisham, a room in a house owned by an Italian woman, Mrs Marenghi, I think her name is.'

'Good God, an Italian,' said Lawrence, 'whatever next? An Arabian valet?'

'She'll clean and cook for me in return for board and lodge.'

'Oh, it gets worse. Italian food? She'll poison you to death with spices and goodness knows what.'

'That sounds perfect, Guy,' said Mary. 'I'm thrilled for you. But listen, I have a better idea – I'll get Josephine to move out, and you could rent her room. There we are – perfect, that would give me an income, wouldn't it, Lawrence, and better company to boot.'

'You jest, I hope.'

'But of course, dear Lawrence, of course.'

After they'd left, Guy was bothered by a nagging thought that troubled him for the rest of the day. It was only later that night as he was falling asleep that Guy remembered what it was – Mary hadn't been wearing her engagement ring. The thought induced within him a strange feeling – he realised he was jealous.

*

The day before he left the Prince of Wales, Guy received his medal. A Colonel Knot came down specifically to award a number of decorations. Most of the recipients had invited family and friends to witness their moment of glory. Guy however could not face such a fuss and without his own personal audience, was able to go through the motions. He shook hands with the Colonel, thanked him for his encouraging words, received his Distinguished Conduct Medal, saluted and looked suitably humbled. A final rousing rendition of God Save the King ended the tedious proceedings.

The following day, two days before Christmas, Guy left the hospital. They provided him with a taxi to take him and his haversack to his new accommodation in Lewisham, where he met Mrs Marenghi. She was very much what Guy had expected a middle-aged Italian woman to be – plump and jolly, with a pronounced accent and wild, grey hair that had certainly once been jet black. His room, at the top of the house on the second floor, was minute but Guy didn't mind, he had so few possessions to speak of. Besides the single bed, which dominated the room, was a bedside table with a lamp, a small writing table and chair, and a moth-eaten armchair in the corner. There was a battered wardrobe and a set of three empty shelves. The faded wallpaper, a pale blue paisley colour, had seen better days and the window let in a terrible draught. Guy spent his quiet evenings at the writing table reading. Next to his room, Guy had the use of a small, adapted kitchen and, down one flight of stairs, a shared bathroom. For now, at least, it was perfect.

Guy spent Christmas Day 1917 with Mary and Josephine. 'Guy!' screeched Mary as she opened the front door, 'you're wearing your medal.' He'd also donned a new red-coloured tie for the occasion and worn his favourite wide-lapelled jacket.

'Doesn't he look handsome,' said Josephine behind her.

Guy purred. He realised he hadn't stepped inside their house since the awful confrontation with Mary and Jack. They had tried to brighten up the living room with Christmas decorations, a tiny tree with painted pinecones, ties of golden ribbon and little baskets of sweets, and on the table a Yule log festooned with holly but still, the place felt dank, the brown wallpaper drab but Guy could think of nowhere else he would rather be.

'I'm afraid, we can't offer much, you know how it is,' said Josephine, passing Guy a tiny glass of sherry.

'Believe me, when I think back to this time last year...'

'Of course. Don't suppose it stops, does it?'

'You hear rumours though, don't you?' said Josephine. 'You know, of soldiers, them and us, playing football. Is it true, does it happen?'

'I heard that too and I think it happened once but I never saw it.'

'Still,' said Josephine, 'you're here now. To your good health.'

'And to all our loved ones,' added Mary.

The trio of glasses clinked and silently they sipped their sherries. Guy's mind went back to the previous year, Christmas Day in the trenches, a day like any other, a day of cold and boredom in a reserve trench, replacing sandbags, perhaps shifting new supplies. Somewhere, not too far away, his brother. So recent; such a long time ago. He thought of the men still out there. How much longer, dear friends, how long can it go on for? And here he was, a cripple for the rest of his life but in a warm flat with rich smells drifting through from the kitchen, with his medal pinned to his lapel, his new tie, in the company of the sisters. Damn the brown wallpaper, he had to stop himself from weeping with gratitude.

'You all right, Guy?' asked Josephine gently.

Guy nodded and kept on nodding, unable to talk.

Both sisters smiled at him, warm, gentle smiles, full of knowing and understanding.

'Right,' declared Mary, 'better see how that chicken is getting on. Chicken, eh? Can't tell you what steps I had to take to obtain that.'

'Nonsense,' said Josephine, 'she just put on this pathetic look and you-know-who came up with the goods.'

'Another word, sister, and it'll be double sprouts for you, you mark my words.'

'Can't we do presents first?' asked Josephine.

Guy had been slightly dreading the moment but his sugared almonds wrapped in decorated paper seemed to go down well with both of them, and in return he exclaimed with delight at another tie and an embroidered handkerchief.

An hour or two had passed and the sisters had retired to a settee, Guy to an armchair, their hunger sated, each clasping a glass of white wine. Conversation flowed, punctuated with frequent laughter. He noticed again the lack of a ring on Mary's finger. Guy was in mid-flow with a tale of the time his father had mixed up his orders and supplied the wrong hats to two sets of puzzled customers when the doorbell rang. 'Who in the graces could that be on Christmas Day?' asked Mary.

'I think we can guess,' said Josephine. Indeed, it was Lawrence, carrying a large present wrapped in bright festive paper.

'Guy,' he said on entering, 'a thorn between two roses.'

'And a merry Christmas to you too, dear cousin.'

'A present for me?' asked Josephine.

'Er, no, it's for Mary, actually.' Awkwardly, he lunged at Mary, the package getting in the way, and kissed her on the cheek.

'Thank you, you're too kind.'

'Well, aren't you going to open it?'

'Lawrence, give me a moment.'

Carefully, she pulled at the sticking tape while Josephine poured Lawrence a glass of wine.

'I won't, thank you.'

'Ah, get away with you, this is Christmas.'

'Well, OK, just the one.'

'Lawrence, it's beautiful.'

Mary held it out for all to see – a red dress, long and flowing, pleated to the umpth degree, with a slash. It was, Guy had to admit, a striking garment and it certainly put his sugared almonds to shame.

'My,' muttered Josephine.

'It's truly lovely, thank you, Lawrence. I just have to find an occasion to wear it now. I'm not sure I move in the right circles.'

'We'll soon see about that,' said Lawrence, allowing himself the faintest smile.

Josephine and Guy passed a sly, knowing look; Mary blushed and for a few moments an awkward silence hung between them. Mary broke it with a cough. 'Lawrence, I bought you a little present, nothing special, it's just… just…' It was a tie, the same as the one she'd given to Guy.

'I'm sorry.'

'No, no, it's lovely, it's, really, just right, thank you.'

*

For New Year, Mary and Josephine were invited to a party. They encouraged Guy to come along too, but he couldn't face the prospect of rubbing shoulders with jolly strangers.

Instead, he spent New Year's Eve in his room. Just before midnight, Mrs Marenghi persuaded Guy to join her and her Italian friends to see in the New Year. Reluctantly, Guy accepted. The Italian Londoners made grand toasts that 1918 should bring an Allied victory and peace. Guy echoed the sentiment and made a silent toast to his friends and comrades still stuck in the trenches.

A few days into the New Year, on a bitterly cold morning, Guy heard the doorbell ring two floors below and assumed it to be one of Mrs Marenghi's many elderly Italian admirers. But seconds later, he heard footsteps jogging up both flights of stairs, across the small landing and towards his room. Guy thought the footsteps too heavy to be Mary's, but who else could it be, it had to be her; apart from Mary, no one knew of his whereabouts. Delighted at the prospect of seeing her again, Guy closed his book and waited. On hearing the knock on his door, he beckoned his unexpected visitor to enter. There, standing in the doorway, his beard trimmed even further, was Lawrence looking somewhat anxious and carrying a large briefcase.

'I'm terribly sorry for calling on you unannounced like this, but I had to come and see you.'

Guy was intrigued. His cousin was such a self-assured man; what on earth would Lawrence want to see him about. 'By all means, come in please.'

Lawrence stepped in, removed his hat and coat, and hung them on the hook on the back of the door. He cast his eyes disdainfully around the small cramped room.

'It's only a temporary arrangement,' said Guy as a way of explanation. 'Please, sit down.'

'Thank you,' said Lawrence as he sat down gingerly on the edge of the armchair in the corner of the room. 'Mary says you're due to start work soon.'

'Yes, a week on Monday. They found me a job at the Quartermaster's Office in Woolwich.'

'Not too bad a journey then, considering your…'

'It'll be fine.' There was a pause while each thought of something to say. 'Lawrence, forgive me, I haven't offered you anything, would you like…'

'No, no, I'm fine. Thank you all the same.'

They sat in silence for a few awkward moments more. Guy decided that as small talk was proving too difficult, they might as well get to the point. 'You were saying, Lawrence, you needed to speak to me…?'

'Er, yes.' He leant forward, fixing his eyes onto Guy's. 'It's a bit delicate, so I would appreciate your discretion.'

'Of course.'

'You see, I need your advice…' He paused.

'Advice?'

'Yes, I do apologise for–'

'Advice on *what* exactly, Lawrence?'

'Well, it's about…' He glanced around the room, as if the cramped space was about to reveal an unexpected occupant. 'It's about a girl.'

'A girl?' Guy suppressed a smile; Lawrence didn't seem to be the type to be worrying about girls. 'I'm not sure I'd be the best person to offer advice on the subject of women.'

'Well, nonetheless, I'd like your opinion. You see, I'm thinking of asking a girl to marry me.'

'Oh? Do you have a particular girl in mind or just any girl?'

Lawrence glared at him. 'Obviously, I'm wasting my time–'

'No, forgive me, I'm sorry, it's just a bit out of the blue, that's all. Please, carry on. There isn't a problem, is there? She's not already married?'

Lawrence laughed. 'Of course not.'

'Is she about the same age as you? She's not Catholic, is she?' Guy was enjoying this.

'No, none of these things, although now you mention it, she is a few years younger than me – but only a few. Actually, you're probably right – quite a few. Anyway, it's just that I thought you might know whether I should ask her or not.'

Oh no, thought Guy, the penny had dropped. 'Why, do I know her?' he asked anxiously.

'Why, yes, of course.'

'It's Mary, isn't it?'

'Yes! Well, Guy, what do you think; do I stand an earthly chance?'

On the two recent occasions Guy had met Lawrence, he'd felt slightly intimidated by him, but now, as his older cousin sat in front of him, waiting anxiously for Guy's opinion, Guy saw a pathetic insecure man who had not the slightest idea about women. What on earth made him think Mary would accept his proposal? He felt almost sorry for the poor, deluded man. 'Well, of course she will. A man of your standing, how could she refuse?'

Lawrence preened at the compliment, but a doubtful frown quickly returned. 'You don't think it's too soon, you know, after the business with Jack?'

'No, she's young, she's resilient.' But, thought Guy, she'll never marry a fool like you.

'Oh, Guy, what a relief, I can't tell you how much this means to me. Maybe, I'll stay for that drink after all.'

Guy feared as much. Lawrence stayed for another half an hour, extolling the virtues of Mary while continually seeking and receiving Guy's reassurance that he would be suitable for her. No fool like an old fool, thought Guy. The man was a bigger fool than Guy remembered him to be, but it wasn't Guy's place to enlighten him to the fact. Eventually, Lawrence got up to leave, shook Guy's hand vigorously and thanked him several times.

As he was leaving, Lawrence said, 'Oh, Guy, I almost forgot...' He fished in his briefcase and produced a large package wrapped in brown paper. 'This is for you.'

'What is it?' asked Guy.

'A late Christmas present from my mother.'

Guy unwrapped the paper bag. Inside was the jumper his Aunt Winnie had been knitting him. He held it against himself. 'It's lovely,' he said. 'Do thank her for me.'

The jumper was of a bright bottled-green colour with a dark red stripe across the middle. It was quite the most hideous thing Guy had ever seen.

Chapter 30: The Marriage – January 1918

'Lawrence has asked me to marry him.'

'I know,' said Guy, adding another spoonful of sugar to his tea.

'You know?'

'Well, I knew he was planning to.'

'How did you know?'

'He came to see me two days ago and sat where you're sitting now and asked for my advice.'

'Your advice? What, on whether to ask me to marry him; what did you say?' Mary sipped her tea.

Guy nodded. 'Well, it was obvious he wanted me to say yes.'

'And... did you?'

'Yes, I did. It's what he wanted to hear, so I said it. So, he asked you then? Popped the question?' He tried to picture Lawrence proposing. Did he go down on one knee, he wondered, or a more dramatic gesture – a romantic meal with champagne or a first-class trip on a luxury train, he could certainly afford it. But somehow, he imagined it was more of a hearty slap on the back: 'You and me, girl; how about it?'

'I said I'd think about it.'

Guy was surprised. 'Did you?'

'Yes, and I'm going to accept.'

Guy choked on his tea. She was accepting? That wasn't part of the plan, she couldn't accept. The man was a buffoon, surely she could see that. 'You can't,' he spluttered.

'And why not?'

'Mary, you know why. It's… it's too soon.'

'Do you mean Jack? Guy, I'm almost twenty, I need to get on with my life and I want to have children; lots of them.' Mary looked at him carefully. 'Is that all that's troubling you?' she asked quietly.

Guy gazed out of the smeary window. It was Sunday; tomorrow he was starting his new job at the Quartermaster's Office in Woolwich. He didn't know what to expect but it was paid employment, another step in the slow process of becoming a civilian. As much as anything else, he needed a job to get him out and face the world. He was fast turning into a recluse within the four walls of Mrs Marenghi's box room.

'Guy,' said Mary, 'don't pretend to ignore me. Is that the only thing bothering you?'

He liked it here in Mrs Marenghi's room, but travelling such a distance over London with a false leg was exhausting, as was having a room at the top of a house. It meant each trip out had to justify the effort of climbing all those stairs.

Mary became impatient. 'Well, don't talk to me then.'

'You know it isn't,' he barked. 'We both know.'

'Yes,' said Mary quietly, 'I think we probably do.'

'And we both know Lawrence is a fool–'

'Perhaps, but a fool with security, financial security and a… a…'

'A future?'

'Yes, if you like, a future.'

Guy guffawed. 'A future for himself maybe, but not for you, Mary, surely you know that. I'm sorry if I sound presumptuous, but you don't… you don't *love* him, do you?'

Mary sipped her tea, avoiding Guy's eyes.

Guy persisted. 'Am I wrong?'

'No, of course not,' she snapped. 'It was Jack I loved and still do, but they took him away from me. And then, I got to know you and…'

'And…?'

'You know.'

'You fell in love with me?'

Mary placed her teacup on the table and gazed idly at her hands. 'No,' she said gently.

'Well, I fell in love with you,' said Guy.

'I know.' She looked at him, her eyes reddening. 'I know, Guy.'

'So why are you crying, Mary?'

'Because I thought I loved you and I wanted to, believe me, I so wanted to. And maybe I do, but I can't allow myself to love you, Guy, and I certainly couldn't marry you. You're Jack's brother and you always will be. It wouldn't be right, you'd be a constant reminder of Jack, you have the same eyes; it would be like living with his memory every day, and that wouldn't be fair – on either of us. Please don't think I want to forget Jack, of course I don't and I never will and wouldn't want to, but I need to move on. Please, Guy, tell me you understand.'

'You want to move on by marrying Jack's cousin?'

'It's not the same. You hardly knew each other as children – he told me, and you still don't know each other – not properly. And Lawrence doesn't look like you two. But you, Guy, you were Jack's brother; you saw him in his last hours. I couldn't live with that knowledge, not day in and day out.'

Guy noticed how white her arms seemed, the blue veins breaking the monotony of the delicate pale skin. 'But why Lawrence, why not someone entirely different? The man is still a

Searight, you'd still carry the Searight name and so would your children.'

'But I wouldn't see the sadness in his eyes as I see it in yours. You may have lost your leg, Guy, but it's nothing to what you lost inside. I need someone who doesn't bear the scars, someone who's settled, financially secure and still young.'

'Young?'

'Well, fairly young. If I married you, we'd never survive on what the army pays you. We couldn't live in somewhere like... well, like this, but on your salary, what choice would we have?'

'So Lawrence is your ticket to happiness and security, is he then? A father figure perhaps?'

'No, this has nothing to do with my father. The devil got into my father; drink took him away from me as surely as a bullet took Jack – I'm sorry, I shouldn't have said it like that. But Lawrence is not some form of substitute father, believe me...'

Guy bowed his head. 'OK, I'm sorry also–'

'I know you think Lawrence is a bit of a prig, but he's a decent man. He says he loves me and no doubt, with time, I shall develop a certain... fondness for him.'

Guy laughed. 'Fondness? Is that all you want from a marriage, a certain fondness?'

'You may laugh, Guy Searight, but I can't sit around all day waiting for a man who hasn't been torn apart by the war; Lord knows, there's not many like him left.'

'I notice you don't wear Jack's ring any more; that didn't last long.'

Her nostrils flared. 'It was getting too small for me.'

'Really? Already?'

'Yes. Already.'

Lawrence's lack of active service seemed so wrong somehow, why hadn't he volunteered, what was so damn special about his job that made him exempt from what ordinary men had to endure? But then an idea struck him, he leant towards her, clasping her hands. 'There *is* an alternative Mary,' he said almost in a whisper.

She raised her eyebrows. 'An alternative?'

'Yes, yes, of course. One word to my father, that's all it would take.'

'The business? No, not while he refuses to acknowledge Jack. Never forget he cast him aside like an old newspaper. You can't take the business from a man like that; you'd be betraying both yourself and your brother. And anyway, it would make no difference; you'd still have that sadness in your eyes...'

*

Lawrence and Mary married in February 1918. It was a grand wedding with lots of guests, a dignified service, a splendid reception, a string quartet and dancing late into the night. Mary looked resplendent in her flowing, intricate wedding dress alongside her distinguished bridegroom. The bridesmaids were a picture, especially Mary's lovely sister, Josephine; Lawrence's mother, Aunt Winnie, cried throughout; the Best Man did a fine job; and Guy's father, in the absence of Mary's father, made a stirring, if overly long speech. In the evening, Mary wore her red dress with its slash, her Christmas present from Lawrence. Yes, it'd been a wonderful occasion – according to Guy's mother. Guy himself had been invited but declined.

Over the coming months, the new Mr and Mrs Searight settled down to married life. Lawrence bought a fine townhouse in Islington and employed no less than three servants. He was doing well at work, as always, and had recently received a hefty but well-deserved promotion. And, to cap it all, Mary fell pregnant.

302

Guy reluctantly left Mrs Marenghi and moved to new lodgings in Woolwich, nearer his work. His mother came to visit him frequently. 'It's a lot bigger,' she remarked on her first visit.

'Yes, not that I have anything to fill up the extra space.'

After she admired the room and talked about increasing prices, she approached the subject Guy knew she wanted to talk about. 'Isn't it time now to bury the hatchet?'

'You mean Father?'

'Of course, Guy, you know that. He's opened the curtains, you know.'

'And has he let the light into his heart?'

'Oh, Guy, how pompous you sound.'

'Well?'

She sighed. 'Since you put it like that, no, his heart remains as dark as ever. He's not a well man, Guy, all this has aged him. Please, come see him, it'd make all the difference. He can't work any more; he needs you to take it over.'

'And what about Jack? Is he still cast out, the son he never had?'

'Please, Guy, come see your father; he needs you.'

*

On 11 November 1918, Armistice Day, Mary gave birth to a baby boy. He was born at seven in the morning while the world was still at war, if only for another four hours. They named him Clarence Jack Searight. His mother rang him at ten. She'd heard the news from her sister-in-law. It had, according to Guy's mother, been a difficult birth, but mother and child were well and Lawrence was delighted at having a son to carry his name while Aunt Winnie was already knitting feverishly. As much as Guy was pleased for her, the thought of Mary settling down to a life of motherhood, married to that oaf, depressed him.

For Guy, Armistice Day was painful. He could hear the celebrations outside, people in the street singing and cheering. At twelve, one hour into peace, he tried to go out. Immediately, he was embraced by a portly man clutching a bottle of wine. Guy resisted the man's calls to join the spontaneous street party. He surveyed the scene – despite the cold and threatening clouds, a line of people were doing the conga up the street, kicking their legs, singing. It was too much for him. He darted back indoors, poured himself a sherry and sat in his armchair, trying to come to terms with the word *peace*. Four years of war and now, like someone turning on a switch, there was peace. It didn't seem possible. His mother, in her phone call, hadn't mentioned Jack; somehow, in the joy of receiving a nephew, she'd forgotten that it was the first anniversary of her younger son's death. He was annoyed she hadn't acknowledged it. Lifting his glass, he said, 'To you, Jack, wherever you may be, and to you, Clarence. May your life never be blighted by war.'

He helped himself to a second glass and drank it while his mind whirled with colliding thoughts – Jack, Clarence, peace. With a sudden realisation, he decided he needed to write it all down. Rummaging round in his bureau, he found a notebook. Sitting at his dining table, he lit a cigarette and began to write. *4th September 1914*, he wrote*, today I joined the army. The nation was at war and it seemed an easy and natural thing to do.* Two hours later, he'd written twenty pages and had covered his first twelve months in uniform. He felt exhilarated but quite exhausted by the process. He vowed that however hard and however long it took, he would continue writing to the end. To whom would he show it, he wondered. No one, absolutely no one.

That evening, his living room seemed bathed in light. He wondered what it was. Looking outside, he saw that all the street lamps had been lit, the whole street illuminated. How strange it was to see the lights again – it'd been four years.

Two weeks later, on a cold Sunday afternoon, Mary and Lawrence paid Guy a visit to show off the latest Searight. Guy had put on his Aunt Winnie's jumper for the occasion.

'He's got the Searight nose,' said Lawrence proudly.

'Yes, poor blighter,' added Mary.

'You seem well, Mary,' said Guy.

'Yes,' she said, 'I feel well.'

Guy smiled. 'Good, I'm pleased for you; for both of you.' And, much to his own surprise, he genuinely meant it.

'It's all thanks to you, Guy,' said Lawrence, removing his glasses. 'I'd never have had the guts to ask Mary to marry me if it hadn't been for your encouragement.'

'Nonsense, you would have got there in your own time.'

'No, I mean it. I wanted to call him Clarence Guy, but Mary says we'll call the next one Guy.'

'The next one?'

'Oh yes,' said Lawrence smugly, 'plenty more where that came from!'

'Guy…?' said Mary. 'Lawrence and I were wondering if you'd do us the honour of becoming Clarence's godfather.'

'Really?'

'Please,' urged Lawrence, 'it would mean so much to us.'

'Well…' Well, why not, thought Guy, why not indeed? 'Yes, OK, I'd be honoured.'

'But, Guy, can I ask you something?'

'Go on.'

'Where did you get that hideous jersey?'

*

And so, during the spring of 1919, Clarence Jack Searight was christened with his Uncle Guy as godfather and his Aunt

Josephine as godmother. The ceremony was as extravagant as the wedding had been, attended by scores of family and friends, followed by another sumptuous spread. Among the many guests was Guy's father whom Guy realised he hadn't seen since his homecoming in November 1917, eighteen months previously.

'Look at them,' said Josephine, sidling up to Guy, a glass of champagne in her hand, 'don't they look a picture?'

'Basking in the glow.'

'Cheers.' The two of them clinked glasses and watched in silence as the happy couple took to the dance floor, gliding around slightly awkwardly.

'It has to be said, it's a funny pairing.'

'Lawrence and Mary?'

'Who else? She's gone from almost marrying a boy to marrying a father figure. You were a bit slow, Guy, couldn't you have saved us all and popped the question?'

'She wouldn't have wanted me. After what your sister's been through she needed security.'

'Unusually perceptive for a man, if I may say so. We haven't seen you for a while, Guy.'

'Yeah, it's the new job, takes it out of me.'

'How is the leg?'

'Wooden.'

She laughed. 'Sorry, I didn't mean to…'

'No, it's fine, I shouldn't have said that. It's fine, I'm used to it now, amazing how the body adjusts.'

'You know, if you ever feel like a bit of company…'

'I'm sorry?'

'Just give me a call one day.'

'Guy, Guy…' It was his mother, waving at him, parting the sea of guests in her approach; beside her a stooped an old man Guy recognized as his father.

'I'll leave you to it,' said Josephine, 'but remember what I said, I mean it, anytime.'

'Thank you, Josephine, I'll–'

'Honestly,' said Guy's mother, 'you two are like a pair of obstinate old fools. At least Arthur has an excuse – he is one. But you, Guy, you're young enough to know better.'

The two men, father and son, shook hands. They talked about the baby, Aunt Winnie's knitting, and commented wryly on how Lawrence was able to afford such lavish dos. They agreed that during such difficult economic times, such extravagance seemed wrong somehow, almost disrespectful. Guy remembered his father saying much the same at his wedding anniversary party three years previously. Guy was surprised by how much older his father looked. He'd lost weight, his hair now totally devoid of colour; his eyes seemed shallow beneath the new, thicker glasses.

'I'm having to sell the business, you know, Guy. But nothing's been signed; it can still be yours. All you have to do is to give the nod.' Even his voice had lost that authoritative edge.

'Mother tells me you've finally allowed the sun to penetrate into the house again.'

'Yes.'

'And er, how about Jack? Have you allowed him to penetrate your heart yet?'

'I've tried, Lord knows I've tried–'

'That means you haven't?'

'People look at me in the street, Guy. People who have lost their sons, their brothers and husbands. Men who died for this country, men who stood by their comrades–'

'Oh for goodness sake, Father, spare me.'

'I can't help it. I've had people walk to the other side of the street rather than say good morning to me. I even had a woman at the factory resign because of what Jack did. Her husband had been gassed at Ypres. I told you it'd bring shame to our family and I was right.'

Guy wanted to feel angry, to lash out at his father; he was an obstinate old fool, as his mother had said. Instead, he was overcome with pity and in need to escape the jollity of the occasion. He had no desire for his father's business and, he realised, he'd never wanted it. Everyone had assumed, including himself, but no one had ever asked what *he* wanted. From the moment of his birth, his future had been predetermined. Looking back with sudden clarity, he realised it was the reason why, all those years ago, he'd volunteered to fight – to escape the inevitability of his future. Hats had been his father's work, but he had no desire for it to be his.

'Sell the business, Father,' he said. 'I don't think I would've cared for making hats anyway. Just don't hold it against me. Sell it and enjoy the proceeds.'

His father tried to smile. Perhaps, thought Guy, they both knew.

*

On a cold mid-December evening, Guy returned from work to find Mary waiting inside his room with Clarence. The baby, now thirteen months old, was fast asleep in his pram. She apologised for arriving unannounced and explained his landlady took pity on her and had opened Guy's room so that she could wait for him in the warmth. Guy sensed that not all was well. He asked after Clarence and the joys of motherhood and she regaled him with tales of the little boy's mishaps, his characteristics and his latest developments. She became animated and Guy thought he'd been mistaken in thinking something was troubling her. Lawrence, apparently, had hired a nanny but apart from night-time, her services were rarely required for Mary was determined to do everything for the little chap. Eventually, once the topic of

Clarence had been exhausted, the look of concern returned to Mary's face. He made her a cup of tea and offered her a biscuit, which she refused. She began talking about Lawrence's work and their house in Islington.

He interrupted her. 'Mary, tell me, why *have* you come?' She remained silent, her mouth tightening as if unwilling to speak. She tried to look at him but was unable to hold his gaze. Guy tried again. 'What's wrong, Mary?'

She spoke so softly, Guy had difficulty making out her words. 'You were right.'

He knew what she meant. 'What do you mean?'

'I don't love him.'

Guy felt no sense of righteousness or glee, he merely felt sorry for the crumpled figure in front of him. 'Lawrence?'

'I tried to love him, I really tried, but I can't and I don't think I ever could.' She was speaking quickly now. 'I thought it would come after Clarence was born but it hasn't. In some ways I feel resentful because I never see him, he's always at work. But as soon as he comes home, I find myself wishing he'd go away again. I don't see anyone, I don't have any friends, I talk to no one. I hardly ever see Josephine now. What few friends I had have all been scared away, for he's the most bullish man I've ever met. He doesn't mean to be and of course that just makes it worse, the fact he doesn't realise it. He's rude, he's arrogant and he's... well, he's no fun to be with and I can't face having...'

Guy thought of a delicate word to finish her sentence with. 'Relations?'

She nodded. 'I used to tolerate it before Clarence was born because I so wanted to have a baby.' She peered into the pram and smiled at her son. 'When Clarence came along, things did get a little better. Lawrence was thrilled; he was like a child with a new toy but the toy soon lost its shine. Since then, we haven't... not once. I've used every excuse in motherhood but after seven months, the excuses are wearing thin. We've been married less than two years and I don't know what to do.'

'I suppose leaving him is out of the question?'

'And where would I go, how would I bring up Clarence? I'd be an outcast.'

'Yes, of course, I'm sorry, I didn't mean to be so tactless.'

'Besides, I know this may sound strange, I still care enough for him not to want to throw him into a scandal. He has his position to think of, I couldn't jeopardise that for him. I keep thinking of what should have been – married to Jack, married for love. You know, I keep thinking perhaps it's all been a big mistake and that Jack will just turn up one day, smiling that smile of his. I even thought about seeing a spiritualist to see if I could get in contact with him, just to know that he's there somewhere, looking over me. I would like that.'

From within his pram, Clarence had woken up and was gurgling and squealing contentedly. Mary peered in at him and made appropriate noises. She lifted him out and rubbed her nose against his. This little boy dressed in ill-matching knitwear instantly transformed her whole demeanour.

'I see my Aunt Winnie's been busy,' said Guy.

Mary laughed. 'She's lovely, but I wish I could stop her knitting!'

'How is she?'

'Devoted.' She sighed. 'How can I do it, Guy? How can I even think of denying her this precious grandson? I just can't bring myself to do it...'

*

Over the following weeks, Mary came to see Guy on a regular basis. Occasionally, they would meet in town and have lunch in a café or go for a gentle walk in a park. Just as Guy had come to rely on Mary's visits during his convalescence at the hospital, the time he now spent with her became the focal point and the highlight of his week. He had to fight the urge to buy little presents for Clarence. It would only have aroused suspicion and he dared not risk losing her again. But this time, he resigned himself to the fact it was different. Before, he'd harboured a smouldering desire for her, a desire which, so soon after the death of Jack, he kept to himself. But at the time, he was always conscious of its presence, a presence which, he felt, with sufficient time, would finally reveal itself. It hadn't of course and this time he knew their friendship was, and had to be, platonic. He felt bound by the unspoken rules on which their rekindled friendship was based. Mary may have been caught in a loveless marriage but it was still a marriage Guy knew had to be honoured for Mary's sake as well as Clarence's.

One bitterly cold afternoon in the February of 1920, she came to see him. She stood at the door breathing heavily as if she'd been running. Guy knew. 'Come,' he said, reaching out his hand. She took it, he pulled her in and instinctively kissed her, urgently. He kissed her with a passion founded on years of want and desire. She reciprocated eagerly, pulling down his jacket, pushing it off his shoulders. There was no hesitation, no doubt. Between breaths, they said each other's name, their lips touching. Still kissing, he managed to yank off his shoes, his socks. He ran his fingers through her hair and breathed in her scent. She slipped off his braces but then the enormity of the moment hit him. It'd been such a long time, and never before had he felt so acutely conscious of his leg, his damn leg.

'Shh,' she whispered in his ear. 'I know what you're thinking. It's fine, my darling, it's OK.'

'No. You won't want me.'

She kissed him gently. 'You listen here, Guy Searight,' she said slowly, 'I want to, I've never been so sure. I want you. You understand, I – want – you.' She took his hand and held it over her breast, 'Kiss me, kiss me.'

Afterwards, after she'd gone, he lay on the bed alone, tears on his cheeks. He reflected that, at long last, he had found what he wanted. So why did he feel so miserable?

*

They met at his lodgings as often as possible, usually with Clarence in tow. While they waited for sleep to overtake the baby, they talked excitedly, in full anticipation of what was to follow. Once Clarence was asleep, they'd make love. Then, in the warm afterglow of sex, they talked freely and with enthusiasm, often fantasising about a life together, just Clarence and the two of them. Occasionally, Guy would push Mary on the subject, taking it out of the realms of fantasy and ask her why she couldn't just leave her husband. Granted, it would be difficult, but they had each other now, he urged. But each time Mary became defensive and placed innumerable barriers to such a possibility. Guy never begrudged her reluctance because he understood only too well. He was unable to provide Mary the security she quite rightly demanded and, for the sake of Clarence, needed. The question of her future stability took on an even greater relevance when, one day, in May 1920, she announced she was carrying Guy's child.

Chapter 31: Goodbye / Hello

'Hello, Father, how are you?'

'I'm dying, Guy, otherwise I'm fine.'

'Yes, of course, I'm sorry.'

'No, I'm sorry, I didn't mean to be rude.'

His father was lying in the middle of the double bed, propped up on several huge pillows, his wife having moved to the spare room months back. The curtains, Guy noticed, were open. On his father's lap, the day's *Times*, and on his bedside table a small pile of books, uppermost Dickens' *A Tale of Two Cities*.

Arthur saw his son look at it. 'Have you read it?'

'No.'

'You should, it's very good.'

'Yes, so I'm told.' His father's cheeks were sunken; his skin the colour of death.

'I see you're wearing your medals.'

'Yes.'

'A DCM, eh? Good boy, I'm proud of you.'

'Thank you, Father.' Guy looked up at the familiar framed sampler above his father's bed.

'I hear you're doing well for yourself – a good job, somewhere to live.'

'Yes, things are beginning to work out.'

'And what about a lady friend?'

'No, I have to say that's not going so well.'

'Well, there's a lot of women about and a shortage of men so it shouldn't take long.'

'Perhaps. It's the leg. Puts them off.'

'Hah, there's a lot worse off than you, my boy.'

This was the point, thought Guy, where he should tell his parents that he was to be a father, that Mary was expecting his child. This was the point to tell them that their greatest desire, to be grandparents, was about to be fulfilled. But how does one inform one's parents that he had got their nephew's wife pregnant, a woman once engaged to his brother. It was better if they never knew.

A knock on the door and Edith came in with a tray of tea and biscuits. 'Couldn't you have got Lizzie to do that?' asked Arthur.

'No, I wanted to do it myself and see my men. Shall I pour?'

'For goodness sake, woman, we can do it ourselves. Leave it here,' he said, tapping the bedside table.

'Thank you, Mother.'

'Mind my books.'

'That's perfectly all right, Guy.' She watched as Arthur stretched over and reached for the teapot. 'I'll leave you to it then, shall I?'

'Yes, yes, I may be an invalid but I'm not a total cripple – yet.'

'I must apologise, Guy, for your father's tactlessness.'

'Oh God, I'm not saying…'

Guy laughed. 'It's fine, Father.'

'Oh blast, look what you've made me do.'

'Arthur, really, the idea is to pour it in the cup not on the tray.'

'Oh, you do it then. Look what's become of me, Guy, can't even pour a bloody cup of tea now.'

'Arthur! Please.'

'What?'

'Your language.'

'Oh, for… I think Guy may have heard worse.'

'Yes, but we're not in the trenches now, are we?'

'At this rate, he'll probably rather be back.'

Arthur slumped into his pillows.

'Arthur, are you all right, dear?'

'Yes, just, just a bit tired all of a sudden.'

'Oh, I'm sorry,' said Guy.

'No, it's not you, Guy,' said his mother. 'It's my fault; I've caused too much excitement. It might do him good to rest.'

'Yes, sorry, son, it just hits me occasionally. Quite often now.'

'I can always come back.'

'Listen, come, come closer.' His eyes were drooping but he took Guy's hand and clasped it. How bony his hand yet the grip, thought Guy, was surprisingly strong. 'Thank you for coming; you're a good lad, and you know what…' His breath smelt rank, the odour of a dying man.

'Go on, Father, go on.'

'Jack. He was too, a good lad, such a good lad.' His eyes closed.

With that, Arthur's grip loosened and his hand went limp.

Guy turned to see his mother. She was standing over him, nodding, her eyes filled with tears, 'I wanted you to hear it yourself, Guy, he's found it in himself to forgive him.'

Guy looked at his father, his chest heaving with deep breaths. He took to his feet and hugged his mother. She buried her face into his shoulder. Guy looked up to the ceiling and beyond, heaven-bound, and smiled.

He never saw his father again.

*

'Guy, this is Robert – your son; Robert, this is your father.' Mary held the sleeping two-week-old baby a little higher so that Guy could see him properly. 'Say hello.'

315

'My word, he's lovely,' said Guy, stunned at meeting his son for the first time.

'Go on, hold him.' She carefully placed the tiny bundle into Guy's arms. Guy was surprised how heavy the baby felt. He felt awkward, terrified of dropping the little chap but Robert seemed contented enough. 'Is he really mine?' he asked.

'Of course, Guy, I told you so. Robert is *your* son, believe me.'

He looked at her, smiled and nodded. Outside, they could hear the sound of a barrel organ grinding its ugly tune. They had met in a small coffeehouse on Liverpool Road behind the Angel. With a two-year-old and a newborn, the trip to Woolwich was too much now for Mary. If Guy wanted to see her, he now had to make the trip north to her neck of the woods, which, in effect, put an end to their lovemaking. 'Dare I ask how Lawrence is?' he asked. 'He knows, doesn't he?'

'Of course, he knows, my name may be Mary but even I'm not capable of an immaculate conception. He's hardly talking to me. He's working in Manchester at the moment but he's due back sometime tomorrow afternoon.'

'Do his parents know?'

'No, they think I've delivered them another perfect grandson. Lawrence doesn't plan to shatter the illusion; he'd be too ashamed to do so anyway.'

'I've bought him a little present.'

'Who? Lawrence?'

'Yes, Lawrence, I've bought him a one-way ticket to Brazil. No, Robert, of course.' He handed the baby back to Mary who placed him gently in the pram. Guy fished around in his bag and pulled out an unwrapped toy soldier. 'I expect it's too big for him still.'

'Oh, but it's lovely. Thank you,' she said, placing the soldier at the foot of the pram. She stared in wonderment at her baby, her creation. 'You know, I look at him and I see both of you there. You and Jack.'

'Leave him, Mary, leave Lawrence and come to me.'

'I can't, you know I can't. Lawrence is still Clarence's father. Please tell me you understand, there's the three of us now, I'm more dependent on Lawrence than ever. I can't live on love alone.'

'Yes, I know.' Guy sighed. 'Bloody ironic though, isn't it?'

She looked at him. 'What do you mean?'

'For the sake of Jack's honour, I threw away the chance to take over the business. If I had, I'd have the means to care for the person he loved most. But it's gone now – sold. I wonder sometimes if this is what he would have wanted me to do.'

'I know, you're right, I've thought of that too.'

'He wanted me to live a full life for him. Those were his words, his very last words to me. And of course, I promised him I would. He also asked me to look after you and I now can't.'

Mary closed her eyes and swallowed. 'I know I'm denying you the chance to fulfil your promise. I'm sorry.'

'It's not your fault. Really, Mary, it isn't. I chose to defend Jack's name from being expunged from our family as if he'd never existed. It's just that in defending him, I threw it all away so now I feel as if I'm failing him. I've already broken my promise.'

Part Four

Chapter 32: The Equilibrium – April 1926

After five years, Guy finally found an equilibrium in his life. Physically, he was fit. He'd grown so used to the artificial leg that it had become as real to him as the flesh version. Financially, Guy was also back on his feet – so to speak. His father's will left him a little, although not so much, once all his numerous friends, acquaintances and relatives received their share. But Guy had left the Quartermaster's office in Woolwich and, using his almost forgotten financial skills, got himself gainful employment in a bank. The experience he'd gained as a youngster helping his father held him in good stead and he soon climbed the promotional ladder to become an assistant manager in a large branch in Holborn. He enjoyed his work – it stretched him and the burden of responsibility was something he relished. Maybe, he thought, he would have made a good officer or NCO after all. With his enhanced salary, he'd been able to save up and lay a deposit on a small house in the Kings Cross area. It was nothing special, but he was more than pleased to finally move away from the successive run of lodgings.

Romantically, Guy had been less successful. He had had a couple of lady friends, one of whom he almost got engaged to. But the relationship fizzled out leaving Guy wiser but not unduly perturbed.

But it was Robert, now five years old, who gave him the greatest pleasure and the deepest anguish. His secret son. Soon after Robert's birth, Guy and Lawrence discussed what arrangements they could agree over Robert. They never actually met, or even spoke by either letter or telephone. Their extended conversation was relayed from one to the other through Mary, acting as their intermediary. For the sake of avoiding a scandal, Guy acquiesced and allowed Lawrence to be named as Robert's legal father. It was more for the child's sake than Lawrence's; Guy didn't want his son growing up with the taboo of illegitimacy hanging around his neck. In return, Lawrence permitted Guy to see Robert every fortnight, but on the strict condition that no one, absolutely no one, should know that Guy was Robert's father – not even Robert himself. Guy knew that the arrangement was as good as he was likely to get, but it hurt. There were so many times Guy had been tempted simply to yell out to the passing crowds, 'Look everyone, this is *my* son.' But he knew better than to risk Lawrence's further wrath. In the winter of '23, Guy's mother had died. Both his parents had gone to their graves without ever knowing that they had a grandson. The thought caused Guy pain.

During these years of equilibrium, Guy saw Mary and Robert every fortnight, as arranged. But apart from the occasion of his mother's funeral, he never saw Lawrence. It wasn't difficult for the cousins to avoid each other, for Lawrence spent most of his time devoted to his work. He often worked weekends or was called away for days at a time to the Manchester office.

Guy treasured his time with his son who seemed to grow immeasurably from one visit to the next. On each occasion, he would buy Robert a little present – toy soldiers, wooden trains, a spinning top, books, whatever he could think of. It was only after a couple of years that Guy realised that on the rare occasion he went to Mary's house, he never saw any of the toys he had bought for Robert. He pressed Mary on the subject, who finally confessed that Lawrence knew instinctively which toys had come from Guy and would immediately throw them away. From then on, Guy kept the toys at his house for Robert's occasional visits to Kings Cross. Clarence was a fine lad too, very physical and brusque. Guy liked him but he reminded him too much of Lawrence, while knowing that Robert probably reminded Lawrence too much of him. Guy loved the way Robert, on first seeing him, would waddle or, as he grew up, run into his arms. One day, when Robert was about four, Mary had left the room, and Guy did something that earned his son's total devotion.

'Robert, come here; do you want to see some magic?'

'Yes, please. I love magic.' Guy adored his son's little pug nose with its freckles, his delicate eyebrows.

'Right. You see how I walk, yes? Up and down, up and down.' Robert nodded, unimpressed thus far. 'Well, if you turn around, close your eyes and promise not to peep, I'll show you some magic. Ready?'

Robert did as told and quickly, Guy undid the buckles and removed the straps, then quietly pushed the wooden leg behind the settee. 'OK, Robert, you can turn around now.'

Robert was distinctly underwhelmed by the sight of his uncle hopping around until Guy suddenly rolled up his trouser leg sausage-shaped. 'Your leg! Where's your leg?' he shouted. 'It's behind you.'

Guy hopped around in a circle. 'Oh no, it isn't.'

He leant against the settee, unfurled his trouser leg then waved it around in a circle.

Robert laughed, running round the room, shouting, 'Where's it gone? Where's it gone? I'm going to tell Mummy.'

'No, don't tell Mummy.'

'Where's your leg then?'

'Do you want to know?'

'Tell me, tell me.'

'It's here,' said Guy, producing it from behind the settee.

Robert gaped, open-mouthed, as his uncle twirled about this piece of wood in the shape of a leg. 'Are you a pirate?'

'Aha, shiver me timbers, that I am for sure!'

From that day, Guy was known as Uncle Hobbly.

*

In the warm summer days of July 1926, Guy and Mary rekindled their affair.

He hadn't meant to, neither of them had, but it happened. Guy had been increasingly tormented that he had never told his parents that he had produced a grandson. Mary had offered him a shoulder to cry on and a reassuring kiss soon led to the bedroom, a passionate postscript to their earlier affair. After the first occasion, they both agreed it had been a mistake and that it had to be a one-off. But the more vehemently they vowed never to repeat the occasion, the more inevitable it became that they would.

So now Guy's equilibrium began to fall apart as he became increasingly besotted with Mary. He dreamt of making her his wife and becoming a real father to Robert. He saw them as often as he could. They still met officially once a fortnight, but additional visits had to be conducted in secret. Guy helped Mary invent increasingly elaborate excuses for her to disappear for a few hours. It was a risky game and Guy hated it; he knew they couldn't go on forever, making excuses and meeting in secret. Something had to give and Guy hoped it would be Mary. She was beginning to show a defiance that she'd previously lacked and, over the weeks, Guy subtly tried to egg her on. The material gap between Guy and Lawrence was shortening; Guy too, had a respectable job now and a house of his own, albeit a modest one. With a son by each cousin, all Mary had to do was to follow her heart and to hell with the inevitable scandal – that was Lawrence's problem. While she was in Guy's company, away from Lawrence, she seemed almost convinced but Guy remained worried, fearing that her new-found courage evaporated the instant she returned home. But the way she enthused about a new life was deeply encouraging; all it needed, thought Guy, was a little push...

What Guy hadn't expected was for Lawrence to appear out of the blue. It was September, the nights had begun to draw in and Guy had just returned from work one evening when Lawrence suddenly stepped out of the shadows. 'I've been waiting for you,' he said menacingly. Guy jumped at Lawrence's unexpected appearance. He could see from the expression on his cousin's face that the visit was far from a social one.

'You'd better come in.' Guy led Lawrence through to his sitting room. Lawrence glanced around at the bareness of the room, leaving Guy conscious of his lack of pictures, ornaments or plants. The only thing Guy had in abundance were his books, which filled two sets of bookshelves on either side of the fireplace. Guy noticed Lawrence run his finger across the sideboard as if he was checking for dust. Sure enough, much to Guy's irritation, he found some. Guy sat down as he watched his cousin pace around the room; Lawrence's whole demeanour was of one deeply unimpressed.

Guy found himself making excuses. 'I haven't been here long, I need to do some work on it, but it's difficult finding the time.' Lawrence made no response. 'Take a seat,' said Guy.

'No, thank you, I won't be staying long.'

'Tea?'

Lawrence cast his eyes over Guy's collection of books. 'You read a lot of Dickens,' he said.

'I do now.'

With his tour of inspection over, Lawrence flung around, his voice simmering with barely suppressed anger. 'I think you know why I'm here.' Guy sat staring up at him, refusing to be drawn into a possible trap. 'I'm not blind, you know.' Guy's continual silence merely fuelled Lawrence's anger. 'You must think I'm a bloody fool. Well, maybe I was the first time around but once bitten, twice shy, as they say. You may have made a fool of me before but not this time, *not* this time...' Lawrence paused, but Guy still refused to respond. 'You're breaking the terms of our agreement; from now on, I forbid you to see Mary... or Robert.'

Finally, Guy spoke. '*Your* agreement, not mine,' he said calmly.

'No matter, you're not to see them again.'

'No, it's not going to happen, you can't stop me from seeing them. Don't forget, Robert is *my* son.'

'Not legally, he isn't; remember, you signed that privilege away.'

'For the sake of *your* reputation; after all, you do have your name to think of–'

'Are you trying to threaten me?'

'No more than you're threatening me.'

Lawrence leant forward, narrowing his eyes. 'No, mine is not a threat, dear cousin, it is a promise, a guarantee if you prefer.'

'The only guarantee, *dear cousin*, is that Mary has had enough. You can't provide her the things she needs, the things she *really* needs. Money and position can only take you so far, but as for the rest... well, I don't have to tell you, you know it, she wants to leave you.'

'Quite the contrary, she's leaving *you*.'

For the first time since the start of this ridiculous posturing, a rush of panic rose within him. 'What... what do you mean?'

'We're leaving,' said Lawrence lightly, relishing his trump card. 'I'm being transferred to the Manchester office. Big step up, you know the sort of thing. We leave tomorrow morning.'

Guy's mind raced; surely this was some elaborate bluff, a monstrous deception to keep him away. 'No, I don't believe you; Mary wouldn't take Robert away from me.'

'Oh, but she is, she's already packed, we all are. No, I'm afraid this time tomorrow we'll be in our new home, albeit a temporary one, in Manchester. Our things follow us up at the end of the week. I still have to return a few times to settle things at this end and...' Guy stopped listening as Lawrence dwelled unnecessarily on the practical arrangements of the move. 'This time tomorrow,' he'd said, 'this time tomorrow.'

'But surely...' he interrupted, but paused, not sure what he wanted to say.

'Yes?'

'But when will I be able to see Robert?'

'I wasn't going to tell you about us leaving; it's only because you are the boy's father that I'm extending this courtesy.' Lawrence finally sat down in a chair at right angles to Guy. He spoke in an almost sympathetic tone. 'Robert is seeing more of you than he does of me, he's always asking for you. He's becoming confused; I think perhaps it's for the best if you did not see Robert for a while. Maybe, after he's had time to settle down, we'll think again, but in the meantime, you are not to try and contact us.'

'What do you mean confused?'

'It doesn't help when Mary lets slip and refers to you as Daddy.' He glanced at his watch. 'Well look, I've still got a lot of things to see to and Mary's sister's coming round to help, so if you don't mind...' He rose to his feet. 'No need to show me out.'

Was that it? thought Guy. Did Lawrence really think he could cut him out of his son's life as simply as that? His mind flashed back to the numerous conversations he had had with Mary, how enthused she seemed at the prospect of leaving Lawrence and starting again. Guy could not believe that she could change her

327

mind so easily and without telling him. 'No, she won't go,' he said quickly as Lawrence was about to leave. 'She just won't.'

Lawrence paused at the sitting-room door and turned to look at him. 'Guy, I won't deny that my wife entertains a strong attachment to you, but you know Mary, the children always come first. I grant you, you may be right, I may not be able to provide the emotional support she needs, but I *can* provide in abundance what's best for her children. Clarence is already enrolled at the best school in the northwest and, when he is of age, Robert won't be denied either. Think of their future, Guy; if you love your son, you'll let him go.' Guy stared at him, unable to respond. 'It's for the best.'

Lawrence disappeared out of the room and Guy found himself alone with Lawrence's presence still lingering in the air. Guy slumped into the armchair, his mind whirling with panic as he heard the front door close with a gentle click. He listened to Lawrence's fading footsteps on the pavement outside. He needed to think. Lawrence was lying. There was no way she would leave him, not now. If only he could see her, speak to her. Tomorrow morning, Lawrence had said. He tried to think. What station did the Manchester trains depart from?

Chapter 33: The Station – 20 September 1926

Ten to seven the morning after Lawrence's devastating visit, Guy was at Euston station. He searched the platform as the few passengers boarded the 7.02 train to Manchester. But there was no sign of them. Surely, he thought, he would have seen them had they been there. It did seem very early for a Sunday. The next train for Manchester was due to leave exactly an hour later, at 8.02. He would wait in case they boarded that train, and then the next one and the next one. Lawrence had said the morning but if need be, Guy was prepared to wait all day. He went off to the small station café and bought himself a coffee and a roll. He also bought a newspaper and tried to read the sports pages. In front of a crowd of 120,000 people, the boxer, Gene Tunney, had defeated Jack Dempsey to become world heavyweight champion. But Guy felt too distracted to concentrate, terrified of missing them. After only ten minutes, he could not bear to sit still a moment more. He slurped down the last of the coffee and, leaving the newspaper on the table, went back out onto the main concourse. He paced up and down, searching every face that passed him – male, female or child. For a moment, he thought he saw them from a distance, a couple with two young boys. He called out her name but she didn't turn around. On closer inspection, he realised his mistake. Perhaps, he thought, he should wait near the taxi rank, but there was always an outside chance they would arrive by tram or Underground. There was nothing for it; he would have to maintain his vigil on the concourse.

Half past seven. Guy glanced up at the indicator board for the hundredth time – still no platform number. He made his way to a bench at the side of the concourse from where he could still watch what was going on, and sat down with a sigh. He was nervous again, his palms sweaty, his head thumping. This sort of dramatic confrontation was alien to him. He tried to think what on earth he would say to her and tried to imagine her reaction at seeing him there. Would she consider his bravado as romantically heroic or merely pitiful? His mind fluctuated between the two extreme possibilities – one in which she falls gratefully into his arms and allows herself to be whisked away to a new and freer life, and the other in which she looks him up and down contemptuously, and then turns her back on him in a defiant gesture of rejection.

After ten minutes, Guy made his way back to have another look at the indicator board. It was quarter to eight, and the platform for the 8.02 to Manchester had been announced – platform eight. He walked quickly to the ticket barrier at the end of the platform. There was already a small queue of passengers waiting as the train from Manchester pulled in. Dozens of carriage doors opened simultaneously and the platform quickly filled with outgoing passengers, and the immediate area around the ticket barrier soon became congested. The number of people waiting to board was increasing by the minute. Guy tried to keep pace with the density of people coming and going. Eventually, the ticket inspector allowed the ongoing passengers through the barrier. Guy looked at his watch; it was just gone five to eight. He heard her before he saw her.

'Clarence, don't run off please.'

He spun his head around. There they were – the four of them, accompanied, much to Guy's surprise, by Josephine, clutching a small handbag, together with three attendants lugging numerous suitcases and bags. As Lawrence and Mary approached the ticket barrier with a child each, Guy called out her name; he was only a few feet away.

She looked up and saw him immediately. 'Guy? Guy, what are you doing here?'

Before Guy could speak, Lawrence stepped between them, his face looming inches away from Guy's, his eyes burning with anger through his spectacles. He spoke quietly but menacingly. 'What in the blazes do you think you're doing, man? Just get the hell out of here.'

Guy saw Robert in the corner of his eye. Sidestepping Lawrence, he dropped down onto one knee and spread his arms open. Robert needed no second invitation; he flung himself against Guy's chest. Guy wrapped his arms around the little chap and squeezed him as tightly as he dared. Guy couldn't speak, couldn't think. He closed his eyes and breathed in as much of Robert's smell as he could. The smell of his smooth, pink skin, the fresh odour of his beautiful, silky hair, the smell of his son, his only son. He could have died in that smell, that unmistakable smell. His mind flashed back to Jack, hugging his brother for the last time, the smell of him beneath the stale sweat, the hint of rum, the stench of fear. Here he was again, using smell as the last desperate thread by which to remember. By this time tomorrow, he thought. 'Uncle Hobbly!' squeaked the little five-year-old, his words muffled into Guy's chest. Guy could feel the tears coming, his heart breaking. 'Robert, Robert, Robert, my darling Robert,' he whispered.

'Robert, Robert let go of Uncle Guy now.' Guy heard Lawrence's piercing voice, bringing to an end his desperate embrace. 'Robert, this instant!' Reluctantly, Guy loosened his grip and Robert stepped back fearful of earning his father's displeasure. Guy pulled himself up. Mary had turned her back, unable to bring herself to watch the scene of severance. Josephine sidled up to her and placed an arm around her shoulder. Guy glanced at Clarence and tried to smile at him. But Clarence looked concerned; he was old enough to know something was not quite right.

'Mary…' said Guy quietly.

Josephine removed her arm and Mary turned around and looked at him beseechingly. 'Guy?'

This was it, thought Guy, in front of Lawrence, in front of Josephine, he had to say it and she had to believe it. 'Mary, I don't want you to leave.'

Lawrence tried again to intervene, but Mary brushed him aside with a withering look to which he quickly submitted. She looked pale, almost petrified by what Guy was asking of her. 'Don't do this to me, Guy.'

'Mary, you don't have to go, you know that, you don't have to take Robert away from me.'

She shook her head. 'Oh Guy, I have two sons, we just couldn't do it.'

'Uncle Hobbly.' Guy looked down at his son. 'Are you coming with us?'

'No, sweetheart, but…' He looked back at Mary. Nearby, the ticket inspector announced two minutes for passengers boarding the Manchester train. 'Mary, please, I love you.' He realised he'd never said it before. He wondered whether Jack had ever said it.

Lawrence spoke, his voice raked with uncertainty, the former confident and menacing tone all but vanished. 'Mary, love, we ought to board, otherwise, we'll miss it.'

Mary looked at her husband, glanced at Josephine and then turned back to Guy, her hand at her mouth. Guy noticed she was wearing Jack's ring again. The two cousins watched her intently;

both men knowing their respective futures with Mary hung on the very words she was currently struggling to find.

'Last call for Manchester please.'

'Mary, please, we *have* to go now.'

'Tickets please.'

'Don't do it, Mary, don't take him away from me.'

She opened her mouth as if about to speak and for a moment Guy feared she was about to faint. But instead, she let out a cry. As her face crumpled under the tears, she spluttered, 'Oh, Guy, I love you too…' She tried to catch her breath through the tears.

Robert tugged at her sleeve. 'Mummy, Mummy,' he said, his little voice filled with incomprehension.

'It's OK, darling, Mummy's all right.' She took his hand to reassure him. 'But Guy, I can't truly give myself to you when not a day, barely an hour passes, when I think of Jack and how much I miss him so, so terribly and how much I *still* love him. It wouldn't be fair on you, or me, and it wouldn't be fair on him. Jack would destroy us, Guy, and you would end up resenting him for it.'

'But…' He couldn't say it; his conscience wouldn't allow him to form the words. But Jack never really loved you, not properly, not in the way I love you. From the moment Jack, dressed in his new uniform, had stepped onto the train bound for France, Mary had lived with the illusion of love. And she would continue to live it to her last breath, thought Guy. He cared too much for her to shatter her love for Jack and, with the realisation, Guy slumped, the moment of resignation. His false leg seemed to have disappeared and for a moment, he feared he was about to tumble. He felt a sudden resentment for Jack. How could Guy live a life for both of them, when Jack wasn't prepared to allow him to live his own life the way *he* wanted to, with the woman he wanted to live it with, and with the son he wanted to be a father to? Why had Jack made such an effort to save him from dying in no-man's-land, if he was then quite content to allow Guy to rot slowly from the inside? He'd gladly forfeited his inheritance for Jack, for Jack's honour, and what did he have to show for it? It was the ultimate betrayal.

The ticket inspector approached Lawrence. 'Sir, if you're planning to catch this train, this really is your last opportunity.'

'Yes, of course, I'm sorry.' Lawrence turned to his wife. 'All set?'

She nodded. 'Come on, Clarence,' she said to the older boy lurking behind the attendants, who were tactfully talking to each other. Clarence took his father's hand as Lawrence led the way. Guy stepped back to let them pass. Lawrence glanced at Guy briefly as he passed, but there was no exultation in his eyes, no joy in his victory, just a fleeting glance of concern. Then Mary followed, holding onto Robert's hand. She paused in front of Guy, leant up to him and kissed him politely on the cheek. 'Goodbye, my love.'

Guy shook his head, his lips pursed, shocked by the sudden and overwhelming sense of Jack's betrayal. He looked down to Robert, who seemed preoccupied by a pigeon that had landed a few paces away. Guy could not face the torture of holding him again, fearing he'd never be able to let go. He bit his lip and, as the little boy ambled past pointing at the pigeon, ruffled his hair. Robert looked up at his unknown father and grinned momentarily before being gently dragged away by his mother. Guy felt a hand tenderly clasp his wrist – it was Josephine. 'Be strong,' she whispered before letting go and following the others.

Guy watched as the five of them walked quickly towards the train, the attendants struggling closely behind. They stopped at an open carriage door, two carriages away from the ticket barrier. First class. Josephine climbed aboard first and helped Mary lift Robert up the steep steps onto the train. Carrying a small suitcase, Clarence followed with his mother directly behind. After various comings and goings with the baggage, Lawrence boarded the train last, slamming shut the carriage door as the conductor blew his whistle and waved the green flag. He didn't look back.

Guy waited, staring at the door, hoping it would suddenly reopen, that there would be a change of heart and a reappearance. The platform became engulfed in billows of smoke, obscuring his view. He watched as the train slowly pulled out of the station. In four hours, thought Guy, they would arrive in Manchester. Only four hours away, just a couple hundred miles but, for the size of the gulf that Jack had driven between him and Mary, it might as well be the other side of the world. At the far end of the platform, the train emerged from the darkness of the station and into the bright morning sun. It began to pick up speed as it turned a corner and slowly disappeared from view. Guy remained rooted to the spot, looking idly at the swirling smoke rise and diffuse. It reminded him of the smoke rising menacingly above the trenches, gradually revealing the sight of the mutilated and dying. Guy closed his eyes and let out an audible groan. He suddenly felt very tired and in urgent need to get home and away from the empty deserted platform in front of him and the crowded concourse behind him. 'I'll see you again,' he said to himself. And in his mind, he heard his brother's voice echoing back, 'Yes, but not too soon.'

He opened his eyes to see a figure slowly emerging from the rising smoke. She paused, strands of curling hair blowing across her face, clutching her handbag. He'd assumed she was going with them, but obviously not. She smiled, almost apologetically, as she approached. 'You know as well as I do, don't you?' she said. 'But you never told her.'

Guy shook his head. 'How could I?'

'It could have made all the difference.'

'But, Josephine, she was besotted with him. I couldn't destroy that.'

She brushed her hair back. 'After Father left us, she wanted a man to fill the gap. When Jack proposed, she was delighted. Jack's death deified him, made their love seem all the more real, a marriage made in Heaven. It would've never worked out otherwise.'

'I know. Jack was just a boy looking for adventure and a girlfriend to go with it. Could have been Mary or anyone… could have been you.' He smiled. 'Especially you.'

'I know. And I know you know – I saw you lurking behind that tree when Jack… you know.'

'At my parents' party.'

'Yes.' She looked at him earnestly. 'Care to buy me a coffee?'

Guy thought of his aching leg. He desperately needed to remove the wooden limb, to ease his throbbing thigh. 'I ought to be going really.'

'I understand. I'm sorry.' A look of embarrassment flashed across her face and she quickly turned to leave.

Guy watched her for a few moments. Perhaps his leg wasn't that bad after all. 'But there again…' he called out. She stopped and turned around to face him, a hint of an expectant smile on her face. 'Why not?' he said. 'I do have the time. In fact…' he added, 'I've got all the time in the world.'

THE END

Dedicated to the three hundred and six British servicemen executed during The Great War of 1914 to 1918.

During the First World War, there were 238,000 British courts martial – 3,080 resulted in the death penalty. Of these, 346 (11 per cent) were carried out – 40 for murder, the other 306 for offences such as desertion, cowardice, falling asleep while on duty, etc. 3.6 per cent of soldiers tried for desertion were executed.

In November 2006, the UK government pardoned all 306 servicemen executed during the war of 1914 – 1918.

The Searight Saga:

PART ONE: *This Time Tomorrow*

PART TWO: *The Unforgiving Sea*
'Ten men adrift on a lifeboat. Only one will live to tell the tale.'

A sequel to This Time Tomorrow, The Unforgiving Sea, set in World War Two, is, on its surface, a tale of murder, survival and loss, while at its core we find a story of deep love, loyalty and forgiveness.

PART THREE: *The Red Oak*
Summer 2004. A chance letter from France takes Tom Searight on a journey to discover his World War One great uncle, Guy Searight. But as Tom learns more about his family's tragic past, his future becomes increasingly uncertain.

https://rupertcolley.com

Novels by R.P.G. Colley:

Love and War Series:
The Lost Daughter
The White Venus
Song of Sorrow
The Woman on the Train
The Black Maria
My Brother the Enemy
Anastasia
Elena
The Mist Before Our Eyes
The Darkness We Leave Behind

The Searight Saga:
This Time Tomorrow
The Unforgiving Sea
The Red Oak

The Tales of Little Leaf
Eleven Days in June
Winter in July
Departure in September

**The DI Benedict Paige Crime Series
by JOSHUA BLACK**
And Then She Came Back
The Poison in His Veins
Requiem for a Whistleblower
The Forget-Me-Not Killer
The Canal Boat Killer
A Senseless Killing

https://rupertcolley.com

Made in the USA
Las Vegas, NV
31 March 2024

88070621R00203